Warfare Qualified

An Icaran Confederation Navy Novel

Michael Kingswood

Contents

About This Book

Join the Navy. See the Galaxy.

Every newly-minted officer of the Icaran Confederation Navy has one goal: to earn the golden warfare device of a fully qualified Stellar Warfare Officer.

In pursuit of that goal, Ensign Matthew Gilbert looks forward to a grand adventure together with his friends on the newest, most powerful ship in the fleet.

Instead, a last-minute change in orders sends Matt, alone, to a backwater station and an aging ship he never would have chosen.

Far from home and surrounded by an unfamiliar culture, with a crushing workload and little chance of seeing any real action, he finds himself embarked on the adventure of a lifetime, on the pointy end of his nation's spear.

He just has to get qualified first.

Technically detailed and accurate to Naval culture and tradition, Warfare Qualified is a fun and exciting excursion into the life of a junior officer on his first adventure in a large and dangerous galaxy.

Enjoy the book! After you're done, please come to Michael's website and sign up for his mailing list at www.michaelkingswood.com/newsletter-signup/. Guaranteed to be spam free, he uses it to announce new releases and special promotions for his fans.

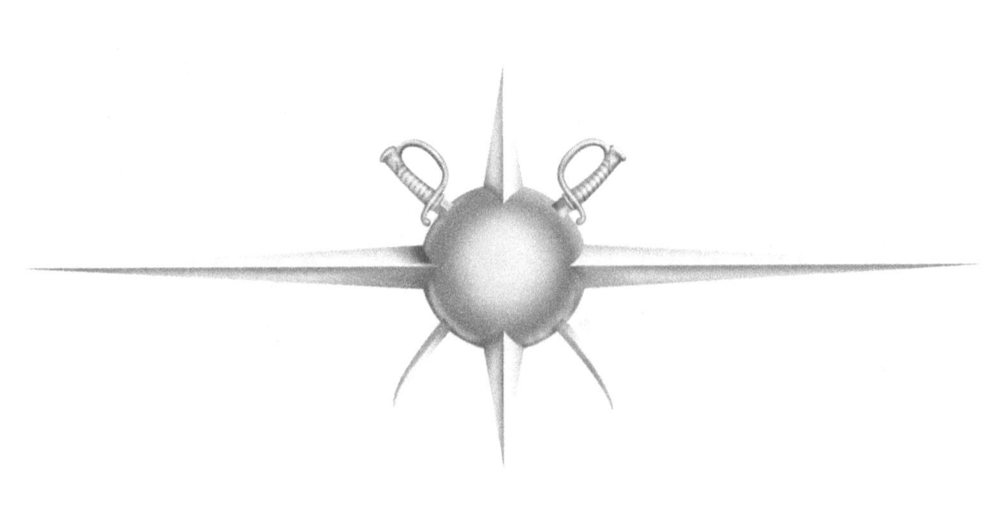

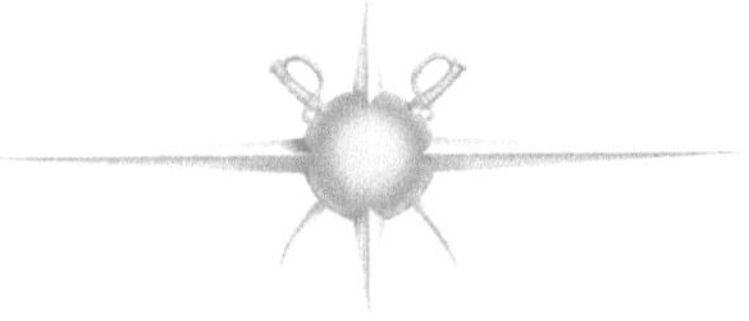

Chapter One

The first indication of a problem was a violent shudder as the ship reeled from impact.

Half a second later, the popping in Ensign Matthew Gilbert's ears advertised an internal pressure drop. Then the Chief of the Watch's voice came over the 1MC.

"Hull Breach on the 02 level, frames 34 through 38. Rig ship for loss of pressure."

The general alarm rang out immediately after the Chief's words, thirteen electronic gongs that on their own would have roused even the deepest of sleepers, had anyone been in the rack just then. Then the Chief spoke over the announcing circuit again.

"Hull Breach on the 02 level, frames 34 through 38. Rig ship for loss of pressure."

With practiced haste, Matt raised his hands over his head and grasped the wrapped-up bundle that rested on the back of his dark blue, single piece underway uniform. The bundle tore open at a quick tug of his fingers, and he drew a thin transparent hood up out of the bundle and over his head. A quick press of his fingers along the bottom initiated the seal at his neck. That done, he checked the seal on his gloves, always worn at battle stations, then tore a tab from his left breast and withdrew a thin, retractable hose from its housing there. Half-standing, he reached up and inserted the metallic tab at the end of the hose into the Emergency Atmosphere System manifold in the overhead above his console. Then he sat back down.

Immediately, air began flowing into his uniform, expanding the hood slightly. The air smelled faintly like onions, and left a bitter taste in his mouth, but it allowed him to breathe freely. Fair trade.

At the same time, coils in his uniform began conducting current supplied through the hose, and the growing chill of the increasing vacuum within the ship fled swiftly.

All around him in the subdued blue light of the Combat Information Center, his fellow Junior Officers, seated at the various consoles, did the same as he had, one and all donning the lifesaving gear within seconds of the casualty announcement. In the center of the room, standing next to the holographic tactical fusion plot, the Tactical Action Officer and the Commanding Officer also donned their gear. Then they waited as, one by one, the tactical stations began calling in status reports in order over the Tactical Net.

"Sensors hooded and ready."

"EW Hooded and ready."

"Plot hooded and ready."

The reports came in through the implant in Matt's right ear; much better than wearing earbuds. It was his turn.

"Weapons hooded and ready."

A second passed, then the Tactical Action Officer acknowledged, "Very well."

In Matt's left ear, over the Command Net, the TAO reported, "Tactical Stations hooded and ready, Captain."

"Very well, TAO. Status of firing solution?"

Without prompting—that was the advantage of having all stations listening in on the Command Net even though only a select few could speak on it—Sensors piped up on the Tactical Net. "Still filtering out EM and Gravitic interference from the torpedo hit. Estimate regain track in 2 minutes."

The TAO relayed that and received a very dissatisfied "Very Well" from the CO. He proceeded to give orders to the helm, but the TAO's follow-up orders to the Tactical party took precedence for Matt.

"Weapons, set torpedoes for short range search. Make tubes one and three ready in all respects."

"Short Range tactics, make tubes one and three ready in all respects, aye," Matt replied, and leaned forward into his console's embrace.

The holographic interface wrapped around him, and he was within the innards of the torpedo launch system. All four of the ship's tubes showed green—loaded for launch—and he selected the starboard side tubes with a quick brush of his fingers.

Immediately, bubble-menus opened, and two more finger gestures powered on the weapons and selected their short-range search settings. Two more swipes at the tubes themselves sent their electromechanical systems through the sequence to ready the tubes for launch. A timer display appeared above each tube.

"TAO, Weapons. Short range tactics selected. Tubes 1 and 3 ready in one minute."

"TAO Aye."

To Matt's left, Ensign George Ramirez, his breathing bubble fogging slightly, worked determinedly at the sensors fusion console. To Matt's right, Ensign Thomas Geiger worked the plot. Both men's profiles were obscured by the holographics of their stations, but the tension in their shoulders gave their urgency away.

The command net piped up in Matt's left ear. "DC Central, XO. XO is the man in charge at the scene. Additional hull patch materials are required. We have two injured personnel and three dead. The hull breach is a meter-and-a-half wide and approximately seven meters long, and extends to the deck on the forward section of the breach. It appears to be contained on this level. Send the secondary DC team to the O1 level to verify. The airtight door at frame 41 has failed. Securing ventilation stops in the adjacent spaces."

The Damage Control Assistant's voice replied, "XO, DC Central, Aye."

The DCA came over the 1MC, repeating the XO's report for all hands' benefit, but the Tactical Net overrode the announcement in Matt's ear as George reported, "TAO, Sensors. EM interference clearing. Commencing active sweep."

"TAO aye."

The timers on Tubes 1 and 3 began flashing red, drawing Matt's attention back to them. Fifteen seconds.

Five.

Ready.

He keyed his comm. "TAO, Weapons, Tubes 1 and 3 ready in all respects."

"TAO aye. Plot?"

"Wait one, TAO," Tom replied.

The CO's voice came over the command net. "Bridge, Captain. Come left to 027 and up ten degrees."

"Captain, Bridge, aye."

The ship's movement should have been imperceptible, but Matt pressed back into his chair as an acceleration struck him. The local gravity plates must have been damaged in the attack.

Funny, he hadn't felt any different until the ship turned. He wondered if—

"TAO, Plot. Regained target. Track Number 72561, range twenty thousand kilometers bearing 145 mark 097. Course 080 mark 125 and accelerating at 12 gravities."

They were heading for the lower orbitals, trying to evade counterfire in Celenia 3's Van Allen belt.

Matt grinned thinly. Wouldn't work.

"Captain, I intend to kill track 72561 with Hammerheads." The TAO couldn't keep a bit of eagerness from his voice.

The CO's reply was cool and calm. "Batteries release."

"Aye, sir. All stations, TAO, firing point procedures, tubes 1 and 3."

CIC became suddenly quiet as every console operator buried himself in his work.

Over the Command Net, the Officer of the Deck reported, "Ship Ready."

George: "Sensors ready."

Ensign Dan Napolitano in Electronic Warfare: "EW ready."

Thomas: "Plot ready."

Matt drew a deep breath. "Torpedo run twenty-three thousand five hundred kilometers. Own ship's protection is GeoBox. Weapons ready."

The TAO ordered, "Shoot tubes 1 and 3."

"Shoot tubes 1 and 3, aye," Matt said. He reached forward toward the launch controls.

Thomas reported, "Set."

Matt hit the controls. "Standby...fire Tube 1...fire Tube 3."

The ship lurched twice as the tubes cycled. Matt's display shifted from a display of the torpedo tube system to a three-dimensional representation of the battlespace around the ship. On it, the two torpedoes accelerated straight forward for five seconds, then dropped and sped to spinward and down, continuing their acceleration as they left the ship's vicinity and flew toward the target.

Matt reported, "Ownship clearance maneuver complete. Weapons running normally."

"Bridge, Captain, come right to 130 mark 115," the Captain ordered over the Command Net before switching to Tactical. "TAO, engage with primaries."

"TAO, aye. Weapons, fire primary cannons as she bears."

The acceleration hit Matt, pressing him forward into his console as he minimized post-launch control of the torpedoes and brought up the primary cannons. "Weapons, Aye," he said, and managed to hold back a curse at his slowness. He should have seen this coming. It was a standard tactic when within cannon range: use the primaries to clear out the target's defensive fire as the torpedoes homed. The incoming fire would distract the defenders, and with luck it would also damage the enemy enough to get a mission kill even if they managed to spoof the torpedoes.

That wasn't as likely, though. Unguided plasma projectiles were relatively easy to evade, and they didn't pack the punch of a well-placed torpedo. Still, every little bit helped.

It seemed to take forever, although in reality only a few seconds passed. The primary cannons' targeting reticle flashed red in his display, indicating that it was lined up with the pip representing the targeting computer's projection of the enemy's course.

Matt fired, and the ship shuddered ever so slightly; far less than it had over the torpedoes.

"Primary Cannons hot, TAO."

"Very well, Weapons. Maintain continuous fire. Break. EW, status of offensive EA."

Dan, in Electronic Warfare, reported immediately, "Electronic Attack in progress, sir."

"Very well."

There was little to do but watch and wait for a few seconds. Then...

"TAO, sensors. Target zig, coming right to 280 mark 035. Detecting Soft Kill emissions."

The enemy's track updated a second later as Plot adjusted its solution, and Matt tracked the primaries to a new leading angle.

As he did that, another burst of acceleration pitched him to the right and threatened to push him up out of his seat, as the Captain maneuvered the ship to follow. He was adjusting the primary cannons again when, in the lower left quadrant of his hologram, the torpedo control window flashed red.

He maximized it, and his eyes widened as he took in the new data.

"TAO, Weapons. Adjusting fire with primaries. Torpedo #1 has entered anti-countermeasure search mode. Active Homing on #3."

"TAO aye. Is it homing on the target or a countermeasure?"

Matt swiped at his display furiously. The telemetry coming back from torpedo #3 appeared on the screen...he cursed under his breath. "Homing on countermeasure, sir. Pre-enabling the weapon and inserting a steer."

He raced to reset Torpedo #3, sparing a moment to check on the status of his cannons. Still firing, and it looked like the leading pip was still good. But it was impossible to tell if he was scoring any hits.

"Sensors, Captain, report status of target."

"Captain, sensors. IR blooms from the forward section of the hull. Assess several hits from the primary cannons. Break. Target acceleration lowering to 10 gravities."

"Counterfire?"

"Negative indications of counterfire, sir."

They must have used their last torpedoes in the attack that struck the ship. It was the only reason Matt could think of that the enemy they hadn't returned fire yet. He would have.

Torpedo #1 flashed blue, then red. "TAO, Weapons. Active Homing, Torpedo #1. Telemetry," he checked the torpedo's enemy data overlay against's Plot's, "matches plot."

"TAO, aye. Sensors?"

"Target maintaining 10 gravities acceleration, sir. Zigging to port. More IR blooms, and we're detecting narrow-band EM transmissions. Probably anti-torpedo systems."

The telemetry from Torpedo #1 filled Matt's display, painting a near-lifelike image of the enemy ship that was derived from the torpedo's Active EM and passive IR and gravitic sensors. A small turret at the enemy's stern rotated, and the torpedo began making random high-gravity accelerations across the plane of its approach.

"TAO, sensors, point defense fire from the target."

"Concur, TAO," Matt said. "Terminal Homing, Torpedo #1." Matt checked the other weapon, and grinned thinly. "Active Homing, Torpedo #3."

"TAO, Aye." Hot satisfaction carried from his voice over the Tactical Net clearly. "Get 'em, Hammerheads."

Matt's grin widened, despite the lapse in circuit discipline. After all, if you couldn't enjoy this just a little bit... "Computed impact in twenty seconds...ten..." The telemetry from Torpedo #1 blanked out. "Lost the link, Torpedo #1."

"TAO, sensors, large IR bloom from the target. Assess good hit."

"Damage Assessment, sensors?"

"BDA, aye. Wait. Lots of interference at the moment."

The telemetry from Torpedo #3 changed. "TAO, Weapons, telemetry update from Torpedo #3. Target acceleration has ceased." The displayed flashed again. "Terminal homing. Impact in 30 seconds....15... Lost the link Torpedo #3."

From Sensors, "Second large IR bloom. Good hit."

"TAO, aye." He broke to the Command Net. "Captain, TAO, two good hits on track 72561 with Hammerheads. Assess as total kill based on weapon yield, sir."

The Captain sounded just as cool as he always had. "Very well, TAO. I concur." He shifted over to the 1MC. "All hands, this is the Captain. We struck the enemy with two Hammerheads and assess he has been destroyed. Secure from battle stations, with the exception of damage control efforts." He paused. "Well done, men."

Around the CIC, Matt's fellow JO's let out a loud, heartfelt huzzah.

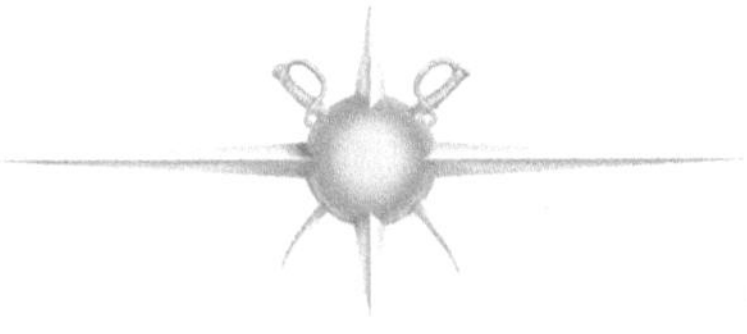

Chapter Two

The white lights in CIC's overhead turned on, replacing the blue that had been illuminating the space and making Matt blink for a second as his eyes adjusted to the increased illumination. The holographics within his console shifted as well, reverting to the in-port systems status display while a single line of text appeared in the upper quadrant: ENGAGEMENT SIMULATION 28A TERMINATED.

He pushed himself back from the console and pulled at the release tab on his breathing mask. The seal around his collar released with a slight hiss, and he threw the plastic back over his head, then stood and unclipped his umbilical tube from the EAS manifold above his station. Then he reached over his shoulders and pulled on two quick-release tabs.

The mask assembly dropped from the back of his uniform, landing on the seat he had just vacated with a soft thud.

George spoke as Matt was leaning over to pick up the mask assembly. "They made our last one fun, huh?"

Matt rolled up the plastic carefully, sparing George a quick look and a grin. "Yeah, that turned out pretty well."

George looked like he was about the reply, but the voice of LT Tolson, the instructor who had been playing CO, overrode him.

"Debrief in the classroom in 10 minutes, gents."

"Just like always," Tom said, no small amount of annoyance in his voice.

Lieutenant Tolson, all of two meters of muscle and bald-headed bad attitude, turned baleful eyes on Tom, and for a minute there Matt wasn't sure the two of them were not going to come to blows. Tom and he had been getting on each others' bad sides since Matt's group had classed up. Oh, Tom had never pushed it into the bounds of actual insubordination: a sarcastic quip here, a little malicious compliance there. But the LT had clearly wanted to take Tom down a peg or six for weeks now.

Problem was, Tom was just too good. Matt had never met someone as smart, or as naturally inclined to Naval tactics, as him. Not that Matt was drawing on a big pool of acquaintances, but even the instructors had remarked on how quickly Tom picked things up, and how well.

So all Tolson had been able to do was give Tom the occasional Extra Military Instruction, and probably get him a reduced military bearing mark on their final scores at Tactical School. Not that that mattered, from what Matt had heard.

LT Tolson's narrowed brown eyes seemed to burn in their sockets for a second or two. Then he just sighed and looked skyward as though praying silently for deliverance. "Yes, Mister Geiger. Just like always." Then the instructor actually grinned. "Last time, though."

He turned on his heel and strode past the other Ensigns in Matt's class, all of whom had stopped stowing their gear in anticipation of the face-off that seemed to be brewing.

One and all, they wore expressions of mixed relief and disappointment as the instructor left the compartment. Tolson hadn't made a lot of friends among their group, and most of them had, at one time or another, fantasized about him getting what was coming to him.

Or at least, of *watching* him get what was coming to him. Tolson was not the sort that anyone would want to fight if he didn't have to. Rumor was, he had been a champion boxer back in the Academy. He certainly had the build for it.

"Jeez, Tom, you never know when to quit do you?" George said. His blond hair, treading the hairy edge of acceptability within regulations' standards, swayed back and forth as he shook his head quickly.

Tom just snorted. "Whatever man. That's guy's a total jackass."

Matt straightened from rolling up his mask assembly and gave Tom a meaningful look. "Yeah, well, what if he ends up as your Department Head someday? You know he's on contract for another tour."

Tom's lips turned downward into a frown, and he actually gave a little shudder. "If that happens, I'll resign." He tossed his rolled-up mask assembly into the air and caught it, then grinned roguishly. "Come on, let's get out of here."

Tom turned to leave, and Matt and George followed along behind him.

CIC was a circular compartment about ten meters across, with tactical support stations ringing the main fusion plot in the center and a single airtight hatch offering egress at the aftermost section of the room. Aside from consoles, cable bundles, lighting receptacles, power panels, and UAS manifolds, it was filled with another half-dozen of Matt's fellow trainees, and they all had the same idea as Tom, Matt, and George.

So there was a bit of a wait to exit the room. But finally they got out, pausing only to deposit their mask assemblies into a receptacle just inside the door.

The passageway outside was broad, about four meters wide, and ran straight from the tactical simulation spaces to the classroom areas at the other end of Tactical School's main building. The left hand side of the corridor, when heading back to the classrooms, was lined with pictures bridging the entire span of naval history from the earliest sailing galleys to the newest interstellar assault cruisers. About every twenty meters or so the line of pictures broke in favor of an airtight door leading into another simulator. The opposite wall was mostly plasteel, allowing views of the bay below the Tactical School's campus and, on its opposite shore, the white-capped peaks of the Hopkins Range. It made quite a contrast with the, for lack of a better term, space-age setting of the school, and Matt always found himself enjoying the walk down this particular hallway.

And he would get plenty of time to enjoy it today. CIC Simulator #6, where his section had played for the last two and a half hours, lay near the end of the corridor, promising a long walk back.

Turning left out of the door, Matt, Tom, and George set off at the brisk pace that had become their natural stride after years of drill and being browbeaten to move with a sense of purpose. Now the ground-covering pace seemed as natural as moving; Matt hardly realized how much quicker he walked than non-service people unless he was visiting his family or old friends. Then he found himself always having to slow down or just pause and wait for them to keep up.

"Can't believe we're finally done with this place," George said, pulling Matt's attention away from the distant mountains and back to the present.

"Not nearly soon enough," Tom put in. "Why, I—"

He stopped talking as an airtight door ahead of them opened and a gaggle of other junior officer trainees walked out into the corridor. Leggy, curvy, and far prettier trainees than Matt's section.

Tom's frown immediately fled, replaced by a broad grin. "Hello, girls," he called out to the female class ahead of them.

A blonde, short and very nearly skinny, stopped and turned to look in Tom's direction. Seeing him, she rolled her eyes toward the ceiling, but the familiar, almost warm, smile she sent his way belied that. "Hey Tom," she said. Then, "Matt. George. How'd the sim go?"

George spread his hands in a helpless gesture. "We could not help but crush it, Selena."

Two others of the female class paused alongside the blonde. Katerina, raven-haired and nearly as tall as Matt, with the lushly exotic beauty that seemed to mark all Russian girls on Selena's left and, on her right, Helen, more darkly tanned, of medium height, with wavy auburn locks that she kept cut short to avoid having to put her hair up while in uniform. All three wore the navy blue underway uniforms that the guys did, and all had the single golden collar device that labeled them as Ensigns in the Icaran Confederation Navy.

"The only things you're good at crushing," Helen said, a dark eyebrow arching toward George, "are beer cans."

George made a slight bow, his grin growing more broad. "Guilty as charged," he said.

Matt shook his head at their banter and went up to Katerina. Slipping his hand into hers, he smiled at her warmly. "Did it go well?"

She returned the smile in kind and gave his hand a squeeze. "As well as could be expected." Her deep blue eyes caught the reflection of the sunlight from outside. Had he thought the mountains across the bay presented a lovely view before? They were nothing compared with her.

"Good."

"Oh good Lord." Tom's mocking laugh broke the moment. "Get a room, you two."

Matt, flushing, shot Tom a look, and he returned it innocently. A second or two passed, then Matt found himself chuckling as well. It was hard to be mad at the man, and he had a point. This was a public passageway, in a professional environment. Not exactly the place for canoodling.

Reluctantly, he released Katerina's hand as the now larger group turned to continue its walk. She stayed at his side, and as their arms swung, their fingers would occasionally brush against each other. Each time, a little tingle of electricity surged up Matt's arm, followed by a warm glow that seemed to emanate from his chest.

"Hope the debrief doesn't take too long," Tom was saying. "I've got Household Goods coming at 1400."

Selena looked at him in shock. "What? We weren't supposed to schedule our moves until—"

"Until after close of business. Yeah, yeah," Tom waved a dismissive hand at the comment. "Whatever. Nothing's going on this afternoon. Better to get it done now." He glanced at the window and scowled. "The sooner I get out of this place, the better."

Matt shook his head. "Don't understand why you hate this place so much."

Tom snorted. "This school sucks. It's the most—"

"The planet's nice." Matt did not agree with Tom's assessment of the school, but they had gone around in circles on this point enough times before that he knew not to push it. The planet, though...

"You gotta understand, Matt," George said. "Tom here is used to the big city life. He's not a nature lover like we are."

Tom snorted. "This place is a backwater. Just wait til we get to Montecino." He spread his hands wide, as though taking the other five of them into a big embrace. "You guys are going to love it. You want to talk happening places. Montecino's the hub of everything and everyone that matters." He looked almost worshipful as he spoke. "It's going to kick so much ass being stationed there."

Helen sniffed softly at his words. "You've said that a million times."

"Because it's true." He wagged a finger at her. "You'll find out soon enough."

The girls shared a look, and all three rolled their eyes in unison.

The corridor curved left, and the window overlooking the bay fell behind them, replaced by the plain grey wall panels that marked the classroom section of the building. Up ahead, a trio of Matt's section mates were lingering beside an open door, conversing quietly.

From nowhere and everywhere, an electronic chime sounded, and Matt's classmates hurried through the door.

Matt turned to Katerina and took her hand again. The electricity flowed freely for a second, and he had to restrain himself from leaning forward to steal a kiss. That wouldn't be appropriate here. Instead, he smiled at her. "See you after."

"Only if I don't see you first." Her smile turned mischievous, and she gave his hand a squeeze. Then she released her grip, and she joined her friends as they hurried to another doorway a few tens of meters further down the passageway.

He watched them go for a moment, until a nudge in his side brought him back to the present.

"Come on, lover boy," George said, a teasing grin on his face. "Don't want to get written up on our last day."

That much was certain. Matt hurried into the classroom.

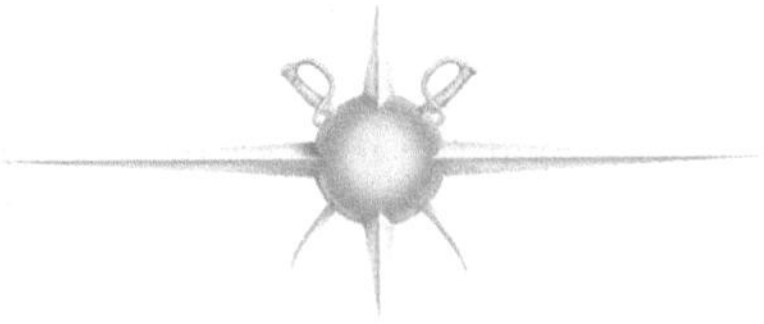

Chapter Three

The classroom was actually three rooms in one; the two ends of the room could be closed off from the central portion by folding partitions that extended out from the rear wall. For most of the past sixth months, those partitions had been closed, separating Matt's class into three sections.

Now, they were fully open, revealing the entirety of the room.

Three groups of thirty desks, all made of faux-wood that almost but not quite looked like oak, with workstations built into the desktop, faced holoscreens built into their respective partition's far wall, behind a raised podium that would allow an instructor to walk from one side of the room to the other while lecturing. As in the hallway, the stationary walls held paintings or photos of warships on sea and in space, all in suitably dramatic angles with weapons firing or storms beating their sails. The rear walls also held large cork boards, on which were hung exams score records, announcements, classroom rules, signup sheets for activities...all the administrivia that a classroom required. The classroom was well-lit by recessed lights in the ceiling, and comfortably cool. It smelled faintly of the remnants from the morning's coffee excesses. And of course, the place was filled with Matt's fellow male trainees.

All of whom, naturally, were in their seats and facing the central podium where the three sections' lead instructors and LT Tolson stood, expectantly.

Tolson looked over as Matt, George, and Tom entered the room. "Nice of you to join us, ladies."

Matt felt himself flushing from embarrassment. Beside him, Tom's features darkened, and he began to scowl.

Tolson spoke again before Tom could say something to get himself in trouble. "Take a seat."

Matt's desk was in the second row of the middle section, third from the left, between two dark-skinned fellows from the tropical region of Carraway's World who could have been twins, they looked so similar to each other. Too bad they despised one another. Matt was certain if he hadn't been placed between them, one would have ripped the other's head off in the first week of training.

Which was probably why he *was* placed there.

Steeling himself, Matt slid into his chair, nodding to Pollos on his left and Devon on his right and receiving an amused grin in return from Pollos, and a disapproving shake of the head from Devon. That's how it always went with those two.

On the center podium, LT Tolson cleared his throat, and Matt turned his attention fully onto him.

"Since this was your final sim run, I'm going to keep this one quick. A few things to keep in mind." He thrust his index finger toward the ceiling. "Section Two, there is no need to sound the general alarm for a casualty when the ship is already at Battle Stations." He paused, eyes narrowing at Matt's section. In the front row, Xander Hollison slumped in his chair noticeably; he had played Chief of the Watch this time. The Lieutenant continued, "Everyone's already out of the rack. Just announce the casualty and move on."

A second finger rose on LT Tolson's hand. "Section Three," his eyes moved left, toward the next group of trainees, "If your target is outside one hundred thousand kilometers, you use *long range* search tactics." Both his eyebrows rose meaningfully, and Matt blanched, embarrassed for the guy in Section Three who messed that up, whoever he was. "We gave you the hit because we're nice, but you should be dead."

Tolson held Section Three with his gaze for a long ten seconds or so, then he turned back to the group to Matt's right. "Section One," he paused again, and the named section seemed to tense in unison. "Good job."

Section One let out a collectively held breath, and their tension broke, replaced by a grins.

LT Tolson continued, "And good job on this course. We've tallied up final scores, and your section has won the Commander's Cup for class 75-02."

The grins were out in force now, and the members of Section One began patting each other on the shoulder in celebration.

LT Tolson turned away from them toward the other two sections. "Three cheers for Section One, gentlemen." He clenched his fist. "Hip-Hip," and he thrust his fist skyward.

"Huzzah!" Matt shouted in time with the fist pump, along with the rest of his section.

"Hip-Hip"

"Huzzah!"

"Hip-Hip"

"Huzzah!"

LT Tolson waited while the commotion of Section One congratulating themselves, and the general murmur of congratulations mixed with disappointment from the other sections, died down.

"The Captain's going to say a lot of things at grad on Friday." LT Tolson resumed pacing along the podium as he spoke. "Naturally, every last word he says will be important."

A soft chuckle spread throughout the room, and even LT Tolson's fellow instructors shared in it. Tolson himself, though, kept a straight face.

"But I want you to remember one thing. When you get to your ships, the configuration of the spaces and the systems will be different from what you've seen here. Two of you, going to ships of the same class just a single hull number apart will find entirely different software versions."

"Don't ever accuse our procurement system of making sense," LT Hapsburg, the lead instructor for Section Three, said.

LT Tolson shot him a hard look that softened after Hapsburg returned it with a raised eyebrow. LT Tolson nodded quickly. "True enough. But we can't change that, can we? Above and beyond the systems differences, the culture of any two ships will be completely different. That's a function of the Captain. But," he thrust a finger ceiling-ward again, "there is something that holds it all together."

LT Tolson peered around the room, his eyes challenging, seeking an answer.

Matt knew what it was. They all did; it had been drilled into their heads enough over the last year and a half of training.

"The Watchstanding Principles," several voices said from around the room.

LT Tolson nodded briskly. "Damn right. Technical knowledge. Tactical Proficiency. Attention to Detail. A Questioning Attitude. Integrity. Procedural Compliance. Forceful Backup. Remember those things, and whether you're going to the newest dreadnaught or a scow barely limping its way to the shipyard for decommissioning, you'll do ok." He grinned then, and his eyes seemed to twinkle with something that almost, but not quite, resembled mirth. "And of course, don't forget the most important thing."

Again he looked around the room as though challenging them to give voice to his thought. This time no one spoke up.

LT Tolson sighed and shook his head. He looked back over at LT Hapsburg, who shrugged and rolled his eyes skyward. "Nubs," he said, in a tone of exasperation.

LT Tolson nodded. "That is the most important thing to remember, gentlemen. No matter how shit-hot you think you are," his eyes seemed to zero in on Tom for a full second before he continued, "when you get to your ship, you're just a new, useless, body. You suck up the oxygen, consume the food, and fill the san tanks. And that's it." He leaned forward. "Get qualified, and do it quickly. That's the single best thing you can do for yourself, and for your ship. Because until you are wearing these," he pointed to the insignia that was painted on the wall above the lecturer's holoscreen in each classroom, "you're nothing."

Matt focused on the insignia, the same thing the instructors all wore on the left breast of their uniforms and he did not. A golden four-pronged starburst, the horizontal plumes long and prominent, the vertical plumes shorter and more stubby, with crossed sabers overlaid. The insignia of a fully qualified Stellar Warfare Officer. Even more than the three bars of rank the Instructors wore, and the greater pay that went with them, Matt wanted that.

He licked his lips in anticipation.

LT Tolson paused for a few seconds, as though going through a list of things in his head. Finally he nodded again. "That's it. The library's waiting to receive your books. If you have any classified notes you want to send on to your ship, they'll bundle them up and send them for you. Otherwise, make sure you've deleted and shredded everything. The security watch will be checking, and I don't want any violations on the last day." He peered around the room for a moment, then said, "Have fun packing out tomorrow," his eyes seemed to zero in on Tom again as he said that, and Matt found himself smirking in amusement. "I'll see you at grad on Friday. Dismissed."

The three sections stood up as one, and the sound of fifty different conversations began to fill the room. Matt turned and offered a congratulatory handshake to Pollos, who returned it with gusto. "Good luck on the HATHERLY, Matt."

"Thanks man." He turned to offer the same to Devon, but found him hamming it up with the guy to his right.

All of a sudden, LT Tolson's voice broke through the hustle and bustle again.

"Ensign Gilbert."

Matt turned to find the instructor had descended from the podium and was standing at the end of his row. He had his usual serious expression on his face, but his eyes had a more severe look than normal. Matt swallowed.

"Yes, sir."

"I need to see you in my office."

"Sir?" Matt got a sinking feeling in the pit of his stomach.

Tolson nodded. "Come by as soon as you're done here."

"Aye sir."

Crap. What had he done now? Well there was nothing to it but to go to the Instructors' Office and see.

LT Tolson turned away and walked toward the doorway back to the main corridor, leaving Matt to sigh in dejection and watch him go. Pollos shook his head, a look of sympathy on his face, and clapped Matt on the shoulder.

"Not sure what you did, Matt. But it was nice knowing you."

Matt looked at him sidelong and saw the Carrawayer grinning mischievously at him. He couldn't help but chuckle.

"He probably wants to give me a private commendation," Matt said, and cuffed Pollos lightly in the belly.

Pollos snorted in response and shook his head, then waved grandly toward the doorway—he even worked a bow into the gesture— and replied, "Your decorations await, sir," in a faux-bass that carried across half the room.

Several sets of eyes turned to regard the pair of them, and Matt had to force himself to stand taller under the weight of them all. "Here goes nothing," he said.

And then he strode firmly out of the room.

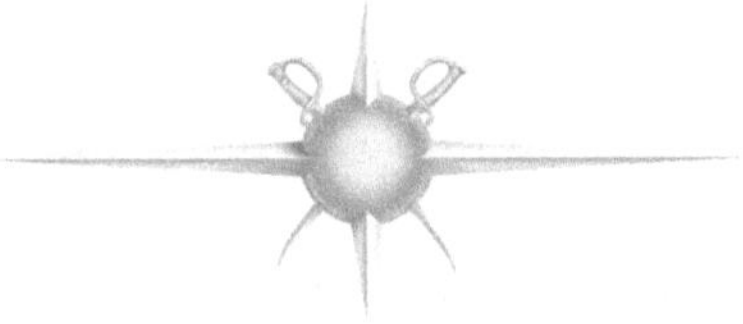

Chapter Four

The instructors' offices lay at the extreme end of the main training corridor, past all the classrooms and the stairwells—ladderwells the Navy called them—that led to the other sections of the Tactical School's campus, until even the memory of the window-laden corridor leading to the simulators had fled from a student's mind and all that remained was the misery of light-grey governmentally bureaucratic decoration.

The office for the male instructors was on the right, as were the male classrooms, the females on the left. Matt had never set foot into the female instructors' office spaces, though from the look of some of their occupants, he would have liked to. But that way lay madness, or at least reprimand, for a student like him. So he had quickly, upon reporting, shoved that curiosity from his mind.

And so it was without effort that he turned away from the female side and tapped the entrance call box next to the door leading to the male instructors' office.

A digital chime sounded, barely audible through the faux wood of the door's construction.

A few seconds later, the door slid open, revealing LT Hapsburg on the other side.

Matt drew himself up to attention and said, "Ensign Gilbert reporting as—"

LT Hapsburg interrupted him. "Come on in, Matt. Glenn's waiting for you."

Matt blinked. That was the first time any of the instructors had called him by his first name. And the first time he had even heard LT Tolson's first name....ever.

He swallowed and stepped into the office.

He had been in here many times before, but as always he did a quick scan.

The room was maybe ten meters squared, and, like all of the other rooms in Tactical School, was decorated with pictures of Naval vessels doing Naval things. The only difference was the greater number of cork-boards interspersed amongst the pictures, the better to keep up with the schedules of the various sections in house.

At any given time, there were three different classes of newly-commissioned male officers on this level, and usually three sections in each class. That made for a fair number of schedules for instructors to maintain, and the office was suitably untidy to make up for it.

And that wasn't counting the instructors' personal items. Each guy had his own postings up in his cubicle, and all of them had something over on the communal wall near the coffee mess. Pictures of women in all manner of dress or undress. Exercise equipment. Sexy cars and aeros. Music bands.

The panoply of interests conflicted mightily with the professional pinups on the surrounding walls, and were it not for the demeanor of the instructors, Matt would be tempted to think this a place of utter chaos. In fact, he had made the mistake of thinking that very thing when he first set foot into the instructors' office at Engineering School, last year.

They had quickly put that impression completely out of his mind.

LT Tolson's desk was in the back left corner of the room. Like the rest of the instructors' stations, most of his area's spare space was hung with pictures and photos. Unlike the other instructors, no images of wife, girlfriend, or kids graced his space. They were all images of him on the bridge, or in CIC, or in some port of call somewhere, always posing dramatically, and never with a woman. Or really, anyone.

Tolson was standing with his back to the door when Matt

approached, talking with one of the instructors who was teaching the class behind Matt's. Thin where Tolson was bulky, but taller than Tolson by a couple centimeters, with a shaggy, by Navy standards, red mop on his crown and green eyes to match, Matt had never actually interacted with the guy, though he knew the instructor's name—Tulliver —from the name tag on his right breast.

As Matt approached, Tulliver nodded in his direction, and Tolson turned around. Seeing Matt, the instructor nodded in greeting.

"Mr. Gilbert." The LT turned to his desk and picked up a clipboard that lay there. He removed a few pieces of paper that were stapled together at the corner and held them out to Matt. "This came on the boards for you this morning."

Matt blinked, surprise fighting with curiosity as he reached out to take the pages. He had presumed he was in trouble for something. But if that wasn't the case... He looked down at the pages, and his mouth dropped open.

"FM DIRECTOR, NAVAL PERSONNEL
TO NAVTACTRASCOL, OLIFANT SYSTEM
ICS HATHERLY
ICS FREDERICK HALSWELL
INFO PERSUPDET OLIFANT SYSTEM
PERSUPDET COPERNICUS
PERSUPDET MONTECINO
COMDESRON TWELVE
COMFRIGRON FOUR
NAVPERS ORDER 2102/1
OFFICIAL MODIFICATION TO CHANGE OF DUTY ORDERS FOR ENSIGN MATTHEW R. GILBERT, ICN/7839
1. WHEN DIRECTED BY REPORTING SENIOR, DETACH IN JUL 2675 FROM DUTY AS STUDENT AT NAVTACTRASCOL, OLIFANT SYSTEM.
2. REPORT TO ICS FREDERICK HALSWELL (SFG 1271) FOR DUTY. HOMEPORT: COPERNICUS STATION, NEW CALIFORNIA
3. REPORT NLT AUG 2675
4. ULTIMATE DUTY STATION IS DESIGNATED AS UNUSUALLY ARDUOUS SPACE DUTY...."

The rest of the message droned on into administrivia, and he could not take it in. Only one thing registered.

"New California," he said, and the dismay that was welling up within him must have shown, because LT Tolson managed a sympathetic frown.

"Sorry, Mr. Gilbert," he said. "I know you and your friends were looking forward to Montecino."

Matt nodded. "We got a house lined up to rent."

LT Tolson returned the nod. "Well, that's how it works some times. Needs of the Navy, you know." He grinned, and it looked unnatural on his normally severe face. "At least New California's nice. Ever been there?"

Matt shook his head, but he did not reply. His mind was racing. Tom and George were going to have fits finding a guy to replace him, and Katerina... Oh crap, Katerina.

"Did any other ordmods come through, sir?"

LT Tolson's eyebrow twitched upward, and he shook his head. "No, not that I saw. Why—?"

"Crap!"

That came out louder than Matt had intended. It drew the eyes of all of the instructors in the room. It felt like being in the crosshairs of a ruby laser, he suddenly felt so hot. With embarrassment. He cleared his throat. "Sorry, sir," he managed, looking abashedly at LT Tolson. "It's just, my girlfriend is getting stationed—"

Tolson rolled his eyes. "Mr. Gilbert, you didn't hook up with one of the girls from the female class, did you?"

There was nothing for it but to nod. It was the truth, after all.

"You know the Navy frowns on that sort of thing."

Matt raised his chin. "It's not against the rules, sir."

LT Tolson glowered at him for a moment before, grudgingly, he nodded. "True. But it's still frowned upon. And this is why." He sighed. "The needs of the Navy come first, Mr. Gilbert. You know that. They're not going to ordmod her too just so you can be together. Hell, it's hard enough to get that for a married couple. And anyway, there are no female ships homeported at New California." The instructor's eyes narrowed. "She is going to Montecino I take it?"

Matt nodded.

"Well." LT Tolson crossed his arms over his chest. "Three weeks travel time between there and New Cali. A day or so for an email..." He shook his head. "You'd better break it off now. It'll just end later, regardless."

Matt flinched. To hear it said so plainly... He shook his head. "We can make it work."

LT Tolson looked at him for a few seconds, his expression portraying his supreme doubt plainly for all to see. Then he shrugged. "Your call." Another second's pause, then he continued, "You'll want to get to the travel office to reschedule your flight and then over to Household Goods so they can redirect your shipment. When do you have the movers coming?"

Crap. Something else Matt hadn't thought of. "Noon tomorrow, sir. I don't have a lot of stuff so they think it'll just take a couple hours."

Tolson nodded. "That's good. Some morons," he shook his head quickly, "always think to push the system, and schedule their moves for this afternoon." He smirked. "Every couple classes, one of those guys gets an ordmod, and it kicks their ass, trying to get their move squared away with so little time."

Matt let out a half-chuckle, for politeness' sake, and tried to keep his poker face on. But then, thinking on it for a second, LT Tolson probably knew exactly which of them had violated that particular rule, and it probably wasn't just Tom.

"I'd better hurry, sir," Matt said, and Tolson nodded.

"Yes, you had better." He half-turned back to his desk, then paused and looked back at Matt. "Good luck, Mr. Gilbert."

Matt wasn't sure whether he meant with the move or his new ship.

Or both.

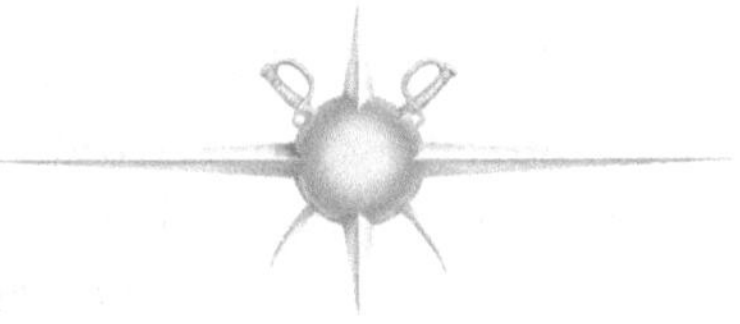

Chapter Five

"New California?" George looked incredulously across the highly polished faux-pine of the table where he, Matt, and Tom sat.

They had all hurried to close out their business at the school and head home, though Matt was busy enough re-arranging his entire life that he didn't see the other two except to arrange to meet up later. Now, as afternoon dwindled into evening, they had changed into civilian attire and met up at The Score Zone. Situated along the shore of the bay, and on the other side of town from the school, the Zone had quickly become their preferred starting-off spot for their evenings out here on Olifant. Not terribly loud, the place nonetheless had a great sense of energy to it, with holoscreens showing live feeds from all the various sporting events in-system, and taped-delayed broadcasts of the major games from across the Confederation. The decor was modern enough, and kept pristinely clean by the platoon of wait staff that was always on duty.

And best of all, it had over a hundred different kinds of beer on tap, and at least another hundred more in the bottle.

Matt nodded glumly, and swallowed a mouthful of a locally-brewed amber that he barely tasted.

George shook his head. "And...HALSWELL? Hull 1271...Jesus, how old is she?"

"Twenty-six years." Older than any of the men at the table. "POTTER class frigate." Matt sighed. She was a far cry from from HATHERLY, the brand new strike cruiser the three of them used to have orders to. "So much for the pointy end of the spear." He raised his half-empty stein to his lips. "This sucks," he said, and took another drink.

Across from him, George and Tom traded looks. Neither appeared any more happy about the change to Matt's orders than he was.

Tom cleared his throat. "Well, it could be worse. Could be Triton..." He trailed off as Matt gave him a flat look, and took a drag from his own stein. "You told Katerina yet?"

Matt shook his head. "Haven't seen her. They should be here tonight though, right?"

"Yeah we told Selena to meet us." George winced sympathetically, then drew a deep breath. "How do you want to handle it?"

Matt swallowed another gulp. "LT Tolson said I should break up with her." He couldn't keep a bite of bitterness from his tone.

It didn't help when Tom nodded agreement. "He's right, you know."

Matt scowled at him, and he leaned back, holding his hands out defensively. "Don't get pissed at me, Matt. It'd be hard enough to keep things going with her in the same homeport and different ships. And New Cali is how far from Montecino?"

"Four jumps, and about three weeks. I checked this afternoon."

"Three weeks." Tom shook his head. "That's basically your entire leave for the year, one way. You'll never see her." His eyebrows rose on his head. "And there are more than enough hotties on New California that after a few weeks, you won't want to."

Matt felt his scowl deepen, though intellectually he knew Tom had a point. That *was* an awful long distance. And New California, with a gravity well just over ten percent greater than Terran norm, tended to produce people who were quite a bit more fit than average. Add to that the fact that more than 80% of the planet's land mass lay within its tropical zone, and they were a well-tanned people as well, with less than stringent dress codes. It made for a great place to visit, or so everyone said.

George noted Matt's increased scowl and looked between the two of them for a second. "Come on, Matt. Tom's right."

Matt turned his glare on him, and George snorted.

"About not getting mad at him," George said, to clarify. "It's not his fault. Or mine."

Matt drew in a deep breath and held it for the count of five, then released it, slowly, and nodded. "You're right, George." He looked back at Tom. "And you probably are too, Tom. But, damn it..." He trailed off, unsure how to give voice to the jumble of thoughts going through his head.

Yes, there was probably no way to make it work. Yes, it would be best for both him and Katerina to just make a clean break now instead of dragging it out fruitlessly for months apart.

But damn if she wasn't an amazing girl. Sharp as a tack, fun, witty. And smoking hot; she was certainly the most attractive girl he had ever been with. It would be hard saying goodbye to all of that.

George waved to get the attention of their waiter, a student at the local college from the look of him. "Get my buddy a refill and put his drinks on my tab," he said, nodding Matt's way.

"Hey, you don't need to do that," Matt said.

"The hell I don't. You're going to need to tie one on tonight, brother." George shook his head. "Can't let you pay for it."

Matt sighed and nodded, but George's gesture already made him feel a bit better at least. He managed a grin toward his friend as the waiter departed to see to his drink.

"Well, as long as you're buying," Tom began, but George cut him off quickly.

"Not a chance, Mr. Trust Fund. Hell, you should be buying all of our drinks."

Tom rolled his eyes. "I told you, I can't touch that until I'm thirty."

"Excuses, excuses." George smirked, and after another second or so, Tom laughed, shaking his head in what Matt was sure was mock consternation.

A movement from the direction of the entrance caught his eye and Matt looked away from his two friends. The beginnings of mirth died within him as he saw Selena, Helen, and Katerina approaching the hostess station. They were dressed to the nines, ready for a club in tight-fitting but tasteful dresses that suggested more than they revealed, but revealed enough to demand attention. Katerina and Selena had let their hair down, and they all looked like they had spent a good hour in front of the mirror getting their makeup just right.

Tom whistled softly in admiration as Helen noticed them and gave a little wave, then led the trio toward the guys' table.

"Gentlemen," Tom said, "we did alright at Tactical School."

That was true enough. Too bad it was going to have to end on a sour note.

"Hello boys," Helen said as the girls arrived at the table.

"Hey," George said, and put on a smile of greeting. Tom gave them a nod and a grin.

Matt's eyes found Katerina's, and the broad smile she was wearing faltered. She paused mid-step and looked quickly over at the others. "What's wrong?"

Matt could feel Tom and George cringing, inwardly at least, but they remained silent. The other two girls focused in on him, their eyes narrowing.

He drew a deep breath and stood from his chair. "We need to talk," he said, and reached out for Katerina's hand.

She slowly took it, the smile gone completely now, replaced by wary concern. "Ok...?" She trailed off into a question, punctuated by a raised eyebrow.

Matt cleared his throat to shove aside the feeling of every pair of eyes boring into his back and led her away from the table toward an empty couple of stools along the bar. "I've got some bad news," he said as he pulled out one of the stools for her.

She slid onto the stool gracefully and took a second to smooth the fabric of her dress before looking back at him again. "Ok," she said again, slowly.

He sat down next to her, reached into his pocket, and withdrew his new orders. He took a moment to unfold them, then handed them over for her to peruse.

Katerina accepted the pages. Her eyes widened as they scanned the text. "No," she said, and all the consternation that Matt had been feeling the entire afternoon came out in that one word.

Matt nodded glumly and waved for the bartender. "That's what I said. But it's real."

She lowered the paper into her lap and sat there for a long moment, apparently stunned into silence as she just looked at him. Finally, she swallowed and gave a little nod, as though to herself. "Well, the needs of the Navy, right?"

Matt snorted softly. "Yeah. Needs of the Navy."

The bartender, Gabriel, pushed a filled stein to Matt. He was a bulky guy in his mid-forties whose black hair had receded halfway back on his scalp, and he wore a t-shirt with The Score Zone's logo on the breast. "Got your refill, Matt," he said, and nodded to the side, where the waiter from their table was standing at their staff service area. "What'll the lady have?"

Katerina gave herself a little shake and turned more fully toward the bar. Her eyes swept over the various taps, then to the bottles of liquor on the shelves above. "Smirnov, please, Gabriel," she said. She looked sidelong at Matt, then added. "Two shot glasses. And leave the bottle."

The bartender blinked, surprise flashing across his face for a second, then he nodded and turned to see to it.

For his part, Matt couldn't help but grin at her. Looked like it was to be the tried and true vodka shots until you can't stand up routine again.

She met his grin with a challenging stare. "We've only got these last few nights together," she said, and both eyebrows rose. "We'd better make the most of them."

"You're...taking this well," he said, after a second's pause to collect himself. "I thought—"

"What, that I'd be shattered?" She sighed and laid her hand atop his. Those big, blue eyes of hers peered deeply into his, and he could tell part of her, at least, was. All the same, her voice was strong and calm as she spoke. "Let's not fool ourselves, Matt. What we've had is great, and it could have gone on being great on Montecino." She shook her head slightly. "Not easy because we'd be on different ships, of course, but it could have worked. But this..."

Gabriel set a pair of shot glasses down on the bar top between them, then unscrewed a tall bottle and poured clear fluid into the two before setting the bottle down and backing away. He knew when not to interrupt, professional that he was.

"I was trying to think of a way for us to keep it going," Matt began, but Katerina interrupted him.

"You know that won't work."

He shrugged slightly. "Yeah." He flashed her a quick smile. "Doesn't mean I'm not willing to try."

She leaned forward and kissed him lightly on the mouth. "That's sweet," she said as she withdrew. "But you don't have to pretend for my benefit. We both knew this was possible." Her eyebrows lifted again. "You can't say you hadn't considered it."

"Well, yeah. I guess."

Katerina shook her head in amusement, and smiled gently at him. "I'm going to miss you, Matt." Then her smile turned predatory. "But I intend to make the most of it while I still have you."

He found himself returning her grin in kind. "I think I can handle that."

"Good." Katerina picked up her shot glass and held it between them.

Matt picked up his own, and the glasses met with a solid tap.

He kept his eyes locked on hers, and she on his, while they downed the shots together.

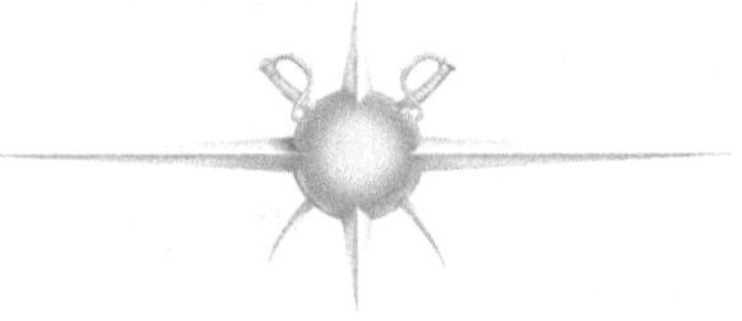

Chapter Six

"New California is aptly named One of two planets in orbit around a small G-type star, approximately 60% as luminous as Sol. Over 80% of its land mass lies within its tropical zone. A small axial tilt, only 7 degrees, makes for only extremely minor seasonal variance in its climate. That lack of variation combined with the lack of a moon makes for noticeably calmer weather patterns than on other planets its size. The result is a world with almost ubiquitous Mediterranean-to-Tropical climate. As most of the original colonists were from the North American continent of Terra, they most closely related it with Southern California and decided to name it to match.

"Despite its pleasant climate, New California has remained relatively sparsely populated in the centuries since colonization, primarily due to limited easily-harvestable natural resources and, more importantly, a paucity of jump points in the system. There are only two, leading to Davidea and to Elysium, neither of which were particularly noteworthy in their own right, being themselves an independent system on the fringes of colonized space and a system of secondary importance within the Confederation, respectively.

"It is doubtful New California would have ever become anything more than a high-quality tourist destination, except that the discovery of a newly-formed jump point between Davidea and Philemon, in the

Tsago Dominance, suddenly presented both Davidea and the Confederation with the possibility of a Dominance incursion into their territories. This prompted Davidea to enter into a mutual defense pact with the Confederation, and led to the establishment of the Naval Base at Copernicus Station in New California.

"Though lightly staffed, with just five Frigates and three squadrons each of interceptor and reconnaissance craft, the Naval Station nevertheless represents a significant investment in the system, and has brought with it the shipyard, cargo, and security facilities that New California had lacked before. That combined with the influx of raw materials and labor force from the increased Confederation activity has led to an economic boom in the system. New California'a population, once barely fifty million total, has increased by twenty percent over the last twenty standard years.

"This has not sat well with some locals, and there have been boisterous, and occasionally violent, protests of the increased Confederation military presence in the system. However, the majority of the populace has welcomed the increase in their fortunes gladly..."

Matt tabbed off his holopad and dropped it onto the table in front of him. He stood from the padded chair he had been sitting in and stretched, trying to hold back a yawn. There was only so much reading he could manage at a time if it wasn't a spy thriller, and besides, he had read this same synopsis, or one very much like it, half a dozen times since boarding the liner from Oliphant to his new home.

They all added up to the same picture: New California was a great place to live, but not necessarily the best place to be stationed. Some—not all, but a fair number—of the locals resented the Navy's presence. They were two jumps from the major trade routes, a week or more at best, and there was next to no danger of the Dominance trying something. Davidea had already been more than capable of taking care of itself, and since the mutual defense pact they had just gotten stronger.

No way the Dominance would try to push through there. Not when there were easier nuts to crack on the other side of the Confederation.

No, it looked like he was going to be far from any action that didn't involve tourist girls.

Not that there was anything wrong with tourist girls.

Over the last week and a half since departing Oliphant, he had come through the grommet over Katerina. The last few days with her, going through Grad and then final departure preps had been good. Good enough that he had almost been tempted to push for making a go of it, despite the hopelessness of it all.

Well, he had been tempted. But the decision had been made, there in The Score Zone. And all the good things that had happened between the two of them had come because they had been grown up about it. Tempted though he had been, he wasn't stupid enough to mess that up.

She certainly wasn't either. When the time came to depart, they embraced, shared one last kiss, then said goodbye. He went to his liner, she to hers. He looked back once, despite telling himself he was not going to. He got a glimpse of the back of her head as she stepped through the boarding hatch, and then she was gone.

It had taken a few days to really get it through his head that they were actually done. But now, with the docking at Copernicus just a few hours away, he had managed to put the worst of his regret aside, as eagerness to see and explore his new world began to creep up over him.

Boring garrison duty or not, crappy aging ship or not, bad attitudes among the locals or not, it was a hell of a nice place to be. Or so they all said. He found he was looking forward to finding out.

The 1MC clicked to life, and two pairs of tinny bells intruded into his thoughts.

Matt blinked and did the conversion from bells to clock in his head. 1800. Time for dinner. He looked around and considered his options.

His stateroom was small, but still quite a bit more luxurious than what he could expect when he got to his ship. A single room with a double-bed mounted to the rear wall, the chair he was sitting in and coffee table adjacent to it, a kitchenette and round breakfast table with seating for two, and a sliding door that led into the head compartment, just between the head of the bed and the kitchenette's counter. The walls were a semi-consoling beige, with a painting of snow-capped mountains hanging adjacent to the stuffed chair. Recessed lighting, just slightly white of warm, cast illumination over the room, making it seem not quite homey.

There was some food in the fridge, the last of the supplies he had purchased when he first came aboard. He could cook himself a bite and then get back to studying up...

Screw that. He had been limiting how much money he spent up to this point on the trip, but he really didn't feel like being cooped up any more. Besides, they were coming up on New California. From the trajectory of their orbital track, there ought to be a good view of it from the port side observation deck.

That settled it.

He took a minute to straighten out his shirt and run a hand through his hair, then he set out.

Matt's stateroom was on the centerline of the ship, almost amidships. He made a right once he stepped into the passageway, marveling as he had every time he had gone out and about the ship at the red carpeted deck. Carpet, on a starship! Didn't they know that was a fire hazard?

You've been thinking military for too long.

That thought made him laugh. He hadn't even really been in the Navy for a year and a half yet—College and Officer Candidate School didn't count—and already he was thinking of everything from the Naval perspective.

The passageway was almost three meters wide, leaving plenty of room for movement in both directions, but surprisingly few people were out and about. He passed one elderly couple, walking slowly, arm-in-arm and talking to each other in low but warm voices. And that was it until he reached the main forward athwartships passageway.

It ran, he knew from his orientation briefings, from the starboard observation deck to the port, and connected the three fore-and-aft passageways on this deck together. So it was natural that the passageway would see more traffic. Still, after the emptiness of his own, Matt gave a start at the sudden comparative press of people, and he had to jump aside to avoid being run over by a gaggle of red-haired children. They were giggling and carrying on, and didn't notice him at all as he pressed himself up to the bulkhead. But their mother, a round-faced woman in her mid thirties, following along behind them with a harried look on her face, winced and mouthed, "I'm sorry," to him as she passed.

Matt shrugged and grinned in return, and she looked relieved.

Kids. What can you do?

His way now mostly clear, he proceeded to port. Another couple minutes of walking brought him to the double-portal that lead to the observation deck. Matt tapped at the control pad on the right-hand side, and the metallic-grey door slid open, soundlessly.

He stepped within and stopped as he beheld the view beyond.

This was not his first visit to the observation lounge, and it was far from his first view of space. Though, he had to admit most of his previous views had been sims or pictures. But still, he had seen star fields before. He had even sat in an observation bubble during the transit through a jump point, and hadn't that been a mind-warping view.

But he hadn't beheld such a view as lay before him now.

His own home world of Trinity was relatively distant from its star, mostly snow-covered except for the regions near the equator, and mostly devoid of oceans. The immense snowcap made drinking water plentiful, but it was not exactly picturesque from space. Oliphant, housing the Engineering and Tactical Schools, was more temperate and Terra-like, but even still its ocean to land mass ratio was fairly low.

New California was another matter entirely. A sapphire-blue globe, punctuated by a multitude of swirling white clouds, that dominated the forward half of the observation deck's curved plasteel dome, it was almost completely unbroken ocean except for a seemingly tiny bit of green just visible at the globe's edge. Matt knew that was illusory; New Cali's land mass made up about 12% of its total surface area. But the liner's orbital trajectory, coming in at about thirty degrees above the system's ecliptic, accentuated the impression of continuous, unbroken ocean to such an extent that his comparatively-landlocked brain had trouble taking it in at first.

A few seconds later, a flash of light from the side of the mostly blue and white globe drew Matt's eye, and he shifted his focus. It took a short while to make out the flash's source, but eventually he found it. A roughly cylindrical metallic structure, just barely large enough to make out with the naked eye, that seemed to hover above the globe.

That was also an illusion, Matt knew. Copernicus Station was far from stationary; it was in geosynchronous orbit with New California, connected with the surface by an array of space elevators that he had no hope of seeing from this distance.

His ship, if she was in port, was moored there. That made it his new home.

What a sight to see.

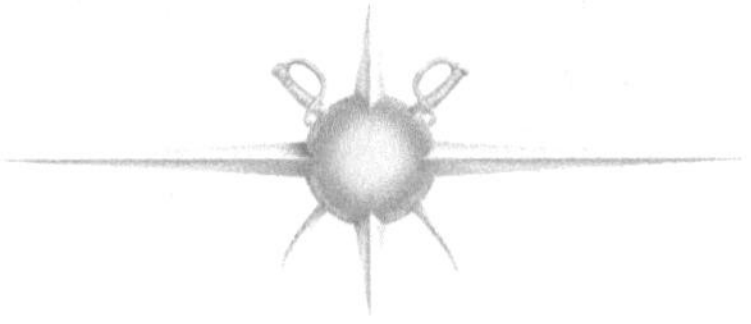

Chapter Seven

"Pretty, ya?"

The low-pitched female voice came from Matt's right, drawing his eyes away from the planet. She sat in a low-backed, cushioned chair, one of four surrounding an oval-shaped glass-topped table. One of several dozen similar placings scattered throughout this area of the observation deck, it was clearly designed more for socializing than for dining. Down in the lower section of the observation lounge by the bar were more traditional tables, but the facility served up here as well; several groups nearby were nursing drinks and appetizers.

Even sitting—more like lounging, Matt's mind corrected itself—he could tell the woman was tall, maybe a centimeter or two taller than he was. The sleeveless cream blouse she wore showed off well-toned muscles in her shoulders and arms. Her deeply-tanned skin gleamed in the mixture of natural and artificial light, giving her a healthy and vital appearance. She wore her dark, nearly black hair cut short at the back and right temple, nearly shaved, but long on top and combed to flow down the left side of her head to her shoulder, partially hiding that side of her face. Yellow-brown eyes looked at him with welcoming interest, and she half-smiled, half pursed her lips as he took a moment to look her over.

The woman arched one eyebrow. "Navy, ya?"

Matt snorted out a little chuckle and spread his hands in what he hoped was a disarming manner. "That obvious, huh?"

She nodded. "You got the look." She leaned forward, resting her elbows on her knees. "First time to New Cali." She said it as a statement of fact, but it took a second for Matt to register her words. The loose blouse drooped down from her neck, revealing impressive, and almost certainly braless, cleavage.

Matt swallowed and forced his eyes back up to the woman's face, and paused again when he saw the knowing look she wore. Coughing lightly into his hand to avoid saying something and sounding completely stupid, he just nodded.

"Welcome t' me home." She sounded like she genuinely meant that.

Of course she was a local. That much should have been obvious from her physique, if nothing else. That was one thing all the information on New California made abundantly clear: higher gravity combined with near-perfect climate made for an extremely fit and vigorous population.

Matt returned her frank gaze with a grin of his own, firmly keeping his eyes above her neckline. "Thanks. I'm excited to be stationed here." He glanced at the other chairs at her table, all empty, and the lack of any food or drink, and decided to take a stab at it. He widened his grin. "Can I get you a drink?"

She pulled back from him, her head cocking to the side slightly, making her hair wave about as she moved. Her left hand raised quickly and tossed her hair back from her face, pushing it past her shoulder. She did it forcefully, almost as though suddenly annoyed at her locks. But she said nothing.

Matt, confused, found his grin slipping. "Is that a no?"

The woman's lips turned downward slightly, and she raised her left hand to her hair again, leaving it there for a long second before raising her eyebrows at Matt.

What in the hell? Matt shook his head. "I don't get it."

The woman's nostril's flared, and for a second Matt thought she was going to launch into him. But then an amused chuckle from off to his left broke the moment.

Matt turned to see a man ascending the stairs from the lower level, down where the bar and dining tables were positioned. Like the woman he had been talking with, the guy was deeply tanned and well-muscled. Also like her, he wore a loose-fitting, sleeveless shirt, though his was a brilliant blue, and baggy, off-white capri-cut pants. But his hair was a couple shades lighter than hers, and his eyes very nearly the same shade of blue as his shirt. He carried a cocktail glass in each hand, both filled with a light pink fluid that bubbled slowly.

The man grinned mischievously. "She tryin tell you she married," he said, nodding toward the woman. "But she forgot t' wear the ring."

Matt looked back at the woman in time to see her jerk slightly as though the man's words had smacked her. She blinked, then blinked again, and looked down at her ringless left hand. Her cheeks turned crimson.

Matt had noticed the lack of wedding ring, or he wouldn't have offered to buy a drink. "I'm sorry," he said, as much to cover the woman's embarrassment as anything else. He looked back at the man and tried to look apologetic. "Didn't mean anything by it."

The man shrugged and slid into the chair to the woman's right, setting one of the glasses down in front of her. "Of course." He smiled warmly at her for a second then looked back at Matt. "My name is Isaiah, and she Maleen." He gestured toward the seat opposite the woman. "Join us?"

Matt hesitated. Glancing at Maleen, he found that her bout of embarrassment had passed and she was back to looking friendly again. She nodded in agreement at her...husband's?...invitation. Still feeling a bit awkward, Matt settled down into the chair and offered his name, but didn't say anything more for the moment.

Probably best to let them speak next.

Maleen broke the ice first. "We coming so close t' home I forgot the ring. Revertin' t' our ways early." She lifted her hand to her hair again, running her fingertips along the dangling locks. "Woman wear her hair this side," she said, "she married. Other side, she available. Wouldn't expect you t' know. I have a ring, for time offworld, but..." She shrugged, flushing again, though not as badly as she had at first. "Apologies."

"You've got nothing to be sorry for. It's a natural mistake."

"For her, ya," Isaiah said, and his earlier smile faded into seriousness. "For you?" He shook his head. "Some places on New Cali, man get forward wit' married woman..." He trailed off, raising his eyebrows meaningfully. Then, putting his glass down on the table, he made a fist with his right hand and drove it into his left palm.

The man's expression said he was deadly serious, and just then Matt remembered how much weaker he probably was than him. The liner had been gradually increasing gravity from Oliphant's 0.96G to New California's 1.11G over the course of the voyage, but that was not nearly enough to make up for the lifetime this guy had spent in that deeper gravity well.

"Seriously, I didn't mean—"

Isaiah's grin returned just as quickly as it had vanished and he spoke quickly, interrupting Matt mid-word. "We know. Just word t' the wise, for when you get planetside."

Over Maleen's shoulder, Matt spied a waitress meandering through the tables and raised a hand to get her attention. Then, seeking to change the subject, he looked at Isaiah. His hair was long, almost shaggy, not even close to shaved short like Maleen's right side. "So how does a man show he's married?" He gestured toward Isaiah's head to punctuate the question.

Isaiah chuckled and, leaving his drink on the table, raised his hands. He had a tattoo on his left wrist: a black band that circled the wrist entirely, almost like the stripes of rank at the bottom of the Navy's Service Dress Blue uniform.

He tapped the tattoo with the index finger of his right hand, and raised an eyebrow.

Matt blinked, taken aback. "That's....rather permanent."

"Is marriage," Isaiah replied in a matter-of-fact tone.

"But, what if you get divorced—"

"No divorce on New Cali," Maleen said, nostrils flaring for a moment and her tone growing hard. "Is blasphemy."

Another surprise. These were coming quickly and without mercy. "But..." He saw their expressions turn toward disapproval, and gestured toward the long hair flowing past Maleen's shoulder. "A woman just shows by her haircut. That's not very...even." He couldn't think of a better way to say it.

"Women live longer," Isaiah said, again in that matter-of-fact tone. "And it not proper t' desecrate a woman's skin wit ink." Another eyebrow raise. "Blasphemy. Also..." He paused, working his jaw as though searching for the right words. After a second he continued, "You see men offworld remove the ring when wife not around, t' try have fun with other women?"

Matt nodded. He hadn't personally seen it happen, but he had heard of the practice, unsavory as it was.

"Hard to do wit this," he gestured at the tattoo. "Or wit a woman's hair."

"But what do you do if she dies first?"

For a second, Matt thought sure he had stepped in it, to ask so crassly, but Isaiah just shrugged and tapped at his right wrist. "Another tattoo here. Then, if re-marry," he tapped at his left wrist again.

Matt understood. A second circlet above the first, to denote the second wife. Made sense.

The waitress arrived just then, and before Matt could say anything, Isaiah made a sweeping gesture with his hand, as though pulling Matt into the table. "His drinks on us."

"You really don't have to do—"

"The least we can do."

Matt hesitated, then, not wanting to give offense and also not really inclined to pass up a free drink, inclined his head in acceptance. "Bourbon on the rocks," he said to the waitress, and she nodded briskly before hurrying off. Looking back at Isaiah again, he said, "Thanks. And thanks for the cultural lesson too."

"Our pleasure," Isaiah said.

Maleen said, more warmly than before, "Not everyone know and friendly with offworlders like we."

Matt nodded. "I read about the troubles, since the Navy increased its presence. Lots of riots. Sailors getting rolled." He left that last dangle out there. Part of him wanted to think those reports were just the typical scare-mongering from the brass. He hadn't been in the Navy all that long, but he'd already figured out that the things they said were horrible in the off-limits notices were almost always nowhere near as bad as advertised.

The couple traded glances, and then after a second Maleen gave a little shrug. "Some on New Cali bitter. Think we do better without Confed around. Want," she raised her hands and made sarcastic quotation gestures with her fingers, "independence."

Isaiah snorted and shook his head. "They don't know how t' do math. Confed money flowin' in what holds our economy up. They think tourist trade will continue t' be what it is if we not allied wit Icarus?"

Maleen reached out and laid a calming hand on his, but didn't take her eyes off Matt. "But they few. Most locals be good and friendly. You'll see. Just learn our ways, respect 'em."

"And stay out of a few areas," Isaiah put in.

She looked at him for a second and her expression darkened, then she nodded with obvious reluctance. "Ya, that. Some places it don't pay t' go if you outworlder." She smiled again as she returned her gaze to Matt. "But again, they few."

Sounded like the Navy actually had the right of it, for a change. The Force Protection briefings Matt had read said basically the same things, and laid out the off-limits areas. Still, Matt wondered if this couple's advised keep out areas would match those in the briefings.

A second or so of silence passed as Matt pondered that, and the couple shared another look.

"Not really very many places." Isaiah grinned. "Come down t' the surface, and we show you around the good ones."

Maleen nodded agreement. "Too many Navy stay up in the station, only come down for bars t' pick up tourists." She raised an eyebrow, and Matt chuckled inwardly at his earlier thought about that breed of young lady. "That no way to know New Cali."

"Thanks," Matt said, as the waitress returned and set his drink down on the table in front of him. He favored the girl with a quick grin and a nod, then looked back at Maleen and Isaiah. "I think I'll take you up on that."

He lifted his glass, and they followed suit. Their three glasses clinked together in the space above the table with the sound of a pact being made.

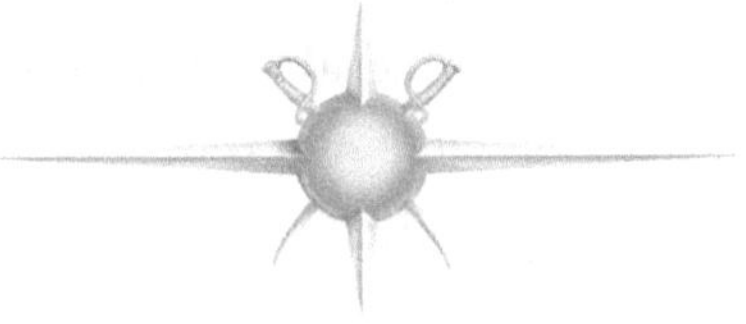

Chapter Eight

Matt strode out of the passenger access tube that connected his part of the liner to one of the many docking gates that ringed Copernicus Station. There he paused for a moment to take in the scene.

It was much like any other passenger terminal that he had seen: off-white paint on the walls, modular semi-padded chairs in the seating area around the gates themselves, a cluster of food and necessities kiosks in the center of the half-circular area that made up this hub of the terminal, four other tubes that disgorged passengers from the other sections of the liner, and a wide passageway leading further into the station's receiving area.

And people. Lots and lots of people.

It was easy to tell the locals from their dress and their toned bodies, but they were a distinct minority here. Most of the folks debarking and milling about were from offworld, and Matt saw many a military man in the throng. Despite the lack of uniforms, the short haircuts, erect statures, and fit physiques were dead giveaways, even if the military men had the same wide-eyed look that he was certain he wore himself.

Because this terminal differed from the others he had been through in one glaring, and disconcerting, way. The floor in the center of the walkways was transparent, allowing an unfettered view of the lush planet, far below. Even he, having spent many weeks on spacecraft during his training both before and after commissioning, found himself feeling a little queasy looking down at it that way.

It was one thing to know you were on a station in geosynchronous orbit, connected to the surface by a few relatively tiny anchoring structures. It was another thing entirely to see it for fact.

And to see, seemingly infinitely far away but growing rapidly closer with every heartbeat, the strobes on one of the elevator lifts as it brought its cargo of goods and people up from the surface.

Swallowing, he looked away from the seeming hole in the floor and got moving, rolling his carry-on garment bag and duffle behind himself, before he could cause a traffic jam. He kept strictly to the normally-tiled section of the walkway though, as did all but a very few of his fellow travelers.

The crowd carried him along almost without effort; everyone was going the same place. Before long, he had descended a short sloping corridor into the station proper, where a group of a half-dozen baggage claim stations stretched out in each direction. They were sizable units, used for larger cargo that passengers either could not, or didn't wish to, store in their staterooms.

Fortunately, Matt only had his clothing and sundries to worry about. Household Goods would deliver his furniture and bulky items separately, once he got a place to stay lined up. Smiling a thankful little smile that he would not have to deal with that annoyance right this minute, Matt turned right and walked past the silent, still baggage units.

The third station to the right would have been his, from the section number that appeared on a status board above it. A crowd had already started to form, the offworlders in the group looking at the unit with consternation as they waited for it to spring to life and disgorge their belongings.

Interestingly, the locals in the group seemed nonchalant about the wait. They stood in groups, separate from the offworlders, chatting away and laughing softly, a distinct difference from the largely silent and solitary offworlders.

In one larger group of locals Matt spied Isaiah and Maleen. She was talking animatedly with a pair of older Californian women. Grey-streaked hair hung over the right sides of their faces, and they wore the sleeveless blouses and capris that Matt had come to expect from the locals. Isaiah, arms crossed over his chest, stood to the side looking bemused.

As Matt approached, his eyes met Isaiah's, and the Californian man's lips turned a bit further upward. He laid one hand lightly on Maleen's shoulder and, when she turned to look at him, nodded in Matt's direction. When she saw him, Maleen grinned broadly and waved for him to come over.

Matt hesitated for a second, the lure of getting to explore this new place tugging him onward, then he shrugged to himself and meandered over,.

"Matt," Maleen said warmly, "Lovely t' see you again." She leaned in, giving him a quick half-hug that consisted of taking hold of his upper arms and moving in to bring their foreheads close together before releasing him. He had read that this was the traditional way for women to greet a man who they considered a friend, but this was the first time she had it done to him. He was supposed to grasp her lower arms as she came in and copy the lean-in, but the suddenness of her movement caught him by surprise, and he missed the timing completely.

"You too," he said, trying not to sound embarrassed, and looked back at Isaiah. "Isaiah," he said, and held out his hand. That way was more familiar, as the greeting between men was what Matt knew and appreciated: a good firm clasp of the hand, even if the exact grip was different from the shake he had grown accustomed too.

Isaiah retained his bemused expression as he released Matt's hand, but he said nothing, just nodded quickly.

Matt glanced at the two women Maleen was talking with, and found them giving him appraising looks, curious expressions on their faces. A trifle uncomfortable under their gazes, he flashed a smile at them and nodded. "Ladies."

They remained silent for a second, then returned the nod.

Matt got the impression he had done something wrong again, but he wasn't sure what.

Isaiah saved him. "You got an idea of where t' go, Matt?"

Matt shrugged. "I think there's a guy from the ship going to meet me. I imagine he'll take me to the base, and we'll go from there."

Isaiah nodded. "Remember, come down and we show you around."

He fished a holopad out of his pocket and lifted it toward Matt, an eyebrow rising on his forehead.

Matt let go the handle on his baggage and pulled out his own holopad. Thumbing the permissions pad on the side of the unit, he tapped corners with Isaiah's, initiating the transfer of their contact information.

"I'll do that," Matt said. "Thanks." He glanced between the four of them, and again found the older women looking at him like he was a curious specimen of some sort or other. And maybe not an appealing one, at that.

"Well," he said. "I'll get going. See you around?"

Isaiah nodded with a smile, and Maleen again did one of their friendly greetings. This time Matt didn't mess up his part of it.

He turned away from them, and he heard Maleen's conversation start up again behind him. But then time he thought he heard one of the older woman say something low, almost below his hearing. Something about trouble from offworlders.

Glancing back, none of the group was looking at him, but he had the distinct impression he was now the subject of the discussion. Only natural, but still something about it made his hackles rise a bit.

The flow of people continuing past the luggage stations carried him along then, and he put the oddness of that last interaction out of his mind. Not entirely certain where he was supposed to go next, Matt decided to follow the flow of people. Everyone couldn't be going the wrong way, after all.

That brought to mind a Terran animal he had heard of that apparently was so stupid it would follow its fellows off a cliff, and Matt couldn't help but chuckle.

Past the luggage stations, the walkway narrowed, becoming a broad corridor with a moving walkway on the left side. A sign on the ceiling confirmed this was the way to the terminal exit. With that extra bit of reassurance, Matt upped his pace, eschewing the moving walkway and the small but growing crowd of people using it.

He never could understand the appeal of those things. They weren't all that much faster, and really, how lazy does a person need to be?

After a few more minutes of walking, the walkway ended at an arched doorway a good ten meters across. It was roped off with the kind of crowd control fixtures Matt had seen many times before at the entrances of high-end restaurants and clubs. A security checkpoint obstructed the flow of people into Matt's walkway on the left-hand side of the arch, a simple affair consisting of two rows of not-so-intimidating rent-a-cops in grayish-blue uniforms whose purpose appeared to be to check IDs against boarding documents, and little else.

The right-hand side of the archway was open, and the crowd that he had been following made their way toward that side, and the station beyond.

A half dozen men and women stood along the wall of the walkway where it ended in the arch, each holding a placard with a name on it.

Matt almost missed the fellow who was waiting for him, until he did a double take and looked back at that little group.

The man was maybe a centimeter shorter than Matt, lean but in shape with dark brown hair, a narrow, serious face, and dark eyes. He was dressed in offworld-style civilian attire: dark grey slacks and a loose-fitting long-sleeved red collared shirt. His hair was long by Navy standards but trimmed tidily enough that it was instantly obvious he was a military man.

And he carried a placard that read "M. Gilbert."

Matt walked up to the man, who looking him up and down quickly, sizing him up.

"I'm Matt Gilbert."

The man nodded, then grinned, and the earlier seriousness of his expression faded into one of cheerful good humor. "Charlie Vicente," he said, and shook hands with Matt. His shake was not the strongest Matt had ever encountered, but it was confident. "I'm the ship's Training Officer. Welcome to Copernicus."

"Thanks."

Charlie glanced down at Matt's two bags. "That all your stuff?"

Matt shrugged. "Except for what Household Goods has."

Charlie nodded. "Alright then. Let's get you checked in."

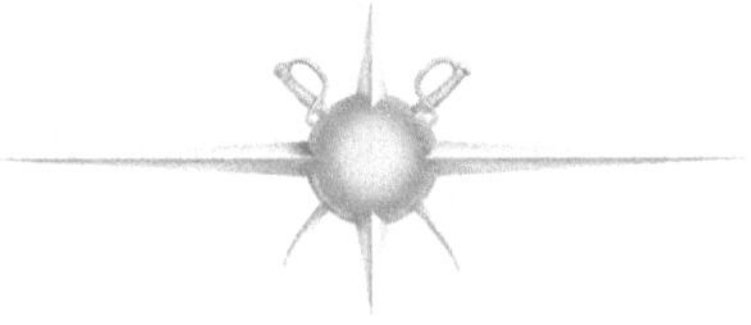

Chapter Nine

Matt followed Charlie out of the terminal complex and onto a broad thoroughfare. Probably fifteen meters across and as many high, it ran straight to the right and left from the terminal entrance. Its ceiling was domed, and the dome projected an image of a bright blue sky with white puffy clouds moving slowly past, and the sun shining brightly beyond. If he hadn't known the terminal structure was located on one of the lower levels of Copernicus Station from the research he had done during his voyage, Matt would have sworn the dome was an actual window looking up into the sky.

There was even an occasional bird flying past.

"Wow," he said, his eyes locked on the dome projection, "they really did that well."

Charlie chuckled, "Yeah they take out all the stops to show the tourists a warm welcome on this level." Implying that the other levels were not so nicely appointed. Certainly the Naval Station would not be. He turned to his left, gesturing for Matt to follow. "This way."

It seemed that every hotel or resort chain in existence had a store-front in this corridor. They passed the Hyatt Grand Californian first, followed by the Sundancer, then the Outrigger. The Hilton followed next, and as the corridor slowly arced to the right around the outer curve of the station Matt could see an apparently endless parade of lavish accommodations with doors wide open to welcome the hordes of tourists to New California.

Of course, storefront didn't really do these things justice. Matt had seen mansions that were less lavish. Once or twice.

"Where are the hotels for the regular folks?"

Charlie glanced back over his shoulder and shrugged. "Don't let the facade fool you. These places have rooms for anyone who wants them." He paused, then added, "Local places and the smaller chains are around in Section D." He made that sound boring, something he couldn't be bothered to pay much attention to.

Matt thought back to the station layout he had studied back on the liner, envisioning it in his mind. On this level the station was split up into four quadrants. Sections A, where they were now, and D were on opposite sides of the hub from each other and were the primary personnel docking areas. B and C were where bulk cargo carriers moored and offloaded their wares.

It said something about the state of New California's economy that the passenger terminals were of equal size with the cargo docks. Tourism for the win.

They came upon an intersection with another passageway, almost as broad as the main corridor, that ran straight in toward the center of the station, and Charlie took it.

Ten or fifteen meters along, the domed ceiling lowered until it became a normal flat overhead, painted grey. Though it still was high, allowing for multi-level businesses on both sides. These tended more toward pubs and restaurants, and general stores for purchasing all the beach gear one could want down on the surface.

Although why someone would come all the way here without bringing that was lost on Matt for a second, until he considered the crews of vessels coming into port.

And people tended to forget to pack things all the time. The places seemed to be doing good business, regardless.

"If you want to go to the surface, follow this straight to the central hub," Charlie said over his shoulder as Matt moved to follow him. "You can take the elevators up or down to the other station levels, but you have to wait for their scheduled departures, so it's better to take the internal lifts once you're on the station."

He pointed toward a structure ahead on the right-hand side of the passageway. All blue and white neon, it advertised "IntraStation Lifts" in signs that were impossible to miss.

No doubt where they were heading.

Half a dozen other people were waiting for a lift, a mix of offworlders and locals, though at second glance some of those who Matt initially took for locals may have been offworlders. They wore the local style but they carried themselves differently from the locals Matt had met and seen, more hunched.

Matt could relate to the hunching. At first he hadn't really felt the burden of the increased gravity here—the slow adjustment on the liner helped, a little—but after a good half hour dragging his baggage through the station's passageways he was feeling the extra effort in his shoulders and arms. And in the soles of his feet.

All the walking, more than he had done in the liner most days, was taking a toll from his new, increased weight.

Matt gestured with his chin toward the offworlders in local garb. "Is there protocol on attire?"

Charlie looked at him curiously for a second, then seemed to get it as he shook his head. "Most people take to dressing the local way, especially down on the surface. Easier to try to blend in." He put a little emphasis on the try, making it sound like he considered that a futile effort. "If you wear civvies to the ship, no one will give you guff either way."

"Ok."

The lift going up arrived, and Matt and Charlie boarded, along with an elderly offworld couple who also had luggage like they had recently arrived.

Charlie pushed the controls for the fourth level, then the third at the couple's request, and they settled back to wait.

It was a short ride up. After the couple got off on three, Charlie said, "Civilian living quarters are on levels two and three. Navy and the shipyard is on four. Station control, security, and the engineering and environmental systems are on five through eight. If your tour goes like mine has, you'll never have any reason to go there, though."

There was an immediate difference between the passageways on Level 4 than those down on Level 1. They were not dinghy by any means, but while the thoroughfares down below were broad and high-ceilinged, the passageways here were smaller, so maybe three men could walk abreast, and the overheads only half a meter above Matt's head. The walls were painted a utilitarian grey, and the floor was tiled in a faux-stone, white with black speckles. Lighting receptacles were LEDs and hung in the overheads, alongside cable runs and pipes.

It was almost like being aboard a ship, except not so cramped.

Charlie led Matt down a long, straight corridor that, Matt thought, ran toward the central hub of the station. Sure enough, after a couple minutes of walking, and passing crossing passageways every ten or fifteen meters, Matt saw that the corridor broadened ahead before opening into a receiving room.

But Charlie turned left at an intersection before they could reach that room. Though he did gesture in that direction and say, "Elevator's over there," in an offhand manner.

Another left and then a right, and the passageway stopped at a pair of sliding security doors, with NAVAL STATION COPERNICUS written in blocky black text above them. A pair of sailors in their dress blues and wearing white gunbelts with sidearms in holsters, their rating insignias naming them Masters At Arms, were stationed there, one on either side of the doors. Matt saw an ID scanner mounted on the wall to next to the guy on the right.

There were also at least two security cameras Matt could see, and he wouldn't be surprised if there were others hidden there as well.

The two sailors tracked Matt and Charlie coming from the moment they turned into the corridor. There was nothing menacing about their demeanors, but it was also obvious they were sizing the two of them up.

"Afternoon, MA1," Charlie said to the higher-ranking of the two, a First Class Petty Officer by the chevrons on his sleeve. He pulled out his ID and handed it to the sailor. .

The MA took Charlie's card, looking over it and him for a moment. Then he touched it to the reader, and an LED atop the reader flashed green. The MA1 noted the LED and gave the ID back.

"Afternoon, sir," he said, and turned his gaze to Matt.

Matt followed the same procedure Charlie had, and a moment later the two MAs snapped off salutes to them both. Then Charlie and Matt stepped through the security doors into the Naval Station.

There was a window on the left side of the corridor just past the security door, alongside an airtight door, looking into what could only be the base security office, as functional and severe as that space looked. On the opposite side of the corridor was a wood-paneled display area with a big "Welcome To Naval Station Copernicus" engraved in gold at the top. Beneath that were pictures of the Base CO and XO, and their department heads.

A few paces further down the corridor on the right was an airtight door labeled PASS AND ID in the same blocky text as before.

And then the corridor continued on ahead, looking the same as it had outside the Station.

A few more twists and turns later, and they came to an airtight door with BACHELOR OFFICERS QUARTERS written above it.

Charlie led Matt inside, and he was relieved to see the decor changed here, at least.

The floor fooled Matt into thinking it was marble for a moment, but a double-take revealed it to be cleverly-styled tile instead. The space itself was wide, and well-lit by recessed LEDs in an overheard that was devoid of cable runs or pipes. A blue faux-leather couch and a pair of similarly-upholstered chairs sat around a round coffee table off to the right, and there was a coffee mess along the wall next to them. To the left was a counter that was topped in the same blue as the couches. Swinging doors directly ahead led further into the space.

Potted plants on either side of the doorway as they came in—Matt couldn't have said what kind of plants they were—gave off a light but pleasant fragrance, and pleasant violin music that Matt couldn't quite name, though it seemed familiar, played softly through hidden speakers.

"Good afternoon, gentlemen," said the woman behind the counter.

She was short and a bit on the heavy side, with curly brown hair that hung to her shoulders and a cheerful smile that brightened the room so that Matt found himself grinning in return without realizing it. She wore a white collared shirt that was emblazoned on her right breast with a stylized star with a comet shooting past it and the words "Copernicus BOQ" stitched above. The nametag on the opposite side of her chest said, "Jenny."

"Afternoon," Charlie said, walking briskly over to the counter.

"Need to check in my guy here." He gestured with his thumb at Matt, and Jenny looked his way.

She nodded. "First space duty station?" she asked as Matt approached, and he nodded.

"What gave me away?"

She giggled softly. It was high-pitched, but not unpleasant. Instead of answering, she said, "Can I see your orders and ID please?"

As Matt was fishing the documents out, Charlie said, "If you're good here, I've got some work to finish up on the ship. I'll swing by after and we'll get dinner. I'll show you around the station a bit, and in the morning we'll get you checked aboard."

Matt handed over his orders and ID, but looked quizzically at Charlie. "I don't have a place to stay yet, don't you think—"

Charlies waved the comment away. "We'll put you right back on leave to find a place. But it's better to check you in so the ships gets custody of you and you're not in limbo." He paused, then added, "Plus, it gets that space pay counter started." He accentuated that last with a sly wink.

Which was an angle Matt hadn't thought of. A new guy like him got a bit of space pay, but it was barely worth mentioning. It was only after he accumulated two years of space duty that the extra space pay would become significant. And while a week or two of house hunting wouldn't delay that all too much, why not get the counter started sooner?

He nodded. "Got it. Ok, see you later on this evening."

Charlie grinned, and they shook hands. Then he left for the ship and Matt turned back to Jenny, to get settled into his new—temporary—home.

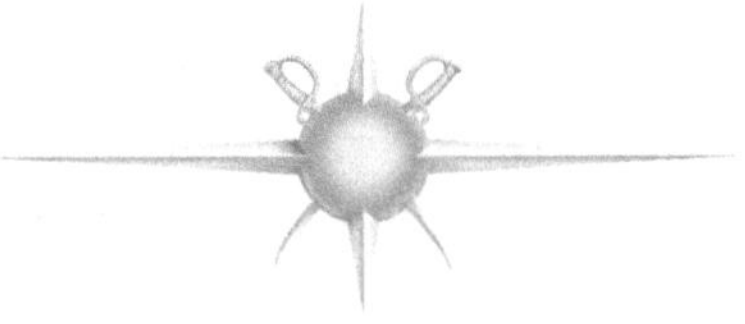

Chapter Ten

O530 came quickly.

Matt should have been used to rising early. He told himself that every morning. But as he pushed himself out of the narrow rack in his BOQ room, his limbs as usual stubbornly refused to comply with this mind. He rose stiffly and shuffled over to the doorway leading into his head. It took several splashes of water on his face to rouse himself fully, and he took a minute to look himself in the eye using the mirror above his little sink.

He didn't look as tired as he felt, but right then he would have liked nothing more than to roll back into the rack for another five or six hours.

No time for that. It wouldn't do to be late on his first day.

He bathed and shaved quickly, then donned his Service Dress Blues, noticeably lacking in ribbons and only bearing the single gold stripe of rank at the bottom of his blouse sleeves. Giving himself a final once-over, and pausing to pick a bit of lint from his shoulder, he nodded to himself in the mirror, gathered up his portfolio bag, and strode quickly to the door.

The little galley adjacent to the BOQ lobby was open, naturally, and he took a minute for a quick breakfast of eggs and toast, then he left to find his ship.

The corridors in the Naval section were more narrow and, naturally, more spartan than the tourist areas Charlie had taken him through the day before. Grey paint on the walls, and on the cableways in the overhead, made for a uniformly boring appearance, but that was to be expected. Still, the sameness of the passageways got Matt turned about, and after a few minutes he realized he must have made a wrong turn. He should have reached the airdock after a short walk, but instead, he found himself facing a four-way junction without a clue which way to go.

A placard hanging from the overhead in the center of the intersection proclaimed the FRIGRON offices to the right and WING offices to the left, but there was no indication where the airdock lay. Biting back an annoyed curse, Matt turned right. The FRIGRON staff ought to be able to point him the right way. It would be embarrassing to have to ask, but...

He tried to take some comfort in the fact that he was an Ensign. No one expected an Ensign to know anything.

It didn't help.

The corridor continued straight for about twenty meters before bending sharply to the right. Maybe five meters later it ended at a sealed pressure door. On the bulkhead to the right of the door was mounted a yellow shield with a red lightning bolt striking downward from upper right to lower left running through it. COMMANDER FRIGATE SQUADRON FOUR was emblazoned in scarlet text above the shield, and PRIMO VICTORIA beneath it.

A call box was mounted on the door's left, and Matt tapped it. No sound issued forth, but a moment later the pressure door opened, and Matt stepped inside, doffing his cover and tucking it under his left arm as he did.

The FRIGRON offices were a stark contrast from the corridor outside. Uniform grey gave way to dark paneled faux-wood, but very convincing faux-wood. Navy blue carpet replaced off-white tile, and the lighting, while still the station standard LED fixtures, was subtly more warm somehow.

To the right as Matt entered, the bulkhead was covered in pictures of the chain of command, from the Prime Minister to the Minister of War, to the Tenth Fleet Commander, to the System Commander, and finally to the Commodore of the Squadron, a sandy-haired man who looked far younger than the late-40s he had to be to have reached his rank and station. He seemed to have a twinkle in his eye, and his smile, though professional, seemed to convey a sly wit. Captain R. S. Neeley, ICN, read the placard beneath his picture.

Below the Commodore was his Deputy's picture, and below him the Squadron Department Heads, but Matt's eyes swept past them all heedlessly as he noted the final row below: the Commanding Officers of the five Frigates under the Commodore's command.

HALSWELL was second from the left, and Matt swallowed hard as he saw the face of his new boss. Thin, with high cheekbones and black hair that was going grey at the temples, Matt's Captain stared out of the picture with piercing grey eyes and a deadly-serious expression. No sly wit from him; he was pure stern professionalism.

Commander J. C. Berkley, ICN was his name, and he looked like no fun at all.

"Can I help you, sir?"

The voice pulled Matt out of his reverie and he tore his eyes from the pictures toward the reception desk that he had noted and then dismissed from his thoughts the moment he had seen the pictures.

It was more of a counter than a desk, made of dark wood similar to the wall panels, and ran across the width of the room to Matt's front. A swinging door section was built into the extreme left side of the structure, allowing access to a corridor that lead back into the FRIGRON offices' innards.

A man of about Matt's age, maybe a year or two older, sat behind the counter. Garbed in standard issue navy-blue underway coveralls, he had the two chevrons of a Petty Officer Second Class on his right collar and the stylized quill and inkwell of a Yeoman on his left. His name, Hersch, was embroidered on his right breast, and on his left was the enlisted version of the Stellar Warfare device, silver instead of gold. He looked at Matt with an expression of professional cordiality beneath his lengthy, by Navy standards, mop of auburn hair.

Matt nodded to him and stepped up to the counter. "Morning, YN2. I'm supposed to check onto the HALSWELL this morning, but," he shrugged and put on an apologetic grin, "I got a bit turned around. Can you point me toward Airdock Two?"

Hersch smirked slightly. "Easy to get lost around here if you're new." He looked to his left, where a terminal monitor was mounted, screen facing away from Matt and toward him. "I think you might be in luck, though, sir. One minute." He tapped an input panel on the countertop and pressed his left index finger to his ear, eyes losing their focus on Matt. "Chief," he said, clearly talking to someone else, "it's Hersch at the front desk. You're heading over to the HALSWELL this morning right?" A pause, and Hersch focused on Matt again and nodded, smiled, then gave him a thumbs up. "Could you show an Ensign the way to the Airdock?" Anther pause, and he nodded again. "He's here at the front desk. Thanks, Chief."

Hersch took his finger away from his ear and said, "Chief Bettancort will be out in a minute. He'll take you over." He looked rather pleased with himself.

Matt nodded gratefully. Far as he was concerned, Hersch had the right to look pleased. "Thanks, YN2," he said.

"No problem, sir."

Hersch looked away from Matt and back to his monitor. Having nothing else to do but wait, Matt went back to studying to pictures of the FRIGRON chain of command, and silently hoping his Captain wasn't going to turn out to be as severe a CO as his picture made him appear.

A few minutes later, approaching footsteps drew Matt's eye back toward the counter as a short man with salt-and-pepper hair that had receded almost completely from the front of his head pushed through the swinging door on the side of the counter. He had broad shoulders, but a pronounced gut, and he also wore underway coveralls. But where Hersch bore his Petty Officer rank and rate on his collars, this man's held matching the matching golden anchors of a Chief Petty Officer. His name was embroidered in gold thread, a juxtaposition to the silver Stellar Warfare device on his left breast, and read Bettancort.

The Chief noticed Matt immediately and stepped over to him. "Morning, sir. Chief Bettancort. Trying to find the HALSWELL?"

Matt nodded and shook hands with him. He put on a self-deprecating smile. "Ensign Gilbert, Chief. And yeah, I made a wrong turn somewhere. Appreciate the help."

Bettancort grinned, and the bushy mustache atop his lips seemed to swell. "That's what we're here for." He glanced aside at the Petty Officer behind the counter. "I'll be back about 1000, Hersch."

Hersch nodded. "Roger that, Chief."

Then Bettancort pulled a battered-looking ball cap with the FRIGRON emblem above the brim from his thigh pocket and plopped it on his head, then turned toward the hatch leading back into the station. "Follow me, sir. We'll get you hooked right up."

Matt took a second to nod thanks to Hersch again, then followed the Chief, taking a second to put his cover back on his head. Two lefts later, they were heading back down the passageway Matt had come down just a few minutes earlier.

"Checking aboard today, sir?" Chief Betttancort said over his shoulder as they made the turn, and Matt nodded despite knowing he couldn't see it. Still, Chiefs being Chiefs, he seemed to anyway. "Good ship. Used to serve on her."

Matt perked up and took a couple quicker steps to catch up so he could walk alongside the Chief. "You did?"

Chief Bettancort nodded. "I ran RC division." That made him a Reactor Technician by rate. "Transferred off four months ago." He looked sidelong at Matt, then added, "CHENG's"—he pronounced it CHANG—"a hardass, but fair. Be straight with him. Don't pretend to know something you don't, listen to your Chief, and you'll be fine."

"How's the Captain?" As soon as he said it, Matt regretted it. It wasn't exactly a politic thing to ask.

The Chief chuckled. "Don't let the picture fool you. He's a good guy. Best Skipper in the squadron, you ask me."

They came to a T-junction that Matt remembered form his earlier travels. To the left lay the BOQ, a few more twists and turns farther on. The Chief turned right. Matt followed silently, finding his earlier anxiety fading a bit at the Chief's words. If the Captain was as good as the Chief said...

Another left, then a right, and the passageway widened, becoming broad enough for four men to walk abreast. Ahead, another airtight hatch, this one twice the size of the hatch leading into the FRIGRON spaces, drew near. A placard above it read AIRDOCK TWO.

"Here we are, sir," Chief Bettancort said, pausing to activate the control pad to the right of the hatch. As the mechanism began opening the hatch, he looked fully at Matt again. "Let's go meet your ship."

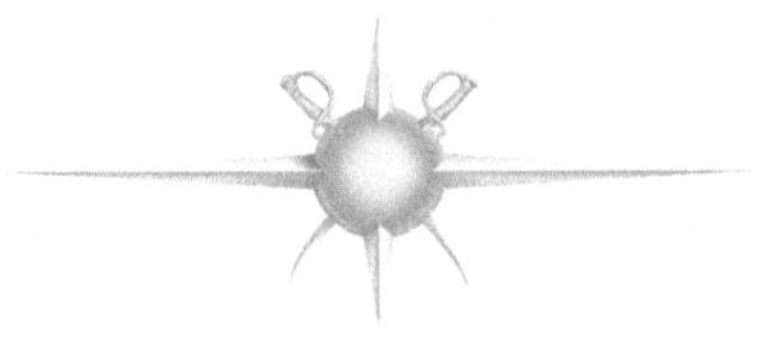

Chapter Eleven

Matt stepped through the pressure hatch into a large anteroom.

Large didn't actually do it justice. The room ran at least two hundred meters to the left and right from where the hatch was located. The overhead, maybe three meters above the deck in the passageways, towered a good ten meters above him. The entire bulkhead opposite the hatch was transparent, composed of plasteel most likely.

And through that barrier, Matt beheld ICS FREDERICK HALSWELL.

He knew the ship's dimensions from reading up on the POTTER class during his transit from Oliphant. Two hundred meters from bow to stern, thirty meters in beam, and fifty meters from keel to her uppermost mast.

But it was one thing to know her size intellectually. It was another thing to see her. She was big. And surprisingly pretty. The newer Cruisers like HATHERLY were severe, almost blocky in their construction. The POTTER class was a throwback, more sleek. From her tapered nose that gently rose into the swell of her body, the bulbous drive nacelles attached to the after third of her length with the ship's primary cannons protruding from nacelles' forward section, to the elevated bridge, almost like the conning tower of an ancient submarine, with its extended bridge wing globes on port and starboard sides, she looked like something that was designed for speed. Almost like she was made for atmospheric flight.

Intellectually, Matt knew the older design, neat as it was to look at, had a number of severe restrictions from a practical standpoint. There were fewer areas where weapons or sensors could be mounted with adequate fields of fire: he counted only four point defense turrets, two on the keel and two on her back. The primary cannons were not trainable past just a few degrees out from the ship's centerline, and she only had two torpedo tubes forward.

Still, it was hard not to like the look of her.

"Pretty, isn't she?" Chief Bettancort said, from Matt's side.

Matt nodded, his eyes running along the line of the ship's hull a second time. He frowned then, noting a hump behind the bridge tower that didn't seem to fit with the rest of the ship's design. He gestured toward it.

"What's that?"

The Chief sniffed. "Self Defense Missile System. They've been installing it this yard period." He paused, then added, "The yardbirds could have figured out a better way to put it in."

Mat blinked. He didn't know that system was going on Frigates this old. It was state of the art, something they had only just begun to teach at Tactical School during the class before his. He grinned a little bit more broadly; things were looking up, even though he had to admit it did spoil the look of the ship a bit.

Speaking of yardbirds, there was evidence of their presence, and the frenetic pace of their activity, all over the ship. Scaffolds were mounted in various places, stretching up from the base of the Airdock, and here and there along the hull the occasional white-hot glow of welding equipment was visible where they were closing up a few hull cuts that he hadn't noticed at first.

Nor was the anteroom empty, either. Dozens of personnel in work coveralls and heavily laden tool belts were moving with a purpose in and out of any one of the six doorways that he now saw were built into the plasteel, leading to ladderwells that descended to the bottom of the dock.

And to the right, about fifty meters away, a single extendable umbilicus stretched from the anteroom to the side of the ship, offering ingress and egress.

"This way, sir," the Chief said, and strode briskly toward the umbilicus.

Matt followed, and shortly they stopped before an open, circular hatch that allowed access into the umbilicus itself. They paused to let a pair of yardbirds step out, and Chief Bettancort nodded familiarly to them before entering.

As he followed the Chief inside, Matt had the impression of being closed in, though truthfully the passage was a more than spacious four or five meters in diameter. But after the expanse of the anteroom, it was a definite difference, especially as there were no view ports through the walls of the umbilicus at all.

This was silly. He was a Naval Officer, and about to check onboard a relatively small and totally enclosed vessel for a two year tour of duty. He was more than accustomed to enclosed spaces and had never felt a hint of claustrophobia. So why the sudden nerves in here?

The approaching open airlock door at the end of the umbilicus, leading into the ship that would be his new home in a just a few minutes, gave the answer almost as soon as Matt voiced the question to himself.

This was it. His first ship. Was he ready for this?

Oh sure, he had studied for years to get to this point. Orbital Mechanics and Physics in University on a Navy scholarship. Officer Candidate School followed by Engineering School and then Tactical School. Tally those all up and it amounted to almost seven years of his life devoted to getting here. And that didn't count the years in Primary School he spent dreaming about warships and pointing himself toward the path to make his dream come true.

But that was all academic. It was about to become real.

Chief Bettancort stepped over the airlock seal and into the ship. His body lowered in Matt's field of view as he took a pair of stairs down from the lock door, and Matt could see into the space beyond.

It was nothing fancy, a space probably seven meters in width and half as many deep. To his right were a number of blanked off pipes and what looked like retractable rigging equipment built into the bulkhead. UNREP STATION #1 was stenciled in blocky yellow letters adjacent to them, standing out easily against the slate grey paint of the compartment bulkhead. A second open airlock hatch lay directly in front of him. To his left, in front of another collection of pipes and cable bundles stood a darkly-stained wooden lectern. And behind the lectern on the left was posted the flag of the Icaran Confederation, white with a red bird emblazoned atop a yellow starburst.

A sailor in Summer Whites with a single red chevron on his left sleeve atop the gear and hammer symbol of the Machinist's Mate rating stood behind the lectern, and a Chief, also in his whites, stood next to him.

The Petty Officer was a couple years younger than Matt, so maybe twenty, but he wore the Stellar Warfare insignia on his left breast atop two rows of ribbons. His name tag said his name was Gonzalez, but he didn't look the part. He was tall and lanky, with fiery red hair and green eyes to match. And freckles.

Matt's eyes traced over Gonzalez's ribbons, tallying them up automatically. Navy Achievement Medal. Space Service Deployment Ribbon. Expert Pistol Medal. Expert Rifle Medal. And the Volunteer Service medal. This guy was off to a good start in his Naval career, looked like.

The Chief had too many ribbons to take in at a glance, six full rows. His name tag read "Stevens". Unlike Chief Bettancort, his belly was flat and he had a full head of black hair. But he had that same something or other that all members of the goat locker seemed to have.

After he returned Chief Bettancort's salute and granted him permission to come aboard, the two of them exchanged familiar and mutually respectful nods before Chief Stevens looked past Bettancort to Matt. The congenial look on his face changed, becoming speculative as he took Matt in.

Matt stepped carefully over the airlock seal and down into the quarterdeck. Turning to face the colors, he snapped off a salute, then turned to Chief Stevens and saluted him in turn. "Permission to come aboard."

Chief Stevens returned the salute quickly. "Granted, sir." He looked at Matt expectantly.

Matt stepped toward the lectern. "Ensign Gilbert, reporting for duty," he said, and Petty Officer Gonzalez nodded.

"Can I have your orders, sir?"

Matt paused, the hard Irish lilt in the man's voice taking him aback for a second. Gonzalez's lips twitched and he gave a little shrug that seemed to say he knew the affect the combination of his name, looks, and accent had on people and he was used to it.

"Bet you've got an interesting story," Matt said as he fished the original printed copy of his orders from his portfolio case and handed it to the Petty Officer.

Gonzalez grinned fully then. "You could say that," he said, and he accepted the paperwork. He scanned the document quickly, then bent forward over the lectern and began tapping on a keyboard that was built into its top.

While he was typing, Chief Bettancort said, "You should be good to go from here, sir. I've got to get down to the MMR."

Matt nodded. "Thanks for your help, Chief." He held out his hand and the Chief shook it with a firm grip.

"Of course. Good luck, sir. Have fun."

And then Chief Bettancort ducked through the inner airlock hatch and turned aft out of sight.

"Ok, sir, I've got you entered into the system," Gonzalez said after another couple seconds of typing. He handed back Matt's orders, then glanced at Chief Stevens. "Call the wardroom?"

The Chief nodded, and Gonzalez turned away from the lectern to a call box behind him. As he picked up the handset to make his call, Matt looked back at the Chief.

"What's your job on the ship?"

Chief Stevens replied, "Communications Division LCPO."

Matt nodded. That put him in Combat Systems Department. Probably they would not work together directly for a while. Matt firmly expected to start out in Engineering Department. That was the typical path for JOs; learn the ropes in the Engineering plant so as to get a good feel for the technical side of the ship and then, later, move up to the operations and tactical side. Though truth be told, Matt would be just as happy to skip, or at least minimize, his time there. He did fine in Engineering School, but he didn't get into this to drive fusion reactors.

He wanted to drive the ship.

Gonzalez said something into the handset and hung it up, then turned back to the Chief and Matt. "Lieutenant Vicente is on his way down, sir."

Matt glanced at the chronometer display above the call box. 0650. He would have preferred to get here earlier, but at least he wasn't late for O-Call. That would have been a bad way to start. He nodded. "Thanks, MM3."

They stood there in awkward silence for a short while, and then a group of three yardbirds stepped out of the umbilicus hatch, and the Chief and Petty Officer got back to the business of their watch, checking their credentials thoroughly before logging them in and allowing them access to the ship.

The trio voiced their thanks and stepped through the inner airlock hatch, turning right to go toward the bow. Immediately after the last of them disappeared from sight, Charlie stepped through onto the Quarterdeck. He glanced around and found Matt immediately. Stepping over to him, he held out his hand.

"Hey Matt. Thought we'd have to send out a search party for you."

Matt shook his hand and shrugged apologetically. "I got a little turned around."

Charlie smirked out a half-chuckle. "That happens." He looked aside toward Chief Stevens. "I've got him from here. Thanks, Chief."

"Roger that, sir." Chief Stevens looked from Charlie back to Matt and nodded. "Welcome aboard, Mr. Gilbert."

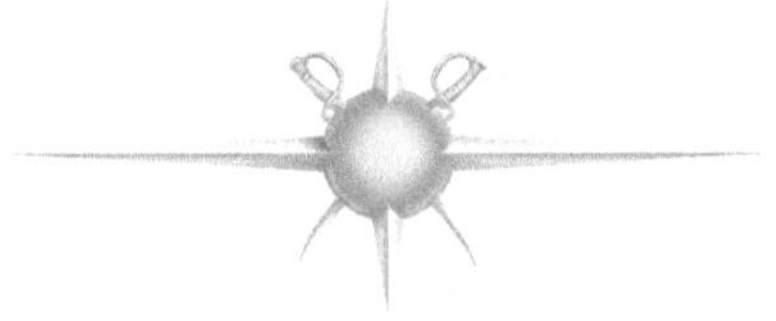

Chapter Twelve

Charlie led Matt through the inner airlock hatch and into the innards of the HALSWELL. Following him, Matt stopped for a moment inside the hatch and inhaled deeply, taking in his first view of his new home.

The difference between the ship and the station was immediate, and striking. Where the station was dull grey, almost dingy, the ship sparkled. The deck tile was a white and grey speckled approximation of stone, and waxed to a shine. The bulkheads were painted a not-quite-white overtop the insulation lagging, but the paint was without blemish as though freshly applied. The lighting came from recessed LEDs in the ceiling, giving the passageway a warm, almost natural glow.

Piping, labeled as everything from Potable Water to Hydraulics to Sanitation ran along the pressure hull going forward and aft, and cable-ways ran along the overhead, positioned so as to not interfere with the light. The passageway was narrow enough that two men could just squeeze past each other, and interrupted every four or five meters with the raised cowling of an airtight bulkhead hatch. Power panels hung on the bulkheads everywhere, bearing identification placards prominently on their access doors. Elsewhere, frame and compartment identification markings and EAS manifold labels stood out to the eye, the later in yellow-green paint that would glow in the dark on a loss of power.

The ship had an odor about it: slightly acrid, slightly tangy. Boat-smell, he had heard it called, and he had smelled it before. It was certainly distinctive, a product of the military-grade atmosphere processing equipment installed on the ship, and he knew it would quickly seep into every piece of gear and clothing he stored onboard.

Directly across the from the airlock hatch was an airtight door with a placard reading "Galley", and Matt realized he could just catch, alongside boat smell, the residual odor of bacon in the air. It made his mouth water and he had the hankering to see if there were any left-overs from breakfast available. But Charlie immediately turned left to head aft, not wasting any time, and Matt had to hurry to catch up to him.

A few meters along, another passageway joined up with theirs, running athwartships, and Charlie turned down it. Almost immediately, he turned right again into a ladderwell and bounded up the ascending section.

At the top of the stairs they turned left and moved forward along the starboard side passageway. To the right as they walked were half a dozen circular hatches embedded in the bulkhead. Matt recognized the distinctive markings of emergency escape craft. Lifeboats.

They came to another athwartships passageway, and Charlie turned left to take it. Ten meters, and they passed an airtight door on the left labelled "Wardroom Pantry". Then they came to two airtight doors across the passageway from each other. The forward-opening door was labelled "CIC", and Matt felt a twinge of excitement as he looked at it.

Charlie took the door to the left, leading aft.

As Matt followed him, he saw the writing on the door: "Officers Country. Official Business Only."

Past the door, the environment changed completely. Gone were the white-painted bulkheads, replaced by what Matt could have sworn was real Icaran Blackwood. It was only when he rain a finger along the bulkhead that he realized the grain was missing; it was false wood. But very convincing false wood.

The deck was also different, becoming tile that nicely approximated pine, or maybe cedar, hardwood.

The overhead retained its white paint and cableways, and he spied a few more power panels on the bulkhead down the passageway, as well as a couple portable fire extinguishers. Regardless, the overall effect was to give this area of the ship an almost homey feel.

A few paces in, a closed faux-wood door on the right with the golden star of command. and above it the words "Commanding Officer" engraved in its surface marked what could only be the CO's Stateroom.

For a second, Matt thought that was their destination, but Charlie continued on until he reached another pair of faux-wood doors facing each other from across the passageway. The one of the right bore a simple brass plate reading "Executive Officer" at eye level. The one on the Left had a similar plate that said, "Wardroom". It was that door that Charlie led Matt through.

"Gentlemen," Charlie said as he stepped aside and swept his left hand out wide to present Matt as he walked in. "The Ensign."

Matt had envisioned a half dozen different ways this introduction to his first wardroom would go. The chorus of boos and exclaimed "Nub!"'s that came rushing at him from every side took him aback, and he was left there speechless for a moment as he took it all in.

The wardroom consisted of a main seating area where a large table that was shaped like a blocky and backwards capital C, with the closed side facing the wall to his right and the open side pointing left. It was covered by a scarlet tablecloth that drooped about a third of a meter over the table's edge and had the ship's name and coat-of-arms, featuring a man in Marine Corps armor who was making a "Follow Me" gesture to unseen people behind him with the Confederation's colors flying in the breeze over his head, embroidered in the center of the closed side. High-backed chairs with crimson cushions surrounded the table, and over on the wall opposite him a holoscreen was mounted. A second holoscreen was mounted off to the left, where a smaller sitting area gave the wardroom an L-shape. Directly to his left was a door that was labelled "Pantry", and he saw what looked like a serving counter around the corner from the door, opposite the larger of the two couches in the sitting area.

The officers of ICS FREDERICK HALSWELL, with the exception of a dumpy-looking fellow with greying temples who was pouring himself a cup of coffee from the serving counter, were seated around the C-shaped table in their underway coveralls, and one and all were staring at him.

And booing.

With great big grins on their faces.

One guy, who had the look of Carraway's world, even threw a wadded up napkin at him, and it bounced off Matt's chest before he could even think to try to catch it or dodge out of the way.

"Who the hell are you, Nub?" asked a guy on the opposite side of the table from Matt. He was head and shoulders taller than any of the other guys seated near him, with a narrow face and hooked nose beneath a completely shaved head. He was a full lieutenant—three golden bars on his collars—and wore the Stellar Warfare device on his breast.

Matt shrugged. "I'm Matt—"

"Shut up!" came a chorus of voices, and another napkin came flying at him.

He ducked this one, dropping his cover onto the deck in the process, which sparked a round of laughter.

"Knows right answer when told," quipped another Ensign who was seated at the end of the nearest wing of the table to Matt.

"Quiet, Nub," said a different guy, casting a baleful look the Ensign's way: like Matt, he was not wearing a warfare device.

"At least he stands watch, Jerry," said a Lieutenant Junior Grade—two gold bars—with curly brown hair who was sitting opposite the speaker.

"Fair point," the first said, nodding. He looked back at the Ensign at the end of the table. "He's not completely useless. Unlike some." His eyes went back to Matt.

He probably should have fired back somehow, but Matt couldn't think of a thing to say. So he stood there feeling, and probably looking, stupid.

A couple seconds later, hook-nose rolled his eyes. "Well don't just stand there like an idiot." He gestured toward an empty chair in middle of the closed section of the table, in front of the coat-of-arms. "Siddown."

Matt looked around at the other officers, and several of them gestured forcefully toward the chair. He glanced aside at Charlie, and his guide nodded, a little grin on his face.

Shrugging, Matt bent over and picked up his cover, then moved to the proffered chair.

It was a tight fit squeezing behind the guys sitting along the closed section of the C. Naturally they did not scoot their chairs in at all to give him a hand. But the guy in the chair to the right of the one hook-nose directed him to was nice enough to stand up and pull the chair out for Matt.

Nodding gratefully to him, Matt plopped his portfolio bag and cover down on the table and sat.

The guy sitting across from him sniggered, and Matt was just about to ask what was so funny when the door he had came through opened again.

All eyes went to the door as a man in underway coveralls stepped through. He was looking behind himself as he entered, but he had the two silver bars of a Commander on his collars and the star of command over the name tag on his right breast.

Matt didn't need to see his face fully to know he was the Captain.

"We're going to have to—" the Captain said, but stopped as he turned fully into the room and saw his officers—and Matt—in the room.

Charlie spoke up. "New guy's here, Skipper."

The Captain nodded, his eyes fixed on Matt and his face severe. "You're in my chair, Ensign."

A roar of laughter followed the Captain's words, and Matt flushed with embarrassment. He glanced aside at hook-nose and found him smirking with glee, his eyes flashing with laughter. Anger flared up in Matt's chest. But this was not the time to press it, not with the Captain staring down at him. Pushing the chair back, he hurriedly stood and moved out of the way, knocking into the guy who had pulled it out for him.

When the laughter had faded, he managed a penitent, "Sorry sir." His cheeks were hot, with embarrassment and anger both. But mostly embarrassment.

He had feared screwing up on his first day, but not quite so immediately, or so blatantly, as this.

The man who followed the Captain in had a single silver bar on each of his collars: a Lieutenant Commander. His name tag said his last name was Earhardt.

The XO.

"It's worse than that, Skipper," he said, and gestured toward the tabletop, where Matt's cover and portfolio case rested.

"My God," the Captain said, and he shook his head. Then he looked around the wardroom at the rest of his officers, and his severe expression cracked as he grinned broadly. "Next round's on the Ensign!"

A raucous mix of cheers and laughter erupted in the room, and Matt felt his cheeks grow even hotter. He knew not to put his cover on the wardroom table. Everyone knew that, but in his befuddlement he had completely forgotten. Two infractions in less than the same number of minutes!

The laughter died down as the Captain raised his hands and made a shushing gesture. "All right, that's enough, gentlemen." He looked back at Matt and the grin remained. It was remarkable; the face that a second ago had been so severely stern, matching the picture on the FRIGRON wall, was now open and cheerful. He walked to the table, and the officers who had not moved before scooted their chairs in so he could pass easily. Reaching Matt, the Captain held out his hand. "John Berkley."

Matt, still feeling off-balance and embarrassed, shook hands and replied, "Matt Gilbert, sir."

"Glad to have you with us, Matt." He gave Matt's hand a firm squeeze and released it. "You got in yesterday, right? You got a place to stay yet?"

Matt shook his head. "I'm in the BOQ sir."

The Captain pursed his lips and shook his head slightly. "That won't do." He looked back at Charlie. "What's the plan for him today, Charlie?"

Charlie, still with an amused half-smirk on his face, gave a little shrug. "I figured I'd get him checked in with Admin and then help him get to work finding a place."

The Captain nodded approval. "Good." He looked back at Matt. "Take next week to get settled in, and report back here the following Monday morning. That work?"

Matt nodded, not quite trusting himself to speak, off balance as he still was.

"Bull!"

The other Ensign at the end of the table, the guy who had spoken up earlier, gave a little jerk in his seat at the Captain's call. "Yessir."

"You've got the Hail and Farewell set up for the SLOB and Matt?"

Bull nodded quickly. "Sunday at 1500, at your place, sir."

The Captain blinked and, wincing slightly, looked sidelong at Bull. "Cindy know about that?"

Bull returned his look with a quizzical one of his own. "It was her idea, sir."

The Captain made a quick, rueful chuckle, and nodded. "Ok then." He returned his gaze to Matt. "I may be Captain, but I don't have any say in my social schedule." A ripple of soft chuckles spread through the room, and Matt got the feeling he was missing half of a joke. "Alright, Matt, I won't keep you. You've got a lot to do. Go get settled in, and we'll see you Sunday."

Matt nodded and picked up his portfolio case and cover. The Captain shook his hand again, and then Matt moved back around the table to meet back up with Charlie, who was already moving to the door.

"Oh, and Matt?"

Matt stopped at the door and looked back at the Captain, who had settled down into his chair, and the XO in the chair to his right. The Captain grinned again, this one a bit more mischievous. "When you come by on Sunday, don't forget to bring the beer."

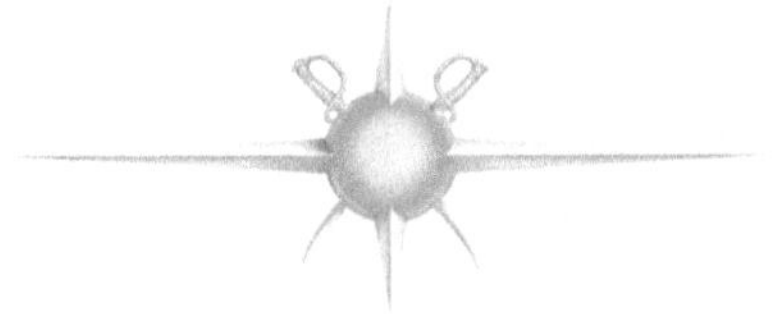

Chapter Thirteen

"What the hell was that?" Matt demanded as he followed Charlie down the wardroom passage.

Charlie looked over his shoulder and flashed a grin. "Better get used to it; you're the new guy." His grin slipped a bit. "First rule of life on a ship: show no weakness. Let these guys know something bothers you..." He raised an eyebrow, his meaning clear.

Matt had heard that one before; his various instructors had warned him about it. The Navy worked its crews hard, and there weren't all that many ways to let off steam underway. So teasing got to be an art form.

Still...

"Who was that asshole with the nose?"

Charlie snorted out a laugh as he opened the airtight door they'd come through before and stepped back into the ship's athwartships passageway. "Shaved head? That's Tim. He's the SLOB."

Matt blinked, pondered, but could not find a definition for that acronym. He followed Charlie through the door and shut it behind himself. "SLOB?"

"Shortest Lieutenant On Board." Charlie turned left, walking toward the port side of the ship as he talked. "He's the senior JO, finishing up his second space tour. Getting ready to roll to shore duty." He glanced aside at Matt and must have seen the look of distaste on his face. "He can be a little abrasive, but he's really an ok guy. Knows his shit."

They came to a t-intersection where a passageway joined theirs from further forward, and paused to let a crewman, a fireman from the three red stripes on his collars, pass. Then Charlie turned right into the passage and led Matt to a pair of airtight doors a few meters ahead on the left. The first was labeled ADMIN, the second SCIF.

"Here we go," he said, as he opened the door to ADMIN and stepped inside.

The Admin office was rectangular, with the longer sides running fore and aft. A reception counter blocked off the customer service area—or whatever the Navy called it—Matt and Charlie entered into from the rest of the space, where three clusters of desks were arranged equidistant from each other along the length of the room. Placards on the walls behind the clusters announced they dealt with AWARDS AND EVALS, ORDERS AND TRANSFERS, and CORRESPON-DENCE, respectively. Another desk sat in the back rear corner of the space, and an additional airtight door allowed for access through the aft bulkhead, for division staff only, Matt supposed.

The desks were all occupied by sailors ranging from Spaceman Apprentices all the way to Yeomen First Class, except the one at the rear. The man sitting there had gold on his collars and the silver of the enlisted Stellar Warfare device. Another Chief; the Admin LCPO apparently.

A single Yeoman, a third class from his chevrons, with a round face, black hair, and slightly slanted eyes that spoke of blood from the Tsago Dominance, or maybe China back on Terra, was stationed at the recep-tion desk, and perked up when he saw Matt and Charlie.

"Morning, Lieutenant," he said, nodding familiarly to Charlie before turning his gaze on Matt and nodding again in a way that somehow seemed more formal. "Sir."

"Petty Officer Cho," Charlie said, "this is Ensign Gilbert. He's checking aboard today."

Recognition flashed on Cho's face and he looked down at the work space behind the counter. "Yes sir, we've got his package ready. It's around here somewhere...ah!" He looked back up and lifted a folder with the ship's name and coat of arms on the front, and slid it across the counter top toward Matt. "Here you are, Mr. Gilbert. You need to verify your Page 2, and enter your information for the Alpha Roster. If I could just get your orders and ID, I'll get started processing you in while you're working on that."

"Ok." Matt again took his orders out of his portfolio and handed them to Cho, then fished around his pocket for a second before finding his ID. It was a hunk of clear plastic, with a holographic image of his face and an encoded chip that held all his vital information on it. In point of fact, it wasn't really necessary, because most of that information was also encoded into his implants. But for the time being, at least, the Navy still used it. He handed it over to Cho, who nodded thanks, then he flipped the folder open.

It was the usual administrivia. First, the ever-present Page 2 with next of kin, insurance, and emergency contact information, none of which had changed in the months since he last updated it, when he checked into Tactical School. But it had to be done.

Behind the Page 2 was his recall data for the Alpha Roster, and there he paused.

"I don't have a place yet; I'm staying the BOQ."

"That's alright, sir," Cho said. "Just put the Q for now, and you can update it later when you move into a place. The really important parts are your holopad address and implant serial number, so we can get in contact with you if there's a recall while you're on liberty."

Matt nodded, and set to filling out the data blocks.

As he wrote, Charlie said, "Given any thought to where you'll want to stay?"

Matt glanced his way and saw that he was legitimately interested. He shrugged. "Not much. Maybe a place on the surface by the beach."

Charlie snorted and shook his head. "Wouldn't do that if I were you."

Matt gave him a quizzical look, and after a second, Charlie rolled his eyes.

"Look, it's a half hour ride on the elevator to get down there, then at least another twenty minutes on a flyer to the decent towns. Then you've got the locals..." He shook his head. "Don't get me wrong, I like most of them just fine. But some of them are a real pain in the ass. Besides," he crossed his arms over his chest and frowned, "after a twelve, fourteen hour day, especially if you're coming off duty, that commute will eat you alive. Trust me, you want to live up here, down on the civvie levels. There's plenty of stuff to do, and you won't have to deal with all that crap. You can always go down to the surface on weekends if you don't have duty, on stand-down, times like that."

Matt frowned. Truth be told, he had thought long and hard about the elevator commute. It was a heck of a lot easier than an orbital hop would have been, but it still was a sizable chunk of time, and that's assuming he didn't miss an elevator car. There was continuous service, but at intervals of fifteen minutes. Tack on one of those intervals and suddenly a forty-five minute commute became an hour. Each way.

That would suck.

But at the same time, he thought back to Isaiah's and Maleen's words on the liner. It would be a pity to be here for two years and never really experience the life and culture of this, very unique, world. Which sounded like exactly what Charlie was suggesting, and had signed himself up for.

Wasn't that part of the reason Matt joined the Navy: to see the Galaxy, and meet interesting people?

"I'll think about it," Matt said, and handed the recall data back to Cho.

Charlie chuckled softly. "I'll take you by my place when we're done here. You'll see."

Matt nodded. It wasn't a bad idea, and it could be Charlie would end up being right. Couldn't hurt to see. Besides, it was just now Thursday, and he didn't have to report back until a week from Monday. There was time.

The rest of the paperwork in the folder from Cho consisted of the ship's official welcome aboard pamphlet, a few pages showing the interior schematics, and a check-in sheet with signature blocks for the medical officer, drug testing coordinator, Command Fitness Leader, Security Manager, and pretty much every key person on the ship up to and including the Command Master Chief, XO, and CO.

That was a lot of signatures.

"I'll go ahead and sign off for Admin," Cho said, sliding Matt's orders and ID back to him, "as soon as we're done here. And I'll forward electronic copies of the ship's information packet to your holopad, now that I have its address. Now," he looked back down and shuffled a few out of sight things around for a second. When he looked back up, he pulled a thin black cable with an adjustable strap on the end up from where it must have been connected into a terminal below. "If you'll hook this up, we'll get your implants registered and talking with the ship's system, and you'll be good to go."

Matt smirked. This part was annoying.

You'd think the guys who designed the implants would make it so that they could be accessed by any Navy system; they were part of the Common Access System, after all. But no. Every Navy shore facility was theoretically on the Navy-Wide Information Network (N-WIN they called it officially, but Matt had heard it called No-Win more often). But the Intel guys had their own system. So did Medical. And the ships couldn't be hooked up to the same network as the shore commands because of light speed latency issues screwing up the network access protocols.

Supposedly QUANTNET would solve that some day, but that came with its own issues.

Regardless, it meant that the ships all had their own networks, with their own logins, and even though they theoretically complied with the N-WIN data security and assurance requirements, there was simply no way for the Common Access System to actually allow Common Access to all of the Navy's networks and installations, regardless of how it was hyped.

Matt rolled up his right blouse sleeve and slid his hand into the strap at the end of Cho's cord. He moved the strap up to a position about a centimeter above the little bone ridge in his wrist and felt around for a second before he found a second raised area of hardness, this one square. He positioned a matching square area of the strap atop the square in his arm, and the strap stuck fast, held in place magnetically to the implant dock below his skin. He pulled the strap tight to ensure it did not become dislodged, then looked up and Cho and gave him a thumbs up with his left hand.

"Alright, this will just take a second..."

A little flashing square appeared in the upper right quadrant of Matt's vision, then scrolled to the right, emblazoning "Welcome to the ICS FREDERICK HALSWELL information exchange network" in green letters on apparent nothingness for a second before they faded away.

Well, that was different. The implants hadn't done that before.

"All done, sir," Cho said, and Matt focused back on him.

"What was that text thing?"

"It's a new texting system the Navy's looking to implement. We're part of a pilot program for it." Cho sounded less than thrilled about it.

Matt pulled the strap free of his arm and handed it back to Cho, frowning slightly as he pondered that. "You don't like it?"

Charlie barked out something that sounded like a cross between a snort and a laugh. "It's annoying as hell. Random words popping up from out of nowhere..." He gave a little shiver. "I can handle an audible call over the implants. It's like a normal conversation. This text stuff is weird."

Cho looked at Charlie and hesitated for a second, then nodded agreement.

"It's only going on for another couple weeks though," Charlie said. "Until we undock. Then they'll take their data and analyze it, and maybe the Navy will can-x the whole thing." He sounded like he hoped, but doubted, that's what would happen. A second of silence seemed to last forever, then Charlie roused himself and clapped his hands together. "Right. We good to go, YN3?"

Cho looked down at the documents Matt had given him, scanned them one last time, then nodded. "Yes sir. We'll send his info to PSD this afternoon, and they'll get his Space Pay started. Should notice it showing up week after next."

That made sense. The Navy paid biweekly, but it was far too late for any changes to show up during the scheduled payroll dispersal tomorrow.

Cho looked back at Matt and raised an eyebrow. "They sometimes screw it up when they make changes though, sir. So I'd check your wallet closely next pay day. If Space Pay doesn't come in, or if something else is messed up, let me know asap so we can get it fixed."

Matt noted the Admin Office's contact information on the check-in sheet. He nodded. "Will do, thanks YN3."

"No problem. Welcome aboard, sir."

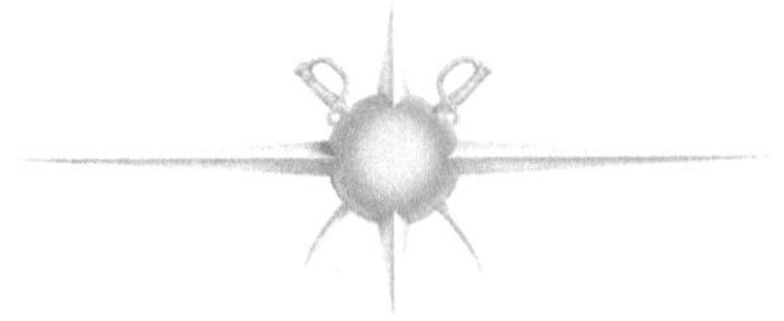

Chapter Fourteen

Matt stepped out of the open doorway in front of him and into warm, moist air, and bright midday sunlight. A gentle breeze washed over him, bringing the scent of growing vegetation and the salt of the nearby ocean to his nostrils, and he felt an immediate calm, like he had shed a twenty kilogram pack. And never mind that he still felt the increased gravity with every step he took.

It might take him his entire tour to adjust to the deeper well here, but so what? Right then, despite the crowd of people streaming past him as they, too, exited the flyer that brought them here from the elevator's surface terminus, his first real taste of New California felt too good to worry over trifles like muscles that were weaker here than they should be, and that were aching a bit from that added stress.

He closed his eyes and drew a deep breath, and when he let it out he was smiling contentedly.

Yeah, he could get used to this.

The town was called Ventura, again after a place in the original California on Terra, and it had come recommended to him by Isaiah.

Matt had spent the rest of the previous day with Charlie, getting to know the station in the civilian area where Charlie lived. And he had to admit, Charlie had a point. There was a lot going on up there: plenty of restaurants, bars, and clubs; simulated outdoor parks; gyms and sporting facilities; a library. And though the apartments were almost certainly smaller than anything that could be found planetside, they were surprisingly affordable. Well within the limits of the local Housing Allowance for an Ensign on his own.

All the same, appealing as the relative lack of commute was, Matt couldn't shake a feeling of distaste over the notion of just staying on the station. So in the evening after he had left Charlie, Matt sent Isaiah a message, and they had agreed to meet up here for lunch, and after that Isaiah would show Matt around a bit.

The flyer station rested on a hilltop a bit more than a kilometer from the shore, and from this location Matt could see the sweep of Ventura Bay, and get a general feel for the town's layout.

The bay ran north to south, widening from its narrow mouth to a total width of about ten kilometers before closing back into a near teardrop shape, when seen from above. A trio of high-rises dominated the extreme south portion of the bay. Two were hotels: from this distance Matt could see the Marriott and Peninsula names. The third boasted no large sign. Maybe it was filled with condos?

The rest of the town was built more low, with few buildings standing more than five or six stories from what Matt could tell, and sprawled across the remainder of the bay's southern shore.

The beach was almost totally white, reflecting the sunlight easily, and no doubt offering a challenge to any barefoot sunbathers. But it looked inviting, and the local palm-equivalents grew everywhere, their long fronds swaying in the sea breeze in a way that seemed custom-designed to entice one to leisure and carefree existence.

First impression was this place did not suck.

A short set of flagstone stairs led down from the flyer station to a road running parallel with the bay shore. The other people exiting the station were going that way, and Matt followed the thinning crowd. Most of them turned right at the bottom of the stairs to a parking lot for private vehicles, but there was also a transport queue to the left, about fifty meters up the road.

Matt considered the queue for a moment, but thought better of it. Instead, donning his sunglasses, he followed the road by foot as it curved off to the right and downward.

His destination was a cafe called La Trattoria. Isaiah had said it was located to the left of the Marriott, and it had a great view of the beach. It seemed an easy enough walk, and Matt had been out of natural light for so many weeks the thought of cooping himself up in another transport, even for a few minutes, was repellent.

Traffic was steady, despite the lack of houses and businesses in the vicinity of the station. No doubt the locals had wanted to avoid the noise, small as it was, from the descending and ascending flyers. And who could blame them? There was certainly enough space, the population of the planet being as comparatively sparse as it was. Very quickly Matt found himself surrounded by palms and undergrowth, and the station passed out of sight behind him.

It was easy to imagine that he was out in the middle of nowhere for a few minutes, and he found the feeling tremendously peaceful.

Then he came to a crossing road, this one larger: four lanes instead of the two that led to the station, and that illusion faded. The new road, leading down to the shore as it continued to descend to his left, was lined with buildings in that direction. They were low at first, one or two-story, stucco-sided and painted in bright pastels, with steep tiled roofs that would easily shed rainfall. But the Marriott and Peninsula high rises, along with their anonymous partner, were easily visible at the end of the road, and as Matt proceeded in their direction, the other buildings grew more dense, and larger.

Of course, dense was a relative term. Every residential lot was sizable; you could easily set up a volleyball court between houses and still have plenty of room to spare. And several of the homes had done exactly that.

Houses gave way to businesses as he approached the high rises, ranging from the usual tourist traps selling souvenirs or beach apparel to restaurants and bars, a martial arts gym, and markets.

Matt took it all in, noting all of it but not focusing in on any particular building as he took in the ambiance. Locals and tourists strolled along the walking paths on either side of the street, the locals easy to pick out as much by their leisurely gait as by their tanned, muscular physiques, and unique style of dress and hair. The tourists were more flighty, moving quickly from diversion to diversion; some had obtained local attire and were wearing it, but they could not manage to mimic the way the locals moved.

The odors changed as he approached the beach. The smell of sea salt and tide pools remained, but spicy aromas wafting from restaurants and sidewalk cafes mixed with it, making Matt's mouth water. And music, driven by hand drums accompanied by guitars or ukuleles in a relaxing but energetic style, seemed to come from all directions at once.

And the scenery.

Holy smokes, the scenery was breath taking. Blondes, Brunettes, an occasional Redhead, and lots of Ravens, all of the locals were curvy, tall, and sensual. The tourists weren't bad to look at either, but...wow.

By the time he reached the end of the road, where it met another four-lane street that ran past the high rises to run directly along the curve of the bay, Matt was wearing a broad grin, and he decided he definitely liked this place.

He liked it a lot.

The Station didn't hold a candle to this, commute be damned.

The Marriott was the left-most of the high rises, and its grounds sprawled over at least three or four acres. Matt crossed the Bayside Road —that was its name, actually—and walked past the resort, taking in what he could of the facilities from beyond the barrier bushes that marked the boundaries of its property. What lay within was partially obscured by the barrier and by the copses of palms and fruit trees that were planted all over, but he could easily pick out at least two wading pools, a water slide, a couple sand volleyball courts, and a half-shell-style amphitheater back near the beach. Pretty nice.

But it wasn't for him. Not today, at least.

He continued on, and came to a long, low building that was set back from the road a ways, fronted by tall palms. The building was beige stucco, the roof burgundy tile, but its construction departed from the local norm after that. Fluted columns flanked an open gate that led into a stone-tiled courtyard that was dominated by a bubbling fountain, which was capped by a replica of The David. More columns stood on either side of the main entrance: three-meter tall double doors of red-stained hardwood that stood open invitingly.

A sign hung over the gate: La Trattoria.

Probably cafe was the wrong word for this place. It looked to be a very nice restaurant and function space. Silently hoping it wasn't going to be as expensive as it looked, Matt strode quickly through the court-yard and stepped inside.

He pushed his sunglasses up onto his forehead, and took a second to let his eyes adjust to the noticeably dimmer interior.

The place was spacious, and impeccably decorated, in a simple style that screamed elegance despite its lack of obvious flair. Wall sconces hung at intervals along the interior walls, but none were lit. All of the light came from the open rear wall of the place, which led out onto another stone-tiled courtyard that allowed access to the beach via stairs at the extreme rear, again between a pair of fluted columns. The entire rear courtyard was covered by a pergola structure that allowed shade while still keeping the natural lighting, and filled with metal tables that would accommodate anywhere from a couple to eight or ten people.

The interior was dominated by a bar along the right-hand wall. Cushioned booths lined the left-hand wall, and the space between was filled with more tables similar to the ones out back. The place was about half-filled with lunchtime customers, about evenly split between inside and outside dining. There were more locals than tourists, but just barely, and the two different classes of people seemed to keep to their own.

"Welcome t' La Trattoria," a woman's voice said, and Matt tore his eyes from his scan of the place to focus in on her.

She stood behind a simple lectern that made up the hostess station, and she was a local; that was obvious from her accent even before he took her in. She was maybe a centimeter shorter than him, and lean, with auburn hair running down the right side of an oval face that seemed made for smiling. As seemed the norm for locals, her blouse was sleeveless and her pants were cut to capris length. The light green of her blouse set off her eyes well.

Maybe it was his imagination, but it seemed her smile broadened a tad when he met her eyes. "Table for one?"

He shook his head. "I'm meeting a friend. Mind if I wait at the bar?"

She swept her hand toward that side of the room. "Be welcome."

"Thanks."

The girl smiled again, and he flashed his best imitation of a roguish grin. Then he strode over to the bar area.

It was nicely made: darkly-stained wood topped by a black, polished-stone counter top, and ran most of the length of the room. The stools were also dark wood, with deep maroon Naugahyde—he had to believe it wasn't actual leather—cushions. Behind the bar were the usual glass shelves displaying bottles from cheap to uber-expensive, and a half dozen taps with colorful, stylized handles showing the brand names.

Matt licked his lips and leaned his elbows atop the bar, studying the taps. It was possible they would have a brand he knew, of course, but he rather hoped they had something locally made. That was always more interesting.

He waved at the bartender, a stocky local man with wavy blond hair was was chatting up a couple of tourist women down at the far end of the bar.

The guy didn't notice him.

Of course.

Matt shook his head, unable to be angry at the snub, just amused. He turned away from the bar and looked toward the open rear portion of the room, and the white sands beyond.

The courtyard was sprawling, oval shaped, and surrounded by a low stone wall that allowed egress only through the stairs at the rear. The tables were laid seemingly at random, though Matt truly doubted that was the case, and now that he was looking more closely he saw a second bar off to the left, along the courtyard's wall. There was a bartender there, but no customers at the moment.

Easier to get a drink there, and it was outside. So much the better.

Slipping his sunglasses back down, he walked the few paces out into the courtyard, then he maneuvered toward the outside bar.

He had only gone a few steps when he heard, "Matt," from off to his right.

He turned to see Isaiah rising from a table that he had not seen from inside the building.

It was up against the courtyard's wall, and set for six. Isaiah had been sitting facing the building, Maleen next to him in the chair closest to the wall. They both were dressed in the local style, his blouse deep green and hers light grey, lined with silver.

Across from them sat a man in his late middle years who was also dressed like a local. But unlike every other New Californian Matt had yet met, he was portly, with a belly that pressed aggressively out against the confines of his burgundy blouse. His hair used to be black, and curly, but it had almost totally gone to grey, as had the bushy mustache above his lips.

"Isaiah," Matt said, "Good to see you again."

Isaiah shook his hand firmly and, grinning, gestured toward his table. "Join us."

Matt stepped over to an empty chair at the end of the table and focused in on the older man. He was about to introduce himself when Isaiah beat him to the punch.

"Vincenzo, Matt be th' Navy man we spoke of."

Vincenzo looked Matt up and down, then rose, and they shook hands. "Pleasure to meet you," he said, in a distinctly not-Californian accent.

Matt returned the shake and settled down into his chair, looking at the older man curiously. "You visiting too?"

Vincenzo barked out a little laugh, and shook his head. "No, not for some time. This," he gestured around the courtyard, "is my place."

Matt blinked in surprise, and looked back at the rest of the restaurant for a second. "You own it?"

Vincenzo nodded. "After my wife passed, I moved here from Veneto. Decided to bring a little slice of home with me."

"And we glad he did," Maleen said, smiling fondly at the older man. "He the best chef in th' hemisphere."

Vincenzo waved away her comment, but Matt could tell it pleased him from the little flush that filled his cheeks.

Maleen turned her attention to Matt and, leaning forward, clasped his hand gently in hers. "Good of you t' come, Matt."

"And fortunate for you, the timing," Isaiah said as he settled down into his own chair again. He gave a little half-nod in Vincenzo's direction.

The restaurateur chuckled softly. "When I get hungry I pick a customer and join them for a meal. On the house, so they don't make me eat alone." He grinned slyly at that. "I was just about to insist we get started; can't keep my belly waiting." He patted his belly briskly with the palms of his hands, and grinned a bit wider. "You almost missed out."

Matt blinked, surprised. "That's awfully nice of you, but you don't need to do that on my account." He glanced between the three of them, hoping this wasn't something special Isaiah and Maleen had put this guy up to.

Vincenzo snorted. "Though I hear you are a fine fellow, it's got nothing to do with you. My tradition, in *my* restaurant," he put extra emphasis on my. "It's been too long since I caught up with these two. You just happen to benefit."

"Oh." Matt felt a little bit better about it, put that way. "Alright then." He grinned. "What's for lunch?"

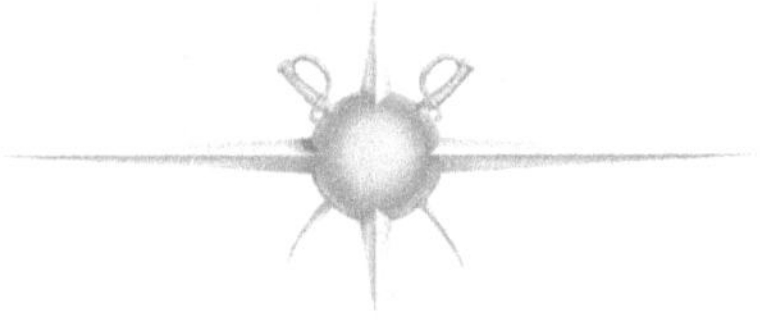

Chapter Fifteen

The sun was setting over the hills lining the west side of Ventura Bay. The winds were light, from the north, driving short waves that caught and distorted the sun's reflection off the water, making it shimmer slightly, and lending the panoramic view from the deck constructed to the side of Isaiah's and Maleen's house an almost mystical quality.

That same breeze carried the scent of roasting meat of some kind or other; down the hill to the the right from where the house was perched another family was holding a party. A couple dozen people in local attire were easily visible adjacent to a fire pit, and Matt could see they had a rotisserie apparatus of some sort set up.

Whatever that was they were roasting, it smelled amazing. And they had the same kind of light-hearted and upbeat music playing that he had heard throughout the town the rest of the day.

It made him want to run over and join them. But...

Isaiah came up next to him and followed his eyes down toward the party, and chuckled.

"Th' Carlsons," he said, nodding in their direction. "Youngest boy getting married next week."

"That's awesome." Matt looked down at the party, and soaked up the music and the scents for a few moments. He almost felt himself pulled away into the joy that he felt emanating from them. Then a thought interrupted, and he looked aside at Isaiah.

"I'm not keeping you from the party, am I?"

Isaiah looked quizzically at him for a second, then chuckled and shook his head. "Tonight just for family. After this is three days of solitude with th' groom, his father, and his priest. Then a party for both families. On the wedding day, all are welcome to celebrate."

"Oh. Ok."

Isaiah clapped him on the arm. "Come."

He led Matt into the house, through a sliding glass door that separated the deck from the interior.

His and Maleen's house was not large, but as Matt stepped inside he could see it was just as well-appointed as any home he knew back home on Trinity, or any of the other worlds in the Confederation he had visited since university and his commissioning.

The main room was open, and inviting. The wall adjacent to the deck was almost all windows, looking out at the bay and the sunset. A dark grey, leather-upholstered couch sat facing the windows, flanked by a matching love seat and a pair of stuffed chairs surrounding a glass-topped coffee table, upon which sat what looked like a picture book and an incense burner.

Across the room was a stone-topped island with a trio of standing stools ahead of a well-appointed kitchen space, complete with every appliance and convenience Matt could want.

Past the kitchen, to the left, was a doorway leading back to, Matt assumed, the bedrooms. The door out to the front walk, darkly stained wood that matched well with the light-blue paint on the walls, lay to the left of the bedrooms. Tasteful art decorated the walls: landscape paintings, and one of a sailboat under sail beneath a star-lit night with gentle waves lapping up against the hull.

A subtle fragrance filled the room, from a stick of something that was burning on the coffee table. It gave a feeling of peace, somehow.

Maleen was just emerging from the bedroom area when they walked in. She had changed clothes, donning a light green blouse that cascaded past her hips to almost be a robe, and she had done up her hair a bit, as well. It was now tied into a braid that draped down her back.

And how had she managed that in just the few minutes he and

Isaiah had spent to walk from their car onto the deck? Better not to ask; the mysteries of women, and all that.

"Karl and Abbie called," she said as she saw them. "They coming over with friends for dinner, if that's alright."

Isaiah smiled. "Always welcome. What are you thinking?"

Maleen looked toward the refrigerator, then shrugged. "They bringing bread and wine. We have the fish from the market yesterday." She raised an eyebrow, and Isaiah nodded in approval.

That piqued Matt's curiosity. He hadn't thought about the local fish, but they had to be different from what he'd encountered before. This might be a treat. "What kind of fish do you have here?"

Maleen paused, considering. "You know the terran breed...tuna I think it called?"

Matt nodded. That was one of the few animals from old Terra that colonists had managed to bring with them when they ventured out to the colonies, before they lost track of the old worlds.

"Not too different from that. We call it Rubba."

"Sounds good," Matt said.

Maleen nodded. "Then you two make salad and set th' table. I see to the rest."

There was a separate dining room in the house, around the corner from the great room and off the hallway that Matt assumed went only back to the bedrooms. But Isaiah shook his head at that, and instead he led Matt back out onto the deck, where they also had a table, under a spreading umbrella, that faced the view out onto the bay.

It was a simple matter to get the table set. The salad was another matter entirely.

Matt had the notion that it would just entail greens, peppers, maybe some onions, and a scattering of nuts or berries. But he quickly learned a salad on New Cali was another thing entirely.

It involved chopping up chilled sausages—or at least he thought they were sausages, but Matt decided not to ask exactly what they were made of—and slicing a collection of fruits and melons of a type he didn't recognize but whose fragrance immediately made his mouth water. And then adding the kinds of greens that he expected. Then Isaiah dripped a local oil and some spices onto the mix, and began mixing it all up by hand.

Literally by hand. He rinsed his hands in water from the sink and then sank them, almost elbow-deep, into the bowl where he and Matt had dumped everything, and began kneading it, a slow, deliberate stirring that soon had the entire concoction mixed and completely coated in the oil/spice combination he had created moments before.

Matt watched, in appreciation but also with a bit of trepidation, as Isaiah performed the almost ritualistic act. It took quite a bit longer than he would have thought.

Isaiah noticed the look on his face, and smirked slightly. "This different from how you do it." It wasn't a question.

But then, it wouldn't be a question, would it? Isaiah had been off-world many times.

Matt shrugged. "A bit."

"It not just a recipe," Isaiah said, as he plunged his hands deep into the bowl for the third time since Matt had set to watching. "This way, we bring th' life of New Cali into the food, t' bless it for our sustenance."

Past him, at the stove, Maleen was working her own magic with the fish, stirring the pieces of meat into a mixture of tubers and peppers within a pot that resembled a wok. She looked over her shoulder at Isaiah as he said that, and rolled her eyes slightly.

Matt got the joke. Or he thought he did, and looked at Isaiah with amusement. "You're putting me on."

Isaiah chuckled. "Not entirely. It come from an old—"

An electronic chime sounded, interrupting Isaiah's words. He looked toward the front door and frowned slightly. "That Karl and the others. Will you?"

His hands were still deep into the salad, so Matt understood his meaning. He nodded. "Sure."

Matt went over and opened the front door.

A quartet of people in local attire were standing there. The older of the two were a married couple; Matt could tell that immediately from her hair and his tattoo.

She was striking, a raven-haired woman of Matt's height with the sort of statuesque figure he had come to expect from the people of New California. But what really stood out was her eyes. They were bright green, reflecting the light from inside the house back at him almost like beacons in the night.

He was taller than Matt, but more plain. In that he was more slender than Isaiah, though still fit, and fairer of hair; his was light brown, almost blond.

The pair with them were both women, single, and young, more Matt's age. One had hair almost as dark as the married woman's, with eyes to match her hair. The other...

She was lush. Curvy in all the right ways, with auburn hair that was tied into a braid that reached to just above nipple-level, and a heart-shaped face that seemed like it was designed to laugh. Or at least, she wore a gentle smile on her face, anyway.

Matt felt a rush as he looked at her, and never mind the married woman. Holy smokes, she was—

"Hello," said the man. There was a question in his voice.

"Oh." Matt tore his eyes from the auburn-haired woman and went back to him. He put on a smile of greeting. "Hi. I'm Matt."

There was a moment of silence, then the man nodded understanding. "Th' Navy man."

Matt spread his hands and shrugged slightly. "Guilty as charged, I guess."

"Karl," the man said. He indicated his wife. "My wife, Abbie. This be Constance," the dark-haired girl nodded, "and Marta."

Matt nodded at Constance, then Marta, and he thought he saw something like speculation in Marta's eyes when their gazes met.

Interesting. He forced his attention back to Karl.

"Good to meet you." He extended his hand, and Karl gripped it. His grip was firm to the point of almost being overpowering. Then Matt stepped back and waved them inside. "Come on in."

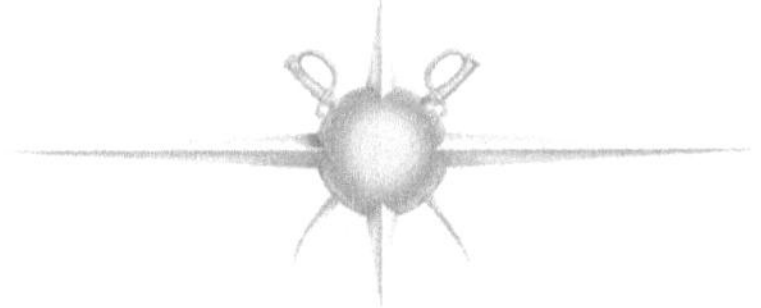

Chapter Sixteen

Captain Berkley lived in Ortega, on the opposite side of the continent from Ventura.

Of course, New California's land mass consisted of just a single continent that ringed the planet near the equator, and ranged in width from fifty to one thousand kilometers in width. So that meant the two towns were really only a couple hundred kilometers apart, maybe twenty minutes by flyer. It was a much different way of thinking about spacial relationships than Matt had grown up with on Trinity, but he found he rather liked the notion.

The flyer station was much the same as the one in Ventura, even down to its layout on a hill overlooking the town. But Ortega's coastline was quite a bit different.

While Ventura rested within a sheltered bay, Ortega lay right on the shore of the southern ocean, at the mouth of a slow-moving river that flowed from the continent's central mountain range, near where the Space Elevator was anchored. A man-made breakwater created a harbor area on the eastern side of the river, and the surrounding buildings had an industrial look about them. A suspension bridge, graceful and delicate-looking in the early afternoon sunlight, spanned the river and allowed access to the residential area of the town.

Also unlike Ventura, Matt could see no sky-rises or obvious hotels. A local town?

He didn't bother walking. The address Charlie had passed him indicated the Captain's residence was a few kilometers west of the downtown area, farther than Matt would have been comfortable going on foot, even if he wasn't carrying a burden.

Matt hefted the cardboard box he had carried over from Ventura and set off down the steps in front of the flyer station to the transport queue, and set to waiting. Fortunately, the crowd was sparse at this hour, and there were only four people in the queue ahead of him. Still, by the time he set the case into the cargo compartment of his transport and settled into its rear passenger seat, his arms were aching from exertion.

The transport driver was short for a local man, with black curls atop his head and a pleasantly uninterested smile on his face. He accepted the address from Matt with a dutiful nod and set to driving, but did not attempt any conversation. Which was just as well, Matt supposed. He had always found the forced friendliness of these sorts of encounters to be rather off-putting, fake.

So instead he sat in silence and watched the scenery pass outside the transport.

The buildings were constructed similarly to those in Ventura, all stucco and tiled roofs. But the residences were larger, fronted by courtyards where transports were parked, or seating areas were laid out, as were the lots they were built on. The businesses lacked some of the tourist-trap flair that those in Ventura had, making the town seem more homey, somehow. Even the industrial area by the waterfront seemed welcoming and wholesome.

They passed over the suspension bridge and through the more congested residential areas on the west side of the river in just a few minutes, and continued on a two-lane road that meandered uphill through a thick palm forest for a kilometer or so before breaking out onto a grass covered—or the New Californian equivalent of grass—bluff overlooking the sea.

The road ran along the edge of the bluff, along a sheer drop-off of a hundred meters or more, and kept on that way for a kilometer or two before veering off to the right and descending into a valley that sat astride another river, barely more than a stream really, that ran north to south.

At some point, the river must have been much more fierce, because it had eroded a v-notch in the bluffs, leading straight down to a lagoon that joined with the ocean beyond.

The transport rounded a bend and then ran down the the little river, and a small hamlet came into view, surrounding the lagoon. A couple dozen houses along the edge of the lagoon itself, a general store and a school, and out near the mouth of the lagoon at the breakwater, a larger building astride a series of docks.

"Ortega Larga," the driver said, his first words since Matt had entered his vehicle, and turned to follow the road around to the right along the bed of the lagoon. The third house on the left was number 2834.

The Captain's place.

The transport stopped, and Matt got out. He took a moment to look at his CO's dwelling, and could not help being impressed.

It was stucco, of course, painted yellow-beige, and two stories tall. The front of the house was dominated by a wide flagstone staircase that went up four steps to the heavy double front doors. A red-stained balcony overhung the doors, running the length of the house with access from a pair of glass doors at either side of the second story. A pair of tall palms grew outboard the ends of the balcony, the swaying fronds seeming to sweep over the house's roof. The front yard was carefully manicured, with a simple flagstone walking path leading from the street to the stairs. Off to the left, a driveway led back to rear of the house, to a detached garage, no doubt. The property was separated from its neighbors by carefully trimmed hedgerows, a little bit taller than Matt, that offered privacy without being standoffish.

"Nice place," Matt said to himself as he opened the cargo compartment.

The driver snorted out a half-chuckle. "Ought t' be, how expensive it is." When Matt gave him a look in response, he merely shrugged and grinned as thought to say, "Hey, what can you do?"

Letting the matter drop, Matt thanked the man and pulled out his holopad, then tapped the command to authorize payment from his wallet. Then he hefted his box and started toward the front doors.

The transport hummed to life behind him and drove away, leaving him to it.

Time to go make an appearance.

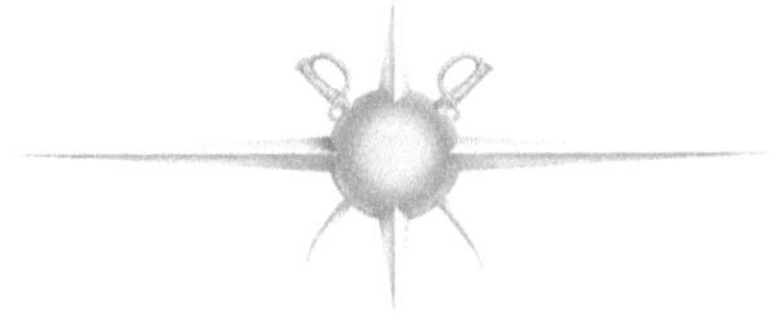

Chapter Seventeen

The rightmost of the double doors opened, and a girl looked curiously out at Matt.

She was maybe fourteen, with pixie-cut brown hair and matching eyes. She was dressed in the local style: light blue, sleeveless blouse and khaki-colored capris, and Matt could see shadows of the Captain's features in her face.

She looked him up and down. "Are you Matt?"

Matt adjusted his grip on the box and nodded.

The girl smiled invitingly then and moved aside. "Come on in. I'm Tina. Mom and Dad aren't back yet, but the George is in the kitchen." She pointed deeper into the house. "He's been waiting for you."

"Thanks," Matt said, and stepped inside.

The foyer had vaulted ceilings that stretched all the way up through the second story, and a hanging crystalline chandelier. The walls were painted blue-grey, matching the inlays in the tiled floor. A doorway to the right led into a formal dining room, complete with a well-crafted table and chairs for eight, and an antique-looking china cabinet in the corner. To the left, a second doorway led into an office space that was dominated by a great wooden desk that faced the doorway. Built-in bookshelves, packed to the gills with tomes, lined the wall behind the desk, and Matt glimpsed the requisite plaques and pictures on the wall adjacent that were the staple of a career Officer's "I Love Me" room. A staircase along the left-hand wall led up to the second story, and a wide hallway continued further into the house.

Matt took the hallway, and Tina shut the door behind him. A powder room on the left and a coat closet on the right, and then he stepped out into a wide-open great room.

The kitchen area was off to the right, dominating that side of the house. The refrigerator was twice the size of the units Matt was used to seeing, the stove and hood gas-fired, the sink deep and broad. The cabinets were painted bright blue. A chest-high sit-up counter ran the length of the room in front of the preparation area, fronted by a half dozen bar stools, and topped by polished blue stone with flecks of white and grey throughout.

Opposite the kitchen was a sitting and recreation area, dominated by a large black leather sectional couch and a matching stuffed chair that sat facing the rear of the house. A stone fireplace sat in the back rear corner, and the entire rear of the room was glass. Drawn curtains let sunlight in, giving the room a bright and cheerful feel.

Swinging glass doors, propped open to admit the outside air, led out onto the rear patio, where outdoor couches and chairs sat around a fire pit on the left side, opposite a bar and grilling area on the right. A path led from the patio down to the edge of the lagoon beyond, where a dock jutted out into the water.

"Wow. This doesn't suck."

A man's laugh drew Matt's eyes back to the kitchen area, where a fellow he remembered from the other day in the wardroom straightened from where he had been bent over behind the counter.

Matt never got his name—but then he had gotten few—but he recalled the man as one of the few Ensigns in the room. He was a couple centimeters shorter than Matt, and lanky, with a curly red-blond hair. He had on a white blouse in the local cut, and he nodded with a friendly grin.

"Rank has its privileges." He wiped his hands off on his pants and stepped around the counter toward Matt. "Jeremy Stevens," he said by way of greeting. "I'm the George."

Matt set his box down on the counter with a sigh of relief, and shook hands. "Matt Gilbert." He paused, then asked the obvious question. "The George?"

Jeremy chuckled again. "The George Ensign." He looked at Matt for a second, and seeing no comprehension, shrugged. "Senior-most Ensign is the Bull. Most junior is the George. I've been the George," he pointed at Matt and grinned again, "but now it's you. Or will be after today, anyway."

"Ok... So what does that mean?"

Jeremy gestured toward Matt's box. "That's beer, right?"

Matt nodded.

"That's what the George does. Come on, we'll bring it to the outside fridge."

Jeremy led the way toward the back patio, leaving Matt to heft the box. He stifled a groan, but picked it up to follow him.

Man, the thing was heavy, and it was only twenty-four bottles. But the higher gravity well here turned what would have taken only moderate effort into a real chore.

Oh well, it would help him adjust all the quicker.

The outside refrigerator was located behind the bar on the right-hand side of the patio. Sized like a normal unit, as opposed to the behemoth inside, it was already partially filled with beer bottles, and some white and sparkling wines as well. When Matt set the box down in front of the fridge, Jeremy squatted down and tore the top open eagerly.

"Ok, what'd you get?" He pulled a bottle out and looked at the label. "Haverhold Brewery," he said, and nodded approval. "Very nice." He looked back at Matt and raised an eyebrow. "You found them quickly."

Matt shrugged and pulled a couple bottles out, helping to move them into the fridge. "I've got a couple friends in Ventura."

"That's convenient. Navy guys?"

Matt shook his head. "Locals."

Jeremy pursed his lips and paused what he was doing, looking at Matt seriously. "Be careful, bro. Some of the people here can be," another pause as he obviously considered his words carefully. "Difficult," he finally said in conclusion.

"Yeah I've heard. Isaiah and Maleen are alright, though."

Jeremy shrugged. "You say so."

They loaded the beer into the fridge in silence after that, Matt not really trusting himself to respond. He knew Jeremy meant well, but at the same time he couldn't help but take his words as an affront to his friends. But then again, how well did he really know them? They had only met a few days ago, after all.

But still, they had opened their house to him. They'd had all kinds of opportunity to cause mischief, and they hadn't. They'd been nothing but helpful and friendly.

Jeremy pulled the last two bottles from the box, but instead of putting them into the fridge, he kicked the door shut and turned to the bar, where a bottle opener was mounted below the counter top. He popped the tops off and turned back to Matt, offering one.

Matt accepted, and Jeremy clinked his bottle against Matt's. "To the new George."

Matt took a pull on his beer. "So I'm the beer bitch then?"

Jeremy shook his head, swallowing a swig of his own. "More like you're the entertainment coordinator. Bull runs the wardroom mess: collects dues, keeps the books, schedules events, arranges for going away presents, things like that. George handles the logistics. I get the food and the beer, make sure everything's lined up. When we go to liberty ports, I set up the Admin room."

Matt raised a questioning eyebrow.

"That's the communal hotel room. Place where any of us can crash if we need to, or where we'll hold Hails and Bails like today, or pre-lube for events. We keep the place stocked with booze and snacks, and I'm in charge of that." Jeremy grinned. "It ends up being a good deal. I get off the ship on the first Liberty launch, or if we're moored, as soon as the ship is secured, to set things up."

"So you spend your own money, or...?"

Jeremy shook his head vigorously. "No. Bull will come up with a budget for the event, and authorize me to deduct from the Wardroom wallet to get supplies." He looked down at the empty box at Matt's feet. "You having to buy this time was just...an initiation."

"Great."

"Happens to all of us, brother." He looked past Matt's shoulder, his eyes focusing on something behind him. "Skipper's back."

Matt turned around, and saw a boat motoring into the lagoon mouth from the open sea. Sleek, and about fifteen meters long, it had a shining white hull and boasted a raised conning station above a deck-level cabin, and it looked like it had stations at the stern to accommodate fishing gear.

"Nice boat."

"Yeah. We've taken it out as a Wardroom a few times. It's pretty sweet." Jeremy stepped past Matt, heading to the dock. "Let's help them tie up."

Matt followed, taking the path down from the patio past the carefully mowed grass that sloped down to the water's edge.

The dock was simply constructed: wood pylons driven into the seabed supporting wooden planks of the deck. It sloped up for the first few meters, getting well above the waterline, then leveled out. Out at the end, the mooring area was free-floating, plastic runners holding the floating deck to the pylons while allowing movement up and down. A ramp on rollers led down onto the mooring platform for access, and there was a shore power and water connection up on the stationary portion of the dock above.

As they walked down the ramp to the mooring platform, Matt pondered over the reason for having it. "There's no tides here, right? No moon. So why the floating dock?"

Jeremy looked back at him and grinned. "There *is* a small tide due to interaction with the sun."

Matt gave him a flat look. That would probably be extremely hard to even measure; it surely wouldn't have been noticeable, from a practical standpoint.

Jeremy nodded acquiescence. "Seriously though, that's a big ocean out there." He gestured toward the mouth of the lagoon, which the Captain's boat had now cleared. "Bigger proportionally than on almost any other colonized world. Lots of fetch for waves. It doesn't happen often, but when a big storm brews up out there, you can get a noticeable surge, even from a thousand kilometers away."

That made more sense. "Do the storms make landfall very often?"

"Every now and then. It's not pretty when they do."

The boat had slowed to barely a crawl, and was heading toward the mooring dock where Jeremy and Matt stood. As it drew nearer, a door opened on the port side of the deck cabin and two people came out. The first, a boy of maybe eleven or twelve, moved toward the bow. The second, a woman of average height and trim figure went to the stern. Both were dressed like locals, the boy in a bright red blouse and the woman in blue, and both moved easily with the motion of the boat, from lots of practice. Glancing upward, Matt saw the Captain clearly up in the conning station, wearing a white blouse, a Navy blue ballcap with the golden scrambled eggs of a Commander on its brim, and dark sunglasses.

Jeremy meandered to the end of the mooring platform and caught a line that the woman threw over to him, leaving Matt to do the same for the boy, and a brief few minutes later, the boat was securely tied up, rubber bumpers holding the hull off from the dock and a short boarding ladder descending from the boat's deck allowing access.

The boy scampered off first, pausing only briefly to say hi to Jeremy before darting past Matt and up toward the house.

Matt watched him go, bemused, but turned around when he heard the woman speaking.

"I'm sorry about that; he knows better than to be so rude." The Captain's wife—who else could she be?—looked to be in her mid-30s. Her hair bordered between blonde and brown, and she wore it in the local style: short on the right side and back, and long on her left, down past her shoulder. She smiled at him, and her eyes twinkled with friendly good humor as she extended her hand to him. "You must be Matt. Cindy Berkley."

Matt shook hands, and was impressed by her grip. "Pleasure to meet you, ma'am."

"Cindy, please," she replied, then looked toward the house. "We'll talk more later. But if you'll excuse me, I need to go teach someone some manners right this moment."

Matt stepped out of the way to let her pass, and watched for a moment as she walked determinedly toward the house, on the trail of her son. He shook his head in pity over the tongue-lashing the boy was sure to get.

"We all set, Jeremy?"

Matt turned back to see the Captain stepping down from the boarding ladder and shaking hands with the George.

"Yes, sir. The roast is in, and Matt came through with Haverhold. The others should be arriving in the next twenty minutes or so."

The Captain nodded and turned his attention on Matt. "Glad you could make it, Matt." They shook hands, and the Captain continued, "Jeremy explained how things work?"

"More or less, sir."

The Captain grinned. "It's not really that complicated. We'll ease you into it." He glanced down at the bottles in Matt's and Jeremy's hands, and shook his head. "You guys are getting a head start on us, I see. Good idea." With that, he turned and started up the ramp leading up from the mooring platform.

About halfway up the ramp, he turned and looked back at them. "Well, gentlemen? Shall we?"

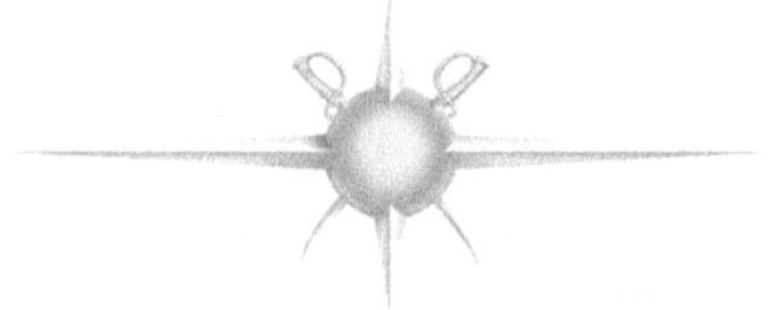

Chapter Eighteen

Jeremy called it correctly. Twenty minutes later, almost to the second, the doorbell rang and the first of the remaining wardroom members showed up. Within the next fifteen minutes, everyone who was not on duty on the ship arrived.

The wardroom of ICS FREDERICK HALSWELL consisted of twenty-five officers, including the CO and XO. Most had wives or girlfriends who came along, and several had children. Very quickly, the numerous introductions went washing right over Matt's head, leaving him hopeless to remember everyone's name, let alone who did what, where. So he smiled and nodded, told everyone how nice it was to meet them—that wasn't a lie, but it felt like it after the twelfth or thirteenth introduction—and stuck close to Jeremy as he went about his George duties for the gathering.

Those duties consisted mostly in making sure the fridge remained stocked with beer. Matt had not brought nearly enough, but fortunately Jeremy had a few more cases stashed away in the Captain's garage. Ever so often he would check the fridge and, when the number of bottles got low, he and Matt would run out, grab a case, and bring it back to restock.

Not too hard.

The roast was Cindy's creation, and she doted over it from the time

Matt got back to the house with the Captain until it was ready, shortly after the last of the guests arrived.

That ended up being a bit of a relief, actually. When Jeremy had mentioned the roast, Matt had gotten a sinking feeling in the pit of his stomach. Surely he wouldn't be expected to cook for everyone as the George? Not that he minded cooking, per se. But he was good for spaghetti or a ham and cheese sandwich, and not much else. And certainly he had never thought of cooking for so many people.

That was one bullet dodged, and a good thing too.

After the initial greetings and pleasantries, the guests split up into several different groups. After a short while, it became very obvious that some of the clusters were based on the officers' positions on the ship: the Supply Officer—Chop the others called him—and his two subordinates seemed to be together more often than not, as did the Operations Officer —OPS—and a couple of his JOs. But there were other demarcations as well. The Ensigns clumped together, as did the more senior Lieutenants, and after a while, Matt found himself in the little Ensign group.

He already knew Jeremy, and he recalled the Bull—turned out his name was actually Ivan—from his greeting onboard ship. He was the Communications Officer, and Jeremy the Main Propulsion Assistant. But there were two other Ensigns onboard. Vasili Kusnetsov, who looked exactly the way Matt would have thought a guy with that name would look—Russian to a T—was the Reactor Controls Assistant. And Jorge Ramos, who unlike Petty Officer Gonzalez actually had the dark hair and deep tan that went with the name, was the Electrical Officer.

"I guess I'll be relieving one of you," Matt said, and received shrugs in reply.

"Probably, but OPS hasn't put out a plan yet," the Bull said. At Matt's raised eyebrow, he explained, "He's the Senior Watch Officer. It's up to him who goes where, long as the XO agrees."

"Ah."

Charlie walked up then and joined the group, and the gaggle of Ensigns parted to let him in. "Get a place yet, Matt?"

He swallowed a swig of his beer and shook his head. "Still looking."

"Where do you have your sights set?" asked Jorge.

"So far Charlie's showed me around the station, and I've checked out Ventura."

Jorge nodded. "Ventura's nice. Lots of tourists, though. I'd say look here in Ortega, but it's a little pricey. I'm up in Moana. Might want to check it out. It's up in the mountains, so you don't get the beach, but it's a little cooler, temperature-wise, and there are some great views. Cheaper, too."

The Bull frowned and shook his head. "You can almost pass for local. Matt might have a bit more trouble there."

"Oh come on, it's not—"

Right then, a ringing bell interrupted, and Matt turned to see the boy from the boat—his name was Peter—looking abashed as he stood beside the door leading into the house, a big bell in his hand. As all eyes turned on him, he flushed. "Mom says the roast's done, and come get it," he said, then looked to the ground, embarrassed.

Didn't have to tell them twice. Very quickly everyone had a plate with a sizable hunk of meat on it, along with some fresh greens and what looked like braised potatoes, but that Matt assumed was a locally-grown equivalent tuber.

"Is this the buffalo?" someone asked as the plates were being passed around, and Cindy nodded.

"Straight from Mira Mesa."

That went right over Matt's head, and he leaned in to Charlie, who was waiting next to him, to inquire about it.

"Mira Mesa's inland about a thousand clicks northwest of the elevator. Big herds of buffalo roam near there. They've got a couple hunting preserves, and a few ranches. Great meat, but the local government caps how many can be taken by hunters and ranchers each year, to preserve the herds. Toward this time of year, as they reach mating season, the meat can get hard to find, and pricey."

That made a certain amount of sense. After Matt got his plate, and he got a taste of the meat, it made even more.

He could not recall ever having a better cut of steak. It seemed to melt in his mouth, and the flavors! No doubt Cindy had worked some magic with herbs, but that couldn't change the underlying quality of the meat.

No wonder the government sought to preserve it. If not, folks would very likely wipe the herds out in short order, the demand would be so high.

The cynical voice in Matt's mind pointed out that the real reason for the limits was to prop up prices, and benefit the friends of the politicians who instituted the policy. But he shut that voice down. It was probably correct, but he preferred to look at the more positive side.

At least for the moment.

There was more than enough roast to go around, and several of the guys went back for seconds, so Matt didn't feel too bad when he decided to do the same. Lord knew the extra gravity made for a good workout every day, whether he actively sought one or not. Surely that meant a few extra calories would be ok. But before long everyone had their fill, and went back to talking amongst themselves in their little groups. Though, Matt noticed the groups had changed, people filtering from one to another. That boded well; cliques on the ship would probably become uncomfortable.

After a few minutes more, the Captain stepped out into the middle of the patio and cleared his throat, loudly. All eyes went to him, and the buzz of conversation died.

"Probably better get down to business before things get out of hand, or the XO falls asleep."

The XO, who had been leaning back on one of the outdoor couches, gave a little jerk and sat upright, then stood up, looking abashed, to the obvious amusement of the JOs who had been sitting nearby. A general ripple of laughter spread through the rest of the officers as well, and the Captain gave him a "Caught You" kind of look for a second before he went back to the rest of the group.

"We're here to Hail the new Ensign, and say farewell to the SLOB. So without further ado...Matt, get up here."

Everyone turned to look at him, and Matt moved hurriedly around an ottoman that was occupied by the Chief Engineer's—CHENG's— three-year-old and his teddy bear, to the Captain's side. The Captain grinned at him and clapped him on the shoulder, then turned back to the assembled officers.

"Ensign Matthew Gilbert hails from Trinity, correct?" He sidelong at Matt, and Matt nodded agreement. "He *didn't* go to the Academy." Fully two-thirds of the wardroom clapped and whistled at that, while the remaining guys, ring-knockers all presumably, booed. "He instead chose the path of the scholar and gentleman." His eyebrows rose as he looked back at the XO, who Matt noted had been one of the boo-ers, and the XO snorted, but grinned. "He's single, and is trying to figure out where to live. And," he reached his left hand into his pants pocket and pulled out a little note card. He studied it for a second and pursed his lips. "Says here you like boxing, and play the piano."

Matt nodded again.

"Anything else to say for yourself?"

He couldn't think of a damn thing, so he blurted out, "Just happy to be here."

"Glad to have you." The Captain turned back to his officers and replaced his note card in his pocket. "Now, Matt's coming is serendipitous, because it means Jeremy gets to turn over the George duties."

"Step increase in performance!" said someone from the back of the crowd, to a chorus of chuckles.

The Captain waved them to silence and beckoned Jeremy forward. "Have you given him a turnover, George?"

Jeremy nodded. "Yes sir."

The Captain turned to Matt and raised an eyebrow. "Are you ready to relieve?"

Matt almost just nodded, but at the last minute he remembered his formality, and he stepped in front of Jeremy, coming to attention. "I am ready to relieve you, sir."

Jeremy smiled faintly and also braced up. "I am ready to be relieved."

Matt glanced at the Captain, who nodded, then focused back on Jeremy. "I relieve you, sir."

"I stand relived." Jeremy fished into his pocket and pulled out a set of Ensign bars. Or at least, they were the right size to be Ensign bars. But instead of being golden, one looked like it had been powder-coated green and the other red. He held them out to the Captain, who accepted them with a solemn look on his face.

The Captain turned and stood in front of Matt. "These," he said as he began working the right side collar of Matt's shirt, "are only to be worn on the ship, while underway. Commodore frowns on them in port." He raised an eyebrow. "Understood?"

Matt nodded.

The Captain finished with Matt's right side and moved to his left.

"We are giving you a sacred trust, Ensign. If you fail, our liberty will never recover." He finished with Matt's left collar and stepped back, looked him up and down, then nodded in satisfaction.

Matt glanced down, and it was as he expected. The green bar was pinned to his starboard collar, the red to his port. Just like the running lights of a ship.

The Captain turned to the end table where he had put down his drink. He bent over, picked up his glass and, straightening, raised it over his head. "To the new George Ensign."

The others gathered around repeated the toast, amazingly enough without any joke of hint of sarcasm, then all took a drink.

"As you were, Matt," the Captain said, and Matt moved back to where he had been standing beside the CHENG's kid. As soon as he had left his side, the Captain continued, "Now for the main event. SLOB!"

More chuckling from the officers, and the crowd on the opposite side of the Captain parted, allowing Tim to step forward.

He did not hold with local fashion, apparently. He wore jeans and an orange, long-sleeved, collared shirt, and hiking boots. Not exactly what Matt would have chosen for the moist warmth of this New California evening.

But whatever floated his boat.

Tim reached the Captain's side, beer bottle in his left hand and bulging satchel in his right. He took a second to put the satchel down at his feet then turned to face the rest of the officers, a mixture of a smile and a smirk on his face.

The Captain glanced down at the satchel and raised an eyebrow.

"Oh, this is going to be good," CHENG said. He was sitting in the chair that went with the ottoman his son had commandeered, and he leaned forward, an anticipatory grin on his face.

"Lieutenant Timothy Granderson has been with us for almost two years, now. When I took command, he made an immediate impression." A round of chuckles followed that remark, and again Matt felt like he was missing half of a joke. "And now he's leaving us for greener pastures. The Navy, in its wisdom, has decided to send him all the way to Icarus, where he will be working in the acquisitions branch of the Parliamentary Liaison Office."

Matt blinked. That was quite a shore duty gig. He wasn't all that savvy on the ins and outs of Navy politics, but he imagined they didn't give a job like that to just any schlub. His initial impression of the SLOB from their first meeting in the wardroom shifted, and he recalled Charlie's words. Tim apparently was more than just a jerk, after all.

The Captain went on, "I really appreciate the hard work you've put in, and the dedication you've shown. We're going to miss you."

Tim smiled, genuinely, and replied, "Thank you, sir."

The Captain nodded, then turned away from him to look out at his officers. "Does anyone want to say anything?"

It seemed almost everyone did. Starting with the Department Heads, the various officers stood, one by one, and thanked Tim for his service on board. Most shared anecdotes, and more than a few of them set the group to guffaws as they recalled things that had happened underway, or on liberty calls, or the like. Finally, the XO stood and summed it up: Tim had done a lot of good for the ship, and he would be missed.

After the XO, silence loomed for a few seconds as the Captain looked around, waiting for someone else to speak. When no one did, he took a deep breath and stepped to the side. "Ok, Tim. Let us have it."

What followed was beyond what Matt could have expected, or even envisioned. Tim's bag was full of gag gifts, which he took out one at a time after telling a story—usually embarrassing, or amusing, or most often both—about the person receiving the gift. And each gift matched the story precisely. No one in the wardroom was safe from his ribbing, from the former George all the way up to the Captain. And all took it with a grin and a laugh.

Matt should have known he wouldn't be spared. As the Captain moved away from Tim's position of honor, clutching a pink teddy bear with a big red heart on its chest and shaking his head in amusement, Tim looked directly at Matt and said, "George!"

All eyes turned on him, and Matt, with no small amount of trepidation, stepped back around the Ottoman to Tim's side.

Tim didn't wait for him to get settled before he turned back to the crowd and grinned impishly. "You all know I like to give the new guys a hard time." A ripple of chuckles rolled through the crowd, which apparently wasn't tired of winning the war against laughter yet. "But it's out of love." Another wave of chuckles, but Matt didn't feel any temptation to join in on it.

Tim looked back at him and saw the skepticism in his eyes. He rolled his. "It's true. So I've got something special for our new George here." He bent over, and reached into his bag. Matt braced himself, but when Tim withdrew his hand he was holding a gold Stellar Warfare pin. But this one was different from the other Matt had seen. Its color was deeper and...was that a flash of red from the port end of the starburst and of green from the starboard?

The crowd hushed, and Matt looked up from the warfare device to Tim's face, which was now deadly serious. "When I reported to my first ship, the SLOB gave me this. He got it from the SLOB on his first ship when he was George, who got it from the SLOB on his first ship, who got it from his first SLOB, and so on and so on until the guy who got it as a NUB Ensign at his first liberty port when he was stationed on the TRIPOLI."

A collective intake of breath from the wardroom mirrored Matt's own. The TRIPOLI had been the first ship to encounter forces from the Tsago Dominance. Everyone knew what happened in that meeting, and how few of TRIPOLI's crew had lived to tell about it.

Tim held out the warfare device to Matt, who took it in trembling hands.

"I think the tradition needs to continue. So when you get pinned, do it with these. And then pass them along to the George when it's your turn to be the SLOB."

Matt looked down at the emblem in his hands. Closer now, he could see that an emerald had been inlaid at the starboard end of the starburst, and a ruby at the port. He would bet good money the thing really was made of pure gold.

Speechless, he raised his eyes back up to Tim's, and the SLOB nodded gravely.

Right then, Matt was sure he could have heard a pin drop from the skipper's neighbor's house.

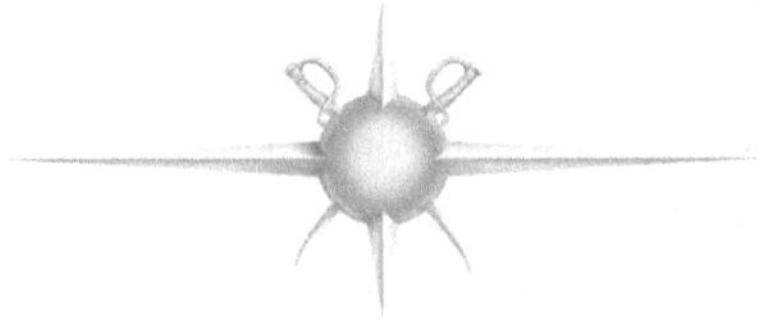

Chapter Nineteen

When the elevator came to a halt, the only indication was a soft chime that rang through the passenger lounge, followed by a recorded female voice saying, "Copernicus Station, O-4 level".

Matt hadn't been dozing, exactly, but he also hadn't been fully paying attention to the goings-on around him. He had started out passing the time on the upward transit with a book on his holopad, but his residual fatigue left him restarting the same page six times, so he put it aside and just reclined in his seat. It would not do to be seen sleeping in public while in uniform, so he didn't.

Not really.

Still, it took him a minute to get himself together enough to stand up and shoulder his sea bag. By then most of the other people who had been riding up from the surface with him had filed to the now wide-open airlock doors that marked the exit.

He glanced at his chronometer: 0600. He had plenty of time to get to the ship and get settled before Officers Call, but still anxiety filled him. It wasn't like he hadn't been to the ship before, hadn't met everyone there, and at the Captain's house during the Hail and Farewell a week ago. But this was going to be his first real day on the job.

Didn't want to make a bad impression. Or had that ship already sailed?

Matt snorted. That was just self-consciousness talking. New-guy joshing aside, the other officers from the HALSWELL seemed to have accepted him just fine. That wasn't a legitimate concern.

Still, it wouldn't do to be late, or anywhere close to it.

He hurried over to the line of people, a mix of yardbirds and civilian contractors from the look of them, with a few Navy thrown in as well, and waited his turn to disembark, then set off toward Airdock 2, and his ship.

It had been a busy week, and a busier weekend, and he still felt the strain of it.

He had considered Jorge's suggestion of Moana, and the Bull's trepidation over it, carefully. Even went to the town to check it out. But after an hour there, and getting not-so-friendly looks from a sizable percentage of the population, he decided it was not the place for him, and returned to Ventura.

When he met up with Isaiah later, he had confirmed that the mountain towns tended to be the places where anti-Navy, or outright separatist, sentiments tended to be more pronounced. Not that you couldn't find those notions on the coasts, of course. But with less tourist money flowing directly into the inland areas, resentment found easier soil to grow there.

Matt supposed that made sense, in a way. But something about it seemed a bit too pat, almost cliche, to make him believe that was all there was to it.

Regardless, he didn't want to live in a place where he might have to watch his back. And there was the tourist girl angle to consider. So in the end he decided on a condo in Ventura, about halfway up the third high rise there, with an ok view looking down the beach. An inland view would have cost less, but he didn't want to just look at a bunch of buildings. And a full ocean view was more than he wanted to spend, so he took the happy medium.

It had taken a day to negotiate the lease and set up recurring payments, then another to schedule his household goods delivery. Finally, the movers arrived on Friday, and he had spent the weekend getting mostly unpacked, in between trips up to Copernicus to check out of the BOQ and reconnoiter the route from the elevator to the ship and back. He did that twice, to be doubly sure he knew the way.

When he finally hit the rack last night, it was much later than he would have preferred, well into the ninety-three minute "CaliTime" that was added onto the normal 24 hour clock to make up for the difference between New California's rotation and a standard day.

So yeah, he was feeling it this morning.

It took ten minutes to walk from the elevator lobby to the umbilicus leading to the HALSWELL. About the same amount of time as it had taken during his trial runs over the weekend. Which brought his total commute from Condo door to the ship to about fifty minutes.

Of course, he only had to wait a couple minutes for his flyer, and the elevator was boarding when he arrived at the surface station. So conceivably he ought to add an extra twenty to thirty minute to that figure, to be safe.

That was a lot of time to spend going to and from work, but it was worth it.

He just hoped he still felt that way in three months.

Stepping over the airlock seal onto the HALSWELL's quarterdeck, Matt did not recognize the petty officer behind the lectern, but Vasili was the supervisor on duty. The Officer of the Deck, rather. Matt snapped off a salute to the Ensign, then to Vasili and requested permission to come aboard.

"You *have* permission," Vasili said as he returned the salute, earning a quizzical look from the petty officer behind the lectern, a dark skinned Carraway's World native who wore a single chevron and the Operations Specialist rating badge.

Matt was confused as well for a second, then he remembered his protocol. Officers attached to a ship had blanket permission to come and go; they did not need to ask for permission to go ashore, or come aboard. That said, he had never been able to figure out what he was supposed to say in lieu of the standard "Permission to come aboard" that he had learned. "I have permission to come aboard?" That seemed pretentious. "Coming aboard?"

"Can I see your ID please sir?" said the petty officer. His name tag read "Okubo," and he was a full head taller than Matt, with a shaved head and lean, bony face that matched his slender torso.

"Sure," Matt said. He set his sea bag down and fished his ID out of the thigh pocket on his uniform trousers. He had chosen working khakis today since he didn't have his underway coveralls fitted out with ship's kit and insignia yet. And besides, wearing underway uniforms off base was against regs.

Petty Officer Okubo scanned his ID and tapped at the console atop the lectern, then nodded. When he looked back up at Matt, his demeanor became a tad bit more relaxed. "Just checked aboard, eh sir?" he said as he handed back the ID.

"Yep," Matt replied. "Time for the adventure the recruiting ads promised."

Okubo laughed.

Vasili interjected, "I think Charlie's in the wardroom, Matt."

Matt replaced his ID and nodded. "Thanks." Shouldering his sea bag, he said, "Good to meet you, Petty Officer Okubo."

"Welcome aboard, sir."

It wasn't hard to remember the route to the wardroom, and sure enough Charlie was in there when Matt arrived, sitting in one of the couches in the offset sitting area by the kiddie table, and watching a news broadcast on the holoscreen there. He looked up when Matt approached, looked him up and down, then grinned.

"Moving in?"

Matt looked him askance. "Well, yeah. Figured it would be a good idea to leave some things here, for duty and all."

Charlie shrugged and hit the controls for the holoscreen, muting it. Then he stood up. "You won't be on the duty roster for a week or so, probably. Skipper likes to give a bit of time for the new guys to get started on quals before we load them down." He grinned. "He's good like that. But yeah, you'll want some stuff here, regardless. Talked with OPS on Friday. You'll be with Tim and Harry in Stateroom Six, until Tim moves out. Good deal for you, because we aren't scheduled to get another new guy for a while. So you'll have some extra space until then."

That was surely a good thing, but Matt wasn't so sure rooming with Tim could be considered a "good deal." He opened his mouth to say so, but thought better of it. Moaning about it wouldn't change anything, and would just make him look like an entitled douchebag. Besides, Tim would be gone in just a few weeks. How bad could it be?

Charlie gestured for Matt to follow him, and he walked around the starboard side of the table, opposite from the doorway Matt had come through, to the Wardroom's second door along the aft bulkhead. "I think Harry's already here. He'll help you get settled."

Matt followed him, and they emerged into a corridor running athwarships. Directly across from the door they took was another, labeled WRSR #1. Another door lay a few paces down the passageway on the aft bulkhead. Another stateroom.

Charlie jabbed his thumb toward a third door, to their left as they exited the Wardroom. "Head's there." Then he turned to follow the corridor to Port. A few meters past the second stateroom door, they came to a t-junction, and Matt recognized the passageway that joined theirs from forward as the one he had taken to get to the wardroom just a minute ago; there were the CO's and XO's staterooms, and the airtight door leading into the main athwartships passageway on this level.

The passageway bent left, past another stateroom door, and then immediately to the right, and Matt saw a door labeled "Storeroom" in the aft bulkhead. Then as they continued to Port, they past two more staterooms opposite each other before reaching another T-junction.

To the right, the new passageway ended at a trio of doors leading to additional staterooms. Ahead, it passed a pair of stateroom doors, one after the other in the aft bulkhead, and then ended at another airtight door. Charlie walked to the last stateroom before the airtight door and knocked.

"Harry, you in there?" he asked, and a few seconds later the door opened.

Matt had not been able to place the name, but he immediately recognized the guy who opened the stateroom door. Of a height with Matt, and ripping with muscles, his sandy hair was receding rapidly and his ears seemed a bit too large for his head. His green eyes flashed with intelligence and he had a broad grin which somehow changed his over-sized ears from oddities to the most natural-looking feature possible. He was the Torpedo Officer, if Matt recalled correctly, and he was in his skivvies and a white t-shirt.

"Hey Charlie," Harry said, then he saw Matt following along and pushed the door open a bit wider. "About time you got here, Matt. Come on in."

Charlie stepped aside to let him pass, and Matt slipped into his new stateroom.

It was small, but not so small as to be claustrophobic. No that it would matter if it was; Matt had never fallen prey to that fear.

Three racks, one atop the other, were mounted against the aft bulkhead, heads toward the port side, and a little step ladder built into their feet to ease access to the top bunk. Inboard of the racks on the aft bulkhead was a small sink with taps for hot and cold water, with a mirror-faced medicine cabinet above. A trio of identical lockers, with opening desks complete with network connections and status displays, lined the forward wall opposite the bunks. There were a pair of EAS manifolds in the room, each with four plug-in connections and marked by the standard red triangular nonskid patch on the deck: one just inside the door and another along the port bulkhead and mounted so the connections were arranged vertically.

Made for easy plugging in while asleep. Matt shuddered at the notion of a casualty so severe and long-lasting that it would require breathing in those damn masks for long enough to require sleeping in them. But they were operating in outer space; had to be ready for anything.

"I've got the top bunk," Harry sad, patting his neatly made mattress with his hand, "and you've probably figured out Tim's a bottom."

Behind Matt, Charlie snorted loudly, then began chortling, and Harry's grin broadened as though to say, "Thank you, I'll be here all week." Instead, he said, in the same even but friendly tone, "That leaves you the middle. Hope you don't mind." Then he pointed at the portmost desk. "That's Tim." The middle one. "Me." And the inboard desk, closest to the door. "You." He paused for a second and looked Matt up and down. "You got coveralls?"

Matt nodded and, unlimbering his sea bag, tossed it onto his new bunk. "Yeah, but I don't have patches or—"

"I've got swag for you," Charlie said. "Be right back." Then he ducked out of the room.

"Hicks, downstairs in the laundry can sew the patches on for you," Harry said. "But no one will care if you don't have them today. You'll stick out like a sore thumb in those, though." He gestured toward Matt's khakis.

"Yeah well, can't wear the coveralls from the surface, so—"

Harry shook his head vigorously. "First rule of surviving a space tour."

"Show no weakness. I know."

Harry paused, then bobbed his head slightly. "Good point. The second rule: don't wear work clothes away from work." He looked at Matt's sea bag, then back at him. "Hope you've got civvies in there."

Well, that was a simple solution to the problem that had been irking Matt all weekend, and most of the morning. Coveralls were one hell of a lot more comfortable than khakis. And looked better too, in his opinion. "Umm...no."

He really should have thought of that. Why hadn't he? Probably because Engineering School had been on a Navy-owned orbital station and coveralls were authorized everywhere, and in Tactical School they only wore coveralls for simulations, and were required to change into them on the premises because coveralls were not allowed off base.

Dumb.

Harry shook his head. "Won't make that mistake tomorrow, will ya?"

"Guess not." He tried not to sound rueful, and almost succeeded.

Harry chuckled good-naturedly, then stepped around Matt to the sink area. On the bulkhead adjacent to the sink, and opposite the feet of the bunks, three sets of hooks were driven into the faux-wood. Towels and a set of coveralls hung from two of them. Harry grabbed the coveralls from the hook nearest the sink and gave them a quick shake, then he began putting them on. He glanced back at Matt and raised an eyebrow. "Better suit up. Don't want to be late for your first ball."

Right.

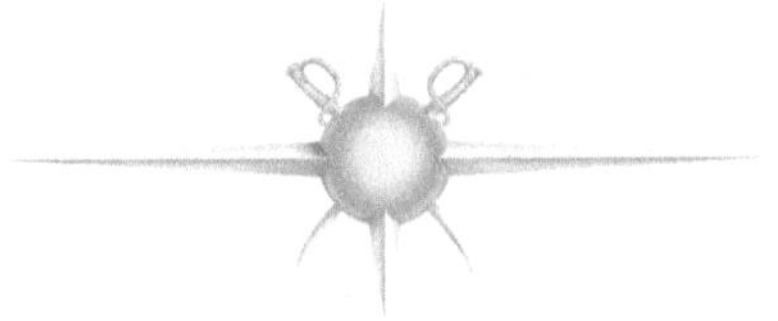

Chapter Twenty

The Navy-blue underway coveralls were distinctly more comfortable. You almost didn't notice that the fabric wasn't standard synthetic material, but was reinforced fiber-weave designed to maintain interior pressure against the vacuum of space, interwoven with heating elements to maintain body heat in the same. Nor was the EAS hose, stowed cleverly in the left breast above where a man's warfare device would have been sewn, if he had one, bulky or even detectable unless one were looking for it.

It really was too bad the Navy brass were such sticks in the mud about not authorizing them for wear off base. It would make life one hell of a lot easier, in a lot of ways.

Charlie had not returned by the time Matt finished changing. But Tim did.

He flung the stateroom door open just as Matt was zippering up the front of his coveralls, and stalked inside, looking annoyed.

"Harry, I tell ya—" he began, but stopped abruptly when he saw Matt there. They just stared at each other for a second, then Tim rolled his eyes slightly. "Right. I forgot OPS put you in here. All settled in?"

"More or less," Matt replied with a shrug.

"Good. Just don't mess with my stuff and we'll be fine. I meant to talk to you anyway." Tim kicked the door closed and tugged the t-shirt he was wearing off over his head, while kicking his sandals off. He took his coveralls down from their hook and dropped his shorts to the ground, then, while stepping into his new garment, continued, "Records say you're a pretty decent shot." He hopped up and down to settle his coveralls in place, then zipped up and turned back toward Matt. "Excuse me," he said, nodding toward his set of lockers. Matt got out of the way and he opened the lowest one to retrieve a pair of black, steel-toed pressure boots. "You interested in VBSS?"

Matt blinked. Visit, Board, Search, and Seizure was one of the multitude of missions a Naval vessel had to be ready to perform on a moment's notice. It involved rendezvousing with another vessel, establishing communications to get their leave to board and inspect—or to compel them to give their leave—and then sending over a boarding team to inspect the ship, crew, and cargo for contraband, or other bits of chicanery.

It didn't rank high on Matt's "Wicked Cool Things To Do With A Warship" list.

He shook his head with a shrug. "Not really. Haven't really given it much thought."

"Well get interested, because you're going to VBSS school next week. Zach's relieving me as First Lieutenant and Boarding Officer, and you'll be his second." He tugged the laces on his boots tight, then stood and grinned back at Matt. It was not a particularly friendly grin, but at least it didn't have the semi-malicious teasing that he had worn at their first meeting. "Sound good?"

"Uh..."

Tim nodded. "Good."

Sitting in his chair, Harry just shook his head and chuckled over the whole exchange. "Come on," he said, standing. "We need to get in to O-call."

Time nodded, then he and Harry swept out of the stateroom, leaving Matt standing there feeling a bit...not quite overwhelmed at the unexpected revelation of his future. More like surprised and irritated and curious all at the same time.

But Harry was right. The chronometer mounted above Matt's stack of lockers and desk space read 0655. Five minutes to O-call.

Time to roll.

The wardroom was full again, the officers all having taken places around the table. All except the CHENG. Just as the last time Matt had been there, he stood hovering over the coffee pot.

Not that Matt could blame him. Chief Engineer was a grueling, and fairly thankless, job from what he had been able to work out so far.

"Hey George," said the Combat Systems Officer, from his seat at the near corner, when Matt came into the space. He was a full Lieutenant, of course. But he was significantly older than the other three-bar guys in the room. His hair was salt-and-pepper grey and he had deep laugh lines around his mouth, and spiderwebs around his brown eyes. Matt recalled he had been an Operations Specialist Chief before getting commissioned—a real Mustang officer. His name was Kaminski, but Matt couldn't remember his first name. To him it would be sir, or CSO, Matt supposed.

"Sir," Matt replied.

The seat caddy-corner to the CSO was open, and he waved for Matt to sit in it. No one else seemed keen on grabbing that chair right then, so Matt obliged.

"Where'd you get a place?"

"Sonora Tower, in Ventura."

CSO nodded slowly, but before he could talk, a Lieutenant Junior Grade across the table from the CSO leaned forward, interested. "That's the tower next to The Peninsula, right?" Matt had met him very briefly at the Hail and Farewell, and again could not remember his name. The name tag said "Flemming", and instead of rank insignia on his left collar, he wore a golden emblem showing a leaf or something flaring around a something else... Matt really didn't know what the heck it was supposed to be. But it looked a little like a pork chop, which is why Navy guys tended called the Supply Officers "Chop" for fun.

"You're Disbursing, right?"

Flemming nodded. "Yep. I make sure your pay doesn't get jacked up, which these days mostly means making sure paperwork for pay changes is submitted as early as possible. I'm also the master of the ship's budget."

"Oh, so you're the guy I should talk to about doing a little embezzling?"

Flemming's lips compressed, and he gave Matt a flat look, which he returned deadpan. After a couple seconds, the CSO barked out a laugh and slapped the table. "Lighten up, Dan. He's screwing with you."

Flemming—Dan—frowned more deeply for a second, then sighed and looked away, shaking his head. "That shit's not funny. Guys have gone to prison, you know."

"Yeah but they're all Chops. We expect that," the CSO said. Then, leaning in toward Matt, he said in a lower, more conspiratorial tone, "Never trust a man whose collar devices don't match." He gave Matt a nudge in the side with his elbow while keeping his eyes, which twinkled with mischief, on Dan the whole time.

Dan rolled his eyes but whatever reply he was going to make was cut off as the port-side wardroom door opened and the XO strode into the space, the CO close on his heels.

"Morning gentlemen," the CO said, and all conversation stopped as the officers gave him their full attention.

The XO stepped around the table and took the same seat he had the other day, directly to the right of the CO's chair, which stood decidedly empty.

In fact... Matt did a double-take. The Captain's chair had a covering on it that wasn't there his first day aboard: scarlet cloth that matched the cushions and tablecloth, with the big golden star inside a ring that marked one as a Commanding Officer. That definitely hadn't been on the chair the other day, or Matt wouldn't have sat in it.

"Son of a bitch," he muttered to himself.

But then again, of course they had removed the cover. The joke wouldn't have worked otherwise.

Still, it rankled.

The CO settled down into his seat and rested his hands on table in front of him. "We've got a busy couple weeks ahead of us. Undocking is three weeks from Wednesday, and—" a ripple of chuckles spread from the other side of the table from where Mat was sitting. Looking over there, it was mostly the Engineering division officers who were chuckling. Behind them, still near the coffee station, CHENG looked pained.

The CO gave the Engineers a level look, and the laughter stopped. His lips twitched. "I know. But we have no control over how the shipyard does its work, besides holding the Project Manager's feet to the fire." His right eyebrow rose, and Matt got the distinct impression he had been doing just that. "That said, if the undocking slips, *we* will not be the cause of it. I want us ready for every evolution: tagouts approved, valve lineups double-checked, briefings and walkthroughs completed well ahead of time. Understood?"

Heads bobbed all around the table, and the CO looked at the CHENG. "CHENG?"

CHENG cleared his throat and pulled his holopad out from his thigh pocket. "Yes sir. I'm closing out the Starboard Plasma Condenser this morning with Jeremy and Senior Chief Tillson. After that, the yard-birds will get started reinstalling piping and lagging. ETA for completion is Saturday afternoon. A day for package signoffs, and we can expect to begin retests on Monday. The RPCP upgrade is on schedule. Final software build and grooming starts tomorrow and will run through the end of the week. The final hull cut welds are scheduled for Thursday, and the battery compartment closeout is next week." He looked up. "Good to go at this point."

The CO nodded and turned toward the CSO, who gave him a familiar but respectful nod.

"SDMS cabling hookups were a little delayed over the weekend, Skipper. A Yardbird tried to start a bulkhead cut without a fire watch." The Captain's brows furrowed, but Matt was fairly sure he had heard this report before; it wasn't the sort of thing to keep from the CO's ears. Hot work without a fire watch had an excellent chance of starting a fire someplace the worker couldn't see, like on the far side of a bulkhead. And a fire in an enclosed area like a starship could get ugly very fast. "The Roving Watch was on the spot and stopped him before he could get started. Still, the yard stopped work for a fact finding. I went to the critique last night." He spread his hands in a helpless gesture. "It was a new guy who was in a rush. He's been disqualified from hot work pending upgrade and requal. They've put different people on the job and will recommence this morning."

The CO nodded, then glanced back at the CHENG. "Is that critical path?"

CHENG shook his head. "No, sir."

"All right. WEPS?"

On the other side of the Captain from the XO, another guy with full Lieutenant bars on his collar perked up. He looked to be the same age as

Tim, but Matt knew he had to be two to three years his senior. He was another ginger, with blue eyes. Matt recalled he had put down an impressive number of beers at the Hail and Farewell, and that his first name was Steve. His name tag named him O'Reilly.

"They're reinstalling the outer door actuator linkages for Tube 2 tomorrow and should finish up Wednesday. Retest Thursday. Reloading team training at the base simulator Wednesday afternoon. And we've got a gun shoot on Thursday."

A couple of the guys around the table let out little groans, and WEPS frowned at them. "Gotta keep in quals, gents," he said, then shook his head in amazement. "What kind of Icaran man doesn't like to shoot guns?"

"I'm not from Icarus, WEPS," said a tall, blocky, shaven-haired Lieutenant halfway down the table. His name tag read Dixon, and though Matt had met him at the Hail and Farewell, they had probably exchange five words total.

"Miriam is still part of the Confederation. If—"

The Captain held up his hands. "Gentlemen." Both men looked at him, going silent. "This isn't a political debate, Terry. You know the requirements. Get it done."

Matt stared at Terry, surprised. He would not have expected to find a citizen from Miriam in a military outfit. As he understood it, the planet was colonized by a bunch of Quakers and pacifists, and had a distinctly non-martial take on life. But then, Terry had the Supply Corps insignia on his left collar. So he wasn't a line Officer. Still...

"Are you current, Matt?" That CO's voice drew Matt's attention back to him. It took Matt a second to recognize that the Captain was asking about his own gun quals.

Matt opened his mouth to reply in the affirmative, but OPS spoke up before he could. "He'll be shooting at VBSS school next week, sir."

The Captain nodded, looking back OPS's way. "That brings us to the billet shuffle."

Around the room, the other JOs shifted in their chairs. Clearly this was something they had known was coming but hadn't received any word about until now.

OPS tapped on his holopad and leaned forward. His left hand went to his ear and began tugging at his earlobe as he spoke. "Matt," Matt perked up when his name was called. He hadn't expected to be involved with this, between being new and going to school next week. And didn't they say he'd get a few weeks to just work on quals? OPS continued, "You're going to relieve Jorge as Electrical Officer and Jorge is going to relieve Rasheid as Sensors."

Matt looked over at Rasheid, the Carrawayer who had thrown the napkin at him on his first day. Rasheid noted his gaze and gave him a little grin and a faked tip of the hat.

"And then Rasheid will relieve Zach as Navigator, and Zach will take First Lieutenant from Tim." OPS looked up. "Clear enough?"

The other named officers all nodded, and Matt followed suit, a surge of anxiety flooding through him at the change in plans.

"Matt," the Captain said, leaning forward to look at him again, "I normally like to give new officers a few weeks to get acclimated, and start on quals, before throwing them into a division. But Tim's leaving the day we undock, and the other guys are at the point where they need to rotate to new jobs on the ship. So I'm afraid you're going to have to start running sooner than we thought."

"No problem, sir," Matt replied, keeping his voice calm and trying to put a cheerful note into it.

OPS spoke again. "We've got four turnovers to do in three weeks, and they have to go in order or it won't work. So Matt, you'll need to finish turning over with Jorge by the end of the week. Jorge, you've got til next week. Rasheid the Friday after that, and then Zach gets the short schedule." He shrugged apologetically. "I suggest you all get started asap."

The Captain nodded. "Anything else, OPS?"

"No sir."

"Chop?"

The Supply Officer was a Lieutenant Commander, like the CHENG and XO, short and skinny, with frown lines and jet black hair. He shook his head. "We're doing the end-of-month audit this week, and then stores load on Friday after field day. That's it, sir."

"XO?"

The XO leaned forward and clasped his hands together atop the table. "I've talked to you guys about this before. We're entering a time of transition, and that's always a dangerous period. The crew has gotten used to being in airdock in the shipyard, not underway. As we wrap up and prepare to undock, and then get underway, we'll have to overcome that inertia as we change mindset. This is when guys will get in trouble out in town, or when we will cut corners and make mistakes, mistakes that could cause delays, or worse, get someone hurt." He turned his dark eyes on each man at the table in turn as he spoke. When they met Matt's, it seemed he was piercing Matt with that gaze. "Each of you need to be on your guard. Enforce standards, and stay involved with your men so we can head off any troubles before they happen." He smiled slightly then. "The Chiefs will be ahead of you on this, but that doesn't mean you can slack on it. We don't want any incidents. It's been a good yard period, and we've earned a lot of points from how we've executed it. It would be a shame to ruin it all at the end."

He sat back in his chair and the Captain nodded emphatic agreement. "Stay on your toes, gentlemen." He looked around the room again. "Any questions or other business?"

Silence.

A few seconds later, he nodded and stood. "Have a good day, gentlemen."

The rest of the officers rose as he did, and Matt followed suit. Then the CO and XO strode out of the wardroom.

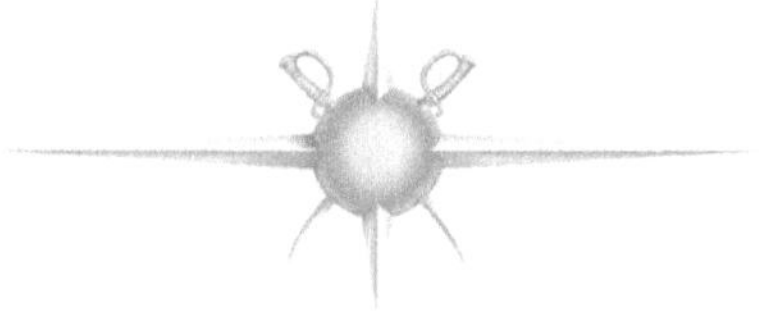

Chapter Twenty-One

The officers began milling about, breaking off into half a dozen different conversations as soon as the CO and XO departed.

"Engineering, stick around," CHENG said from his place near the coffee mess, and his division officers began to move toward him.

Matt stood. "Guess that means me," he said, and the CSO gave him a wry grin.

"Nothing like hitting the ground running," the older man said, and clapped him on the shoulder.

Engineering Department consisted of the CHENG and five Junior Officers, six now, counting Matt. Jeremy and Vasili got there ahead of him, and Jorge met him on the way. He gave Matt a nudge and a grin that almost looked apologetic as they reached the sitting area.

The last two Engineering officers were both Lieutenants Junior Grade, 2 gold bars on each collar, and wore the SWO pin on their left breasts. And of course Matt had met them at the Hail and Farewell. Sam Covington was the Auxiliary officer, a skinny guy from Icarus who was halfway between Jorge's and Rasheid's complexion, with the black hair and dark eyes to match. They had exchanged pleasantries at the party, but that was about it. Gideon Schulz was the Damage Control Assistant. He had a bookish look about him, despite his broad shoulders and muscular frame. He too was raven-haired, though his eyes were hazel.

Matt recalled he had been affable and fun at the party, and that he seemed to have a hundred jokes. He looked serious now, though.

They gathered in a loose ring with the CHENG, who studied his holopad with a frown for a few seconds before speaking. "We've only got a couple minutes before quarters, and we've got a lot going on this week. Real quick, any issues I need to know about? Anything you need help with?"

Jeremy piped up, "Shipyard QA will be in the MMR at 0900 to begin the condenser closeout. Senior Chief's already done a once-through and corrected a couple minor issues, so it should be ready for us."

CHENG frowned. "0900? I thought they said 0800."

"Yeah well, they called this morning to change it. Didn't give any specifics as to why, just that the inspector was running late."

"Fuck." CHENG looked down at his holopad. "I've got the availability status update at 1300...I'll have to call the PM to see if we can push it an hour." He sighed and looked back up. "Anything else?"

Head shakes all around.

"Ok." He zeroed in on Matt then. "Matt, you'll need to hook up with Charlie after quarters to get your qual cards and the rest. Ordinarily I'd tell you to focus on that, but you're going to have to juggle two things right off the bat."

"Yes sir. I was wondering, though. I guess I'm supposed to go to VBSS school next week. How will that—?"

CHENG answered the question before he could finish asking it. "You're just going to have to do divisional work and quals around the school. Going to be some long hours and late nights." His eyebrows rose. "Normal space duty, in other words. Hope you like swimming in the deep end."

"Yes sir."

CHENG glanced at the chronometer mounted over the sitting area's holoscreen. "Let's get to quarters, gents."

The little group broke up, and Jorge gestured for Matt to follow him. "E-div holds quarters down in the MMR, in front of the starboard generator sets," he said, and led him through the inboard wardroom door then forward to the athwartships passageway Matt had taken so many times before. They turned to starboard and and then aft at the outer bulkhead until they reached the ladderwell leading down.

The wardroom was located on the O-2 level. Matt almost expected Jorge to step off the ladder at the O-1 level where the quarterdeck lay, but instead he continued down to the first deck. There he stepped out into a corridor running forward and aft along the starboard side of the ship, and for a second Matt could have sworn it was the same corridor they had just left.

That illusion faded completely when he looked forward, because this deck's main athwartships passageway broke off immediately forward of the ladderwell. Past that, the passageway continued forward and he could see a couple of airtight doors on the inboard bulkhead, opposite a bank of escape pods, much farther forward than they had been above. Then it looked like the passageway bent to port to run athwartships.

"LPO berthing's there," Jorge said, gesturing toward the doors on the inboard bulkhead, then turned aft. "Classroom number 3," he said as he passed another airtight doorway on the right as they walked. Then they passed a clearly labeled Head opposite a red and white striped pressure door that was labeled Repair Locker, in yellowish green lettering that would glow in the dark.

Just before the corridor turned outboard, Jorge stopped in front of yet another airtight door and jabbed his thumb toward it. "Our office." Sure enough, a standard placard over the door read "Engineering Office." "I'll show you that later. For now," he turned outboard to where a pressure hatch, just as solid-looking as the main airlock, stood shut. A placard reading "Main Machinery Room" was mounted above the hatch. Jorge said, "MMR's in here."

There was a round window mounted in the upper portion of the hatch, maybe seven or eight centimeters across. Jorge bent forward and peered into it, then, nodding to himself, took hold of a hand wheel that was mounted inboard of the door at head-level. He began rotating it quickly counterclockwise and the hatch slowly opened inward into the MMR.

"We can dog this hatch shut, but that makes it real easy for pressure in the MMR and the Forward Compartment to lose equalization, and then it's a real bitch to get open. So we normally leave it un-dogged except for battle stations or other emergencies. But we never leave it open." He raised an eyebrow. "Plasma Line Rupture, you know?"

Matt knew enough about starship engineering plants to know how exceedingly unlikely that was. He just returned Jorge's look with a level stare of his own, and after a second the other Ensign chuckled and shrugged.

"Well, it's true." He ducked his head and stepped through the hatch. "Come on."

Matt followed him through the hatch and took a minute to close it behind them, using an identical hand wheel that was mounted on the aft side of the bulkhead. By the time he had finished, Jorge was several paces ahead, and he hurried to catch up.

On either side, as they entered the MMR, were enclosures that Matt recognized immediately as electrical distribution switchboards. Each panel was painted grey and heavily constructed, so it could contain an explosion or fire and prevent it from spreading, and each was filled with breakers and switches ranging from small thumb switches to super heavy duty mainline power breakers that required hydraulic assist to close them.

It wasn't all that dissimilar from the entrance to the MMR at the training prototype at Engineering school, though Matt could see signs of age here, where that one had been an obviously newer design. Some of the indications were LED instead of holotape, and the power junctions that accepted cables from the cableways running in the overhead were a locking quick-disconnect design, as opposed to the permalinks the new plants used. Still, it was familiar enough that it made Matt feel almost at home.

Then they stepped out from between the panels, and that feeling left completely.

Unlike the prototype, which was long, but narrow, HALSWELL's MMR was wide, spanning the width of the ship. The upper level, where he stood, was fairly open, the ever-present cable bundles in the overhead having been mostly left behind amongst the power panels. In their place, two large pipes, covered with insulation lagging and a good meter across each, traveled athwartships in the overhead from one side of the compartment to the other. They both twisted and turned, forming a series of s-shapes as they went, to protect against fractures from thermal expansion and contraction when the plant heated up or cooled down. One of the pipes was labeled ANION, the other CATION.

Those would be the main plasma lines, running from inside the Reactor Compartments, probably amidships and forward from here, to the Engine Rooms outboard.

Matt shook his head, correcting himself. Reactor Compartment, singular. The prototype he had trained on was the design used in the new STALWART-class cruisers like the HATHERLY, where he was initially slated to go. Those ships had two reactors, each powering engines and primary cannons on one side of the ship. Frigates like HALSWELL just made do with one, and it pulled duty for the entire ship.

A hefty difference indeed.

Jorge continued aft, and Matt followed, ducking a bit to step beneath the plasma lines.

Aft of the piping on the starboard side of the compartment, two large, grey-painted, boxy devices were mounted on platforms about half a meter above the decking. Smaller pipe branches came off the plasma lines, one from the CATION pipe and one from the ANION, and ran into each of the boxes. The stern section of the outboard box was enclosed by a white plastic enclosure that stretched from the box to the starboard bulkhead.

Those would be the two starboard Ships Service Electrical Generators, and the enclosure must be where the shipyard had gone into the Plasma Condenser, which the CHENG would be closing out this morning.

Matt looked to his right, and found his view of the port side generator sets blocked by a grey metallic enclosure that spit the compartment in two, except for narrow passages forward and aft. The enclosure was boxy, nestled below the two plasma conduits, and without windows. An especially solid-looking sliding pressure door was visible on his side of the enclosure, with a manual latching mechanism to allow access.

That had to be Maneuvering, the nerve center of the Engineering spaces.

"Morning, Mr. Ramos," said a smooth baritone voice, and Matt looked away from the Maneuvering space toward a gaggle of about a dozen men in underway coveralls who were gathered between the two

SSEG sets. The speaker was the eldest among them, lean and muscled, with brown hair that was flecked with grey, and a closely-trimmed mustache. He wore chief's anchors on his collars. His nametag said "Evans".

"Morning, Chief," Jorge said, and Chief Evans's eyes moved from him to Matt, an eyebrow rising questioningly.

The other members of Electrical Division also looked him up and down, and Matt had to resist the urge to squirm under their obviously assessing gazes.

"Gents," Jorge said, gesturing toward Matt, "This is Ensign Gilbert. He and I will be turning over this week."

"Welcome aboard, Mr. G," said a third class petty officer to the Chief's left, with a cheeky grin.

The Chief rolled his eyes slightly, but didn't say anything. Instead he stepped forward and extended his hand toward Matt. "Good to meet you, sir." He grinned then, as his hand crushed Matt's. "Don't worry. We'll get you settled in nice and neat."

And then they got to work.

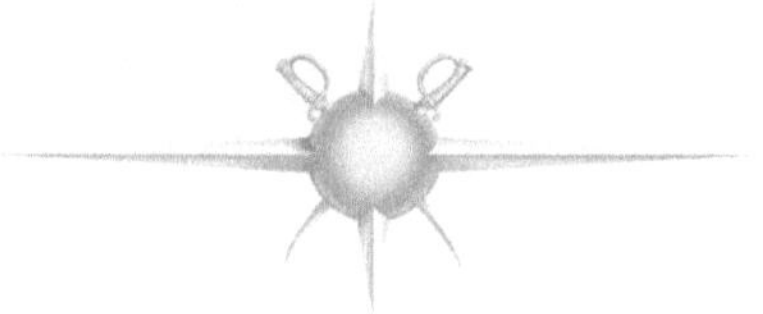

Chapter Twenty-Two

The door to Matt's condo slid shut behind him, and he stumbled across his small sitting area. His welcome home playlist started up, and he cringed. Too much energy right then.

"Music Off," he barked, and the tunes stopped; only a small comfort.

He barely made it to the threadbare beige couch that he had bought at the beginning of his senior year in university before he collapsed onto it. He didn't even notice how deceptively comfortable it was, so exhausted was he; he fell immediately to sleep.

When he awoke to an electronic beeping, some indistinct time later, his mouth was gravelly and he had a kink in his neck from having curled up awkwardly on the couch. He blinked and licked his lips, then took in the dim night-lighting of his rooms. He couldn't have been out that long...

The chronometer that he had hung over the counter of his little dinette shown blue in the dimness: 0430. Not yet dawn, but time for his wakeup alarm all the same.

Matt groaned. Too early; he needed more rack.

It had been a long day to finish off a long couple of weeks. When Matt and Jorge did their turnover sit-down with CHENG the week before, he had grilled Matt on the status of divisional work, personnel qualification progress, who had what collateral duty...every little detail. It had been brutal, and left Matt feeling like a known-nothing. But CHENG had assented, and he and Jorge had officially turned over Electrical Division Officer duties.

Of course, things only heated up from there. He had VBSS school, and the divisional duties as soon as he got done with that. And since E-Div was closing out the Battery Compartment this week, he was lucky to get off the ship by 2000. He had thought he would get a break yesterday, since VBSS school let out early on Friday, but when he got back to the ship Chief Evans was just starting up final closeout of the Battery Bus switchboard. Matt couldn't not supervise that; it was a major evolution. And even though his supervision consisted of him watching, while the Chief ran the show and showed him what he needed to look out for, his role was vital.

Or so he told himself, and so the CHENG told him when he came by to check on status.

Then there was the end of week paperwork, and Preventive Maintenance System signoffs. And he remembered he hadn't gotten in his weekly PMS spot check yet. And he needed to get a least a couple Basic Engineering Qualification checkouts done if he wanted to keep on schedule with his expected qualification date...

He finally got off the ship about 2200, and he had barely managed to stumble from the elevator to the flyer to the cab down to his building. It had to have been midnight when he got back.

Midnight on a Friday, and he never even thought about going out. At least this was Saturday, he could...

He groaned louder.

He could get right back to the ship. He had his first duty day today, and duty section turnover was at 0730. Later than normal, because it was a weekend.

Small comfort.

Right then, he questioned the logic in living down on the surface. What good was being by the beach if he never saw it? What good tourist girls if he never met them?

At least he'd have tomorrow off.

At least things would calm down once he finished VBSS school next Friday, and he would only have to worry about one job at a time.

Yeah. Right.

Muttering softly to himself, he pushed himself off the couch and stumbled past his dinette to the head. A quick shower and a shave, then he brushed his teeth, switched into fresh clothes, and headed out, back to the ship.

Right then, his Mom's idea of him becoming an accountant didn't seem so unappealing after all.

Harry looked up from where he was sitting and reading from his holopad at the wardroom table as Matt walked in. He was the offgoing Command Duty Officer. He wore his coveralls, and looked bright eyed and bushy tailed. When he looked Matt up and down, he pursed his lips and shook his head in disapproval.

"You look like crap."

"Feel like it, too," Matt said, and he walked—more like stumbled— over to the coffee mess.

He needed caffeine badly. The ride up the elevator and the walk to the ship had not been fun at all. He'd managed to get a few more winks in on the elevator, but it was far from comfy. And he had the sinking suspicion he was going to have to mainline coffee today if he was going to be even approaching useful.

One of the nice things about joining the wardroom was he got his own mug, emblazoned with the single golden bar of his rank and his last name, which hung from a hook on the wall above the coffee mess, along with all the other officers's. It was easy to tell who was new. The porcelain of Matt's mug was still pristine off-white on the inside. Not so with the others.

You'd think the CHENG's was originally mahogany-brown, the coffee stains were so entrained into his.

As he poured his mug, the fragrance of the brew perked him up, almost as though the caffeine could get into his bloodstream through his nasal cavity.

"How late were you here last night?"

Matt considered sugar and creamer, then decided against it. He needed it black and bitter today. As he raised the mug to his lips he looked back at Harry and shrugged. "Late."

The brew tasted burnt, and no wonder. Harry was a tea guy; he probably hadn't touched the coffee mess at all this morning, or last night for that matter.

To hell with it. Matt wasn't drinking it for the flavor.

Harry shook his head again. "Bad plan, dude. Especially the night before duty. Third rule of surviving space duty." He raised three fingers. "Marathon, not a sprint. Gotta know when to go home."

Matt shrugged and took another sip. "School, maintenance, quals, paperwork, quals, more maintenance..." He shook his head. "I've got a lot to do."

Harry snorted. "There's always a lot to do." He looked at Matt, disapproval still on his face, for a long several seconds, then shrugged, apparently deciding not to press the issue. "Whatever. Your funeral." He gestured toward the Wardroom's aft bulkhead. "John headed back to Maneuvering a few minutes ago. Better hurry back there." Unspoken went the next comment: Matt didn't want to be late for turnover, and cause the offgoing duty section to be delayed getting out of there.

Not to mention missing important information about the day's planned evolutions.

Nodding in response, Matt turned toward the door.

But he paused to top off his mug before he went. He was definitely going to need all the coffee he could get today.

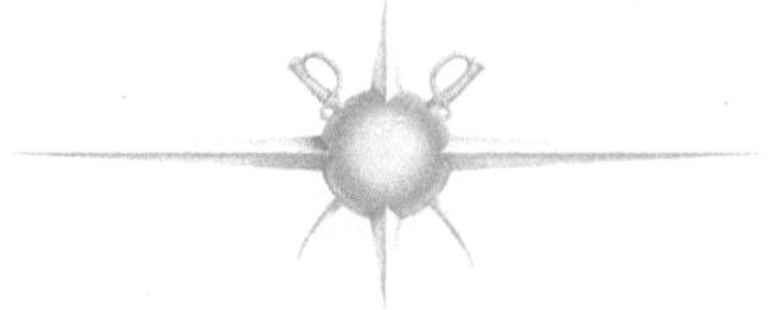

Chapter Twenty-Three

Maneuvering was not a particularly large space, for all that it was the central brain of the ship's propulsion plant. It consisted of two panels set up right next to each other on the forward bulkhead: the Reactor Plant Control Panel (RPCP) on the port side and Electric Plant Control Panel on the starboard side, with the Engineering Officer Of The Watch's (EOOW) desk behind them and centerline between the two. Pressure doors on either side allowed ingress and egress. Both were open with chains stretched across the openings for passage control, since the plant was shutdown. Behind the EOOW's station and on either side of the rear bulkhead were various alarm and breaker panels and a pair of shelves holding paper copies of manuals containing the plant's operating and casualty procedures, in case the network went down. A microphone on a stretchable cable dangling from an interior communications console above the EOOW's desk completed the watch station's kit.

The place was filled to overflowing with personnel. Two members of Reactor Controls (RC) Division were at the RPCP, and two from E Division were at the EPCP, talking quietly to each other as they turned over notes from the watch. Two more members of E Division were going through the panels behind the EOOW desk, also engaged in turnover, and a Second Class Petty Officer with Machinist's Mate insignia stood on the port side of the EOOW's desk, opposite the doorway Matt used, a small stack of papers in hand.

Vasili sat at the EOOW's desk, talking with a short, dumpy guy with scraggly blond hair and a round baby-face who looked like he was perpetually pouting about something, and who wore the two golden bars of a Lieutenant Junior Grade on his collars and a SWO device on his chest: John Connelly, the Gunnery Officer.

John glanced up from where he had been talking with Vasili as Matt said, "Request to enter Maneuvering," and frowned a bit deeper, if possible. "About time you got here," he said.

Vasili cast him a look that spoke volumes then focused on Matt. "State reason."

Matt shrunk back on himself inwardly, but tried not to show it. That was basic protocol, and he had blown it: one must always state why one wanted to enter Maneuvering, so the EOOW could decide if it was valid business or not.

"Request to enter for turnover."

Vasili nodded. "Enter."

Matt unhooked the chain from the doorway and slipped inside, re-hanging it behind him before stepping up to the desk. "Morning," he said.

Vasili grinned at him in greeting. "It's going to be a busy day for you guys," he said, gesturing toward a clipboard that lay on the desk in front of him.

John grunted and turned the board so Matt could read it more easily. At the top of the papers held in place on it were the Chief Engineer's Night Orders for the weekend. Friday took up most of the first page, so Matt flipped to the next one. He felt his eyebrows rise.

"16-RC-A-2R?" He looked up at John, who smirked slightly.

"High-Range Nuclear Instrumentation Alignment and Alignment Check," he said. "The Yard replaced the instruments when they replaced the RPCP. Have to make sure they work right, now that the panel's up and running."

Matt nodded as though he knew what John was talking about.

Of course, he did. Sort of. He had gone through Engineering School, of course, and had memorized detailed schematics and explanations for how the instrumentation worked, along with the basics of RC Division maintenance requirements. But he hadn't known the PMS designation for that procedure on this class of ship. Nor had he ever actually seen a full annual Alignment Check done before.

Oh well, fake it till you make it.

He looked back down at the schedule for the day. Machinery Division was performing an open, clean, and inspect on the plasma medium collecting tank. Auxiliary Division had CO_2 Scrubber PMS to perform. E Division had clean and inspects on a trio of power panels in the plant.

Gunnery Division was conducting a closeout inspection of the starboard primary cannon's anion accumulator.

He looked back up at John and grinned, pointing at that item. "I see why you got the duty today."

John shrugged. "Made sense. I'd be in here anyway." His scowl broke for a second. "It's actually pretty cool inside there. You should check it out. Good for a checkout on your OOD and SWO cards, too."

Matt blinked. He hadn't thought that far ahead; engineering quals came first. But John had a point. No sense not getting ahead on those later qualifications now, when he could.

Plus, the primary cannons were a hell of a lot more interesting than the bowels of atmosphere control equipment, however vital those might be for his everyday life on the ship.

"Sounds like a plan," Matt said.

Vasili had been looking over the MM2's paperwork while Matt and John conversed, and he picked right then to pipe up. "This tagout looks good. Want I should hang it for you, or do you want to review it yourself?" He posed the question to Matt, but it was obvious he really was talking with John.

Matt hesitated. It would certainly be easier to have Vasili do it, and he almost said as much. Though he remained silent, the way John was looking at him made Matt fairly certain he would rather not do it. But... quals. He had to review and approve tagouts for his EOOW qual card. And he would also need to be able to draw and explain the plasma flow system, to include the plasma medium collecting tank. Reviewing a tagout for that system would certainly help him get that knowledge into his head.

So he shook his head and said, "I think we should do it, if the maintenance is happening on our day."

The MM2's lips thinned a bit; he had just gotten through explaining the tagout to Vasili and no doubt didn't want to have to do it again. But John gave an approving nod.

"Makes sense to me," he said. He glanced over at the mechanic. "Sorry, MM2."

"No sweat, sir." He glanced at the chronometer mounted on the bulkhead above the port side entrance. "Right after turnover?"

It was 0715 and the turnover briefing was in fifteen minutes. MM2 was right. There probably wasn't enough time to get a good turnover from Vasili and review the tagout before then. Matt nodded agreement, and John followed suit.

The mechanic returned their nods and turned to leave Maneuvering, and Matt got back to reviewing the schedule for the day.

The turnover briefing for Engineering Department took place in Classroom #3, right next to the Engineering office. The section was composed of about twenty personnel from the various Engineering divisions: Electrical, Machinery, Auxiliary, and Reactor Control; plus the day's Engineering Duty Petty Officer, who was, in fact a Senior Chief today. The brief went smoothly, with Matt mostly standing there trying to look confident while John did most of the talking, and lasted about fifteen minutes. Five minutes later the trio of officers were back in Maneuvering, and Matt commenced with the ritual of watch relief.

He turned to Vasili and stated, "I have toured your spaces and reviewed your logs. I am ready to relieve you."

Vasili replied, "I am ready to be relieved. The reactor is shut down to cold layup. Electric Plant is in a shore power lineup with the battery bus secured. Evolutions for the day are as previously discussed."

Matt looked at the two panels at the forward section of the space again. The RPCP's vertical display showed power levels at background, and coolant flow through the primary heat exchangers at their lowest setting. The plasma loops showed pumps secured and containment fields shut down, with the Plasma Medium Collecting Tank empty. Bulkhead stops at the Reactor Compartment and the two Engine Rooms were shut. Just as he would expect, from Vasili's litany. The EPCP was similarly predictable, with all breakers closed including the forward and aft shore power breakers, and buses powered, except for the two battery bus breakers and the breaker to the battery itself, which showed open. Battery bus voltage read zero.

He nodded. "I concur," he said, and glanced at John, who also voiced his concurrence with the condition of the plant.

Matt turned back to Vasili and said, "I relieve you, sir."

"I stand relieved," replied Vasili, and he reached into his pocket and removed a set of keys on a lanyard, which he had looped through his belt loop. He took a moment to unwind the lanyard then handed it off to Matt before turning to his logbook and making an entry.

"Attention in Maneuvering," John said, and the two watch standers at the panels turned in their chairs to look back at him. "Lieutenant Connelly is the Engineering Duty Officer. Ensign Gilbert under instruction."

"Shutdown Reactor Operator, aye," said the man at the RPCP.

"Shutdown Electrical Operator, aye," said the other. Then he smirked and added, "God help us all," with a raised eyebrow in Matt's direction.

The Shutdown Reactor Operator—SRO—snorted out a little chuckle, and Matt got the sinking feeling it was going to be a very long day.

Matt finished tracing out the plasma system schematics, and found the last of the valves that the M Division PMS required to be danger-tagged shut. As with all of the others on the tagout, it was already shut. And tagged. The shipyard had thoroughly danger-tagged most of the ship's systems in order to facilitate the work they were doing during the availability. But even though it would be piggybacking on the shipyard's tags, M-Div's tagout had to be verified as accurate, and complete, before Matt and John could authorize them to proceed.

He fully understood the rationale behind that policy, and agreed with it. It didn't stop the process from being annoying.

Matt nodded and ticked off that final tag on the sheet the MM2 had brought back to Maneuvering after he and John had returned from their post-turnover call to the CO, and looked up at John. "Looks good to me."

John nodded concurrence, then tapped the EOOW's network access portal to life and selected the tagout database. Two commands later, and the M-divison tagout was officially hanging. The database recorded their work as being connected to the existing tags and would not allow their removal until that work, and all others associated with the tags, had been completed and signed off.

He turned to the MM2 and signed his name on the Work Authorization Form the petty officer had brought with the tagout. The WAF had two copies. John kept one for their records here in Maneuvering. He gave the other to the MM2 to post at the job site, and said, "Commence open, clean, and inspect as briefed."

"Commence open, clean, and inspect, aye sir," said the mechanic with a clipped nod. Then he spun and exited Maneuvering, moving quickly forward toward where his divisional comrades, no doubt, were waiting eagerly—or just as likely waiting with annoyance over the delay —to get to work.

Matt watched him go, and for a second thought about following, so he could have a look at the inside of the Plasma Medium Collecting Tank, but John brought him up short.

"So, Ensign," John said, "why do we need a collecting tank, anyway?"

Matt blinked and looked back at him, perplexed for a second, before it dawned on him what John was doing.

A checkout. Not a bad idea, that.

Matt grinned slightly. "The medium injection pumps need a certain amount of head to function properly without cavitating. The volume of the tank provides that."

John shrugged. "Yeah, but we could get that done other ways. Why not just a simple loop: medium to the core, fuse to plasma, to the mains and the generators, to the condenser, and back to the core? Seems like an added bit of complication."

That was too easy. "Surge volume. As the plant warms and cools, the plasma medium will expand and contract. Without that volume the system pressure would fluctuate wildly. Also, there needs to be a makeup volume for system losses—"

"Losses? This is a closed system. What do you mean losses? It's not like we have plasma leaks all over the place."

Matt had to fight to keep down a surge of annoyance. This was second-month Engineering School stuff. Surely he got the benefit of the doubt for knowing that much, at least. But John had a serious, probing expression on his face, making it clear he, at least, did not consider this a light matter at all.

Matt took a breath. "You get mass loss from firing the primary cannons and from running the Main Engines."

"How so?"

The primary cannons were obvious, so Matt went straight to the mains. "The gravitic field is generated by the interaction of the charged particles from the plasma streams with the gravmat plating inside the engines. During the interaction, some of the plasma mass is converted to energy in the form of a localized field distortion. The summing of the distortions caused by the interactions throughout the gravmat plating creates the gravitic bubble that propels the ship."

John nodded slowly, tapping at his lips with his left index finger. "If that's the case," he rapped his heel onto the deck, "why don't we have plasma lines going to all of the deck plates? They have gravmat plates to keep our local gravity vector correct."

Matt shrugged. "Electric current from the SSEGs is enough to power those."

"But what about mass loss? Wouldn't loss of electrons from the current flow cause trouble in the electric plant?"

Another hanging curveball. "It's a matter of scale. The deck plates only need to generate a field that covers a few cubic meters and affects a few tens of kilograms. The Main Engines have to generate a field large enough to encompass the entire ship, and affect several thousand tons of mass. The mass loss for the deck plates is small enough that it only amounts to slowing the electrons down a bit as they traverse the plate."

"How many tons?"

Matt blinked. "Sorry?"

"What's the mass of the ship?"

That he did not know offhand, and from John's expression it was obvious it showed.

"Look that up," John said, and he opened up the plasma system schematics again. Pointing to the Plasma Medium Collecting Tank, he asked, "What are the high and low level alarm trip points for the tank, and at what point do we have to refuel?"

Anther pause as Matt considered.

"Look that up. How long at max acceleration between refueling?" John only paused for a second, then said, "Never mind. Look that up too." He looked up from the schematic toward the panels at the front of Maneuvering. "Any questions for the Ensign, RT1? EM2?"

The SRO looked back over his shoulder at them and smirked briefly, then shrugged. "Think you've got it covered, sir."

His companion watch stander just winked at Matt and shook his head.

"Alright. Alignment at 1300 still, RT1?"

"Yes, sir."

"Right." John straightened and looked back at Matt again. "Let's go look at my cannon."

Then he turned and left Maneuvering, out the starboard side doorway.

Matt shook his head and chuckled softly, then moved to follow.

"Have fun, Mr. G," said the SEO.

Loads of fun.

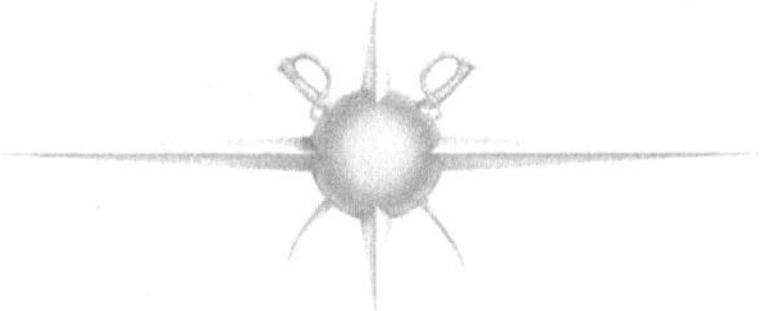

Chapter Twenty-Four

The chronometer on the wall in Matt's condo read 1030 when he—finally—walked in the next morning. Kicking the door shut behind himself, he crossed the short distance from the entryway to his couch and slumped down onto it. Leaning back until the back of his head touched the wall behind him, he let out a long, tired breath.

Dear Lord, he had so many lookups.

The entire duty day had essentially been one long checkout. During every tagout, every maintenance approval, every tour through the spaces, at lunch and dinner, before the evening movie—which he was forbidden to see because NUBs need to be studying and getting quals, not wasting time—and before bed, John had quizzed him on system parameters, procedural guidelines, damage control, safety precautions, alarm setpoints, and on and on and on and on...

His list of lookups took up three and a half pages on his holopad's secure memo app.

"That. Sucked," Matt said to himself, and let out another breath that was more of a groan than anything else.

A couple minutes later, after he had allowed the residual tension and stress to flow out of his muscles and into the cushions of the couch, he had to admit that, as much as it sucked, it had also been good.

Yeah, he had a lot of lookups. But John had also signed off half a dozen items on his qual card. And once he got the lookups done, he would sign at least that many more. That was one hell of a lot of progress for a single day's work.

When he got his qual cards and assigned qualification due dates, Matt had taken the time to count up the total number of signatures needed for each of his quals and figured out how many he had to get each day in order to get qualified on time. That duty day had set him three days ahead; or it would as soon as he finished the lookups.

And he also had to admit that he had learned a hell of a lot. A thorough checkout leaves you much better off than one that somebody blazed off.

So he wasn't bitter about it.

Still, he was drained. Right then, all he wanted to do was sit and not move for a week.

Or at least for nineteen hours. He did have to get back to the ship, and to VBSS school, in the morning.

When his holopad started to beep, he groaned again. He thought about not answering it. But then he fished it out of his pocket and saw that it was Isaiah calling. He shoved that thought aside, straightened, and tapped the connection open.

Isaiah's face appeared on the screen. He grinned, and Matt heard his voice through the implants in his ears.

"Hello, Matt. How was duty?"

Matt shrugged and put on a smile. "A little rough, but not too bad."

The other man's expression said he saw through that show of strength, but he didn't let it show in his upbeat tone. "Good." He leaned toward the screen a little. "We having a cookout here today. Lots of people coming. Marta too." His lips turned further upwards and he raised the eyebrow over his left eye. "She been asking about ya."

"Really."

"Thought that would get your attention." Isaiah's grin grew even more broad for a second. "Come by at one." Then he nodded as though the entire thing had been settled.

Matt found himself returning the nod, and realized he was grinning as well. "Ok, then. Want I should bring anything?"

"Beer is always welcome."

Matt snorted out a chuckle at that. Seemed like he was detecting a trend, when it came to his presence at social events. "I'll be there."

"Good. See ya then."

The connection closed and the holopad reverted back to its default home screen.

Well, that sounded promising. Suddenly Matt didn't feel quite so drained after all.

Isaiah wasn't kidding.

There were a lot of people at his and Maleen's house when Matt got there. A *lot*.

Matt took a transport from his condo to their place, and brought a case of Haverhold with him. But when he got there and saw over a dozen people on the deck at the side of their house, and several more through the windows on either side of the front door, he realized he hadn't brought enough.

But at least he'd fixed his wardrobe. In the last couple weeks since, he'd jettisoned his off-world civilian attire and purchased new clothes in the local style, so while he still didn't look the part to fit in, at least he didn't clash completely.

It also helped that his muscles and joints had mostly stopped aching from the higher gravity.

He thought to just go up the side walkway to the deck, but he didn't see Isaiah or Maleen there, so he went up to the front door and rang the bell.

It took a while for someone to answer, and when the door opened, he found himself looking at an older local woman with grey-streaked hair.

"Who you?" she said, and he recognized her as one of the people who had met Isaiah and Maleen at the spaceport when they docked.

Matt put on a smile. "I'm Matt. Isaiah asked me to come by." He lifted the case of beer, to show he came in friendship.

The woman looked him up and down, and sniffed. "I remember." Then she stepped aside and pulled the door more fully open.

Matt considered whether or not to say anything more to her, but decided against it. Instead, he just nodded and made his way into the great room.

There were eight or nine people around, most of them perched around the coffee table and chit-chatting. A couple more were sitting at the kitchen island. About a third of them turned to look at him as he entered, and their expressions ranged from curious to...displeased.

Well. This was awkward. He lifted the case of beer again, and grinned. "Isaiah around?"

One of the men, a guy about Matt's age who was sitting in a stuffed chair by the couch, scowled at him. "What you—"

But just then Isaiah came in from the hallway leading back to the dining room and the bedrooms beyond. He smiled broadly when he saw Matt.

"Matt, my friend," he put a bit of an emphasis on 'friend,' and Matt saw his eyes flick toward the guy in the stuffed chair for a second. "Good t' see ya."

"Happy to be here," Matt said.

They shook hands, and then Isaiah helped him unload his beer into the fridge.

Matt felt stuffed chair guy's eyes on him the entire time, and sure enough, as he looked over his shoulder, he saw that the guy was staring daggers at him.

"Who's that guy?" he said, as he handed Isaiah the last two beers from the case.

Isaiah frowned, glancing at the grumpy guy again. He put the beers into the fridge and shut the door. "Jonas," he said, softly. "Son of my oldest cousin. Didn't know he was coming." He gave Matt an apologetic look.

Matt nodded, slowly, and glanced back at Jonas again. "He doesn't like off-worlders?"

Isaiah shrugged. "He don't get along with anyone." Then he clapped Matt on the shoulder and grinned, gesturing with his chin toward the sliding glass door, and the deck beyond. "Come on. Colder beer out there." He waggled his eyebrows. "And Marta."

"You trying to set me up?"

Isaiah gave him a look that said he knew Matt wouldn't object, and headed toward the deck.

Matt followed him, taking care not to look Jonas's way. Maybe he'd just let things lie.

On the deck, he saw Maleen holding court over on the far end, with the other of the grey-haired women Matt has seen at the spaceport, and a young man who looked thirteen or fourteen, at most.

Then he was struck by the smell of cooking meat, and that caught all of his attention.

Isaiah had a large grill set up along the side of the house, back from the railing overlooking the bay. The grill's top was open, and there was a veritable cornucopia of meats soaking in the heat from the grill's burners. He saw chicken and steaks, and sausages, all covered in a red-orange cooking sauce of some kind.

A large man, with muscles that bulged so much, his arms looked about as thick as Matt's thighs, was basting the meat when they approached. He looked over at them, smiling, and Matt saw an immediate resemblance with Isaiah. They could almost have been twins, except that this guy was probably ten years older, with the grey in his hair to go with it.

"Tomas," Isaiah said, and gestured at Matt. "Meet Matt, th' Navy man I told you about." Then he said, "Matt, my brother, Tomas."

They shook, and Matt was surprised to find that Tomas didn't break every bone in his hand. But then, Tomas clearly knew his own strength. Still...

"Heard a lot about you," Tomas said. As he released his hand, Matt noticed he had a marriage tattoo.

"Nothing bad I hope," Matt said, and sent an accusing look Isaiah's way.

Isaiah chuckled and went over to a cooler that was off to the side. He came back with a can from a brewery that Matt hadn't seen before, which he popped before handing it to Matt.

Matt looked at the can. It was decorated with the image of a hunting cat pouncing on a creature that he didn't recognize. It had six legs and a long, trunk-like snout. The label said "Bewnat Amber."

He pointed at the creature, "What's that?"

Tomas said, "A Bewnat. Will eat th' tiles off yer house if ya let it," he said. "But is good eating."

"Interesting name for a brewery." Matt took a draw from the can, and found himself impressed. It was hoppy, but not too much, and semi-sweet. Smooth. "Good drinking, too."

Tomas laughed.

The meat was hypnotic, and the sauce Tomas was basting it with smelled...Matt couldn't really place it. It smelled spicy but also a bit tart, different from grilling sauces he'd encountered before. He presumed it was a local blend, made from indigenous herbs.

He was just about to ask about it, when Maleen came over, along with the older woman and the young man.

Turned out that was Tomas's wife and son, and Matt lost himself in introductions and the like for a moment. But the smell of the sauce brought him back...until saw, over by the railing overlooking the bay, Marta, and her friend Constance.

Marta was looking back toward him, and their eyes met, and Matt felt that rush again. The slight upturning of her lips said he had an opening, so he made an excuse that sounded lame even to his own ears, and made his way over toward her.

Constance saw him coming and leaned in to say something quietly to Marta. She made a little nod, and Constance stepped forward.

"Nice t' see ya again, Matt," Constance said. Then she slipped past, heading inside.

Matt watched her go for a moment, bemused. Then he looked back at Marta and shrugged. "Guess I'm not fooling anyone here, am I?"

She laughed.

"How've you been?"

Marta had a bottle of Haverhold in her hand; the same as in the batch Matt had brought with him. She took a sip and shrugged. "Been a good couple weeks," she said. "You settle in well?"

Matt nodded. "Got myself a place right down there." He stepped up next to her and pointed at his condo tower, off to the left from where Isaiah and Maleen's house stood, at the southern-most part of the bay.

"You sleep at the hotel?" Her eyes twinkled teasingly in the afternoon sunlight. "Is expensive."

"Ha ha." Matt grinned at her. "No, the place right next door. How about you?"

Marta's eyebrow quirked upward. "You think I want you knowing where I live?"

"Yup."

Her other eyebrow joined the first, and for a moment Matt thought he might have pushed the banter a little too far. Then she laughed again, more fully this time, and touched his arm with her free hand.

It was like a little zap of electricity.

"You funny."

"Funny looking. But you know, I could use a guide, to help learn the lay of the land. Feel like—"

A movement from the corner of his eye brought his attention to the sliding door, and the man walking through it. Matt hoped it wasn't—

But it was. Jonas came out, and he made a beeline toward the cooler.

Just getting a beer. That was good.

Marta noticed him as well, and her good cheer faded a bit. Matt could see disapproval on her face.

"You don't like him either, huh?"

She looked quizzically at him for a moment, then, almost reluctantly, nodded. "He bring trouble with him."

"Yeah, I know the type." He paused, watching as Jonas dug around in the cooler. "Wanna get out of here? Away from..." He gestured with his beer can toward the grumpy man.

She shook her head. "No, is alright. He not make a stir here, in front of family."

Matt wasn't so sure, but he figured she probably knew better; it was her culture, after all. So he turned back to facing her fully. "In that case, as I was saying, I—"

"Hey!"

He had only heard Jonas speak that one time, but his voice was easy to recognize. Matt looked back, and he saw the man stalked toward him and Marta, an unopened can of Bewnat in his left hand.

"Not good enough ya come here, steal our land and our space, but ya think you can steal our women too?" Jonas's words were slightly slurred, like he had already had a few...and maybe he didn't need that new beer at all.

"I not your woman, Jonas," Marta said.

"More mine than his," he spat. "Or do ya want t' mother voidspawn?"

The others on the deck had stopped their discussions, and Matt sensed several sets of eye turning toward the three of them. But when Jonas said that last, he heard someone gasp.

Marta stiffened, and her jaw set with anger.

Matt set his can on the railing and stepped between her and Jonas. "She can talk with who she wants. I think you better go." He pointed toward the sliding door.

Jonas snorted and straightened. He was at least three centimeters taller than Matt. "Watch yer mouth, off-worlder. I'll—"

But he didn't get to finish his thought. A mammoth arm wrapped itself around him from behind, and Tomas bore him down into a head-lock that had to hurt like a sonofabitch.

Jonas let out a squeak, and flailed his arms, but he was no match for Tomas's strength. Tomas strode through the sliding door, dragging Jonas along behind him. A moment later, Matt heard the front door slam, and Tomas came back into view. Alone.

Isaiah, still on the deck, had a face like a thundercloud. He looked over at the first woman Matt had talked with, the one who greeted him at the door, who had made her way out onto the deck at some point.

He pointed his finger at her, and it was like he was shooting a bullet from it, from the force he placed in the gesture. "I've had enough of your son, Theresa. He not welcome in my house again."

Theresa's nostrils flared. "You would side with...this," she waved her hand toward Matt, using a finger gesture he did not recognize, "over yer own kin?"

"If need be."

Theresa shot Matt a baleful look, then spat on the deck and turned around, stalking through the sliding door after her son.

Silence loomed. Matt felt he could cut it with a butter knife, it was so thick.

"Well," he cleared his throat, and looked around. "I don't want to cause trouble with your family. Maybe I should go?"

Maleen shook her head emphatically. "No, Matt. He just ignorant. You welcome here, as a friend."

Matt had no doubt about that. But friends were one thing. Family was another. He opened his mouth to say just that, but Isaiah must have seen it on Matt's face, because he mirrored Maleen's head shake with one of his own.

"That boy been pushing his welcome for years. Stay."

Matt looked around at the other faces on the deck, and saw agreement on most of them. And more than agreement on Marta's.

He nodded. "Ok." Then he grinned. "Glad you said that, because I'd hate to miss out on that." He gestured toward the grill.

Several chuckles issued, and the tension relaxed. A bit.

Serving the meat a few minutes later removed the last of it, and soon everyone was wearing smiles, and chit-chatting in between bites.

Matt found he couldn't talk much, though. That sauce was just too damn good, and before he knew it he'd eaten two whole chicken breasts...or at least they tasted like chicken, but who knew?

Marta watched him with amusement the whole time.

Finally, a hunk of steak and a couple beers later, he was stuffed to the gills, and all of a sudden he felt completely wiped out. The efforts of the previous day's duty, and the near miss with Jonas, came crashing down on him. If he hadn't been standing by the deck's rail, he just might lean back on whatever he had been sitting on and drifted off.

Marta raised an eyebrow at him. "Ya ok?"

Matt nodded, setting his half-finished beer down on the railing. "Yeah. I had a late night on duty yesterday, and it just hit me, hard."

She laughed softly. "Post-meal coma, ya mean."

Matt shrugged. "That too." He pushed himself off the rail and looked across the bay. The sun was most of the way down toward the hills on the other side; he had been there longer than he thought.

"I think I'd better get going. I've got an early morning tomorrow," he grinned at her. "And I don't think Isaiah and Maleen want me crashing out on their couch."

"If ya think it best." Her tone was neutral, but Matt was certain he saw a flash of disappointment in her eyes.

And for a moment, he considered listening to the brash voice in his head that was screaming that he was being a pansy, and it was way too early to take off, not with this hottie obviously wanting him to stay.

But the rational voice, which began running through the litany of things he had to do tomorrow, and how early he had to start, won out.

"Yeah, I'm going to roll. But you know," he grinned at her, "I could still use that guide about town. Want to volunteer?"

Marta's face was unreadable, and for a moment Matt thought maybe he'd read her wrong. Then she turned and walked through the sliding door, without a word.

Matt blinked, surprised by the suddenness of the rejection.

Beside him, an older man whose name Matt couldn't remember—there had been a lot of names—shrugged and gave him a look of commiseration.

Matt shrugged in reply, then set off to find Isaiah and Maleen, to say goodbye.

They were talking to Tomas and his wife by the kitchen island. When he told them he was going, all four of them looked disappointed, but Isaiah nodded understanding.

"We do this again when you not have a duty day," he said.

"Sounds like a plan to me."

He shook hands with Isaiah and Tomas, then did the half-hug thing with the women. He was turning to go when Marta came into the room from the hallway to the rest of the house. She looked around quickly, and when she saw him with the others, something flashed over her face.

Relief?

She hurried over, and it looked like she was flushed. "Sorry," she said, and held out her hand toward Matt. "Realized I left my purse." In her grasp was a small chip, the kind that holds identification data for interface with holopads.

"Call me," she said, with what could only be called an almost bashful half-smile. "I show you around."

He accepted the chip, and decided it wouldn't be worth it to press her over her apparent rudeness on the deck. For all he knew, that wasn't the sort of thing that the locals would be bothered by. And anyway, all's well that ends well.

"I'll do that," he said.

Her smile became more full. "Good."

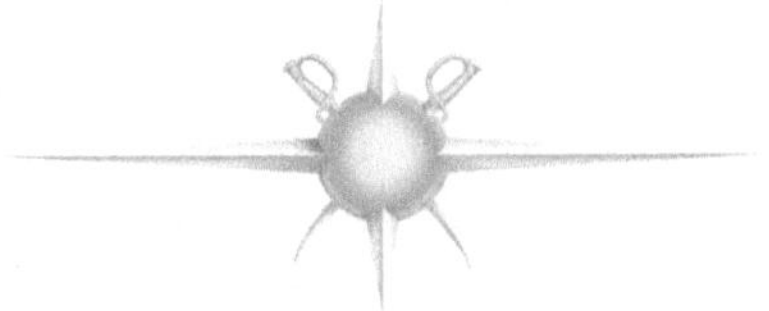

Chapter Twenty-Five

The last day of VBSS school, and time for the capstone training event.

Matt had been looking forward to this with a mixture of excitement and dread for the last week and a half, and now it was here.

His class consisted of three officers and twenty-four enlisted of varying rates, though none above Petty Officer Third Class. The officers, all Ensigns like him, had been put in charge of a group of eight men each, and they had gone to the range together, sat in lectures together, done practical evolutions together, and planned for the capstone together.

As Matt stepped up to the lectern at the front of his section's classroom, he thought sure they had covered all the angles for their assigned task in the capstone. All the same, this was the first time he had been involved in an exercise of this sort, to say nothing of having to lead it. The fact that he would have an officer instructor at his side the whole time, as his over instruction, didn't make the butterflies go away.

Not one bit.

The classroom was small, no larger than an average conference room, and laid out similarly, with a briefing table in the center facing the lectern and wall display where presentations were given. The table was made of faux-wood a few shades darker than the wardroom passageway paneling on the HALSWELL, and had vidcom microphones and cameras built into each sitting position, so the room could be used for long distance briefings as well as in-person. A dozen padded swivel chairs sat around the table, and half again as many stationary chairs lined the walls on either side of the table.

Today, his section sat along the wall to his left. The table was filled with a collection of officers and chiefs: his instructors at the school and their assistants, along with the Department Head in charge of this section of the local Naval Tactical Training Command branch. He was a Lieutenant Commander named Tolburt, with greying black hair, dark eyes, and frown lines around his mouth. From his skin tone and musculature, he looked like had been on New California for quite some time.

Matt glanced from Tolburt toward his section. He'd gotten to know them a bit over the last two weeks and they were a good bunch, from what he could tell. Eager and smart, and at least passingly dedicated.

Two of them were from the HALSWELL: Peters and Holbrook. And it relieved Matt to no end to find that they were among the best of his group. Good thing since he was going to have to deal with them for the next two years.

Peters gave a nod in response to Matt's glance. He was the oldest of the bunch by a couple years, a black-haired Boatswain's Mate who had worked as a crewman aboard a merchant vessel before enlisting in the Navy, and he had gone out of his way to be helpful, not just to Matt but to the other members of the section. So the instructors had put him in the Leading Petty Officer role for the capstone.

Good call, as far as Matt could tell.

"Ensign." LCDR Tolburt's tone was clipped, businesslike.

"Yes sir," Matt said, and got down to business. He tapped a control on the lectern and the presentation on the screen behind him advanced a slide. A smaller screen inlaid into the lectern allowed Matt to see the new slide without having to look back.

As expected, it showed the layout of the system in the immediate vicinity of New California. A number of vectors showed the current trajectories of vessels moving to and from the system's jump points, as well as a pair of ships on course for the system's lone other planetary body. Of those various tracks, a single vector was highlighted in yellow, its orbital path set to take it around New California in a high polar orbit before sling-shotting back toward the outer system.

"This is the Space Vessel Cygnus," Matt said, indicating the yellow vector. "We have been assigned to board and inspect her cargo for contraband, and the ship's master has consented to inspection. I intend to take the Pegasus, intercept her at perigee," he highlighted the point of Cygnus' projected orbital track that would bring her closest to the planet, "and match trajectory. Once we come along side, we will dock with her starboard side airlock and board. Myself and Petty Officer Monaghan," a thin guy, maybe twenty years old at most with reddish brown hair who was sitting at the end of Matt's section's seats, perked up as Matt named him, "will proceed to the bridge and liaise with the Master. Petty Officers Peters and Lim will take their teams, and inspect the crew spaces and cargo areas. Once they have completed their inspection, we will depart."

LCDR Tolburt nodded. "What are you searching for?"

"Intel suspects merchants like the Cygnus have been running illicit stims into the system. We will use drug sniffers to ensure there are none present aboard."

The senior officer frowned, as though displeased by something Matt had said, but he didn't say what. "Your armament?"

Matt clicked to the next slide, which showed his team's chosen equipment load-out. "We'll each have an M87 with 120 rounds and a Steg with three mags. Tactical communications through implants, with earbud backup. And we'll be in EVA suits with the plating inserted." Which meant that instead of the normal maintenance suit load, which was proof against vacuum only, theirs would have ballistic plates slipped into vital areas, to provide extra protection. "But this is a consensual boarding and we don't expect resistance or trouble."

"If that should change?"

Matt swallowed. "If the master withdraws consent or tries to evade before we dock, we back off. If his crew resists after we've boarded, we defend ourselves and retreat back to the Pegasus. Then we launch and call for a Level Two or Three team."

"But there are no Marines or Specwar units in this system."

Matt had to stop himself from shrugging at the LCDR's statement. "We're not certified for an opposed boarding, sir."

"Very well." LCDR Tolburt turned his gaze away from Matt and toward the lead instructor for VBSS School. "Mr. Caldwell?"

"Yes sir." LT Caldwell was no more than five or six years older than Matt, but to Matt's eyes he looked younger. He had one of those round, boyish faces that seemed stuck in time in his mid-teens beneath an unruly—by Navy standards—mop of black hair. Looks were deceiving though, because, of course, he wore the SWO pin over his left breast, and if he'd shown anything over the last two weeks, it was that he was highly competent, and didn't take crap from anyone.

LT Caldwell leaned forward, returning the LCDR's look with a steady, sure gaze. "My people are briefed and ready. Role players boarded the REPTARV this morning. Comms checks sat, and their consumables are well in the safety zone." He nodded in Matt's direction. "I will accompany ENS Gilbert. Chief Tennanbaum will monitor Petty Officer Peters, and Petty Officer Garza will monitor Petty Officer Lim. Safety monitors will be stationed in each space with role players assigned, and with each section of the students's party."

The LCDR pursed his lips and mulled this over for a few seconds, then nodded. He looked back at Matt and drew himself further erect in his chair. "Ensign, execute the operation as briefed."

Matt brought his feet together and assumed the position of attention. "Execute as briefed, Aye sir."

He held gaze with the older man for a short moment, then the LCDR said, "Dismissed."

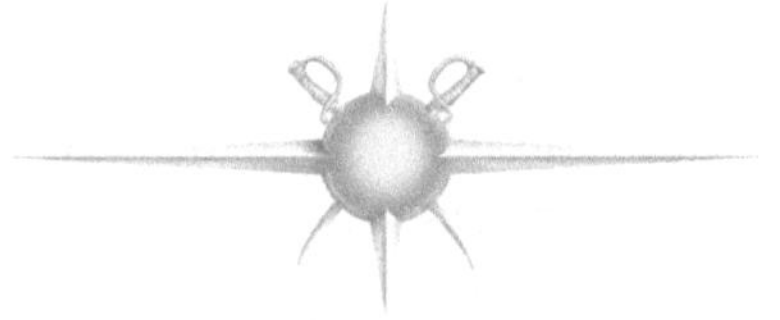

Chapter Twenty-Six

Matt did another check of his weapons.

The M87 rifle had a short barrel, only thirty-six centimeters long, a collapsible shoulder stock, and a drum magazine that held his entire VBSS loadout of 120 rounds. He had counted them out himself when he and his team geared up, and the counter on the left hand side of the rifle read accurately. So that was good.

The rounds were 4mm in diameter and magnetically fired, to minimize the recoil and for seamless functionality in vacuum. In a real scenario they would be designed to shatter against a ship's hull, so as to avoid the obvious problems of over penetration in that venue. But for today, he was using simrounds, which would leave a welt and a splat of ink on a target, and were distinctly non-lethal.

His Steg sidearm fired 8mm rounds, designed similarly to the rifle rounds, though the magazines carried only twelve of them.

Everything seemed in order with both weapons, so he nodded to himself, slipped the Steg back into its holster, and dropped the rifle so it hung in easy reach from its tactical sling. Then he turned to look over the rest of his team.

They were loaded onto the Pegasus, which was essentially a small shuttle that the local training command had for use in all manner of training scenarios. This week, VBSS. The craft was long and narrow, with bench seating along each bulkhead that left just enough room for the men who were sitting there to stand up and turn around without bumping into each other. Airlocks on both the Port and Starboard sides, up forward where Matt was standing just aft of the cockpit, allowed egress.

His men were busy getting ready. One and all were dressed in EVA suits, as Matt was, and they all looked jumpy. They were doing last-minute checks of their gear, and double-checking each others' suit seals. He caught sight of Petty Officer Peters near the stern of the craft. Their eyes met and Peters grinned, then gave a thumbs up.

"All set, Matt?" LT Caldwell's voice came over the private circuit he and Matt had set up between their EVA suits, so he could give instruction or correction without calling Matt out in front of everyone.

Hard not to appreciate that sentiment.

Matt turned to port, where Caldwell stood easily in his own EVA suit. Unlike Matt, he carried no arms. Nor did any of the other safety observers and instructors present. Also unlike Matt, he looked totally at ease with this scenario.

Small wonder; he'd done it dozens of times.

Matt made an OK sign and said, "Yes sir," trying to sound as upbeat as he could.

In truth, his stomach was leaping in his belly.

He got that way every time he faced a new test or obstacle in the Navy, and it was damn annoying. He hoped one day he'd get used to all this constant testing and being pushed, so he could just show up and do it without the jitters.

Caldwell shook his head. "I told you, we're all JOs here. Call me Eric when we're talking in private."

"Ok...Eric." It didn't feel right, calling an instructor by his first name. But Matt did it anyway.

Eric shook his head, his expression amused. But he didn't comment on it any further. Instead, he asked, "Get the jitters yet?"

Matt looks askance at him. "Huh?"

"The jitters." Eric chuckled softly. "I probably did forty boardings when I was Boarding Officer. Thought I was going to throw up before each one."

"It never went away?"

Eric shrugged. "Nope. You just get used to it. So...jitters yet?"

Matt managed a sheepish grin. "Yeah."

Eric reached out and cuffed him on the shoulder lightly. "Walk in the park, man. Just remember what we went over in class, follow the procedure. You'll be fine."

Matt was about to reply when the pilot's voice came over the command net. "Coming up on the Cygnus, Mr. Gilbert."

Eric's semi-joking demeanor switched off immediately, and he drew himself erect, gesturing toward the cockpit door. But Matt was already moving.

The door slid open and he stepped forward into a panorama of space.

The cockpit was arranged almost like the observation blister on the side of the liner he took from Olifant: a plasteel dome affixed to the Pegasus' bow, with only the platform that held the pilot and crew chief's stations interrupting the view of the surrounding void. A HUD was projected onto the dome, with ship's systems status in what would be the lower section of the crew members' visual range when seated, and velocity and heading higher up.

New California dominated the view below the piloting platform, the brilliant blue, speckled with white, of the northern hemisphere's great ocean the largest feature, with only a small swath of green visible along the nearer edge of the visible portion of the globe.

It took Matt's breath away to see the planet this way, even more than it had on the liner. That view had been impressive, but this piloting bubble gave much more of a feel of being right there, in it.

Eric nudged him, and Matt realized he was gaping. He looked sidelong at the instructor, who gestured to the HUD above the planet a bit.

Matt focused where Eric was pointing and saw, to the left of Pegasus' heading and depressed about fifteen degrees from their plane of travel, a projected yellow square with the label Cygnus, and below that a series of numbers that represented the target ship's range, velocity, and acceleration vectors. The ship itself wasn't visible yet, but there she was.

The pilot spoke up again. "About 200 kilometers out. ETA 2 minutes."

Matt nodded, though the man, seated with his back to where Matt stood, could not see it. "They're still consenting to the inspection?"

"That's affirm."

That was good, and what Matt fully expected. It wouldn't be much of a capstone evolution if the boarding team had to turn away before ever reaching the target ship. There might be unexpected resistance on the Cygnus, but nothing would happen before docking to prevent them going aboard.

Or at least, nothing would if Matt were designing the scenario.

The HUD image over the Cygnus shifted as the pilot adjusted the Pegasus's vector slightly, and the range began counting down at an increasing rate.

Eric gave Matt another nudge as the range approached 100 kilometers.

Time to check in with Command.

Matt shifted to the external command network and keyed his transmission. "Command, this is Pegasus. Target vessel in sight. Boarding team is ready. Intend to close and dock with the Cygnus, over."

A couple seconds passed, then a hiss-click in his ear preceded Command's response. Matt recognized the LCDR's voice. "Pegasus, this is Command. Roger, Out."

Well, that was quick and to the point. He switched back to the internal command net. "Proceed with docking."

The pilot didn't look back at him, just nodded and replied over the net, "Roger."

As the seconds passed, the Cygnus came into view, first a small spec at the outer range of perception and then rapidly growing until Matt was able to make out details.

It was blocky, basically a rectangle in space with a few protrusions for communication and sensor arrays. It didn't look like much. But then, it didn't have to.

Matt had received briefings on the REPTARVs at Tactical School, and again here during VBSS training. Remotely-Pilotable Target Vehicles were used for many aspects of Naval Training, from VBSS scenarios like this, to tracking exercises, to live-fire certifications. Little more than a gravitic drive attached to a cargo box, their interiors could be reconfigured to support a variety of boarding or breaching scenarios, and their transponders and emissions signatures could be configured to simulate almost any kind of vessel, from a merchant to one of the Tsago Dominance's warships. There was a basic navigation system inside, and capability to pilot the ship remotely for live fire events, but no internal life support. The role players had to bring all their support gear with them when they came aboard.

Which was why Eric had briefed the LCDR about consumables. They had a limited timetable to complete the event before his team would have to evac the REPTARV, and return to the nearby support ships.

That probably would not be necessary on this one. Everything was proceeding smoothly, as far as Matt could tell.

The pilot adjusted the Pegasus's approach, and the closure rate between the two vessels slowed noticeably, and kept on slowing until the Pegasus came to a relative halt along the Cygnus's starboard side, about 100 meters away.

"Cygnus, this is Pegasus. Standby for docking," the Pilot transmitted over the bridge-to-bridge circuit.

A few seconds passed, then a voice came back. "Pegasus, this is Cygnus. Ready to receive you."

"Roger."

A slight twitch on the control yoke, and the Pegasus eased to the left, toward the blocky target vessel. There was an audible thunk and a slight shudder, then motion stopped and a green indication lit up on the pilot's display.

"Hard dock, Mr. Gilbert."

"Very well," Matt replied, then he turned and left the cockpit, Eric on his heels.

His team was assembled and standing in two columns. Petty Officers Peters and Lim stood at the head of each column, and Monahgan, who would accompany Matt, was off to the right, in front of the port-side airlock hatch.

"Report," Matt said, over the internal command net.

Petty Officer Peters replied, "All personnel ready, sir."

"Very well." He turned to Monaghan at the airlock hatch. "Open the airlock."

The Pegasus's airlock only had room for four at a time. Even though they were in hard dock with the Cygnus, procedure called for not leaving both hatches open until the ship had been secured. That way, if Cygnus tried something unexpected like a severe maneuver, the Pegasus could safely break off without risking damage, or injury to the personnel remaining behind. It also added a measure of security against incursions from the Cygnus's crew.

So Matt, Monaghan, and Eric were the first through, and would be without backup for the fifteen seconds or so it would take for Peters to cycle his people through the lock.

As the Pegasus's inner hatch rolled shut behind him and the outer hatch cycled open, the jitters in his gut grew larger, and he began to question the wisdom of those safety procedures.

They stepped into the Cygnus's airlock, which was slightly smaller than Pegasus's, and Matt looked sidelong at Monaghan. "Be ready, but remember we don't expect trouble here."

The sailor nodded within his helmet and took up his rifle in a low ready position. Matt did the same, but used his left hand to actuate the inner hatch mechanism.

The outer hatch cycled shut behind them and a second later, the inner hatch rolled open.

There were four people waiting to greet them. Matt recognized them all as various instructors from the VBSS school, but the jumpsuits they wore were shabby and grease-stained. And even though they all had their military haircuts, and there was no way to not keep the bearing that they had learned over so many years of service, they did a reasonable job of looking like a hard-working crew who was riding the hairy edge of profitability.

Matt stepped across the airlock seal and a man in his thirties with prematurely greying brown hair—Matt knew he was a Senior Chief—greeted him.

"Welcome to the Cygnus. I'm Matias Harborg, ship's master."

"Ensign Matthew Gilbert, Icaran Confederation Navy," Matt replied, using the formal introduction that he had drilled under Eric's tutelage over the last several days. "By Authority of Parliamentary Edict 67-432, we are here to conduct a contraband inspection of your ship, Captain."

"Harborg" shook his head, an ingratiating smile on his lips. "No contraband here, sir. Honest traders, the lot of us."

"Well then, I expect this will be quick and easy."

The hatch cycled open behind them, and Peters led his team onto the ship.

"This is Petty Officer Peters," Matt said, indicating him. "Will you have someone escort him and his men to the engineering spaces?"

"Harborg" nodded and a short, stocky man to his right stepped forward. He did not identify himself, but gestured for the team to follow him, and they proceeded aft.

When Lim's team entered, they followed a similar process and his men went athwartships to begin their inspection forward.

Matt turned to "Harborg". "Captain, will you show me to the bridge?"

"Harborg" nodded.

It wasn't a long walk, nor was there very much to the bridge itself. No spectacular piloting bubble here: just a couple holoscreens and a no-frills piloting and navigation console that was manned by an older fellow, who Matt recognized as a Master Chief.

He must really like to fly.

The rest of the bridge consisted of a beat-up chair that may have been upholstered in black Naugahyde at one point, but was so cracked and peeling that it was more worn grey fabric now, a couple of electrical panels on the walls, two filing cabinets, and a safe on the aft bulkhead.

"Captain Harborg" sat down in the open chair and leaned back, luxuriating in its apparent comfort. He spread his hands wide. "As you can see, sir, we're a simple crew. Not much to look at, but have at it."

Matt nodded, and gestured for Monaghan to get to it.

The Petty Officer commenced looking through the file cabinets while Matt regarded the Captain closely, trying to read him. "Can you open the safe, please, sir?"

"Harborg" grinned. "Sure, sure."

He stood and walked over to the safe then, keeping his body between it and Matt, he entered a code onto the safe's keypad. It clicked open, and "Harborg" stepped aside. Still smiling, he swept his hand out to the now open safe as though to say, "All yours."

Matt stepped forward and looked inside the safe.

"Right," Eric said, from the front of the classroom that Matt and his fellow trainees had used for the last two weeks. "What did you guys mess up?"

The answer to that was Legion, Matt had no doubt.

At first, Matt thought they'd done well. Petty Officer Lim had found a carton of narcotics tucked away in a cleverly-concealed wall panel behind an entertainment system in the crew's lounge. Or at least, the simulation of a crew's lounge.

When that happened, Matt and the rest of the boarding team had shifted into apprehension mode, and they had the Cygnus's crew handcuffed and mustered for detention in what Matt thought was a pretty short period of time.

Once that happened, Eric had called the evolution to a halt and Matt felt pretty good about himself.

But then, after they released the role players, the instructors showed Matt and his men the stash of weapons they'd tucked away in the engineering spaces. And "Harborg" pulled a folded up document from out of his pocket that had the banner of the Tsago Dominance at its top.

And then there was the tripwire inside the galley that no one saw, and no one tripped on.

Because no one actually went in the galley.

So, yeah...not so good.

Matt looked around the room at his men, seated at their desks and looking dejected. No one looked like they were going to offer up any ideas, so he took the lead.

"I guess we just didn't look close enough, sir. Attention to detail."

Eric nodded. "That sums it up, Mr. Gilbert. But we have to be more specific. Let's start on the bridge." He looked at Matt intently. "You allowed the ship's master to conceal what he was doing when he opened up that safe. If you'd watched more carefully, you would have seen him take that document out."

Matt flushed, but there was no denying that was true. He nodded glumly.

Eric saw his reaction, then glanced around the room at the rest of the students. Seeing their equally downbeat demeanors, he sighed and changed tack. "Remember what we told you on your first day here. Our objection wasn't to make you experts in finding every nook and cranny on a ship. It was to give your the skills and knowledge to carry out a boarding operation in accordance with law, regulation, and procedure and, most importantly, safely."

He looked each student in the eye as he continued. "You guys did that. The rest is us giving you something to think about as you go back to your ships and join the VBSS team." Eric grinned broadly. "Believe me, you'll get plenty of opportunities to practice, and me and my team will be there to help."

A soft chuckle went around the room, and Matt could see that little speech made everyone feel better. At least a little.

Eric paused for a second, then nodded. "Now, let's go on to the next point."

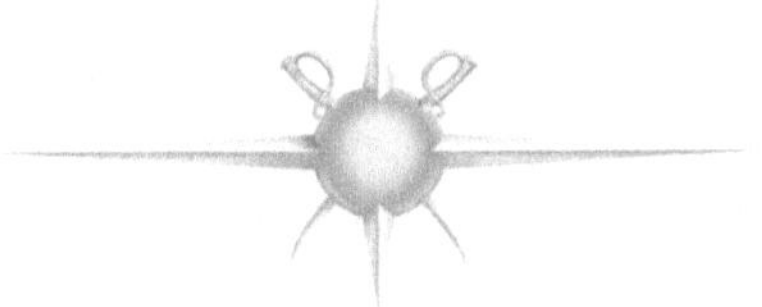

Chapter Twenty-Seven

The bar was named The Queen Bee, and it was located in Leucadia, about twenty-five kilometers east of Ventura, also on the northern coast of New California's main continent.

Matt hadn't been in it before. Had never heard of it before. But the Bull had called for a JO retention meeting, and this was the designated meeting spot.

As Matt walked up to the bar's entrance, he found himself questioning the Ivan's judgment, though.

Leucadia was a small town, probably only a couple thousand people, and picturesque, with single-story, bungalow-style houses lining the top of a high bluff that ran down to cliffs that fell into the sea. But there wasn't a lot to the town, and it didn't seem nearly as well-kept as Ventura.

The bar itself stood farther out on the bluff than any other building in the town, at the very edge of a steep descent to the cliffs. Where it sat was completely exposed to the wind that seemed to want to whip across the bluff like an angry jockey on a tiring racehorse, and the bar's siding showed that fact. It looked like it hadn't had a good power washing in decades. The sign proclaiming the bar's name was faded so as to be very difficult to read. And the illuminated OPEN sign in the window closest to its front door was missed its E.

Not exactly top shelf.

For a moment before he went in, Matt wondered if this wasn't another joke at the new guy's expense. Maybe this was one of those places where you really shouldn't go unless you're a local, and he was about to get an ass whooping.

He quickly wrote that off as overly paranoid. For one thing, he was pretty sure the XO and CO would come down—hard—on the kinds of pranks that got people actually injured.

And he didn't want to think his fellow Ensign, even if Ivan was of higher status qualification-wise, would do him like that.

So Matt steeled himself, pushed the door open, and walked in.

The interior was dim, even with the windows at the front streaming sunlight inside. Matt stood just inside the door for a moment to let his eyes adjust, and to get the lay of the land.

It was surprisingly nice. When it was originally built, the building probably had been subdivided into a number of smaller rooms, but now it was one long open space that led back to the bar at the rear. Against the right wall, about halfway back to the bar, was a small, narrow stage that stood two short steps up from the rest of the room, and could probably fit a four-piece band if they were friendly with each other. Surrounding the stage were half a dozen round tables with seating for six, and the wall opposite it was lined with booths that could probably accommodate four each.

The bar dominated the rear wall, and looked to be made of hardwood, but even from here Matt could tell if it had been stained in the past, it was now scratched and faded. Two levels of wooden shelves behind the bar held bottles of all types, and a sextet of taps were set up in the bar's center. The stools in front of it were backless, and looked to be upholstered in dark, cracked Naugahyde.

But what truly drew Matt's eye were the pool tables, filling the gap between the last of the tables and booths, and the bar itself. There were three of them, and looked to be well-maintained. And they were manned by half a dozen familiar faces.

Surprisingly, there were only two other customers besides his shipmates, a pair of local guys who were nursing beers at a table near the door.

As Matt meandered over to the pool tables, music, a bass-heavy composition that was a mix between blues and techno, but somehow worked quite well, washed over him from speakers tucked away in the corners of the room. The music almost seemed matched to a musky fragrance that was overlaid atop the scene, like there was incense being burned somewhere.

Ivan was just rising from sinking the 5 ball at the furthest right of the tables, while Dan Flemming looked on in chagrin, when Matt approached. He nodded Matt's way. "Glad you could make it."

Charlie and Jorge were at the next table, but talking instead of actually playing, and Sam Covington and Harry were in the middle of getting ready to break on the last table.

Matt returned Ivan's nod, and gestured at the room in total. "This place is a lot nicer than it looked from outside."

Ivan grinned. "The owner says it keeps out the riffraff." He pointed with his thumb over his shoulder toward the bar. "Grab a beer. We just need Jeremy, and we'll get down to business."

Matt wasn't sure what that meant. If beer and pool wasn't the afternoon's business, what was? But he wasn't going to say no to a good brew, so he went.

The bartender was a woman, obviously local and married from her musculature and hair style, though her dirty-blond hair barely came to her shoulder. She looked to be in her late 30s, and regarded Matt with wry amusement as he approached the bar.

"You new to the HALSWELL, are ya?" she said, by way of greeting.

That took him by surprise, and Matt spread his hands as if he were disarmed and surrendering. "It shows, huh? How do you know the ship?"

She gave out a quick laugh. "Your crew been coming here for years, t' unwind." She pointed to the side of the bar, and Matt saw the ship's plaque hanging in a place of prominence, alongside others from what looked like local sports teams and civic clubs. "I'm Mel."

"Matt. Nice to meet you, Mel. Does your husband work here as well?"

She raised an eyebrow at him, and he thought he saw approval in her expression. "You learn our ways quick."

"I made friends." He paused. "And I just started seeing a local girl."

Mel raised the other eyebrow, and her smile turned a bit saucy.

"Lucky for you," she said, in a tone that implied quite a bit. Then she cooled, as though turning on a dime. "My husband and me own th' place. What'll you have?"

Matt scanned the taps and saw the amber from Haverhold, and he indicated it. Mel again looked approving, and she poured him a glass, then slid it across the bar to him.

"Ivan opened a tab," she said, and Matt nodded.

He picked up the beer and raised it to her in toast, then went back to the other JOs at the pool tables.

"So," he said when he got back to Ivan. "What's this business you have in mind?"

Harry stood from sinking his 4 ball. "You didn't tell him?" he said to Ivan.

Ivan shrugged. "You learn by doing." He looked back at Matt. "First, we're going to play pool and give Mel some business. Then, once Jeremy gets here, we're going into Leucadia for an early dinner. Then," he grinned broadly, "we're going on a pub crawl."

"A pub crawl."

Ivan nodded emphatically. "The rules are," he said, pointing at Matt with his own glass, which was halfway filled with a light-gold colored beer, "we get a beer at each pub, and each of us has to complain about something the Department Heads did since our last JO retention meeting. Whoever's complaint is the lamest has to do a shot as well as his beer."

Matt was beginning to get a sinking feeling in his belly. "How many pubs?"

Jorge laughed. "Until we've visited all the pubs in town. Tonight we're going back to Ventura, right Bull?"

Ivan nodded.

Matt did a quick reckoning in his head. He didn't know Leucadia well, but there were a *lot* of pubs in Ventura. That sinking feeling got bigger.

Ivan must have seen it on his face, because he grinned a bit wickedly. "Make sure you eat a lot."

Matt took a draw from his beer, and hardly noticed the flavor as he contemplated what they'd just told him. Oh well...

He pulled out his wallet. "Well, let me settle up with you on this, before—"

Ivan raised his hand. "Put that away. This is a wardroom event."

"Say again?"

"It's a wardroom event." Seeing the confusion on Matt's face, he went on. "I don't know if other ships do it this way—"

"They don't," Harry said. "But they should."

Ivan frowned slightly, then shrugged. "Anyway, I convinced the skipper that it's beneficial for the JOs to get out without the senior officers, for some morale building. So once a quarter..." He spread his hands wide, as though to encompass them all. "We get to have a retention meeting, on the wardroom's dime."

That didn't sound at all kosher, but what the hell, if the CO approved it...but wait.

"If this is a wardroom event, why just us?"

Ivan shrugged. "Brad, Rasheid, Gamal, and John have the duty. Terry is a teetotaler, so he never comes to these." That figured. "Zach said he has a date, but I don't believe him."

Harry snorted out a laugh and shook his head, his expression saying he agreed with Ivan.

"The others will be joining us later."

"Or they better, anyway," Charlie said.

Ivan nodded emphatically.

Matt thought it over, and decided that answered that. Inwardly, he girded up his loins. "Well, I guess this is going to be an interesting evening," Matt said.

Ivan grinned broadly.

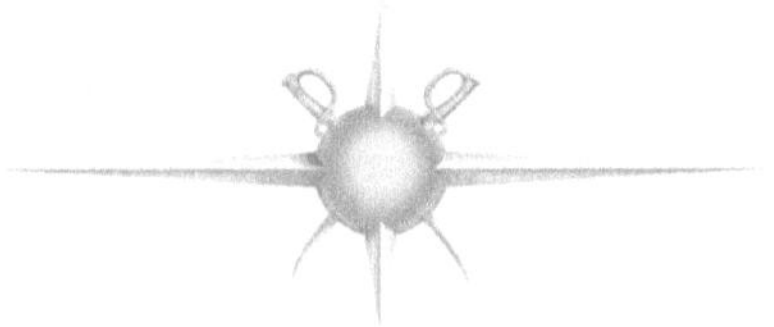

Chapter Twenty-Eight

Even though Matt didn't have duty over the weekend, it was difficult riding up on the elevator Monday morning. He still hadn't completely recovered from the JO Retention Meeting on Saturday. And he hadn't gotten a lot of rest last night, either.

But that was Marta's fault, so he wasn't going to complain too much about it.

He really should have been excited. They were undocking the ship this week. Finally out of airdock, if not from the shipyard entirely. One step closer to doing what he'd had a goal of doing for a lot of years now.

All the same, walking into the Wardroom, Matt didn't feel particularly ready and excited to face another full week. Still, he supposed it could be worse. At least he didn't have to go to school any more, in addition to his normal duties. That was something.

Matt took a moment to fill his mug with coffee—black and bitter again—and sat down at the far end of the table from the compartment's entrance, next to Zach, who nodded in greeting to him.

"Enjoy VBSS school?"

Matt shrugged and took a sip from his mug. "It had it's moments." He paused, then added, "They sure seemed to enjoy sticking it to us on the capstone event."

Zach laughed softly. "Eric can be a bit melodramatic sometimes."

Noting Matt's surprised look, he continued on quickly. "Don't get me wrong, he's a good guy and he knows his shit. But I think he gets off a little on showing how much more he knows than you do."

"Isn't that kind of his job, if he's the instructor?"

"Yeah. But there are ways to go about it."

Another sip, and Matt actually noticed the coffee's flavor this time; he must be finally waking up all the way. Whoever brewed it this morning used a different blend. He looked down at the cup and inhaled the rising vapors. Yeah, definitely different. It was actually really good.

"Did we get a new supply run or something?"

Zach raised an eyebrow. "Tim's going away present to the mess. He went out to Temecula over the weekend and brought some back from a boutique roaster who's holed up there."

"Temecula?" Matt had heard of the island, a couple hundred kilometers northeast of Ventura, though he hadn't ventured out there yet. "Thought that was mostly wine country?"

"Yeah well, apparently not." Zach shrugged, then glanced across the table to where Tim was sitting and chatting with the CSO. "But then, Tim has a knack for finding cool not-so-well-known places. No matter if it's here or in a liberty port."

"Must be his enhanced sense of smell."

Zach burst out laughing, this time loudly enough that all the people in the Wardroom—and pretty much everyone but the XO and CO had arrived by then—looked at him with a mix of curiosity and amusement.

For a second, Matt thought Zach was about to repeat his joke for everyone, or demand he share it. Instead, Zach made a dismissive wave to the room, then looked back at Matt and grinned. "See, *that's* how you do it."

Matt shrugged. It wasn't something he'd planned. He looked back over at Tim, and couldn't help but focus in on the SLOB's nose. It was his most prominent feature.

Still...

He decided to change the subject. "You guys finish turning over?"

Zach gave a quick shrug. "Sitting down with the Skipper this afternoon, then it'll be official." He gave Matt a no-nonsense look. "We're going to need to do a lot of training with the VBSS team. We've been in the yards for five months, and everyone's rusty. So look forward to lots of live boarding events with the schoolhouse."

Which meant a lot more of Eric and his team...as he had predicted.

Matt had a hard time finding that idea unwelcome. "That will be good."

Zach was about to reply when the port side door opened and the CO and XO strode into the space.

All conversation stopped, and those who had not yet found a place at the table did so.

The CO strode over to his chair and sat down. As always, the XO sat to his right.

"Good morning, gentlemen," the CO said. Though he voiced the words with a grin, his tone was all business. "As you know, we undock Wednesday. If there are any last minute issues, now's the time."

XO looked over at the CHENG, who for once was actually seated at the table. He shook his head.

"Good to go on my end, sir."

The CO put on a look of shock. "Really? No issues at all?"

CHENG snorted. "There are always issues, Skipper. Nothing that will stop the undocking at this point, though."

The XO rapped his knuckles on the Wardroom table. "Knock on wood. CSO?"

"We finished the last of the SDMS testing that we can do in the dock over the weekend. All the new hull penetrations have been tested and are looking space-ready." He shrugged. "Ready as we can be."

The CO nodded, and XO said, "WEPS?"

"No issues."

"OPS?"

The OPS cleared his throat. "Pre-evolution briefing is scheduled for tomorrow at 1000, in the Crew's Mess. I've got the watchbill ready to go—"

"You made those changes we discussed?" the CO asked.

"Yessir."

"Ok, good." The CO leaned back in his chair and turned his eyes to look over the entire group. "We're going to do things a little differently on this evolution. I've asked OPS to man the watchbill with only JOs as watch standers. The Department Heads will observe as safety monitors, so you kids won't be totally on your own." A few of the older JOs chuckled at that statement. "And we'll be putting as many Under Instruction watches on station as we can. Any stragglers will be assigned observation stations." He smiled thinly. "We don't dock or undock these ships all that often. Looking back on it, we missed a good opportunity for training when we docked. Don't want to make the same mistake twice."

The CO stopped talking, and OPS added, "Since this is a dead-stick maneuver, we have a lot of flexibility with the watchbill, so some of you will be in positions well past your current levels of qualification. That's intentional."

That sounded interesting. Matt found he couldn't wait to have a look at the watchbill.

Or maybe not. In all likelihood he'd be in Maneuvering as EOOW U/I. With the plant shutdown and no prospect of doing a reactor startup for weeks still, that seemed an incredibly dull prospect.

XO moved on to the Chop, who voiced no concerns with undocking. So the XO went ahead and leaned forward in his chair, before affixing the rest of the officers with a grimly-serious gaze.

"Undocking is dangerous. And not just because we'll be exposing newly welded hull joints to vacuum for the first time. It's a big transition, and the new mindset you and the crew will need, once we're out of airdock, is going to require a rapid shift in thinking. Hold the line on standards, with yourselves and with the crew."

"That's no kidding, gents," the CO put in. "We all know what can happen if an undocking goes bad. You've read the incident report from the MORRISY." Matt actually couldn't place that one. As if he had read his mind, the CO added, "And if you haven't, you should." He grinned. "Consider it a homework assignment."

The MORRISY incident was, frankly, terrifying.

Matt had read it toward the end of the working day, per the CO's suggestion. And found he had to read it a second time, because it was at once so unbelievable that so many blunders and unlikely accidents could happen at once, and so scary to realize that it all really had occurred, that he couldn't take it all in on a single reading.

He found himself dwelling on the incident, and the dozens of deaths that had resulted because of it, the entire evening.

He woke several times during the night from nightmares involving first burning, then freezing, and feeling his blood boil from unexpected and sudden exposure to the vacuum of space.

So when he sat down in the Crews Mess for the pre-evolution briefing, he was both less than fully alert and feeling a lot of trepidation about the evolution they were going to undertake the next day.

He sat next to his Chief at the same table with his division, all of them who were not on watch at least. The older man looked him over as he sat, and shook his head slightly.

"You look a little rough this morning, Mr. Gilbert."

Matt blanched; he had hoped it wouldn't show. "Didn't get a lot of sleep last night." The Chief opened his mouth to reply, and from the look on his face Matt knew he was drawing the wrong impression. He continued quickly, "I didn't go out, but..." He paused, feeling suddenly stupid about the whole thing.

But he might as well get it all out.

He sighed. "Captain told us to read the MORRISY incident report. And, well..." He trailed off with a shrug.

The Chief winced. "Yeah, that was a bad one."

Across the table from them, EM1 Brossard, E-Division's sandy-haired Leading Petty Officer—the Chief's second—winced. "That's a no-shitter," he said, and shook his head. He grinned at Matt then, his eyes twinkling. "No worries of that here though, Mr. G. HALSWELL's a solid boat. We treat her right, and she returns the favor."

The Chief eyed his LPO askance for a second, then slowly nodded. "More to the point, we've held the yardbirds's feet to the fire the whole avail."

Matt nodded as well. "Yeah, I know. It's silly."

Nothing else needed saying about that, so he decided to change the subject. "You ok with the watchbill, Chief?"

A quick nod. "OPS didn't mess with my inputs, so yes. Good to go." He paused, then looked inquiringly at Matt. "Saw they've got you at Chief of the Watch U/I."

Matt had been shocked when the watchbill came out, and he saw himself placed there. Not that he wouldn't have to do some U/I time as

COW; it was required as part of his Officer of the Deck quals. But that was far down the line for him. "Yeah, I expected to be in Maneuvering."

EM1 Brossard snorted. "It's a shutdown watch with less than nothing going on in the plant. Condition Two in name only. It'd be a waste of your time, and CHENG and Skipper know it."

Chief nodded agreement and opened his mouth to speak, but just then OPS strode to the center of the room, where a holographic projector was mounted in the overhead just for briefings such as this.

It was time to begin the brief.

OPS brought the projector online, and the watchbill popped into view.

"Gentlemen. We're here to brief tomorrow's undocking evolution. If you came looking for the stream of the La Jolla Pipeline competition, you've come to the wrong place."

A chuckle swept through the room, leaving Matt feeling like the odd man out of that particular joke. He looked at the Chief and raised his eyebrow in question. The Chief gave a little shrug.

"OPS is a big surfer."

"Ah."

"I assume you've all reviewed the Watchbill," OPS said, "So I won't belabor it, except to point out the large number of Under Instruction watches we have planned. We want to get the maximum training value out of this evolution as we can, but not at the cost of safety. Keep that in mind if you've got a U/I tomorrow."

With that, he turned to his left, where Jeremy and Zach had stood and moved toward center stage. "Lieutenant Cornwell is Officer of the Deck, with Ensign Stevens as Conning Officer. Gentlemen?"

At OPS's introduction, Zach stepped forward. As OOD, he would have overall control of the evolution, so he and Jeremy would deliver the meat of the brief.

Zach spoke in a clear and controlled tone that carried easily to the entire gathering. "Liberty will expire for all hands at 0500 tomorrow morning. Rig for space at 0600. Condition One in-port watches will remain on station until 0800. At that point we will station modified Condition Two watches in the Bridge and Maneuvering and begin evacuating the dock. Watch relief for Underway watches as specified on the watchbill for lunch, then we will station the full Condition Two underway watch at 1230. Expect the dock to be fully evacuated by 1300."

Jeremy spoke up then. "Once the evacuation is complete, we will shift our electric plant to a fuel cell generator lineup, and transfer gravity control to our internal systems. At that point the dock will secure its internal gravitation and detach our umbilical support. Tugs will enter the dock and attach to our towing points on the port bow and starboard quarter. Under the direction of the shipyard's Docking Officer, the tugs will maneuver HALSWELL out of the dock. Once clear of the airdock sill, they will tow us to Platform 4 at the Naval Station, where we will moor starboard side to the station and take on dockside support feeds. Expect to shift back to Condition One watches by 1800."

CHENG piped up from the side. "The duty section will conduct a battery charge tonight so we will have a topped off battery going into the evolution."

There was a slight pause as Zach stepped forward and clicked through a couple presentation slides that he, Jeremy, and CHENG had just talked through. Then he grinned and looked back at the assembled crewmen.

"That's the overview. Now we talk the specifics."

Matt suddenly realized why there were no utensils laid out on the tables he and the other briefing attendees were sitting at.

If there were, they all would probably be gouging their eyes out before the hour was up.

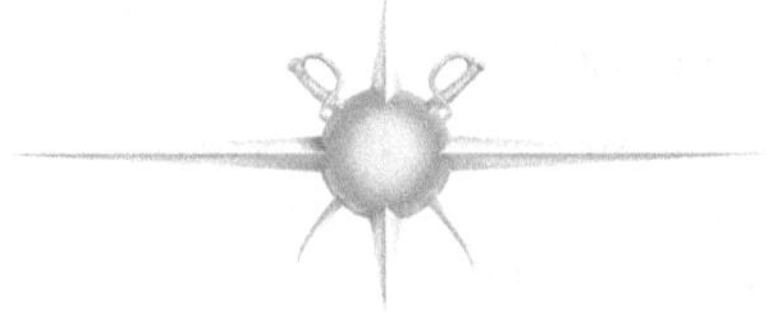

Chapter Twenty-Nine

The bridge of ICS FREDERICK HALSWELL was panoramic. That was the only way Matt could think to describe it.

He had been up here before, during his first week aboard, when Charlie had taken him on a tour through the various ship's spaces. And Matt had appreciated the layout then. But for whatever reason—probably because the ship was actually getting underway now, even if only for a brief dead-stick mooring shift—the sheer expanse of the place took him aback for a moment, as he ascended the ladderwell from the levels below.

The ladderwell emerged in the forward port area of the bridge, just inboard on the XO's chair in the forward port corner. The helm station sat immediately inboard and astern the ladderwell. A spaceman apprentice who looked about twelve years old was at the station, a slightly older petty officer standing behind him as Over Instruction. The station's holographics were online despite the fact they would not be using the engines or ship controls at all during the evolution.

Matt supposed there would be training value anyway, though.

Astern of the Helm, Zach and Jeremy were talking to the Captain next to a raised faux-wood lectern that house the OOD's turnover log, printed binders of procedures, and his computer terminal. Zach had a clipboard and was carefully reviewing some paperwork attached to it; the evolution checklist most likely.

Behind them and to port, the Quartermaster of the Watch (QMOW) had his station up and running, a small-scale chart depicting the planet's lower orbitals and Copernicus station, with HALSWELL's position annotated right where it was supposed to be in the airdock, projected so that it would be clearly visible from anywhere on the bridge.

Opposite the QMOW on the starboard section of the bridge was where Matt would be spending the day's evolution: the Chief of the Watch's station.

Matt should have hurried over to his station; his Over Instruction was already there getting things ready. But the view outside held him entranced.

The entire bridge was surrounded by a bubble of transparent plasteel almost like the cockpit of the Pegasus. Except that HALSWELL had a deck and an overhead with levels above and below, so while on the Pegasus, one had a 180 degree field of view in all directions, on HALSWELL you could look all the way around the azimuth but elevation and depression was more limited. Except for on the bridge wings. Those were plasteel globes protruding out from the port and starboard sides of the bridge, completely unencumbered by structure except for the deck plating, so the OOD could better conn the ship while mooring and getting underway, or for Underway Replenishment (UNREP).

When Matt had first seen the bridge layout, it was impressive. But it struck him that it wouldn't be very practical in a combat situation. Plasteel was tough, but hardly armor-plating tough, and you really wouldn't want the bridge to be shot through very easily. Voicing that had prompted Charlie to point out the mechanisms, above and below the plasteel bubbles, that contained retractable armor to enclose the bridge during combat.

That answered that.

When Matt had last been up here, the bridge's systems were all shut down. Now...

Just as on Pegasus, status display graphics were projected on the plasteel bubble in easily-seen and read locations: ship's heading, velocity, acceleration vector, position information, systems status...and a dozen other things that Matt could guess at, but was uncertain about.

It made an already expansive view all the more involved.

In the airdock outside, the activity was frenetic. Cranes in the overhead lifted the last of the scaffolding that the yardbirds had been using in their exterior work out from the bottom of the dock, and into storage partitions at the far end. Personnel scurried to and fro, carrying various pieces of gear out of the dock. On HALSWELL's topside aft, a final inspection of the new SDMS hump was underway; Matt saw the CSO and WEPS there, along with a trio of shipyard supervisors, making final checks of the new equipment. Other personnel were inspecting the forward-most of the dock access hatches in the mezzanine, no doubt closing them out prior to vacuum.

Busy day.

"Mr. Gilbert."

Matt turned at the sound of his name and saw Chief Stevens, the Comms Division LCPO who had first checked him onboard. He was in his underway coveralls and looked trim and alert, and he was to be Matt's Over Instruction at COW today.

"Morning Chief," Matt said, and grinned. He gestured at the activity outside in the dock. "Busy day."

The Chief nodded. "Yes it is. Ready to get going?"

That brought Matt back to the task at hand. He nodded, and followed the Chief back to their station.

The COW's console dominated the aft starboard corner of the bridge, leaving only a bit less than a meter between the console's back and the plasteel bubble beyond for the OOD or Conning Officer to walk around and view the outside. It had a single red Naugahyde chair hard mounted to the deck in front of it that Matt slid into, and an EAS manifold within reach in the overhead above. Chief Stevens plopped down onto a round stool that was padded in the same red Naugahyde to Matt's right.

Unlike the QMOW's station, which appeared to be mostly holographics-based, Matt's console for the day housed a rather imposing grouping of physical meters and gauges, an entire panel of alarm and warning indications, and an inlaid one-line diagram of each level of the ship, along with indications for every airtight bulkhead and hull penetration that could be actuated.

That, at least, seemed custom-made for a holographic display instead of an old school panel, but when Matt pointed it out, the Chief shrugged.

"That's an upgrade in Field Change Fifteen. They've got it over on the RODNEY JACOBS, but we aren't scheduled to get it for another couple years."

Matt blinked. "Holographics aren't all that new, Chief. I read they started being rolled out a decade ago."

Chief Stevens gave him a level look and a wry smile. "That's Navy acquisitions for you."

Matt was about to voice another protest, but then LT Tolson's words from back in Tactical School came back to mind. No two ships in the fleet had the exact same configuration, because of the vagaries of the acquisitions system, combined with the scheduling of maintenance availabilities, combined with budget limitations. This was a case study in that fact.

He let out a sigh and shook his head.

Chief Stevens just chuckled. "It actually works better this way. Simpler. Look over here."

With that, the Chief began a crash course on the ins and outs of his console.

It was much more intuitively laid out that it appeared at first glance, with Tank Level Indicators for the various onboard fluids—water, oxygen, hydrogen, high and low pressure air, sanitation, and even Deuterium, Helium, and Plasma Medium in the Engineering plant—arranged even with the one-line diagram of the level those tanks were located on, and in order from bow to stern and port side to starboard. So after only a quick orientation, Matt could quickly find the TLI for a particular tank—assuming he could remember where it was physically located on the ship—at a quick glance.

The alarms and warnings were similar. The top row were the ship killers: loss of pressure, fire, plasma line rupture, reactor containment. Each had its own actuator handle so the COW could sound the alarm, with its own stylized and uniquely-patterned handle so the COW could identify them by feel in the dark and actuate the correct one.

Matt didn't want to think about the kind of situation that would eliminate all illumination on the bridge, though he knew it was possible.

But it would really suck.

The rest of the alarm panel was more mundane, though no less important for its lack of flash. Probably he would see a lot more casualties like a loss of hydraulic pressure in the external hydraulic system than a Plasma Line Rupture. Or at least, Matt hoped so.

The one-line diagrams appeared pretty self-explanatory, at least at first glance. But of course, upon further inspection and under the Chief's instruction Matt found that impression, while true, to be only the first piece of the puzzle.

There were indicator lights for every airtight bulkhead door, but controls only for the major dividers corresponding to athwartships passageways or compartment boundaries. The major exterior penetrations: airlocks, hangar doors, and UNREP stations, were indicators only, no controls. He did have controls for the mooring gear mounted forward and aft on each side of the ship. And he had controls for the major internal systems like the hydraulic pumps. But he could only monitor the atmosphere control equipment.

It was a bit of a mixed bag. Matt wondered if—

"Chief of the Watch." That was Zach's voice.

Chief Stevens turned to look over toward the OOD, and Matt did the same.

Zach, Jeremy hovering next to him, was looking at them from over the top of his clipboard. "Report status of the rig for space."

The rig for—? Matt turned back to his panel and cast about, but saw no indications for that. He knew what the rig for space was, of course: a systematic check, space by space, of all hull penetrations on the ship to ensure hull integrity. It was checked by an enlisted crewman and then verified and signed off by an officer, and it required the OOD's or— inport—Command Duty Officer's permission to break for an evolution, after which it had to be re-checked and verified. There should be a place to record the status of the rig, but Matt sure couldn't find it.

The Chief saw his confused scan of the panel and looked back at Zach. "Report Status of the rig, aye sir. Wait." Then he placed a hand on Matt's shoulder. "Got a binder for that, sir." He kicked the toe of his boot lightly into the lower section of the panel, by Matt's knees.

Matt followed the sound of the kick and saw that there was a closed two-level bookshelf down there that he hadn't noticed at first. There were a number of binders, but one that was clearly labeled "Rig For Space" immediately caught his attention. Matt leaned over, opened up the shelf, and pulled the binder out.

The Chief took it from him and flipped it open. The cover page was a laminated sheet with a listing of all the spaces on the ship, with a pair of check boxes next to each of them. A grease pencil was clipped to the top of the page, to fill in the various boxes. Behind the front sheet was a tab labeled "Exceptions", which fronted a stack of pages with printed out lines and check boxes, to check individual items that had their rigs broken during evolutions, Matt presumed.

He looked up for the binder to the Chief. "Paper? I thought there would be a database to track this, or something."

Chief Stevens shrugged, then gestured toward the right-most portion of the COW console, which held an old-school access terminal and keyboard. "There is. But Skipper prefers to track it this way."

That was all that needed saying about that. What the Captain wanted, the Captain got.

Matt nodded and flipped back to the front page. A quick scan showed him all he needed to know. "Officer of the Deck," he called out.

"Officer of the Deck, aye."

"Rig For Space is set and verified in all compartments except for the Auxiliary Machinery Room and Torpedo Room. First checks are done on those but second checks are not."

"Very well."

A moment later, the CO's voice drew Matt's eye back toward where he stood next to Zach and Jeremy. His brow was furrowed into a look of displeasure. "Chief of the Watch, report which officers were assigned those spaces."

"Aye, sir," Matt said, and looked back in the binder. On the inner flap of the binder's front cover was a printout of the Rig for Space Watchbill. He traced his index finger down to the two spaces in question. "LTs Ramos and Connelly, sir."

"Very well." The CO turned away and said something more quietly to Zach, who bobbed his head quickly in response.

Chief Stevens shook his head and made a tsking sound, but didn't say anything. Instead, he tapped the access terminal to life. "Let's get you logged in as Under Instruction and get your implant interface set up for the watch."

They were just starting to enter Matt's information in when the 1MC crackled to life. Jeremy's voice said, throughout the ship, "LT Ramos. LT Connelly. Contact the bridge."

Matt traded looks with the Chief, who just shook his head again, and went back to the terminal's setup function. A couple seconds later, green text flickered across the top of Matt's vision. "JA circuit connected."

Then an electronic beeping sounded in his ears. From previous experience, he recognized it as the sound of the internal communications (IC) net announcing an incoming call.

Chief Stevens must have heard it too—of course he had, as Over Instruction—and he pointed to the left side of the COW console, where a small IC matrix sat beneath the various Tank Level Indicators. Matt found the JA circuit controls and tapped it to life.

"Chief of the Watch."

Jorge Ramos's voice came over Matt's ear implants. "Chief of the Watch, LT Ramos."

"LT Ramos, Chief of the Watch," Matt replied. "Request status of verifying Rig For Space in the AMR."

A pause, then Matt heard a quiet, "Shit." More loudly, Jorge said, "Verification complete. I'll be right up to sign the log."

"Chief of the Watch, aye." Matt tapped the JA circuit off and glanced back at the Chief, who nodded.

"About what I figured," Chief Stevens said.

The JA beeped in Matt's ear again, and he got more or less the same response from John Connelly.

Ten minutes later, both men had put their initials on the signoff blocks for their respective spaces, and the Rig for Space was complete. Matt reported that to Jeremy, who replied with a clipped, "Very Well."

A moment later, Jeremy said, "Captain, Rig for Space is set throughout the ship."

Matt looked over his shoulder and saw the CO nod, accepting the report without comment for a moment. His eyes swept the bridge, then looked out at the dock beyond. The last of the activity outside the ship had subsided, and at least from this perspective it appeared the dock was clear of personnel.

"Inform the dockmaster we are ready for evacuation."

"Aye sir," Jeremy said. He then stepped over to the OOD's lectern next to Zach and tapped a control on its top. That must have activated an external comms circuit, because a moment later he relayed the Captain's message. Matt could not hear the reply, but Jeremy nodded, then turned back to the Captain. "Dockmaster has commenced dock evacuation, sir."

"Very well."

Matt imagined he could almost hear the hiss of air being drawn out of the dock around the ship. That was just his imagination, of course.

"And now we wait," Chief Stevens said.

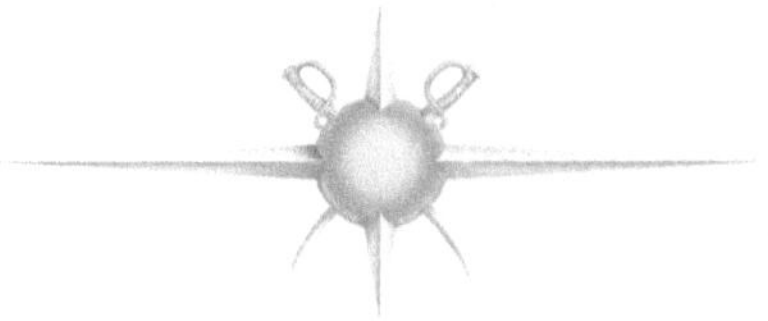

Chapter Thirty

The undocking was boring. Until it wasn't.

One minute Matt was sitting, watching five different air pressure indicators from locations around the dock, their data fed to his terminal by the dockmaster's crew. The next, pressure was gone, or near enough to it, and the ship was a bubble of life in a vacuum, the dock's doors no longer protecting them from the ravages of space.

It took him a moment to register the change, but Chief Stevens was on it immediately. He cleared his throat. "Sir," he said, and the word conveyed entire levels of meaning.

Matt shook himself and drew upright in his chair. "Officer of the Deck, hard vacuum in the dock."

From the corner of his eye, Matt saw Jeremy cock his head as though listening to something, then he nodded. "Very well, Chief of the Watch." He turned to the Captain. "Hard vacuum, Captain. Dock-master concurs."

"Very well, shift the electric plant and gravitational plates."

"Aye, sir." Jeremy tapped a button on the top of the OOD's lectern. "Maneuvering, Bridge, shift the electric plant to a Fuel Cell Generating lineup."

That went out on the 7MC, the intercom channel between the Bridge, Maneuvering, CIC, and the Auxiliary Machinery Room (AMR).

A second later, Maneuvering acknowledged, "Bridge, Maneuvering, Aye."

A minute later, Maneuvering reported the electric plant shift complete, and Jeremy ordered, "Chief of the Watch, prepare to shift to local gravitation."

The order was expected; Matt and Chief Stevens had walked through the steps he would have to take several times over the last couple of hours. All the same, Matt gave a little jerk and found himself almost stammering as he acknowledged the order. He tapped the communication controls button for the 1MC, and took a quick breath.

"Prepare to shift to local gravitation," he said, and heard his own voice echo throughout the space. It seemed to resonate, as if he could hear it going out everywhere at once. Which of course it was.

He was being silly.

Matt tapped the 1MC off and rotated in his chair to face the right-hand side of his console. Next to his terminal, a simple metal placard had been riveted to the edge of the console. Engraved in the placard were the names of each major space on the ship, and next to them a metal slide that could cover the words "Rigged" or "Not Rigged". It was a simple method of tracking the rig that hadn't changed in centuries, maybe a millennium, regardless of changes in technology.

Some times the old, simple ways were best, Matt supposed.

Over the next several minutes, he took reports from the various spaces over the JA, as each reported readiness. When the final space called in, he reported, "Ready to shift to local gravitation," to Jeremy.

He ordered, "Chief of the Watch, shift to local gravitation."

Matt repeated the order over the 1MC, then he waited.

He knew the watch standers down in the AMR were busily going through the steps in their procedures to bring the local grav plates online. He thought he felt a subtle shift in the tug on his body for a second, but that was probably his imagination; there shouldn't have been any noticeable difference at all.

A moment later, a report came in over the JA from the AMR. "Bridge, AMR, local gravplates online."

"AMR, Bridge, Aye," he replied, then relayed to Jeremy, "Officer of the Deck, the ship is on local gravitation."

"Very well, Chief of the Watch," Jeremy replied. He tapped his

OOD console again. "Dockmaster, this is HALSWELL. Ready to disconnect umbilicals."

There was no reply that Matt could hear, but he didn't expect to; he wasn't tuned in to that comms channel. But a few seconds later he felt a slight vibration through his seat, and a pair of indicator lights on his console shifted.

He blinked. Had he seen those indications before? He must have, but... He drew a blank.

Chief Stevens stepped in. "Officer of the Deck, umbilical connections indicate cleared."

Matt gave himself a mental slap for missing that, as Jeremy acknowledged the report. Then—

"Chief of the Watch, retract mooring connections."

Enough self-flagellation. Matt replied, "Retract mooring connections, Chief of the Watch, aye." He reached toward the controls for the forward starboard mooring gear.

"Remember the interlock," the Chief said, and Matt stopped himself.

The mooring connections and the umbilicals were interlocked so that the moorings could not be retracted with umbilicals connected. With them indicating clear, the interlock should have reset. But the procedure called for a second check of the umbilicals anyway, just in case. If the indication shifted because of a fault and the umbilicals were still attached, retracting the gear would cause serious damage to both dock and the ship.

Not life-threatening serious, but a couple weeks to effect repairs serious. And Matt would bet good money that had happened to some poor ship or other at least a couple times in the past, or the procedure would not have been written that way.

So it bore double-checking.

Matt turned to his terminal and tapped a command. The screen flashed to display a camera's view of the forward starboard mooring gear, where it clamped onto the dock. He squinted, and leaned forward.

"There," Chief Stevens said, pointing at a trio of attachments that were clearly uncoupled and retracted back to the dock. "Good to go forward."

They checked aft, and found the same. Then Matt retracted first the starboard forward then the aft mooring connections. The port side forward connection had not been made up, so the ship was free.

"Officer of the Deck, mooring connections retracted," he said. As soon as the OOD made his "Very well" of acknowledgment, Matt tapped the 1MC and announced, "The ship is underway."

"Not yet," Chief Stevens said, looking chagrined.

"We're not made fast to the station," Matt said. That was the requirement to... "Oh."

Woops.

The definition of underway was not at rest or made fast to a mooring station. The ship was no longer connected to the station, but she was still resting on the blocks at the bottom of the Airdock, until the dock secured its own gravitation.

Matt had forgotten about that little detail.

He gave the Chief a sheepish grin. "My bad."

Jeremy gave Matt a bemused look, then tapped his comms control button again. "Dockmaster, this is HALSWELL. Moorings are clear. Ready to release gravitation."

Almost a full minute passed, and then the view outside the bridge shifted. Since they were on internal gravitation there was no sense of movement, but the ship had definitely shifted upward ever so slightly.

They were no longer resting on the blocks.

"The ship is *now* underway, Mr. Gilbert," The Captain said, and grinned at him from where he stood next to Jeremy and Zach. There was good-natured teasing in that grin; no judgment that Matt could see.

"Yes, sir," he replied.

There wasn't much more for Matt to do for a while. He watched as the inner and outer Airdock doors opened, and then two blocky tugs maneuvered into the dock. They took up positions on the port side forward and starboard side aft, their magnetic grapples getting a solid grip on the ship's hull.

Then slowly, carefully, they slipped HALSWELL out of the dock.

Matt only *thought* the view from the bridge had been panoramic before. As the ship cleared the dock, that view changed to awe-inspiring.

Copernicus Station stretched up and down ahead of them as the tugs backed them away, its charcoal grey exterior lit with dozens of exterior lights and portholes. New California's sun blazed from the port quarter, and the plasteel bubble automatically polarized before it to avoid excessive brightness. But everywhere else was the vast sea of space, extending on forever in every direction.

At first it struck Matt as odd that he could not see the planet, but then he remembered how Copernicus Station was arranged: in vertical levels atop the space elevator connections. So when the ship had been in dock, her keel had been resting parallel with the planet's surface at the equator.

If he hadn't been sitting at his console, and been able to walk out to the bridge wing where the plasteel bubbled out, Matt could look down and see New California below them. But the angle wasn't right from where he was seated.

More's the pity.

But then, he would have plenty of opportunities to see that particular sight, so he didn't feel all that bad about it.

The tugs turned the ship to the left and began pushing her in a slow circuit of the station. Twenty minutes later, they reached their new mooring assignment: Platform 4 in the Navy section of the station.

Platform wasn't entirely an accurate description. It was really just a pair of mooring gear attachment points and a waiting umbilicus for connecting to their main airlock hatch at the quarterdeck. But Matt had heard back in the early starfaring days, before the Confederation had been formed, and when humanity was still using spin to simulate gravity, ships used to actually touch down on platforms attached to the various stations' rings, so the ships could have gravity while moored.

And the name stuck from there.

"The pilot confirms we will be mooring starboard side to, Captain," Jeremy said; he must have received another communication over his channels.

The Captain nodded. "Very well."

Over the next several minutes the tugs brought HALSWELL to a halt, then the aft tug shifted over to the port side. The two Junior Officers and the Captain moved out to the starboard bridge wing globe, and Matt lost sight of them through the bulk of his console. But he heard the Captain's and OOD's discussion over the Bridge's internal communications implant link, so he heard when Jeremy contacted the pilot and ordered him to breast the ship in to the Platform.

A second later, the ship began visibly to creep to starboard, and Matt noted the velocity vector indications on the plasteel bubble changing to match.

It seemed to take forever, but in reality was just a couple minutes, when Jeremy ordered to him over his implants, "Chief of the Watch, extend the starboard forward and aft mooring connections."

Matt acknowledged the order and actuated the controls. The mooring connections went from indicating housed to deploying, and on his terminal he watched as they reached out to the station's mooring receptacles.

They seemed to creep together until there was only about a meter between them, then the sensors in the mooring connections registered mini-beacons mounted in the stations's receptacles, and the mooring connections visibly adjusted themselves to align with the station.

The two mated, and the connections latched on.

Again there was the smallest of vibrations through the ship as the connections snapped to, then the indications on Matt's panel shifted from deploying to attached.

"Officer of the Deck, moorings indicate connected," He said, parroting the report Chief Stevens had coached him to say earlier.

"Very well."

A couple minutes later, the Quarterdeck Airlock connection indication shifted to indicate the umbilicus from Copernicus Station had mated and sealed with them, and that was that.

He leaned back in his chair and relaxed. He hadn't realized he had been stressed until just that moment, but it seemed like a river of tension was leaking out of him.

Chief Stevens grinned. "See? Piece of cake, sir."

Matt had almost forgotten Tim was leaving that day.

Undocking had been a long evolution, and though not physically taxing, it had taken a lot of mental work to learn the lay of the COW station, become familiar enough with the controls and procedures that he didn't screw them up completely, and sit through it all while still paying attention.

So when he got down to his stateroom, he was bone tired, and wanted nothing more than to get out of his uniform and into real clothes, then hit the elevator down to his condo and get some rack. And thank the Lord he didn't have duty the next day.

But Tim was sitting at his desk when Matt arrived, dressed in his offworld-style civvies: khaki trousers and a short-sleeved, green collared shirt. He was packing what looked like the last of his gear into a duffel bag that lay on the deck.

He nodded in greeting when Matt walked in. "Have fun playing Chief, Nub?"

Matt rolled his eyes at the term of address, but didn't say anything about it. There was no point. Nub was mostly a term...not really of endearment, but of initiation. Most everyone used it, but rarely and then only to impress a point, like "don't screw that up again, Nub!"

Tim was the only one who really seemed to make a point of rubbing it in Matt's—and the other unqualified guys's—face.

It was annoying. But he knew better now than to let Tim see that.

"Learned a lot," he said. He paused for a moment, then added, "I was a bit annoyed at the lack of holographics at first, but Chief Stevens was right. It really was easier and more efficient with the physical panel. Or at least, compared with the COW station they had at Tactical School, anyway." Which wouldn't be the same equipment as a Field Change Fifteen on the POTTER class. But something told him that didn't matter.

Tim grunted. "Yeah. My first ship had that upgrade. It sucked. Count your blessings."

He bent over and stuffed one last thing into his duffel. Then he zipped it up, stood, and slung it over his shoulder.

"Brad and some of the other guys are doing drinks at Caparo's before my liner leaves tonight." Tim raised an eyebrow at Matt. "You coming?"

Caparo's was a well-known, or at least well-spoken-of by some of the crew, bistro down on the civilian levels of the station. Matt had meant to check it out at some point, and he had heard some of the more senior JOs talking about going there tonight, but he hadn't thought he was invited.

He blinked. "I, uh—"

Tim made a half-snort, half-chuckle. "Even Nubs are allowed to have fun every now and then. 2000," he said, then stepped around Matt to the stateroom door. "Be there."

The door closed behind him, and Matt looked around at the suddenly empty space.

That was unexpected.

So much for just heading home for some rack.

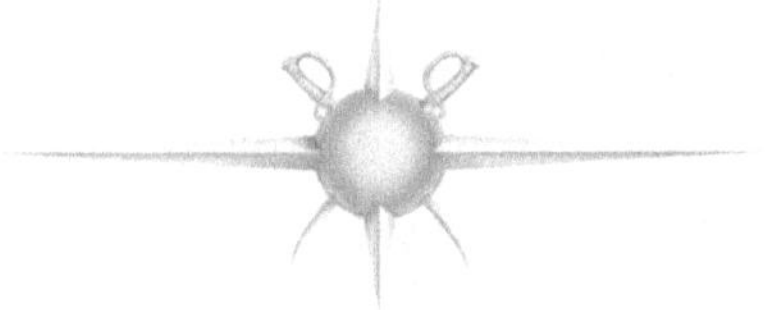

Chapter Thirty-One

"Fuck those fucking fuckers. They're all fucked up! I mean..." Chief Evans's face was red. He waved his hands around in a gesture of helpless futility, spluttered, then finally said, "Fuck!"

It was impossible to spend any time in the Navy without hearing salty language, but Matt had to give it to the Chief: he hadn't heard that many separate uses of the word fuck, in so many different grammatical functions, and in such a short period of time very often, if ever.

It was six weeks after undocking, and Matt was sitting on a bench between two of the Reactor Instrumentation panels, forward of Maneuvering in MMR Upper Level. He had the Reactor Instrumentation Tech Manual open, and had been tracing out the schematics of which connection went to which lead, and triggered that interlock to enable this subroutine.

He had been at it for a good long time, and it was beginning to make his head hurt. But he had to learn the system inside and out, so he'd kept at it.

Still, when his Chief first approached him, he was frankly grateful for the distraction. But the look on his Chief's face, and his words of frustration, swept that first impulse aside.

Chief Evans was normally pretty even-keeled. Did Matt even want to know what had him so riled up?

"Sounds like we've got a problem, Chief?" he asked, slowly.

Chief Evans nodded emphatically. "You could say that." It came out in a rush, a more than a little sarcastic and angry rush, that had a barely-concealed undertone of, "What are you, a fucking idiot?"

Matt felt his hackles rise.

The Chief must have seen it in Matt's face, because he lost a bit of bluster. He drew a breath, then let it out. Loudly. When he spoke again, though, he was more calm.

"Sorry, sir." He shook his head. "You know Morrison and Jimenez had a clean and inspect on Power Panel 41 up forward today, right?"

Matt nodded. He had seen it when he signed approval on the weekly PMS schedule three days before, and E-Division had discussed it, among their other work items, at quarters this morning.

"And you know, that supplies primary power to the navigation systems."

Matt actually didn't know that. He hadn't gotten around to learning many of the non-engineering systems on the ship yet. But he knew it now, thanks to the Chief. "Ok," he said.

"Well those...fucking morons..." Chief's face began to grow red again, and he looked off to the side at the instrumentation panel Matt had just been studying, jaw clenched.

"What, Chief?"

The Chief visibly ground his teeth. "They just went forward, and opened the breakers, and started their clean and inspect. Didn't hang a tagout. Didn't open a WAF..." He trailed off, but that was all he needed to say.

Matt winced. It was a serious safety violation to not hang danger tags. Any joker walking by could have re-closed the breaker while they were inside the Power Panel, possibly shocking or electrocuting them.

It was also a serious work control violation to not open a Work Authorization Form with, in this case since it wasn't an engineering system, the CDO. Without doing that, their work could have interfered with some other division's...

Growing realization dawned on Matt, and he felt the bottom of his stomach fall out.

Navigation division had been doing a full groom and alignment of the ship's navigational gyros this morning. If power had been cut to them in the middle of the alignment and they went through an uncontrolled spin-down...

"Oh shit."

He looked at the Chief, and he knew before Chief Evans said anything that this was exactly what happened. His two electricians had crashed the navigation system, hard.

And they were supposed to have Fast Cruise in two days, then finally get underway next week.

Chief Evans nodded. "Looks like you get to go to your first critique, sir. And it's going to be an ugly one."

The CO was back to his stern face, but he had taken it about three shades farther into stern than Matt had ever seen.

They were all in the Wardroom: Matt, Chief Evans, EM2 Morrison, EM3 Jimenez, Rasheid, Senior Chief Mulkahey—the Navigation Division LCPO, Charlie, John Connelly—the on-duty CDO, Sam Covington—the EDO, OPS, CHENG, Senior Chief Demos—The Engineering Department Master Chief, XO, CO, and Master Chief Gorman—the CMC.

Matt hadn't interacted much with the Command Master Chief since their initial check-in interview. Approaching thirty years of service, he was grey-haired and had deep smile lines around his mouth, flashing green eyes beneath bushy eyebrows, broad shoulders and a chest that spoke of a love of weight lifting, and a paunch that shouted of an even greater love of beer. He had struck Matt as utterly professional, but also cheerful and very personable.

That good cheer was gone now. He looked at Matt's two electricians even more sternly than the CO.

Everyone was seated, even the two electricians, filling the chairs immediately surrounding the CO's. Charlie had his holopad out, taking notes on the proceedings, both for an official record and because he, as Training Officer, would be the one tasked with briefing the officers and men of the HALSWELL on what, exactly, had gone on, the root causes of the incident, and the corrective actions to be taken to correct this mishap and, hopefully, prevent any recurrences.

The critique had already been going on for an hour and a half. They had gone over the events leading up to Morrison and Jimenez's screw up from every conceivable angle, drilled everyone with questions in an attempt to get to the root of what had gone on.

It had truly sucked.

Matt fully understood how important it was to do these critiques. If you didn't understand the root cause of an event, you could not possibly take good actions to correct it, and you would very likely end up having the same bad thing happen again.

It still sucked.

And, frankly, he couldn't see how there were any new lessons to be learned here. His guys had been rushing because they were coming off a duty day and could cut out as soon as their maintenance was done. So they violated procedures. It was that simple.

Nothing that hadn't happened a thousand times before in the lifetime of the Navy, Matt was sure.

Which didn't make it ok, of course.

The XO spoke. "Anything else to add, Mr. Connelly?"

John shook his head. "No, sir."

"Mr. Covington?"

"No, sir."

"EM2?"

"No, sir."

"EM3?"

"No, sir."

There was a pause as the XO and CO glanced at each other. Nothing was said, but Matt had the impression they had communicated deeply, nonetheless. Finally, the XO said, "You four are dismissed."

The two duty officers and the electricians stood and filed out of the room, Morrison and Jimenez looking slightly green with dread.

As the door closed behind them, the CO's stern facade cracked, and he raised his right hand to rub at his forehead. After a moment, he turned eyes that still were disapproving onto Chief Evans. "What the hell, Chief?"

Matt felt an impulse to speak out in his Chief's defense. He hadn't been the one to make his guys go off the reservation. But Chief Evans spoke before he could.

"No excuse, sir. I didn't specifically tell them to tag it out and open a WAF, but they've both been around long enough to know better." He spread his hands helplessly.

The CO nodded. "Damn right they do." He lowered his hand and shifted his gaze to the CHENG. "Do we upgrade them, CHENG, or take greater action?"

CHENG frowned, and so did Matt. Greater action could mean a lot of things, maybe even Non-Judicial Punishment: Captain's Mast. The CO could conceivably bust them each down a rank and dock them some pay for failure to obey a lawful order.

And, Matt pondered, maybe he should, to set an example.

He kept silent, though, as CHENG thought for a moment.

OPS piped up. "The secondary gyro suffered minor damage, but it's nothing we can't fix. Should be up and running tomorrow afternoon. We can work late getting the alignment done, and still start Fast Cruise as scheduled."

Matt wasn't quite sure how to feel about that. On the one hand, he was glad there wasn't any major damage. On the other...

He wasn't looking forward to Fast Cruise, where the entire crew would get on the ship, and they would start up the reactor, close all the hatches and detach shore connections, and pretend to be underway in space for three days even though they were still made fast to the platform.

The rationale behind doing it made sense: put the crew through their paces one last time before getting underway, to shake the rust off and get the underway procedures and routine down, after a long time being moored.

But still, the notion of just pretending to be underway seemed... dumb. And maybe extraneous.

No one asked his opinion though.

The CO nodded understanding of OPS's words, but continued to look expectantly at CHENG.

CHENG sighed. "We'll certainly disqualify them both from

performing PMS duties pending an upgrade. And I'll seriously consider whether or not EM2 Morrison should regain his Maintenance Leader quals at all." He shot a meaningful look at Chief Evans as he said that last, and the Chief nodded. Then CHENG drew a deep breath. "But this wasn't just an unintentional screw up. It was a willful violation of procedures. So I think we have to go further."

CMC spoke up. "I concur, Captain. I hate to do it, but we've got to make an example of those two."

The CO nodded slowly, glanced at the XO, who also nodded, then said. "Agreed. XO, start the process. We'll convene Captain's Mast tomorrow afternoon."

XO said, "Aye, sir." He didn't sound happy, but he also didn't sound surprised either.

The CO drew a quick breath. "Gentlemen, we cannot have screw ups like this. We're putting to space for real in a week. Get your people's heads in the game."

He stood then, and all the rest of the men at the table stood as well. Then he turned and strode from the room.

"Dismissed," the XO said after he was gone.

Instead of the normal crimson tablecloth with HALSWELL's ship seal in front of the CO's chair, for Captain's Mast the wardroom attendants had put down a green tablecloth, as well as a pitcher full of ice water and a half dozen glasses in front of the CO's chair. They had also cleared all the chairs except for the CO's and the two on either side of him.

The CO sat in his chair, flanked by the XO on his right and the CMC on his left. Matt, Chief Evens, and CHENG stood at attention along the inner curve of the wardroom table to the XO's right, facing the centerline doorway that Matt had come through the first time he'd set foot in this room.

The CO had a black three-ring binder open on the table in front of him. He glanced at the pages contained there for a moment then poured himself a glass of water. Taking a sip, he glanced around at the men present. "Ready?"

No one said no, so after a moment, the CO nodded to the CMC. "Bring them in."

The CMC rose and walked over to the door. Opening it, he called out into the passageway beyond, "Petty Officer Morrison. Petty Officer Jimenez. Post."

The two marched into the room in single file. Unlike everyone else in the room, who were in underway coveralls, Morrison and Jimenez wore their Dress Blue uniforms and the white Dixie Cup covers that went with them. Their silver Enlisted Stellar Warfare Specialist pins flashed on their chests above a single line of ribbons for Jimenez, and a line and a half for Morrison. Their uniforms were crisp, as though newly starched, and their black shoes gleamed.

They halted at the CMC's command in front of the CO, then he barked, "Right. Face," and they executed simultaneous right turns to face him.

Matt was actually impressed. They hadn't forgotten much of their drill order since boot camp. Not a mean feat, when serving aboard a ship.

"Hand salute," the CMC ordered, and the two Petty Officers saluted in unison.

"Report."

A second's pause. Then Morrison said, "Electrician's Mate Second Class Benjamin Morrison reporting for Captain's Mast, sir."

Jimenez followed immediately after him. "Electrician's Mate Third Class Ramon Jimenez reporting for Captain's Mast, sir."

The CMC ordered, "To," and they dropped their salutes.

The CO looked at them for a second, then down at his binder. "Petty Officer Morrison. Petty Officer Jimenez. You are accused of violating Article Seventeen of the Confederation Code Of Military Justice, Disobeying a Lawful Order, in that on the morning on 6 September you did willfully violate procedure by failing to hang danger tags and open a Work Authorization Form with the Command Duty Officer before beginning a clean and inspect of Power Panel 41 on board ICS FREDERICK HALSWELL. This resulted in the uncontrolled spin-down of the Navigation system, causing damage to the secondary gyro."

He paused, then looked back up at them before continuing.

"You are advised that this is not a court of law, and any finding of guilt will not reflect as conviction by a court. If you prefer, you may request a Court Martial at any time." Gesturing at the binder, he says, "I have signed statements from both of you saying that you have been apprised of your rights and giving your accounts of the incident at hand. Do you have any further statement you would like to make at this time?"

"No sir," said Jimenez immediately. Morrison followed right behind.

"How do you plead?"

There was a brief pause, then Morrison said, "Guilty."

Jimenez swallowed. "Guilty, sir."

"Very well." The Captain looked back down at his binder for a long moment, then sighed. "I find you guilty of the charges, and impose the following punishment."

There was a pregnant pause, and Matt realized he was sweating.

They had discussed this before bringing the two men in. There really was no doubt as to their culpability; it just came down to what the appropriate punishment should be.

Chief had argued for leniency, pointing out that Morrison had only just put on Second Class, and he wasn't yet getting paid for it. He was "frocked"—wearing the rank and having its privileges and responsibilities, but not getting the pay until the paperwork cleared the system and his official promotion date came. So if the Captain busted him down, he would be taking Morrison from Second Class to Spaceman.

That was a hefty cut in rank, authority, and pay, and Morrison had a wife and a three month old daughter to take care of.

The CO's lips compressed and he looked back up at the men. "Reduction in rank by one pay grade, and a 200 credit fine for two months."

The men both recoiled slightly, their bearing breaking for a second as the CO's words sank in. Morrison in particular looked pole-axed.

Several seconds passed, then the CO added. "However, I am suspending the reduction in rate for a period of six months. Any further misconduct during that time and the reduction happens immediately, before any additional proceedings take place." His eyes narrowed. "This was completely unacceptable, gentlemen. We are getting underway next week, and I can't have any members of the crew not having their heads in the game. Get your acts together. Understood?"

Both men nodded. Morrison looked as though he had just gone to the gallows, but the rope broke when the trap door opened. Relief radiated from him in palpable waves.

The CO nodded in return. "Dismissed."

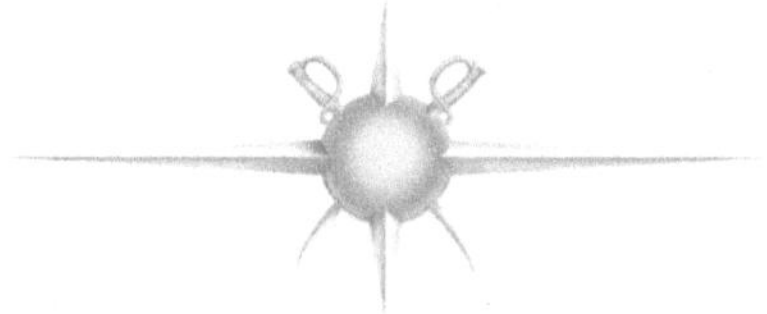

Chapter Thirty-Two

Matt knew Fast Cruise was going to be an underway watch routine, the same as they would use when they got underway next week. He also knew that fact shouldn't have made him nervous. But as he filed out of the wardroom at the close of Captain's Mast and saw the OPS standing in front of the bulletin board the officers used to promulgate watchbills, qualification progress, events, and other wardroom needs, a lump came up in his throat.

Chief Evans was walking ahead of him, and he turned his head to say, "I'll make sure Morrison and Jimenez get squared away. Don't think we'll see another incident like this again, but still..." He trailed off when he saw Matt's attention was elsewhere and stopped, following Matt's gaze with his own.

A knowing grin appeared on his face. "First underway for you, right sir?"

Matt also stopped, and nodded.

Chief chuckled. "They don't bite too hard." He paused, then said, "I'll go check in with the guys and let you know how they're doing."

"Thanks, Chief."

Chief Evans walked away, and OPS turned away from the bulletin board. He nodded in Matt's direction, then headed down the passageway, following the Chief out of officers country.

Matt stepped over to the board and looked at the watchbill.

It was four-section. He'd be on watch the same time each day, so that was good.

He was in Section Two: the afternoon watch, with Sam Covington, the Auxiliary Officer, as Over Instruction.

Matt felt that lump in his throat ease a bit. He hadn't had occasion to spend very much time with Sam yet, but he seemed like a decent guy. He certainly knew what he was about.

But then, Matt had to admit that compared with himself, everyone met that criterion.

"This should be amusing," he said to himself, and chuckled.

Glancing over at the Plan Of The Day for tomorrow, and seeing that liberty was set to expire at 0600, his spirits dropped again.

Apparently, it wouldn't be *that* amusing.

But he could worry about tomorrow's early start tomorrow. For now, he had a bunch of admin to get done and, of course, quals to study for. He'd completed most of the required checkouts for his Basic Engineering Qualification, and the level of knowledge exam was looming. There was an exam scheduled for next week, after the ship got underway, and he wanted to take it then. If he missed it, it might be another month before the department convened another. And while that wouldn't necessarily slow his quals down—he could work on practical factors in his EOOW card whether or not he had completely finished BEQ—he wanted to get it done as soon as he could.

One of the few remaining systems he still had to get checked out on before he could take the test was the Waste Reclamation System. He'd put it off because it wasn't exactly glamorous. And the processes looked to actually be pretty complex; in some ways more complex than even the Fusion Chamber itself.

But he couldn't put it off any more.

It was 1400. He could get that paperwork done in an hour, probably, then he would have a good two hours to get the system down in his head before he had to leave, if he was going to be on time to meet Marta for dinner.

Sucked that he would have to make it an early night, though.

Or, maybe, that could be good.

But for now, to work.

Matt made his way back to his stateroom and, finding it empty, grinned in satisfaction. No distractions.

Sitting down at his desk, he tabbed on his terminal, and got to work.

The alarm rang out, and Matt flinched in his seat. He knew the drill was coming; this was day three of the fast cruise. The first two days had consisted in starting up the plant and then putting each watch section through normal steaming evolutions, to work out the kinks of day to day operations. But today would be drills. He and Sam had briefed the watch team to be prepared, and the Engineering drill team had set up all over the propulsions spaces in the previous hour, while he and Sam had gotten themselves squared away, and settled into the watch.

Still, when it actually came, Matt found himself frozen in place for a moment.

It was one thing to know it was coming. It was another thing when the conversation he and Sam had been having about the intricacies of the power converter units in the DC section of the electric plant was interrupted by a high-pitched warbling from the Reactor Plant Control Panel.

Matt blinked, seeing but not recognizing the flashing red alarm indication at the center of the panel's display for a moment.

"Emergency Reactor Shutdown," Reactor Technician First Class Kertz, the Reactor Operator, called out as he raised himself from his seat to silence the alarm.

A glance at the other indications on the panel confirmed Kertz's analysis. Power ouput was decreasing rapidly toward zero and plasma header pressures were lowering as well.

The immediate actions for the casualty raced through Matt's mind, but he couldn't quite put them in the correct order for a second, until Sam nudged him in the side with a stiff elbow.

He traded glances with Sam, who raised both eyebrows and made a "Get on with it" spin of his index finger in air between them, and Matt snapped out of it.

"Very well. Secure Main Engine throttles," he ordered.

Kertz acknowledged, but Matt saw that he had already begun

dialing down the throttle controls. Of course he would do that without orders; it was the first immediate action to take.

The Main Engines were the greatest plasma draw in the plant, and until they could correct the problem that had caused the reactor shutdown they had to conserve the reserves in the plasma headers. If they ran dry before the crew could get the backup fuel cell generators online, the ship would be left with only the battery for electrical power.

Speaking of which...

Matt grabbed the corded microphone clasped to the EOOW's station and flipped to the 2MC channel.

"Emergency Reactor Shutdown. Engineering Watch Supervisor, investigate. Machinery Room, start up #1 and #2 Fuel Cell Generators," he said, and heard his voice carrying throughout the spaces via speakers mounted all over, and paralleled in the implants in his ears.

There was the smallest of delay between the two transmissions, sounding almost like an echo. It hadn't been that way at Engineering School, and the first few times he had made announcements here, it had thrown him for a loop. He had mostly become accustomed to it now, but right then, in the throws of the casualty, it almost made him feel dizzy for a second.

He swallowed hard, ignoring the momentary disorientation, and shifted to the 7MC. "Bridge, Maneuvering. Emergency Reactor Shutdown. Main Engine Throttles secured. Request the Casualty Assistance Team."

The Officer of the Deck on the bridge acknowledged, and a moment later the call went out over the ship-wide 1MC circuit. Now, the offgoing watch section would begin streaming back to the engineering plant to help with the casualty.

But for the next few minutes, it was just up to him and his team.

The Electrical Operator was EM1 Brossard, his divisional LPO. No doubt CHENG had given him senior personnel as his watch standers on purpose, and right then Matt was happy for it as Brossard effortlessly flipped through a sequence control dials and breaker switches before leaning back in his chair.

"Bus shift complete, sir. SSEGs are at minimum loading," Brossard reported. "Battery discharge is at the three hour rate."

"Very well," Matt acknowledged.

Three hours. If they didn't get the fuel cell generators up, that was they limit of ship's power. But it should only take ten minutes or so for the fuel cell to be ready to pick up load, and by procedure the crew was now hard at work securing non-essential electrical loads.

So that discharge rate would not remain for very long. Indeed, as Matt watched, the battery discharge rate lowered steadily. Then, almost as if no time had passed at all, the call box for the engineering internal communications circuit chirped.

Brossard picked up a headset and listened for a moment, then nodded and said, "Maneuvering, Aye." Then he glanced back at Matt. "Fuel Cells 1 and 2 are ready to receive loads. Shifting the electrical plant to a Fuel Cell Only Lineup."

Matt nodded. "Very well, Electrical Operator."

A moment later, Brossard had the loads shifted again, and the battery discharge rate was reduced to the point of barely being noticeable.

"Request to enter and report," came a deep voice from the port side entrance.

Matt looked to his left and saw Senior Chief Demos waiting at the door. He was a dark-skinned native of Faraway's World, and the CHENG's right-hand man. And Matt's assigned Engineering Watch Supervisor.

Stacking the deck in the new guy's favor once again.

"Enter," Matt said, and Senior Chief stepped within the confined space.

"The Reactor Shutdown was due to a short in the control circuit of the #1 Reactor Protection Breaker," he said. "RC Division is racking out the breaker to troubleshoot it now."

Matt winced. "How long?"

Senior Chief shrugged. "Two, maybe three hours, probably." He looked over at the Electric Plant Control Panel, and nodded in apparent satisfaction after a quick scan of it.

Matt did some quick numbers in his head. "That long..." He looked over at Sam. "We won't be able to do a Quick Recovery Startup."

Sam nodded, and waggled his eyebrows at him. "Guess you'll get your normal reactor startup practical factor signed off today as well."

Matt blinked, and looked back at the Senior Chief, to find him grinning wryly.

"Didn't think we'd let you off so easy, did you, sir?" He stepped back from the EOOW station, to the doorway out of Maneuvering. "I'll brief the watch standers in the spaces. Recommend you start making preps in here."

Matt had thought he might get to do the startup two days ago, since it was one of the practical factors he had to accomplish for his quals. But his weren't the only quals in the works, and one of the First Class Petty Officers from M-Division needed it as part of his Engineering Watch Supervisor Quals. So Matt figured he'd have to wait until the startup for the ship's actual underway next week.

Apparently CHENG had other plans.

Sam grinned at him. "Let's break out the procedure, and get working on the startup computations."

In front of them, RT1 Kertz chuckled. "Welcome to the party, sir!"

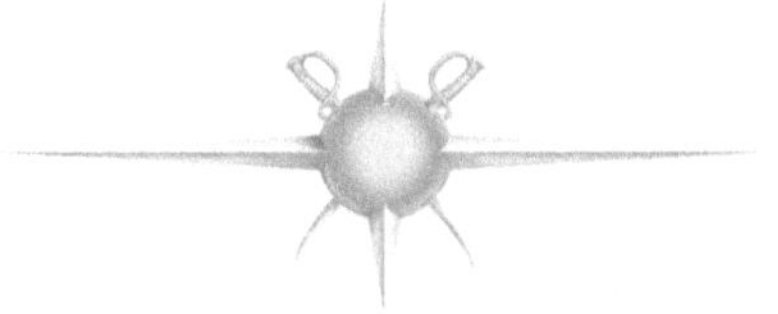

Chapter Thirty-Three

The bridge was different this time. Nothing had changed, of course. The equipment was all in the same place, the number of watch stations just as it had been before. But this morning, it all felt new, like some invisible, ontological alteration had been made, lingering just beyond his vision so that it whispered at Matt's consciousness without fully revealing itself.

The ship was still moored starboard side to the station. The grey-white bulk of the station's structure still dominated the view out the starboard side completely. On the other side of the ship, infinite blackness loomed, interrupted only by the multitude of pinpoints of starlight that were plainly visible now, during New California's night.

In the blackness, shapes moved. Distant, only visible as faintly blinking strobes from running lights, and by the contact identification graphics that the ship's tracking systems overlaid onto the plasteel of the bridge's panoramic windows.

Three contacts were visible: two white squares denoting civilian commercial vessels and one blue circle, indicating it as another warship of the Icaran Confederation Navy. They crept slowly from forward to aft down the ship's port side, slowly enough that Matt didn't even need to look at the range data at the lower left of each contact box to know they were very distant, well into New California's upper orbitals or beyond.

He watched the contacts drift abeam and then beyond, and his mind wandered a bit. What were those crews doing, and how long had they been underway? HALSWELL was putting to space in the morning; maybe his ship would interface with theirs once she finally set out into her proper environment.

Perhaps—

A nudge in his side brought his reverie to an abrupt end, and Matt turned to his right.

Rasheid looked at him with a quizzically-raised eyebrow. "You awake, man?"

Heat rushed into Matt's cheeks from embarrassment, and he cleared his throat. "Yeah. Sorry." He gestured with his left hand toward the contacts, and thought to explain. But instead, he just shrugged.

Rasheid grinned, and, gesturing for him to follow along, headed away from the ladderwell, where Matt had been standing staring, toward the Chief of the Watch's station.

The bridge was not fully manned. No helmsman at the wheel, and no Officer of the Deck. But the Chief of the Watch was at his station, and a pair of Quartermasters were huddled over the plot.

It was Chief Stevens again, and he pivoted in his chair to face them as Matt and Rasheid approached.

"Gentlemen," Chief said. "Here for the Rig for Space?"

Rasheid kept silent, turning his body to allow Matt to take the lead.

Matt stepped up to the chief and held out the check sheet he had been going through with Rasheid for the last hour and a half. Rasheid had been overseeing him as he verified the Rig for Space in the Auxiliary Machinery Room, as part of preparations for tomorrow's underway.

And boy, were there a lot of valves, hull fittings, and EAS manifolds there. Probably more than in any other space on the ship besides the Torpedo Room.

As part of Matt's qualification to Rig for Space, he had to be supervised checking the rig on at least two spaces on the ship. He hadn't figured the first one he'd be assigned to do would be that most complicated on the ship.

But then again, it made sense. He supposed.

It was still rough.

Chief Stevens looked at the check sheet and nodded, then pulled the binder that he and Matt had checked during the undocking from the shelf where it was kept. He flipped it open and turned it around to face Matt.

A moment later, Matt had the block for the AMR initialed, Rasheid counter-signed, and they were done.

Easy as pie.

Kind of.

At least his wasn't the last space to be verified; there was that.

"Ok," Rasheid said as he led Matt back to the ladderwell leading down. "If you can do the AMR you can do pretty much anywhere. Got any questions?"

Mat shook his head. It was, after all, pretty simple. Just the practicality of it was what became complicated: locating all those components and valves, when you haven't before.

"Just takes a bit of practice I guess," he said.

Rasheid nodded. "Soon enough, you'll be able to do it in your sleep." He glanced at the chronometer display at the center of the forward section of the plasteel windows. "And we've still got twenty minutes before the pre-underway briefing."

"Fun, fun."

Rasheid chuckled and clapped him on the shoulder. Then he led the way down the ladderwell.

As Matt followed Rasheid into Crews Mess, he blinked in surprise.

It was more crowded than during the briefing for the ship's undocking. Much more crowded. And many of the faces were people he didn't recognize. All throughout the space, interspersed with the representatives from the ship's departments and divisions were personnel who also wore the standard Naval underway coveralls, but they were unfamiliar, mostly older.

And over next to the head table where the CO and XO usually sat, were two other senior officers. One had three silver bars on his collar—a full Captain—the other the two bars of a commander. Both had the stars of command on their breasts, but the commander's was beneath his warfare insignia as opposed to above his name tag, unlike the CO and the Captain.

The Captain had to be the FRIGRON Commodore. Matt had seen his picture in the FRIGRON spaces his first day, though he had given it only a passing glance, focusing more on his own Captain-to-be.

Who was the other guy?

He moved over to the table where Chief Evans and EM1 Brossard were sitting and took an open seat across from the Chief. As he did, he gestured toward the commander.

"Who's that?"

Chief Evans followed Matt's gesture with his eyes and snorted softly. "Commander Cafferly, the squadron's deputy for maintenance and training."

Matt raised an eyebrow at the Chief's tone. Chief noticed and made a little shrug of his shoulders.

"He had command of LEFCOURT before transferring to the FRIGRON," he said. "Buddy of mine was the M-div Chief on there." He paused, pursing his lips for a second as though considering his words. "Not the best command climate, if you know what I mean."

"Ah," Matt said, looking back at the commander.

He was tall, taller than the CO by three or four centimeters, and thin, the kind of thin that claimed he had never seen the inside of a weight room. Or an ice cream sundae. But his face was round and he looked to have a lot of smile lines, and his blond hair was devoid of even a hint of grey, even though he had to be a few years older than the CO.

He didn't look unpleasant. Maybe Chief's buddy was judging harshly?

Then again, Matt had thought for certain the CO would be a total hard-ass, from his picture. So who knows?

The CO and the Commodore finished exchanging words, and they took their seats as a few last stragglers entered the space and took theirs. Then the CO gestured to OPS, who was standing adjacent to the head table.

OPS stepped forward and cleared his throat, and the strains of conversation that had been wafting through the space quieted quickly.

At a gesture from him, a crewman dimmed the lights and the briefing projector came to life, showing the ship's logo.

"Captain. Commodore," OPS said, nodding respectfully to the two men, before turning to the rest of the gathered personnel. "Gentlemen. We get underway tomorrow at 0900 for space trials. We will have personnel from the squadron and shipyard aboard to assist us as we get our feet back under us and complete the post-availability testing, and the schedule is going to be tight. The watch rotation after we secure the Maneuvering Watch will be the same as for Fast Cruise, so we should all be comfortable." He grinned slightly at that. Then he gestured to the left, where Zach stood waiting, with Gideon at his side.

"Lieutenant Cornwell is Officer of the Deck for the underway, and Lieutenant Schulz is conning officer. Gentlemen?"

Zach swallowed visibly and stepped forward, Gideon at his side, and turned to face the CO and Commodore.

"I will relieve the CDO at 0700, sir, and station the Maneuvering Watch at 0800." The briefing display shifted, showing a top-down view of Copernicus Station, close-up on the section where HALSWELL was moored. "Tugs T4 and T6 will be alongside at 0830. I intend to make them up to the ship on the port side but not use them for maneuvering; they will be in standby to give assistance if needed."

"I don't expect we will need them," the CO said, his tone saying, "We'd better not."

Zach nodded quickly. "Yessir. At 0845 we will detach shore support connections, and then, at 0900, we will detach moorings and breast out from the station on maneuvering thrusters. Once we are clear of the station, we will engage the main engines and transit to navigation box 23-15."

The display zoomed out and rotated, showing New California and Copernicus Station surrounded by a spherical grid of boxes. Matt hadn't gotten too involved in his tactical qualifications yet, but he recognized the basic layout from Tactical School.

The planet's orbitals were divided up into quadrants for traffic control, and numbered based on the latitude and longitude of the planet, projected up into space, and on orbital level. So box 23-15 would be between 20 and 30 degrees north latitude, 20 and 30 degrees east longitude, and orbital levels 15 and 16.

That was a high orbital; Copernicus Station, at geosynchronous, occupied orbital level 8, and level 20 skirted the edge of the planet's gravitation well.

So they would have a good amount of space to maneuver while they carried out their post-availability testing.

Zach continued, "Once we reach the navigation box we will detach the tugs and secure the Maneuvering Watch."

The CO nodded, and looked back at OPS.

OPS said, "The testing schedule will take three days," he said, and the briefing shifted from the navigation view to a time line showing those three days. And they were filled solid with evolutions, briefings, and interviews with squadron staff members.

Matt cringed inwardly when he saw it. That was a lot of events, scheduled one right on top of the other, all throughout the ship. Sure, he saw several that they had performed already during Fast Cruise, but still...

"As you can see, there is a lot to do," OPS said. "We will be embarking the test team from the shipyard to assist. And," he gestured toward Commander Cafferly, "the FRIGRON staff will be observing and providing oversight. CHENG?"

CHENG, who had been sitting with M-Division, rose at OPS's invitation and took over his spot.

"Here is the plan."

The next hour felt like a day, as CHENG detailed each and every planned retest, who was assigned to which, and the procedures and precautions the ship would use to ensure they were conducted safely.

At first Matt was a bit confused, because the testing was going to involve more than just Engineering department. Then it clicked: CHENG had been overall in charge of ensuring the availability went on schedule. He had met with the shipyard's project manager each day, and must have conferred with the other Department Heads as he did so. So he would be the one man who had the overall view of what was happening, and where, for the entire time the ship had been in the dock.

So it made sense he would coordinate the testing as well.

Matt didn't envy him that.

Finally, after what seemed like forever, CHENG sat back down.

There was silence for a few seconds as everyone took in all that had been discussed.

The CO broke the silence.

"We've haven't been underway in more than six months, and this is going to be a very busy time. Fast Cruise knocked some of the rust off, but your men will be adjusting to a different routine than they've been used to. So all of you need to keep a close eye on what they're doing. Remember, slow is fast. I'd rather we take an extra day to get everything done than push it, and have an incident." His eyes narrowed. "The void is an unforgiving mistress. Attention to detail, and safety, is the priority. Understood?"

Heads nodded all around the room.

The CO's lips compressed slightly, then he nodded as well and turned to the Commodore. "Commodore?"

The Commodore scanned the room quickly. His grey eyes seemed to burrow into Matt as they swept over him, and he felt like the man had taken his entire measure in that fraction of a second.

Maybe it was just the serious expression on his face.

"I want to reiterate what your Captain just said. You did a great job throughout the availability. Don't spoil that by letting your guard down out there. I want you all back in port safely, not being featured in an incident report. If something doesn't pass the smell test, or seems like it's being rushed, speak up."

Matt found himself nodding, and thinking back to what they had said back in his training: Forceful Watchteam Backup is the name of the game.

"Dismissed, gentlemen," the CO said.

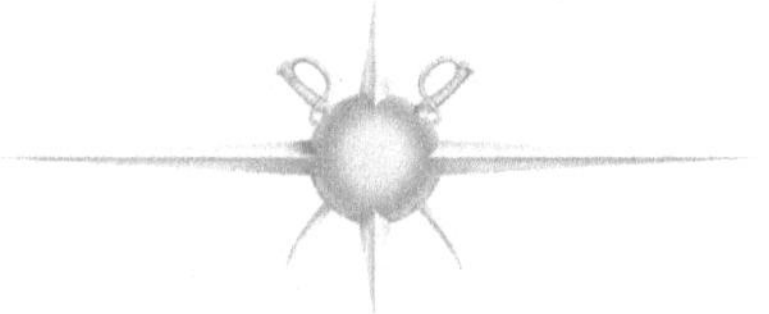

Chapter Thirty-Four

No panoramic views from the bridge for this underway. Instead, Matt spent the maneuvering watch as Engineering Watch Supervisor under instruction.

It was a necessity for his EOOW qualification, but it meant he had to come in earlier than he would have liked to do the reactor startup. Which was pretty interesting from the EWS perspective, actually. Senior Chief Demos led him through the entire engineering plant, and he got to supervise and observe all the various watch stations as they performed the choreography required to bring the plant—and the ship— to life.

Still, Matt hadn't joined the Navy to plug away in the bowels of an engine room. The bridge, or CIC, was where he wanted to be.

All in due time. Gotta walk before you run, said the voice of wisdom in the back of Matt's head.

Sometimes he hated that voice, and all the more because it tended to be right.

Still, it was a good watch and he learned a lot, and when the maneuvering watch was secured, and they turned over to the section one EWS, he got a whole bunch of signatures on his qualification card.

So Matt was feeling pretty good when he walked into officers country.

It was 1030. A half hour until lunch, and then he had to go back to the plant for EOOW under instruction on the afternoon watch. The coffee pot called, but he couldn't go into the wardroom just yet. The stewards were getting the table set up for the meal, and it was no entry to everyone—even the CO—while that was going on.

So Matt bypassed the wardroom and went back to his stateroom instead.

Harry was at his desk, typing away, when Matt walked in. His eyes flicked Matt's way and he went to nod greeting, but paused mid-nod.

"You're out of uniform," Harry said, and tapped the rank insignia on his collar.

Matt blinked, confused for a second. He looked down at his own collars. The single gold bar of rank, same as he always had. He wasn't eligible for promotion for another year or so, so what else...?

Then it hit him. The George bars. He'd almost forgotten about them.

"You didn't lose them, did you?"

Matt shook his head and went to his own desk. He pulled open the lower of the drawers below the fold-down desk. The green and red bars were in a little plastic container that he'd found; just the right size for them.

He straightened and began pinning the bars over-top the sewn insignia on his collar, and Harry nodded approvingly.

"Don't want to let the skipper see you without those," he said, and waggled his eyebrows. "You know how seriously he takes traditions, especially fun ones."

"I kinda noticed," Matt replied. He got them pinned and checked them in the mirror. The pins weren't exactly the same size as the sewn insignia, but close enough that the gold was only partially visible beneath the red and green.

"You're taking the BEQ test tomorrow right?"

Matt frowned. "Not looking forward to it."

Harry nodded agreement. "Yeah, it's a ball buster. Necessary evil, though. How's the rest of your EOOW card looking?"

"I need a few more drills, and half a dozen practical factors." Matt kept his card, printed out because the CO liked to do qualifications the old school way, folded up in the thigh pocket on his coveralls. He pulled it out, unfolded it, and handed it over to Harry.

He looked it over, flipping through the pages quickly. His lips moved slightly; probably counting out the number of signatures Matt had left. When he got to the final page, he nodded and handed it back to Matt.

"You ought be able to get most of those pracfacs done during this underway."

"That's what I'm hoping. Then finish up the last few things, take the test, and maybe have the qual board while we're in port for the post-avail."

HALSWELL was scheduled for a three week post-availability maintenance period after space trials, to fix anything that broke while they were doing their testing. And then things got interesting. A month and a half of certifications and inspections to prove they were ready to re-enter the standard tactical training and deployment cycle, then a short time in port, followed by a two months straight underway for tactical weapons certification and some other events Matt didn't recognize.

Matt wasn't entirely certain exactly what those certifications entailed, but it wasn't engineering-related. So he really wanted to be done with his plant quals before then.

Harry chuckled. "I think the Bull's got his OOD board scheduled for then, too. Maybe you guys could tag team it."

Matt rolled his eyes. Pretty sure that wasn't how that sort of thing worked. Though it might be amusing to try.

Or not.

He glanced at the chronometer on the wall and saw that it was ten minutes til meal time. The stewards should be ready by now. "Well, lunch is calling."

Harry shrugged. "Not hungry," he said, and went back to whatever he was working on.

Matt was right, the stewards were done. The main wardroom table was fully set: white plates with the ship's seal in the center atop the usual red tablecloth, and knives, forks, and spoons laid out just so. Faux-crystal glasses before each plate with decanters of water spaced out the entire length of the table, along with baskets containing sliced bread.

The bread lent the space an earthy odor that was a marked

improvement from the "boat smell" from the CO_2 scrubbers. Though Matt had mostly gotten used to the boat smell, so that he hardly noticed it.

Mostly.

For a wonder, Matt was the only one here. He heard the two stewards talking in the pantry area, but no one was in the wardroom proper.

Lucky him.

The counter by the sitting table in the forward section was set out with a salad bar, and he picked up a bowl and began filling it with lettuce, cucumbers, shaved carrots, and bell peppers. As he was working on that, the door from the passageway opened and two men entered. Matt noted them in passing, but the shredded bacon bits at the end of the salad bar commanded the lion's share of his attention, until one of them stepped up next to him.

"How's it going, George?" he said, and Matt focused in on him more fully.

It was Commander Cafferly.

It shouldn't have been a surprise. Matt knew he, and several others of the FRIGRON staff, were coming aboard for the testing. But he hadn't seen the man yet, and he had been far from Matt's mind.

So, surprise it was. Matt blinked, then after a second his mind got back into place.

He shrugged. "Going fine, sir. Excited for my first underway." Which was true, but even as he said it, Matt cringed inwardly over how trite it sounded.

Commander Cafferly chuckled and scooped a bunch of cucumbers onto the substantial bed of lettuce he'd already accumulated.

"I remember how that felt," he said, flashing a grin Matt's way. "Getting your space legs under you for the first time, eager to take on the galaxy."

He shifted and plopped a few baby tomatoes into his bowl, then turned toward the main table.

Matt looked down at his own bowl, and decided he'd already designed the perfect salad, so he followed the Commander.

Others of the wardroom were filtering in now. Matt saw CSO and WEPS, and several of his fellow Junior Officers. They began filling salad bowls as Commander Cafferly circled around the table to take the spot at the CO's right, where the XO normally sat. He placed his bowl down atop the waiting plate, but did not sit.

He had his eyes on Matt still, though, so Matt moved over to take the place across from him.

The others filled their salad bowls and took other places around the table, all remaining standing, and the Commander looked away from Matt to examine them, one at a time. Then he chuckled again.

"What's you name, George?"

"Matt Gilbert, sir."

"Well, Matt, I'll tell you a little secret." The Commander leaned forward slightly and waggled his eyebrows. "It only gets better."

From off to the right, someone snorted out a half chuckle, and the Commander shot him a look that was part annoyance, part amusement. Then he looked back at Matt.

"Some people love this job. Lots more hate it. But if you love it, there's nothing better in all the universe."

The Wardroom door opened again, and the CO walked in, XO on his heels. The small conversations that had been going around the table quieted as the CO got his salad, and then moved over to his seat next to Commander Cafferly. The XO took the seat to his left.

The CO looked around at the assembled men and nodded. "Gentlemen," he said, then he took his seat.

On cue, everyone else seated themselves and began digging in to their salads.

Matt decided quickly that he had done up the salad just perfectly. After all, everything was better with bacon. Including bacon.

As he was chewing, the stewards came in from the pantry. The senior of the two, a First Class Petty Officer, though his rank was invisible beneath the crimson tunic that the stewards always wore during mealtime, came over to stand across from the CO, to Matt's right.

"Well, Davidson," the CO said, "what do you have for us today?"

Davidson grinned. He was about Matt's height, late 20s, and sported jet-black hair, and piercing green eyes. His face was narrow, his nose pronounced, but the way he smiled made Matt certain he got lots of attention from the ladies.

"Your favorite, skipper. French Onion soup, and braised beef tips atop fettuccine."

The CO pursed his lips appreciatively. "I knew I liked you for a reason, Davidson." He stabbed at his salad with his fork and halfway raised it to his lips, but paused to wave the utensil at the other men at the table. "Don't wait for me. These guys have actual work to do."

Davidson chuckled and inclined his head politely, then turned away to join his assistant in their duties.

"Well, skipper," Commander Cafferly said, "that was a tidy underway. How many times has Mr. Schulz conned the ship away from dock?"

The CO chewed for a moment, considering. As he swallowed, he looked toward XO. "I think that was only his second time, right XO?"

XO nodded. "Yes sir."

"Well, nicely done." Commander Cafferly looked away from the CO, and back toward Matt. "I imagine you're chomping at the bit to do that yourself, right?"

Matt shrugged. "I'm still not done with EOOW quals, sir."

The Commander raised an eyebrow at him, then shrugged. "Soon enough."

The CO, though, was looking at Matt with a considering gaze. "That reminds me, Matt. You have the afternoon watch, right?"

"Yes sir."

"After you finish turnover and eat dinner, grab the Bull and come see me and the XO. I've got a mission for you two."

"Sir?"

The CO must have seen the uncertainty that suddenly flared up within him, because his expression softened a tad. "Nothing serious. But," he pointed at Matt with his fork, again skewering a bunch of lettuce along with a bell pepper, "it is vital for our morale."

XO grinned broadly, and Matt understood in a flash.

Looked like the George was about to get some tasking.

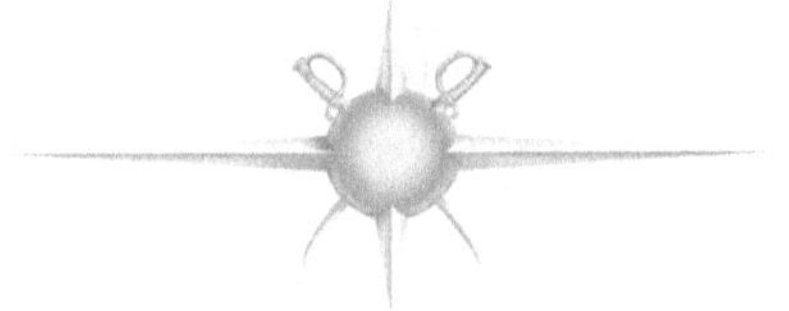

Chapter Thirty-Five

Ivan wasn't at dinner, so Matt had to hunt around for him. It didn't take long, though. He was in the Radio Room, to port and forward of the CIC on the O2 level. Where else would the Communications Officer be?

When Matt entered the space, Ivan and his LPO were hunched over a piece of gear that had been racked-out on the forward bulkhead. Two of the radiomen were standing off to the side, looking not very happy. An open tool bag was between one of the radiomen's feet, and the other carried a tablet that looked to have a technical manual open on it.

The center of the Radio Room had a work bench dominating it, so Matt had to maneuver around a bit to get to them. As he did, the LPO, a First Class Petty Officer who obviously was from Carraway's World from his deep tan and tight black curls, was talking.

"—totally fried," he finished up as Matt came to a halt next to the little group.

"Well that sucks," Ivan said. "How long to fix?"

The LPO shook his head. "RM2 Woo is checking with Supply. We're supposed to have the part onboard, but it's an infrequent use item so they'll have to pull it from their bulk stores. It'll be a couple hours at least, probably, before we can get started working. From there…" He straightened, scratching at his chin for a second before looking at the senior of the two technicians, a Second Class. "What do you think, Coppel? Three hours? Four?"

RM2 Coppel nodded. "At least."

"Well into the midwatch," Ivan said, also straightening. He shook his head, frowning, with what Matt thought was sympathy, at the technicians. "You guys are set for all sorts of fun, aren't you?"

The junior guy, a Radioman Spaceman by his rank insignia, actually grinned as he nodded. "You know it, Mr. L."

Ivan chuckled and looked back at the LPO. "I assume Chief knows?"

The LPO nodded. "He went to brief the CSO right before you got here."

That was stepping over Ivan's head, but Matt had learned enough from his time aboard to know it was futile to take offense over it. After all, the Chiefs were the ones who really ran the divisions. The JOs were in charge, of course…nominally, anyway. But no one had any illusions over where the expertise lay.

Matt remembered his check-in interview with the XO. He had said something that Matt hadn't entirely understood at first, but was beginning to now: the Junior Officer tour was an apprenticeship tour. The JOs got shuffled around the ship to learn how its various processes work and gain experience, so when they came back as Department Heads they would know enough to really shepherd the ship in its path.

Learning, learning, learning was the name of the game for the next 3 and a half years of his life, so Matt should remember that, and remain humble. Guys get into trouble when they try to throw their officer's bars around and be the know-it all big man on the block when they aren't, and everyone else knows it.

Not that Matt ever had that impulse, but he had met some guys who just might trip over that obstacle.

He wondered how Tom was doing? And George?

Funny, he hadn't thought of them in weeks. But if any of their little group would have that sort of humility trouble, Tom might. Or maybe not. Maybe—

"Well, I've got to meet with the Captain," Ivan said, breaking Matt's train of thought. He looked away from his people, toward Matt, and nodded. "You all set?"

"Yeah, just waiting on you."

"Right. Let me know if you need anything, RM1," he said to the LPO, then Ivan led Matt out of the room.

As he closed the airtight door behind them, Matt asked, "What broke?"

Ivan puffed out a sigh. "The primary Tight Beam amplifier circuit. We've got a backup unit, but it's not as high wattage as the primary, so we're limited on ship to ship comms until it's fixed."

That explained why the division was working it as a priority, Matt supposed.

As they turned aft, past the CIC, he considered their assigned space box. Supposedly no other Naval vessels would enter that area until they completed their testing, but there was nothing to stop some civilian from venturing into their area.

Which wouldn't be dangerous in and of itself, but with communications limited, Matt imagined the OOD up on the bridge would be a bit less comfortable until it was fixed.

They reached the midships athwartships passageway and turned left, and after ducking past a couple Yeomen transiting the opposite direction, came to the doors for officers country and the CIC.

"Captain tell you what the deal is?" Matt asked as Ivan opened the airtight door for the wardroom area.

He shrugged. "I assume another party. Come on."

OPS was stepping out of the CO's stateroom, Charlie in tow, when Matt and Ivan got there. There was a moment of slipping to the side and semi-pirouetting as the four of them passed each other, but after only a little bit of awkwardness, the CO gestured for them to come in.

Matt had been in the CO's stateroom a couple times, but it still took him aback how spacious it was, by ship standards anyway. His rack was in the far corner from the entrance, stretched out along the forward bulkhead, and it was a full-sized mattress, not the thin coffin mattresses that the other staterooms, and crews berthing, had. A pair of floor-to-ceiling lockers stood at the foot of the bed, each about twice the size of Matt's.

And then there was his work desk. It was L-shaped, running along the aft bulkhead before curving to make a receiving area in front of the door, complete with two chairs cushioned in the red Naugahyde that was used everywhere in the ship. A pair of file cabinets were behind him, along the port side bulkhead, and above them was an oil painting of the ship before a brilliant blue and red starscape. Floating shelves on the aft bulkhead above the bulk of his desk completed the layout, and Matt was pretty sure it would rival many executive offices in civilian businesses.

Small ones, anyway.

The CO was in his chair when they walked in. The XO was standing, just beside the doorway that led into the head that he and the CO shared; his stateroom, not quite so posh as the CO's, was on the other side of the head compartment.

"Gentlemen," the CO said by way of greeting. "We have important work to plan."

XO chuckled softly, and Ivan nodded. "What did you have in mind, sir?"

"That depends. What's the balance in the wardroom fund?"

Ivan dipped his hand into the thigh pocket of his coveralls and pulled out his holopad. He tapped on it a few times, frowning slightly, then after a minute he nodded. "A couple guys are late with this month's dues. But once they square up we'll sitting on about twenty-five hundred credits. I've set aside five hundred for going away gifts for Gamal and Charlie, though, so only two thousand are usable."

Matt blinked. Gamal and Charlie were going away soon? Gamal was a second tour JO, like Charlie—the Fire Control officer. Matt had met him, of course, and talked a few times over meals in the wardroom, but he hadn't interacted with him all that much besides that. He had gotten sucked into the world of Engineering, and his qualifications, and Gamal never stood EOOW except to retain proficiency. Matt had never stood watch under his instruction, so as far as he was concerned, Gamal almost wasn't on the same ship. Except for those meals.

Still...

Matt thought back to the last time he'd looked at the projected billet rotation plan that the OPS posted after they completed divisional turnover, before undocking. Gamal was going to be the first to leave, but that wasn't for eight months yet... Scratch that, it was closer to four months, now.

Wow, time was flying.

The CO and XO exchanged looks. XO looked a trifle unhappy, but he nodded.

CO looked back at Ivan. "We've got three weeks in port, and then we're chock-a-block for the next four months. I want us to have an evening out with our spouses before we enter that churn." He glanced back at XO. "We'd talked about making it a formal dining out, but doesn't sound like we have the funds for that."

Ivan shook his head. "Not unless we want to make everyone pay a bunch of money out of pocket, no sir."

CO nodded. "In that case... Matt, I'd like you to find a place that can accommodate us, as a group, for dinner. Doesn't have to be fancy, but remember we're bringing our wives with us, so no dive bars." His eyebrows rose, and Matt wondered if he hadn't heard of the JO retention meeting at The Queen Bee.

What was Matt thinking? Of course he had.

He considered the CO's words for a second. Four guys on the ship to take the duty for the night would leave twenty-one wardroom members. With wives and dates... That would require seating for forty-two.

Most of the restaurants he'd seen on New Cali were smaller places, mom and pop shops. They couldn't take so many at a time, not without shutting the doors to other customers. Maybe The Peninsula next to his building would have something they could use? Or...

Ah-ha!

He grinned. "I think I know just the place, sir."

The CO nodded. "Good. I'd prefer to not make anyone have to shell out more than thirty or forty credits apiece, but hold the wardroom outlay to fifteen hundred, max."

XO spoke up then. "Plan the dinner for three weeks from this Friday. We're underway the following Monday, so knock on wood," he paused and rapped his knuckles onto the side of his head, evoking a soft chuckle from the CO, "we'll have all the repairs and upgrades done by then, and we'll be able to enjoy the weekend."

Matt nodded. His mind was beginning to churn. He didn't have Vincenzo's contact information, but Isaiah surely did. He'd fire off an email message to Isaiah as soon as he was done here. And while he was at it, he really ought to check in on Tom and George.

And maybe Katerina?

Matt felt a little lurch inside. He hadn't thought of her in weeks, and anyway, he was with Marta now. So why re-open that wound, when nothing could come of it?

Then again, it couldn't hurt to remain in contact, on friendly terms. If—

The CO spoke up, interrupting Matt's train of thought.

"Enough of work." His eyes narrowed as he focused in on Matt. "CHENG tells me you're almost ready for your board."

Matt blinked. Enough of work? Did the skipper think this was turning the subject toward fun?

Then again, maybe he did, considering what Commander Cafferly had said before.

Matt nodded. "Yes sir. I've got the BEQ test tomorrow, and just a few more pracfacs and other checkouts to go after that."

The CO nodded. "Good. Ivan's got his OOD board after we pull in. And you'll be ready for your final SWO board before you promote at the end of next month, right?"

Ivan stiffened slightly. His face tightened, and Matt thought he saw a flash of uncertainty, but it faded quickly. "Yes sir."

The CO looked over at XO and raised his eyebrow.

XO said, "We've been delayed on tactical quals for some of the guys since we've been in the yards for so long, Matt, so we need you to have your EOOW board before the next underway. That way we can move Ivan to the OOD watchbill, and shift Gamal down to CIC, so he can finish his TAO quals before he rolls to shore duty, and the Department Head screening board."

"No worries, sir."

XO nodded. "Good."

"You'll need to see me for the checkouts on Battleshort Operations and Emergency Core Ejection procedures before we convene the board," the CO said. "Get with CHENG to make sure you're ready, then the XO will put you on my schedule." He looked between Matt and Ivan, and grinned. "I'd like that dinner to celebrate both of your qualifications."

"Yes sir," Matt said, in unison with Ivan, and the CO nodded.

"Dismissed, gentlemen."

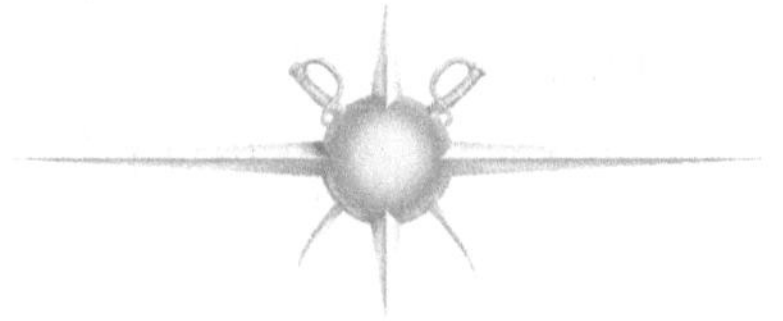

Chapter Thirty-Six

Matt was writing feverishly, the fingers of his right hand gripping his stylus like it was his sole connection to life, and the electronic letters and numbers it created on the examination tablet built into the desktop in front of him were the key to his being able to claim that life.

Because, sort of, they were.

But there was so much to tell, so much depth to the question he was answering. He had already described the relation of the reactor protection interlocks with the primary power bus and battery bus, but now he needed to also explain how that fed back into the engine throttle circuits, to ensure that engine settings weren't changed too quickly so as to induce a feedback loop that the protection circuitry might not be able to keep up with. Because if that were to happen...

"Time's up!"

The man's voice barely scratched Matt's consciousness.

There was so much, still, that he needed to write down, or there was no way he was going to pass.

He kept on writing.

A shadow blotted out some of the light shining from the overhead as a shape moved in front of his desk. Two palms settled down on his desktop, one on either side of the examination tablet.

"Time's up, Mr. G." The voice was serious, no-nonsense. Not mean, and not disrespectful, but it would brook no objection.

Matt sighed and pushed back from his desk. The feet of his chair made soft scraping sounds as they slid across the linoleum of the classroom's floor, and the stylus tinked where it fell onto the desktop.

"Aye, Senior Chief," Matt said, and looked up to meet the gaze of Senior Chief Tilson, the M-Dive LCPO. He let out an explosive breath. "Gah! Man!" He shook his head. "No way I passed that."

To his right and left, he heard snorts and expressions of similar chagrin from the half dozen other guys who had been taking the BEQ exam with him this morning. They were all third class petty officers, a couple of whom he'd recognized from Engineering School when he first checked aboard, but none were from E division.

His new guys weren't scheduled for the exam until next month.

Senior Chief chuckled and shook his head. "Everybody thinks that after one of these tests." He looked around the classroom, to include all of the examinees in his remark. "I'm sure you all did fine. Results should be posted in twenty-four hours."

That stopped some of the side grumbling, but everyone had the same uncertain, doubtful expression that Matt was sure he had.

There wasn't much for it but to wait and see, though. So he stood, pushed his chair in, and filed out of the classroom.

Engineering Department usually made use of Classroom #3, on the 1st Deck just forward of the Engineering Office and the starboard hatch into the MMR. But from its layout, it could have been any of the half dozen classrooms there were crammed into HALSWELL's volume.

It wasn't that dissimilar from any number of classrooms Matt had been in during his school years, except in size. This was smaller, just room for four rows of five student desks and an instructor's lectern at the front, with a retractable screen for showing presentations built into the overhead adjacent to the lectern.

There were lockers built into the left-hand wall, and bookshelves into the right-hand, crammed with printed-out manuals for all the various ships systems, as well as operating and emergency procedures. The lockers held damage control, diagnostic, and maintenance gear for hands-on training on those subjects.

And, of course, there was real DC gear strapped in place all over, as well. It was a ship, after all.

When Matt slipped through the airtight door into the starboard side fore-and-aft passageway, he paused, looking aft, toward the Engineering office.

He still had to do his weekly PMS spot check, and Brossard had mentioned needing to talk with him about something. EM1 was off watch now, so...

Matt felt the tugging toward the office, but resisted. Harry's words, "Marathon, not Sprint," rang in his mind, and he turned away, toward the ladderwell up to Officers Country, and some coffee.

After that ball-kicking, he needed a break before he went on watch.

Five minutes later, he had that coffee—black and bitter, to fit how drained he felt—and he went back to his stateroom.

Harry was seated at his desk when Matt walked in. He looked up from the novel he'd been reading this underway—some sort of spy thriller from the title and cover art, but Matt hadn't pressed him on it—and half-smirked, half-winced.

"I was going to ask how the BEQ exam went, but it's written all over your face."

Matt grunted and nudged the door shut with the heel of his boot, then sat at his own desk, moving carefully to avoid spilling his coffee.

"Dude. That sucked. No way I passed it."

Harry laughed softly. "Everyone says that. You did fine."

He echoed the Senior Chief's words so closely, Matt wondered if the two hadn't planned it.

He raised an eyebrow Harry's way, and Harry spread his hands in a helpless gesture.

"What? It's true. That test is supposed to be a ball-buster. But I've graded it a few times. There's lots of leniency built in, lots of ways to get partial credit. Really, you'll be fine."

Matt considered his words for a moment, then shrugged. "You say so." Then he took a long drink from his mug.

The coffee was hot, and surprisingly flavorful today. There was an almost chocolate undertone to it. That made him pause, and he held the mug away for a moment as he swallowed.

"Wow, did Terry order a different a blend of coffee beans?"

Harry shook his head quickly. "No, that's all Commander Cafferly."

Matt blinked.

"He likes to bring little presents when he gets underway with a ship. This time, he brought a different bag for each day of the underway. Gave them to Davidson yesterday at dinner."

Ah, that explained why Matt hadn't known about it. Coming off the afternoon watch, he had dinner in the second sitting, so naturally wouldn't have seen that happen.

Yet another thing with Commander Cafferly that didn't seem to add up.

"That's surprising," he said.

Harry gave him a questioning look.

Matt shrugged. "I just heard he wasn't the best at keeping up morale when he was CO."

Harry was silent for a few seconds, just looking at him. Then he rolled his eyes toward the overhead. "Who told you that?"

Matt spread his hands silently. He wasn't going to sell out the Chief.

Harry snorted, loudly. "I've been on two ships now, Matt, and one thing I can tell you for certain is the absolute truth." He leaned toward Matt a tad. "A bitching sailor is a happy sailor. I know a couple guys in the LEFCOURT wardroom, and they all practically worship Commander Cafferly. Their goat locker does also." He shook his head and made a dismissive wave of his hand toward the stern of the ship, and engineering. "EM3 Schmuckitelli's cluebag of a buddy on the LEFCOURT complaining about something means precisely dick for how things really are." Both his eyebrows rose. "In fact, the more he complains, the more he probably really likes it."

Matt felt his cheeks flushing, but from irritation as much as anything else. The Chief wasn't just spreading some junior guy's clueless complaints...

Or was he? Matt hadn't asked for clarification, and anyway maybe Chief's friend was in the minority opinion?

"Don't just take deckplate rumor as fact, dude," Harry said. "I saw a quote from an ancient Naval Officer's Guide, like real old, going all the back to old Terra before space flight even existed."

Matt blinked. "That's kind of cool."

"Want to know what it said?"

Matt nodded, and Harry straightened in his chair. His voice turned deeper, more formal, almost scholarly.

He said, "The enlisted man is sly and devious, requiring constant supervision." The formal facade broke and Harry grinned again. He pointed an index finger Matt's way. "It's funny because it's true. Then, and now."

"Fair enough, I guess," Matt said. He paused, considering, then decided to drop the subject. Instead, he took another sip from his cup and set it down next to his desk terminal. He flipped the terminal open and tabbed over to his email.

He had twenty-five un-opened emails. A quick scan showed most were routine nothing-to-worry-abouts. But there was one from OPS...

"New watchbill's out for the maneuvering watch on Friday," he said.

Harry grunted, and Matt tabbed the watchbill open.

"Looks like..." He stopped, surprised. "I get CIC Watch Officer U/I?"

"Makes sense. You're just about done with EOOW, so they'll want to get you knocking out OOD requirements."

"Guess so..." Matt finished looking the watchbill over, and couldn't stop laughing as he came to the end of it. "You get EOOW."

"Glorious," Harry said. His tone did not agree with that. He let out a sigh after a second or so. "Well, I guess there are worse ways to get in a proficiency watch. But speaking of that, why don't you see if Sam will cut you loose as U/I a little early today? We're shooting slugs down in the torpedo room to retest Tube 2, starting at 1600. That's an OOD pracfac."

"Can he do that? I'm written onto the watchbill."

Harry shrugged. "If there's nothing major happening, it shouldn't be a big deal. But if not, no worries. We'll be shooting slugs weekly now that the ship's back into her normal routine. Just thinking ahead for you."

"Thanks. I guess I'll talk with Sam about it." Matt's terminal beeped, and he saw a new email had entered his queue, from Isaiah.

A flash of eagerness swept through him as he opened it up. Had he—?

Sure enough, Isaiah reported Vincenzo was open to hosting the wardroom, but wanted more information before he could commit for certain, and then passed along Vincenzo's contact information: email and voice.

Outstanding.

He set to typing out an email to the restaurant owner, visions of smashing success on his first George tasking making him smile with anticipation.

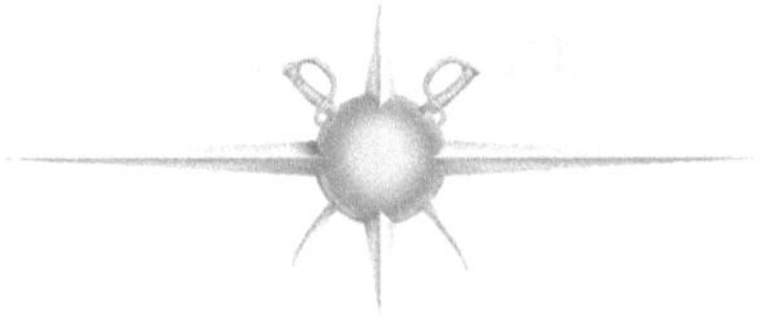

Chapter Thirty-Seven

CIC wasn't all that much different from the simulator back at Tactical School. A bit smaller, but the basic layout was the same. A central holographic tactical display where the Tactical Action Officer and/or the Captain could assess what was going on in the space around the ship. A ring of support consoles surrounding that, staffed by personnel who were focused in on specific specialties: the various sensors, weapons control, target tracking analysis, management of the fusion plot, and others.

The whole space was bathed in a dim blue light, the better for the holographic displays to stand out and be easily seen.

And for a wonder, all of the various stations were, in fact, holographic, just like they had been in Tactical School.

Matt had wondered if they would be, between LT Tolson's discussion about the rate of modernization in the fleet and the lack of holographics up on the bridge. But apparently the ship had gotten the latest updates even before her most recent yard period, in CIC at least.

So while his time as CICWO U/I during the maneuvering watch was uneventful, it was also pretty cool.

He'd been in CIC before, of course, many times. But only in passing, as a part of his initial familiarization tour when he first checked onto the ship, and then later because he had to go in on some business or other.

But most of the time he'd been in before this underway, the systems had been shut down, so he couldn't really see what they were doing. And then, the two times he'd popped in during this underway, it had been just to deliver a quick message, and then he had to be back about his business.

So this time, he had a full ninety minutes to bask in the glory that was the tactical heart of ICS FREDERICK HALSWELL, and Matt had to admit it was pretty great.

There was nothing going on, of course. Nothing that required a ton of attention or that was worth stressing over, otherwise the TAO would have been stationed. But it was still great to see the various stations going about their duties, updating track parameters to ensure they were properly displayed in the fusion plot, both in holographics here and projected onto the plasteel of the bridge, and running drills to assign firing parameters to various defensive systems...because why not? Might as well keep sharp.

It was over soon enough, though, and the ship was moored. Port-side to, this time, and two moorings down from where they had been before they got underway a few days ago.

Matt stretched in his seat, next to Ari Renquist, the ship's Force Protection Officer and his Over Instruction for the maneuvering watch, and held back a yawn. It had been a long last couple days of the underway, between working through the last of his pracfacs, overseeing his divisional testing schedule, and studying. And now, as the blue lights shifted to in-port white and the various watch standers around the CIC secured their stations, he felt like a nap was in order.

But of course, that wasn't in the cards and he knew it, so instead he just grinned at Ari.

"So that's life in CIC, huh?"

Ari shrugged. "On an easy day. But they say that was only yesterday, so..." He chuckled. He was a second-tour JO, and due to put on full Lieutenant in a couple months, but he looked young enough that the more senior enlisted liked to joke whether he even needed to shave. He wore his black hair far shorter than regulations required, almost Marine Corps short, and he had the muscles to match it.

"Yeah, I heard that. I—"

The CO's voice came over the 1MC circuit, and Matt shut up to listen.

"HALSWELL, this is the Captain. Good job on this underway. We accomplished the testing regime, and the Project Manager and Squadron Deputy told me this morning how impressed they were with your performance and professionalism. We've got some items to fix over the next couple weeks that we discovered during the testing, but we are looking good to get back into normal operations on the next underway. Secure the Maneuvering Watch; set the normal in-port watch, section three. We'll be putting down liberty by LPO after lunch, once the CMC is satisfied that the ship is stowed and ready. Have a great weekend. Have fun, and be safe, and I'll see you on Monday. Well done, gentlemen."

The 1MC cut out, and the personnel in CIC moved with a bit more energy as they went about squaring their positions away. Eager to be off the ship, Matt was sure.

He could relate a bit.

"Well," Ari said, standing from his chair. "Let's get some lunch, eh?"

It was Friday, which meant burger day. Hard to say no to that.

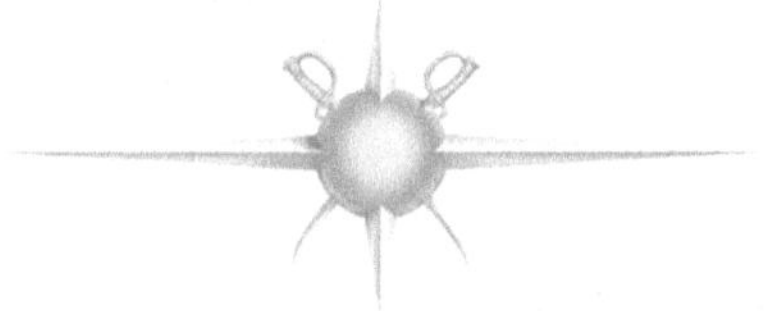

Chapter Thirty-Eight

As the CO advertised, the CMC came on the 1MC about forty-five minutes after lunch to put down liberty. But there was an Officers Call on the plan of the day for 1500, so while the enlisted crew began filtering off the ship, Matt got to take care of business for a bit.

He probably wouldn't have left anyway. He still had to review next week's PMS schedule, and there was a little project CHENG had asked him to work on that he needed to finish up.

And it wasn't all that long an underway. But still, he had duty tomorrow, and the surface was calling him.

Whatever, quit griping, said the grown-up voice in his head.

Matt sighed. He hated that voice, sometimes.

He tabbed out of the PMS application after signing it, and noticed that the notification bubble was lit on his email. He opened it and found messages from Tom, and from Katerina.

Four whole days for them to receive his earlier messages and reply; light speed latency was fun sometimes.

He opened Tom's first.

Turned out Tom and George weren't having as much fun on the HATHERLY as they all had assumed they would. The ship had been underway almost the entire time since they checked aboard. Which was good for quals; both he and George finished up EOOW a month ago.

Matt felt a little jealous about that. But he'd had a fair amount of time on the beach, hanging with Isaiah and Maleen...and Marta. Sounded like Tom and George had been severely liberty-challenged.

And Tom sure bitched about it in his email. But even worse...

Matt almost choked from laughing so hard, as he read the final line from Tom's message. He had to read it twice to be sure he hadn't misunderstood, and that only made him laugh even harder.

LT Tolson had orders to the HATHERLY as OPS, and Tom was assigned as the Navigation Officer, who worked for the OPS!

"When are you dropping your resignation letter?" was Matt's quick reply.

He shook his head, the laughter still coming in waves, and opened Katerina's message.

His laughter faded as he read the quick note she sent. She was doing well on her ship, and was happy to hear he was as well.

And she was seeing a great guy who worked as an engineer at a prominent firm on Montecino.

His heart shouldn't have lurched at reading that. They had broken things off months ago, and anyway he was seeing Marta now. But still, as he closed her note, without replying, he felt a bit of heartache.

Stupid, said grown-up voice again. And it was right.

But as he got up from his desk and went to the wardroom for O-call, he couldn't put aside that glum feeling.

CSO noticed it as soon as he sat down, and cocked his head Matt's way. Matt could tell the older man was about to ask him what was up, but the CO and XO walked in, and instead everyone shut up and stood.

The CO looked around at his officers for a second, his expression measured. Then he nodded and sat.

The others in the wardroom did as well, all attention on the CO.

"Gentlemen," he said, "like I told the crew, good job during this underway. We got a lot accomplished in a short period of time, and the PM and Deputy were impressed. That said, we have a lot going on in the next few weeks, and I wanted to take a minute to lay it out so we're all on the same page." His eyes moved across the gathered officers again, then settled on the OPS, who alone was standing. "OPS?"

OPS nodded and tapped his holopad. At his tap, the lights in the overhead dimmed and a briefing screen lowered from the overhead in front of the kiddie table by the coffee mess/salad bar area.

Matt turned in his seat to get a better look at the screen. OPS had put up a calendar showing the next three weeks, which covered their planned in-port time.

It was chock-full of events.

"As you can see, the schedule is full," OPS said, and a couple people chuckled ironically. "Next week is Security Response Force training by duty section, at the force protection training center, and the week after that is weapons load. WEPS?"

The WEPS was seated at the end of the table near the wardroom door. He nodded in acknowledgment, and spoke up. "The SRF training is step one in our force protection certification. Each duty section will get a morning of refresher training in the classroom and then experience hands-on simulated scenarios in the afternoon. Instructors at the training center will give feedback, and we'll conduct training to fill in the gaps. Later in our underway the training center will embark to run more scenarios, and finish our certification. But that first week will be key."

He pulled out his holopad and tapped it awake.

"The next week we'll bring aboard our self-defense weapons load out. Monday we'll load two warshot torpedoes and two training shapes. Tuesday will be ammunition for the point defense turrets—a full load. Wednesday we'll bring aboard two warshot SDMS canisters and two training canisters. And Thursday will be countermeasures." WEPS narrowed his eyes as the looked around the room. "The torpedoes will come in through the weapons shipping hatch, and the SDMS and countermeasures are loaded externally, so unless you're involved in those evolutions they will be transparent. But the point defense ammo load will require cordoning off passage from the starboard side quarterdeck to the magazines. No one will be allowed along the route except for personnel involved in the ammunition load. So make sure your divisions plan their work accordingly."

The CO nodded gravely. "For those of you who haven't seen this before," Matt felt his eyes burrow into Matt's head for a second, "that is no joke. Anyone violating the cordon will cause the evolution to stop for safety and security reasons. They've got a lot of material to move, so we can't afford to have that happen."

He gestured WEPS's way, but WEPS shook his head. "That's all I've got, sir."

OPS said, "While that's going on we've got VBSS team training scheduled, and an ASV load on Friday of that week."

Matt perked up a bit at that. He hadn't even thought about VBSS in ages. There had been some team training the first couple weeks after the undocking, but nothing since, and he'd almost forgotten about his collateral duty. He wondered what—

"How many are we getting, CSO?" the CO asked.

"Four, sir. Standard recon drones, not the interceptor type."

From tactical school and his subsequent studies, Matt knew frigates like the HALSWELL could accommodate up to ten Autonomous Space Vehicles in external storage bays below the landing deck at the stern of the ship. Un-manned, they could be controlled by personnel in CIC, set to autonomous tasking, or slaved to embarked surveillance and reconnaissance skiffs.

It would be neat to see them in operation.

"I don't expect we'll need to do any strafing runs any time soon," the XO said, evoking more chuckles from around the room.

"Well, we can hope," OPS said. He pointed at the third week. "Last week is Control Tower team refresher training at SSR-37 Monday through Wednesday and Tracking Party team training at the TACTRACOM Det simulator Monday through Thursday. The Bull has his OOD board on Tuesday—"

Charlie whistled through his fingers, evoking a series of "Go Bull!" chants from several of the more senior JOs for a second.

OPS looked at them levelly for a second, and they stopped, but the little smile he wore said he wasn't too mad about the interruption. He turned back to the calendar.

"And Matt has his EOOW board on Thursday."

A little shot of adrenaline went up Matt's spine. "I do?" He had been working toward that, and planning it. But to see it laid out on the schedule in black and white...well, that was quite a bit more real, wasn't it?

From the other side of the table, CHENG raised his eyebrows. "Yes. You do."

Several of the JOs laughed at that, and Matt felt his cheeks heat briefly.

OPS continued, "Then we've got a stores load on Friday. Aside from that, it's fixing all the little things that broke during testing."

"CHENG?" the CO said.

"Like OPS said, whole lot of little things, skipper. The biggest item is the glitch in the #2 SSEG inverter circuitry. The yard thinks that'll take about a week to fix, and then we can retest it upon startup."

The CO nodded, and looked at Ivan. "That leaves the most important item. Bull?"

Ivan cleared his throat. "Yessir." He looked around at the gathered officers. "We are planning a wardroom dinner, with spouses or plus ones, the last Friday before we get underway." Someone groaned, and he rolled his eyes, but the CO spoke before he could.

"Mandatory fun, gentlemen. Consider it an order." He raised his eyebrows. "But if you really don't want to go, trade duty with someone who's scheduled that night." He gestured for Ivan to continue.

Ivan said, "The George will be locking down the venue this weekend, but looks like we can plan on it costing about forty credits each, plus drinks."

"Is that forty per couple or per person?" Jorge asked.

Ivan looked at Matt, who spread his hands slightly. "I'm meeting with them on Sunday to iron out the details. Let you know on Monday?"

"Fair enough," Jorge said.

"Once we get underway, the schedule is very busy the next several months," the CO said. "I think it's important that we take some time to let our hair down." He grinned. "And remind our wives that we do actually exist."

The CSO chuckled at that.

The CO continued, "So prepare to have fun, gentlemen. That's an order." His grin broadened a bit, then he turned serious again. He gestured toward OPS again. "The schedule for the next underway isn't fully nailed down, but I think you should know what we're looking at."

OPS tapped his holopad and the screen shifted to another calendar view. But this one covered three months.

It was also full.

"The first week will be a lot of refresher training. Coxswain training for Deck Division all week—they'll be taking the ship's boats out to freshen up their skills and give the Control Tower team some practice. ASV flights for the CIC controllers. Personnel from the TACTRACOM Det will be embarked, and we'll do classroom training for the tracking team, VBSS team, and damage control teams."

"Week two is Deck Landing Quals with units from SSR-37, and VBSS training using REPTARVs from the TACTRACOM Det. We'll also be doing SRF drills to complete our force protection certification."

"Week Three we'll leave the orbitals and commence a two-week Track-Ex, with ICS RODNEY JACOBS playing OPFOR. We'll start with simple scenarios and work our way up to a cross-system scenario with JACOBS in stealth mode."

He tapped at the holopad and several of the day-boxes changed color to blue.

"And we've got UNREPs every Friday." He raised his eyebrows. "So lots of opportunities for close-quarters ship handling training for the new guys."

Underway Replenishment was one of those evolutions that sounded simple but was actually pretty complex, and easy to go very wrong. Matt knew conning the ship during an UNREP was a key skill he'd need to learn for his OOD quals. And since he'd be done with EOOW by then...

He rubbed his hands together an anticipation. EOOW was the thing he *had* to get through. OOD was what he *wanted* to do. Almost time for it. He realized he was grinning.

"After the Track-Ex we're in port for a day to disembark the TACTRACOM Det staff, who won't be coming with us. And we're picking up Gamal's relief, who's transferring over from the RODNEY JACOBS. Then we're underway to the range in Olifant System for our Tactical Weapons Certification. It'll take about two weeks to get there, then the certification itself will be another three weeks. Two new Ensigns will report aboard from Tactical School at the start of the certi-fication."

Matt perked up a bit at that. A couple of new Ensigns? He hadn't even completed his first tasking as George, and he was going to be turning it over soon.

Well, a couple months from now, so not all that soon. Still...

OPS paused, then shrugged. "After that, the schedule is a bit more fluid. We might head back here directly, or there's talk about maybe passing through Melrose for a liberty call."

That evoked murmurs around the wardroom table.

Melrose was an independent system, not part of the Icaran Confederation, though on good terms with it. It was general policy to send ICN vessels to visit neighboring polities to spread goodwill—or rattle the saber—from time to time. But being homeported in New California, Matt hadn't considered going to a place like Melrose to even be a possibility.

Davidea, New California's neighboring system with the jump gate to the Tsago Dominance? Certainly they'd visit there, despite Davidea also not being part of the Confederation. But Melrose?

The murmurs around the table continued, and the CO held up his hands, palms out. After a moment, silence returned.

"Like OPS said, that part is far from set in stone. And frankly, it depends on how well we do on our certifications these next couple months. So let's focus on the job in front of us, and if we get a good deal later, we get the good deal. Understood?"

Heads nodded all around.

"Alright. What else, OPS?"

OPS shrugged. "After we return from Olifant—whichever way we go—is up in the air at this point, sir. We're slated for a deployment later in the year, but that's still in the planning process."

Matt blinked. A deployment? To where?

Again, he hadn't really considered that possibility. New California was essentially garrison duty against the Dominance pushing through Davidea. Other ships in other homeports were often deployed elsewhere, but he hadn't thought that any more likely than a liberty call to Melrose. Where would they be sent?

The CO shook his head. "Way too early to talk about that," he said, as though answering Matt's unspoken question. "For now, let's focus on the tasks at hand. Any question about those?"

No one spoke up, and Matt swallowed the speculation that had begun to whirl about in his mind over the possibility of a deployment.

Worry about that later.

"XO?"

XO leaned forward and clasped his hands together on the table. "Like I always talk about, we're about to go through another transition to a more full optempo. The crew's not used to this sort of schedule," he gestured toward OPS's calendar. "And neither are we. Keep your people informed and keep a close eye on what they're up to. Keep your standards high. Better to get a thing done right the first time than to rush it, and have to redo it after a fact finding. Or worse, after someone gets hurt."

CO nodded agreement, then added. "And don't forget to have fun. If you're not having fun, you're doing it wrong." He chuckled at his own words. Then he nodded again, briskly. "Have a good weekend, gentlemen. See you Monday."

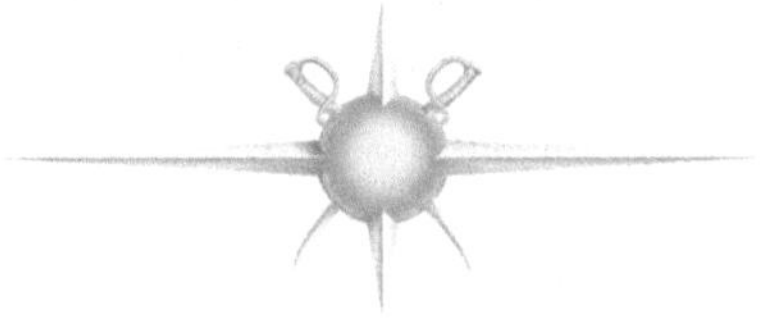

Chapter Thirty-Nine

La Trattoria was one-third full when Matt walked in Sunday afternoon.

He felt great. He had actually managed to get a halfway-decent night's sleep while on duty; almost five hours down!

It really helped to be basically signature complete on his qual card. He only had those two checkouts with the CO, scheduled for later in the week, and the written exam next week, before his board the week after. So there wasn't much extra to do besides weekend duty stuff. And weekend duty tended to be less intense, for obvious reasons.

Still, he got a short nap in after he got home, and rose a bit before noon feeling ready to roll. He donned a light blue shirt in the local cut and khaki trousers, sandals, and descended to the floor level of his building excited for a great afternoon.

And La Trattoria did not disappoint.

The same cheerful girl who had been on duty the first time he set foot in the place was behind the hostess stand again. She beamed a smile at him as he approached, and he returned it in kind. But just like before, he had to disappoint her.

He pointed toward the inside bar, where he saw Marta waiting. "Meeting my friend," he said.

She followed his finger, and her smile became a little bit more know-ing. But did he see a bit of something else in there as well?

"Enjoy th' afternoon," she said, and he nodded.

Marta looked great, as always. Her auburn hair was loose and long on her right side, flowing down the front of her shoulder to just below nipple-height. Her blouse was in the local cut, of course, loose and deep red, offsetting a flowing white skirt that fell to mid-calf. She cradled a wine goblet in her left hand, filled with golden fluid, and was in mid-laugh when Matt walked up to her, and the fellow she was talking with.

He had the look of a tourist, in decent shape on another world but struggling a bit with the deeper gravity well here. Matt could sympa-thize, of course. It had been several months since he arrived, and he only now felt fully adjusted to the difference.

The guy had on flowery board shorts and a short-sleeved, yellow-cream, collared shirt that buttoned up the front. He was leaning against the bar facing Marta, and had a half-empty glass of golden-brown beer in his hand.

"I'm telling you, it's true," the guy was saying, but he broke off when Marta looked away from him toward Matt.

"Matt," Marta said, and stepped up next to him. He slipped his arm around her waist as she came in and kissed him lightly on the cheek. "Good t' see you again," she said.

"Feeling's mutual," he said, giving her a squeeze for a second before releasing her so she could restore the distance between them...if she wanted.

She did, but only slightly. "Sorry I couldn't see you Friday."

He had called when he got off the ship, but she had to help her brother and father with some family business. She hadn't been clear on exactly what, and he hadn't pressed her on it. He just asked her to meet here today, instead.

"No problem." And it wasn't. He had been a bit disappointed, but since he had duty Saturday, a quiet evening at home and an early bed time was actually not such a bad thing.

The tourist guy was looking at Matt uncertainly, his eyes flicking between him and Marta with the obvious question unspoken.

So Matt stuck out his hand and smiled. "Hi. Matt Gilbert."

The fellow's grip was firm enough, but it didn't measure up by local standards. Naturally so.

"Roger Matteson," he said. "I'm visiting from Davidea. Just got in yesterday." He had an interesting lilt to his accent. Not quite like an Irishman, but similar...Matt couldn't quite put a place to it.

Except Davidea. Clearly.

"You're the first person I've met from Davidea."

Roger looked him askance, like he thought Matt was joking with him.

Marta broke the tension by chuckling softly. "Matt be an officer on one of th' Navy ships here. Only arrived a few months ago."

"Ah." Roger nodded, looking Matt up and down as though in new understanding. "Well, I guess that explains it. Lots of us Davideans come here on holiday, and folks from New Cali visit us quite a bit as well."

"I suppose that makes sense. How long are you here?"

"Two weeks." He winced, with a self-deprecating chuckle. "Just enough to make the muscles sore, but not enough to really get stronger, you know?"

Matt nodded. He did know, at that.

He looked away from Roger toward the rear patio. "Have you seen Vincenzo?" he asked Marta.

There was a fairly large party taking up two tables for ten over to the right, but the restaurateur wasn't with them. Where was...

Ah!

Mat saw him, conversing with the patio bartender, just as Marta said, "At th' bar."

Matt nodded and grinned at her. "If you'll give me a minute, I have to talk some business with him. Shouldn't take too long, and then we'll get lunch?"

She nodded.

"Good meeting you, Roger," Matt said, and shook hands with him again. Then he said, "I'll be right back," to Marta, and headed over to where Vincenzo was holding court at the bar.

He had on a dark green shirt today over white trousers, and his belly protruded just as much as it had the first time Matt met him. As Matt approached, he was gesticulating at the bartender, or rather at the bottle the bartender was holding, and his cheeks were a little pinkish.

"No, no. This is not how you handle a bottle of fine wine, my friend," Vincenzo said. He held out his hand and the bartender handed the bottle over.

There was a goblet on the bar between them, partly filled with a dark purple-red fluid. And a few drops were visible on the stone of the bar top adjacent to the glass.

"It is not just sloshed around," Vincenzo said, waving his free hand at the spilled drops. "It must be dispensed lovingly, gently." He picked up the glass and tilted it slightly, then ever so gently angled the bottle so a stream of the wine eased into the glass. "It must be allowed to breathe as you pour it. To maximize the flavor, you see?"

The bartender was a young local man, just out of school unless Matt missed his guess. His hair was so blond it was almost white, except at the roots where it was darker, closer to Matt's own color. As Vincenzo spoke, he bobbed his head up and down. He looked a little embarrassed.

"And that way it doesn't spill," he said.

Vincenzo set the goblet down with a strong shake of his head. "It's not about the spill." His index finger raised toward the nearly-cloudless sky overhead. "It's about the presentation. The artistry of it." He looked down at label on the bottle he was holding and got an almost wistful expression on his face. "We are here to accentuate the experience. To help our guests soak up life! And then soak it up more ourselves."

He handed the bottle back to the young bartender, who now also looked confused.

Vincenzo saw his expression and chuckled softly. "Don't mind an old man, Kieran. You're doing a fine job. Just a few things here and there, for improvement, you see?"

Kieran nodded, looking a little less embarrassed, at least. Then he saw Matt and perked up. "Good afternoon, sir. Can I get you something?"

"Actually, I need to speak with Vincenzo."

Vincenzo looked at him curiously, and Matt continued.

"You probably don't remember me. I'm Matt Gilbert. We talked over email—"

The light came on in Vincenzo's eyes and he bobbed his head up and down. "Of course, of course. Isaiah's and Maleen's friend. I remember." His hand engulfed Matt's, and it seemed his eyes twinkled from more than just the sunshine overhead. "And now you want to bring me more business from your ship!"

Matt nodded. "I need to brief the Captain this week on venue, so I was hoping we can work out the details this afternoon."

Vincenzo nodded again, and looked past Matt's shoulder. "I have a few things to see to right this moment, Matt. Why don't you and your lady friend get a table, and I'll join you in a couple minutes to discuss it."

Matt followed Vincenzo's gaze back toward where Marta and Roger were continuing their conversation. "How did you know we are together?"

Vincenzo laughed, and gave Matt a little nudge with his elbow. "An old man has eyes," he said.

Matt had no real response to that, so he just chuckled and nodded. He took a step away, toward Marta, then stopped as a thought occurred to him. He looked back at Vincenzo.

"You're going to join us, to discuss it."

Vincenzo nodded.

"Vincenzo, I know your rule about joining guests."

He nodded again, and Matt laughed for real this time.

"One of these days you're going to let me actually *pay* for a meal here, aren't you?"

Vincenzo grinned broadly. "My friend, soon your ship will be paying for forty meals! I think that will make us even."

Matt was still shaking his head in amusement when he returned to Marta's side.

Roger was just finishing up a joke, apparently, because they were both laughing, though Marta a bit less boisterously than he was.

She laid her hand on Matt's shoulder. "Your business complete? Was fast."

Matt shook his head. "Vincenzo's dealing with some things. Let's get a table; he said he'll come join us later."

Marta's eyebrows rose, but she didn't reply. Instead she looked back at Roger and smiled. "Great t' meet you, Roger. Enjoy your stay on New Cali."

"I'm sure I will," Roger said, and made a little almost half-bow to her. His eyes flicked Matt's way as he returned to his full height, and Matt practically heard him say, "but not as much as if this guy wasn't here," without saying it.

Oh well.

Matt shook hands with him again, then he and Marta went over to the hostess stand. A few moments later they were seated in the back patio beneath the semi-shade provided by the pergola, and Matt ordered a Riesling to get things started.

As their waitress, a local woman who was probably approaching thirty and who wore the hair style of a married lady, headed off to see Kieran, Matt said, "Everything went well with your brother and father?"

Marta leaned back in her seat and took a sip from her glass, and shrugged. "Good as can be expected." Her face darkened a bit. "Jafi had...a run-in...with th' police."

Matt blinked, surprised. He hadn't pressed the matter, but he also hadn't thought it was something along those lines. "Is he..." He stopped, unsure how to ask the question. "Is it serious?" he finally said, feeling, and sounding, lame as he did.

"Don't think so. His friend decided t' joyride in his father's car, and Jafi came along." Marta winced. "No real worry, but he skidded and hit a street lamp pole. Car wreaked, and the lamp..." She shook her head. "Fair amount of damage."

Matt winced as well. "I imagine his father was not pleased."

"T' say the least. He decided t' not bail out his son. We paid for Jafi, but Hubert not getting out til he sees the judge tomorrow."

"What sort of sentence does a thing like that get around here?"

Marta made a so-so kind of wave with her left hand. "If no damage, just pulled over and caught, not much. But with this... They going to have to pay for repairs, probably do some more service." She sniffed. "Not likely jail though."

"Still sucks."

She nodded agreement. Her face remained dark for a second, then she gave a little shake and focused in on Matt. "So. Tell me about your first time in space."

"Not my *first* time."

Marta rolled her eyes at him. "You know what I mean. Was good?"

"Not too bad," he said. He proceeded to give her the rundown of the underway, its ups and downs, and what happened. He even mentioned the emails from Tom and Katerina. Her eyes narrowed as he finished up, and he got the idea he had just made a mistake.

"This Katerina. She the one you mentioned before, that you broke up with?"

"Yeah."

Marta nodded, her face unreadable. "That why you not friendly with Roger."

"Come again? I wasn't unfriendly."

She gave him a level look that said he was full of it. "You worried I gonna go off with him, like your last girl?"

"Wha— I'm not sure what you mean. I mean, he was obviously trying to make a move, but—"

She laughed then, not entirely a humorous laugh. "You *are* jealous!"

Matt realized he was spluttering a bit. He hadn't seen this turn of the conversation coming, and wasn't entirely sure how to dig himself out of the hole he seemed to be standing in.

She saved him by reaching across the table and giving his hand a squeeze. "S'ok. A little bit jealous is cute." The squeeze increased in pressure, and for a moment he felt the increased strength New California's gravity well gave her. "But not too much."

"Cute? Puppy dogs are cute. Men are supposed to be handsome."

Marta laughed for real this time and waggled her eyebrows at him, and he felt the tension that had flared up so suddenly fade away.

Their waitress picked that moment to return with Matt's glass of Riesling, and he welcomed the semi-sweet flavor, and its coolness, as he took a drink.

The waitress was turning to leave when Vincenzo walked up. He made a little whirling motion with his fingertip, containing Matt, Marta, and their table within it. Then he pointed at himself.

The waitress nodded, and Vincenzo grinned. He turned back to Matt.

"Matt, my friend, may I join you and your young lady?"

Matt gestured toward one of the empty chairs at their table; it had been set for four. "Of course. Have you met Marta?"

"I am sorry to say I have not had the pleasure." He took her hand as though to shake, but instead bowed slightly as he raised it so that he almost was kissing the back of her hand. "Enchanted, my dear."

Was Marta actually flushing a little? Matt wasn't sure; she was well-tanned so it was hard to tell. She did giggle, though.

Vincenzo settled down in the empty chair closer to Matt and spread his hands expansively. "Now, my friends, let us enjoy today's special." He grinned Matt's way. "And you and I can settle business for your ship, eh?"

"Sounds good."

Matt wasn't sure what the day's special was, but it didn't really matter. It was bound to be great.

And it was.

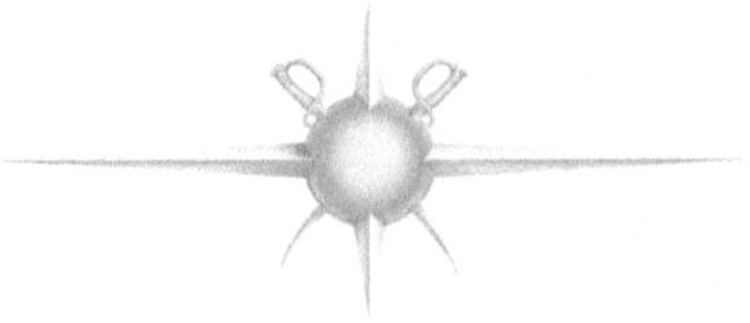

Chapter Forty

Matt wasn't sure what to expect from Security Response Force training, but he definitely didn't expect to be drenched with sweat by the end of it.

He'd done plenty of running in the past. Carried a rifle a number of times, and worn protective ballistic armor. But he'd never actually worn the armor, carried a rifle, and had to run through simulated passageways on a ship, ducking from cover to cover and taking and returning simulated fire, before.

If he wanted to do that, he would have joined the Marines.

But a ship had to be able to handle security breaches, and repel borders. So the crew had to train on the basics, at least.

But man, it was rough. Fun, but rough.

Good thing they only had to re-certify on an annual basis, not once a quarter.

His section had training on Tuesday and then duty on Wednesday, so he took it easy Tuesday night, just came home, showered, and cracked open a spy novel for the first time in several weeks.

Duty on Wednesday, then he had his meeting with the CO for those two checkouts on Thursday. He spent the duty day studying up, in between hanging tags and opening WAFs, while his Over-Instruction just sat back.

It was like that on watch, and during duty days, now. He was just about qualified, and was used to the routine of the watch and the duty day, knew the systems and procedures, so he ended up doing most of the work, with his O/I just countersigning for him.

It made Matt all the more eager to have it done with. He knew what he was doing, so just let him do it already!

The checkouts with the CO only helped reassure him of that. The CO didn't quiz him so much as talk through the philosophy behind the Battleshort and Emergency Core Ejection procedures, and some of the nuances behind them that weren't immediately obvious from just reading the procedures through on their own.

When he left, two command-level signatures on his qual card, Matt felt primed to go for his board.

But first, there was the EOOW exam the next week.

He only *thought* the BEQ exam was a ball-buster. The EOOW exam about made his head explode, from the details it expected him to go into on some of the most obscure procedures in the reactor plant manual, procedures that were done infrequently enough that he didn't see why they needed to be memorized. In fact, engineering watch standers were not *supposed* to memorize the procedures at all, but refer to the book each time they performed even the simplest of them.

So why in the hell did the qualification exam expect him to have the procedures memorized when it was against procedure for him to do so?

And it was all the worse because, since he had VBSS training all day, every day, at the TACTRACOM Detachment facility, he had to take the exam in the evening with the duty section's training coordinator, even though the exam was scheduled on a day when he didn't have duty.

Harry's words from his first couple weeks aboard rang in his ears as he finally turned in the exam and left, exhausted and frustrated, for the lift down to the surface, home, and bed.

"Marathon, not sprint. Don't spend more time at work than you have to."

Damn, but the truth of that was sinking in hard.

So the rest of the week, when he wasn't on duty, he pushed hard to get home early. Fortunately, Marta's schedule was light that week, so he spent a bunch of time with her, exploring the area around his still—relatively—new home.

He got a little surprise on Tuesday of the final week—CSO sent him to Tracking Team training at the training detachment's simulator.

"If you're not ready for your EOOW board by now, there's not much for it," CSO said. "Time to brush the dust off before you start working on your tactical quals."

Matt thought CHENG would object, but no. He just nodded agreement, and Matt went.

It was almost like being in Tactical School again. Almost. The biggest difference was he didn't man a station like he had back then. That was the enlisted crew's job; he had learned all the stations back in school, but it was the officer's job to evaluate the data the stations presented, cross-check it, and make tactical decisions based on it.

So he got to play understudy to the TAO during the simulator session.

Way cool.

But it also meant he didn't have time to cram for his qual board during the day. As he left the TACTRACOM Det offices in the Naval Station, he heard Harry's voice in his head, telling him to go home, grab Marta, and go dancing at that place they'd found last week with the great band and the nice dance floor.

Sounded great, except he knew he'd just be distracted by thoughts of his board in a day and a half. So instead, he went back to the ship for some last minute studying.

He probably would have just stayed the night on Wednesday doing the same, so it was just as well he had duty again. There wasn't much duty work; the vast majority of the post-testing repairs were complete, with only a couple WAFs still open, and they didn't need him to do anything. So the day was almost just a normal work day, plus his required tour through the plant every six hours and having to stay late—and the evening call to the CO to give him the standard 2000 report on ship's status.

So he spent most of the day in Maneuvering, having the watch standers and his O/I quiz him.

When he finally hit the rack Wednesday after completing his midnight tour through the engineering spaces, he wasn't sure if he was ready for his board the next day or not. But there was not much else he could do, was there?

Despite the fatigue of a late night, he tossed and turned—as much as he could in his narrow stateroom bunk—as system schematics, procedural steps, and the errors he'd made on the BEQ and EOOW exams kept streaming through his mind. At some point, he drifted off into real sleep, but when reveille sounded over the 1MC at 0500, he felt like he hadn't slept at all. His mouth was dry, and sour-tasting, his eyes gravelly, and it was all he could do to force himself up onto his feet.

But there was no time to gripe. He had to do the 0600 tour of the spaces and then get ready for duty section turnover, so he splashed some water on his face, brushed his teeth, and was thankful for the high-and-tight that eliminated the need to brush his hair. Then he donned his uniform, hit the head, and headed aft to the MMR.

The morning was a blur. Duty section turnover followed by quarters and then divisional training—he couldn't remember the subject matter twenty minutes after they broke from it, though he thought it had gone well—and then it was almost 1000.

And his board was at 1230, right after lunch.

His stomach clenched as he considered how little time remained. The moment of truth approached.

He was sitting at his desk in his stateroom when the hour of lunch chimed over the 1MC—three two-stroke bells that sounded like they were made of real brass, though of course they were just a recording—and for a moment he considered not eating.

But he'd skipped breakfast and his stomach growled in protest, so he forced himself to close out his terminal, and the RPM procedure he had been reviewing, and go to the wardroom.

It was almost completely full when he stepped in, and they were all seated. The CO looked over as Matt closed the door behind him and raised an eyebrow.

"Permission to join you late, Captain?" Matt said.

For a second, he thought the CO might say no. He normally didn't, of course. The requesting of permission to join the mess late was more tradition and protocol than a real threat of not being allowed a seat. But on-edge as Matt was feeling, he wouldn't be surprised if—

"Take a seat, Matt," the CO said, and that weird tension flowed out of him.

Feeling a bit of a fool, Matt hurried over to the salad bar/coffee mess and filled a bowl of greens, topped with bacon, of course.

There was an empty seat between Rasheid and Terry, across from WEPS. As Matt sat down, WEPS gave him a wry look.

"Almost time for your board, right?" he said, and Matt nodded. WEPS chuckled. "Nerves set in yet?"

"About three days ago," Matt said, and chomped down a mouthful of his salad.

WEPS chuckled again, and Rasheid grinned.

"Don't worry, Matt," Rasheid said. "I'm sure it'll go fine." He paused, then looked sidelong at him, his expression turning serious. "You've got the gummies though, right?"

Matt blinked. "Gummies?"

Rasheid groaned, and stared hard down toward the end of the table, where Ivan was sitting next to Gamal. "Bull!"

Ivan stopped what he was saying, and zeroed in on Rasheid, a question on his face.

"You didn't brief Matt on proper qual board etiquette?"

Ivan blinked, then spread his hands with a, "What are you looking at me for?" sort of expression as he shook his head.

"Oboy." Rasheid scowled Ivan's way, then leaned in toward Matt. "It's tradition. When you go to a qual board, you bring candy for the board members." He nudged Matt lightly with his elbow. "Soften them up, you know? Captain's a sucker for gummy bears."

The sinking feeling returned, and intensified to the point of near despair. That sense of impending doom that he had been trying to ward off the last couple days crouched and leaped onto him, and he felt his blood go to ice.

Across from the two of them, WEPS was looking at Matt with pity. It didn't help.

"What does CHENG and XO like?"

"Chocolate for CHENG. XO likes licorice."

Matt glanced at the chronometer on the wardroom wall. 1110. Just an hour and twenty minutes. No way he could get the required items in time. Unless the ship's store had some?

Wait. He recalled there being a little convenience kiosk over by the airdock that HALSWELL had occupied when he first checked aboard. It had a well-stocked snack aisle.

He ran the distance in his head and did some quick math. If he hurried he could get there and back in a half hour, maybe forty-five minutes.

Matt stood, scooting his chair back from the table abruptly enough that it made a loud scraping sound against the deck tiling.

Several eyes turned his way, but Matt ignored them. He turned to the CO.

"Excuse me, please, Captain."

The CO raised his eyebrows at Matt again, and Matt could see the question in his eyes. But he just nodded.

Matt hurried out of the wardroom, then off the ship.

There was no time to lose.

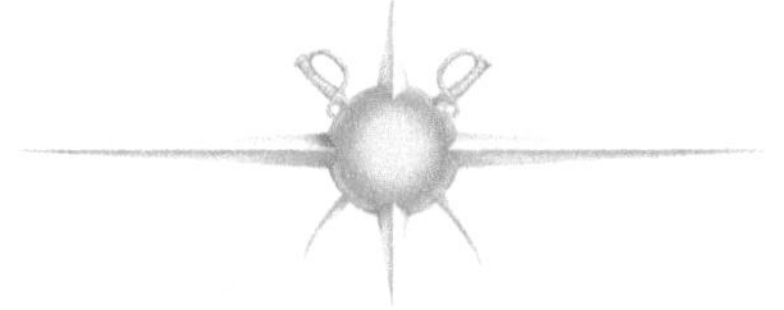

Chapter Forty-One

It was 1220 when Matt finally crossed over the airlock seal onto the quarterdeck of ICS FREDERICK HALSWELL, and he was gasping from exertion. He felt sweat running down the back of his underway coveralls, and he thought sure his armpits had stains.

But dammit, he got that candy!

Jerry Despirito, the Electronic Warfare Officer, was the Officer of the Deck, and Matt recognized Petty Officer Gonzalez manning the welcoming podium.

Jerry was a second-tour JO in Combat Systems department, so Matt knew him, but not nearly as well as the younger guys in Engineering. He was sandy-haired but had dark, almost black eyes, and a tan that could match Jorge's. But that might be because he lived down on the surface, right on the beach, and spent almost every waking off-duty moment on a surfboard on the outside of Ventura Bay.

So his hair got bleached and his skin got dark, so who knew where his heritage came from. Not even him. Matt had asked; from his name he figured Jerry was from one of the Spanish-derived nations of old Terra. But Jerry just shrugged. He had been adopted as a baby in a closed adoption, so he had no idea who his birth parents were, or where they came from.

That left Matt at a loss for words. He had never met someone from that situation, and he wondered whether Jerry wanted to try to find out.

He didn't ask, though. Not his business, and anyway they hadn't spent all that much time together to make it less than two-thousand degrees of awkward to bring up.

Jerry looked him up and down as Matt finished saluting the colors and stepped down into the quarterdeck, a perplexed, and amused, expression on his face.

"You're supposed to put on PT gear before you work out, you know," Jerry said, and Gonzalez snorted out a laugh that he quickly stifled.

But he couldn't suppress the comedic expression on his face. He clearly thought Matt looked even more funny than Jerry did.

"Last minute board preps," Matt said, then he darted through the hatch into the fore and aft passageway beyond.

He popped into Crews Mess and grabbed up three bowls from the stack waiting on the end of the serving line, then stuffed them into the plastic bag containing the required candy, which the kiosk had *not* carried or he wouldn't have had to run to make it back here, and hurried down to Classroom #3, the Engineering classroom.

CHENG was waiting in the passageway as Matt approached, a displeased look on his face. He looked Matt up and down with decidedly less amusement than Jerry had.

"Where have you been?" His brow furrowed and his lips turned decidedly downwards. "It's not good form to be late for your board, Matt."

The pulsing of his blood was throbbing in his ears like a pair of bass drums—Matt's heart rate was still at high cardio levels—but he forced himself not to breath heavily as he shook his head.

"Not late, sir. It starts in three minutes."

CHENG's lips compressed for a couple seconds, then he nodded. "Wait here," he said, then he opened up the classroom door and stepped inside.

Matt sagged against the bulkhead beside the door, willing himself to get his breathing down to a normal level, and for his heart rate to follow.

Enlisted crew members passed by constantly, every one of them eying him weirdly, or so it seemed. Until EM1 Brossard exited the Engineering office, heading forward. He stopped when he saw Matt.

If he noticed Matt's disheveled condition, he didn't say anything. He just reached out and clapped Matt lightly on the shoulder.

"Good luck, Mr. G," Brossard said. "Crush it!"

Then he continued walking forward, turning left at the athwartships passageway and passing out of sight.

It felt like an hour before the classroom door opened again and CHENG poked his head out.

"Come on in, Mr. Gilbert," he said.

He held the door open while Matt entered, then closed it behind them.

The classroom was as it always had been, except the CO and XO were seated in two of the desks in the front row, and all the rest were empty. CHENG moved to take a seat at a third desk, and Matt made his way slowly toward the front of the room.

His breathing was slower, but he could still hear his pulse pounding in his ears; just a bit lower in volume is all.

He got to the front, next to the briefing board built into the front bulkhead. It was switched on, and a free writing/drawing application was called up. Matt saw a writing stylus on a magnetic holder on the bulkhead next to the board, for his use.

He turned to face the CO, sitting between the other two, and found him giving Matt a strange sort of probing look.

"Well, Mr. Gilbert, you know why you're here. Are you ready to go?"

Matt nodded. "One moment, sir."

He reached into the plastic bag and pulled out the bowls, and placed one down on each of the men's desks. Then he put the bag down on the floor and bent over to pick out the candies.

The chocolate was first to hand, so it looked like CHENG was going to get his first.

Matt was beginning to tear open the bag of chocolate squares as he straightened, but paused when he saw the three of them looking at him with quizzical expressions on their faces.

"Matt," CHENG said. "What are you doing?"

"Candy," Matt said, holding out the chocolate bag so CHENG could see its label more clearly. "For the board members."

"Why?"

What did he mean, "Why?"

Matt looked at him, bafflement making him lose his train of thought completely for a second. He swallowed. "Well... They said..."

XO rolled his eyes to the ceiling and began shaking his head. His cheeks were flushing and he looked, if anything, highly amused.

The CO, though, frowned. "I think someone's been messing with you, Ensign."

"What?"

"Is that why you left lunch so quickly?"

Matt nodded, his cheeks flushing with embarrassment now, more than his earlier exertion. "They said it was a tradition to..." He held up the chocolate bag again and shrugged. "I didn't have anything, so I ran out to get some real quick and..." He scowled, looking at the classroom door, firmly shut. "It's really not a thing?"

XO shook his head. So did CHENG.

"Son of a bitch!" Matt said, anger now competing with embarrassment within him.

He was going to strangle Rasheid next time he saw him.

"You've been literally running all over the station..." The CO did not look pleased, but Matt thought he saw a bit of humor threatening to crack through there. Was his lip turning upward ever so slightly?

He blew out a breath and turned to look at the CHENG. "CHENG, he's obviously flustered, and half soaked with sweat. Let's reschedule for—"

"No, sir!" Matt said, and the CO looked back at him.

Matt cleared his throat and stuffed the chocolate back into the plastic bag at his feet. "I mean, we're here now, and I'm ready. I'd prefer to proceed."

"Are you sure?"

Matt bobbed his head, and the CO nodded in return.

"Very well. Put this stuff away," he gestured toward the bowls, and the candy bag.

Matt moved quickly to comply, and a moment later the bag of pranks that Rasheid played was off against the side bulkhead. He came back to stand before the board at parade rest, waiting.

The CO just looked at him for a moment, then turned to CHENG. "CHENG?"

CHENG nodded. "Mr. Gilbert, please draw a schematic of the fusion chamber, including all fluid inlets and outlets, and all electrical connections."

"Yes, sir," Matt said.

Anger at Rasheid still burning within him, he snatched up the stylus and began to write.

Two and a half hours later, Matt walked into the wardroom. The main table was empty, but four men were sitting at the kiddie table in the coffee mess alcove: Charlie, Vasili, Gideon...and Rasheid.

Matt zeroed in on Rasheid, and he stalked over toward the little group.

Gideon was sitting next to him, and saw Matt coming. He nudged Rasheid with his elbow, and Rasheid turned to look.

He saw Matt immediately, and broke out in a great big grin. "Hey Matt! How'd it go?"

"You asshole!" Matt said.

All four of them broke out in laughter.

Good-natured laughter, not the malicious kind. That took some of the wind out of the sails of Matt's anger. But only some of it.

"I spent more than an hour hunting around for this damn candy," he said, holding up the bag of goodies for them to see. "And I had to sprint back to the ship to make it back in time. I almost didn't!"

Rasheid was still grinning broadly. He nodded. "Yeah, but you weren't tearing your hair out worrying, were you?"

"What? Yes I was! I—" But he stopped, as the memory of his wild dash through the station came back to him.

He had been anxious to get the candy, but he hadn't thought for even a second about what he was sure he had forgotten, or what he didn't know, or what questions they were going to ask, and what if he screwed up, and...

He had only been thinking about the need to find that damn candy, and fast.

He could tell Rasheid saw the realization come over him that

Rasheid had been right: his stupid prank had stopped Matt from driving himself nuts with worry. And his grin increased.

"So," Rasheid said again, "how'd it go?"

"I've got a bunch of look-ups to give CHENG, but I passed."

It was only as he said it that it really sank in. He had passed! He was qualified!

Or would be, once he finished the look-ups. But that was almost a non-event. He was qualified!

Anger at Rasheid's prank fled completely as that realization filled him, and he grinned ear to ear.

"Outstanding!" said Vasili, and he rose from the kiddie table.

The others did as well, and they took turns shaking hands, patting him on the back, and generally congratulating him.

To hell with being angry; he didn't even want to be anymore. It was time to celebrate.

And as he looked down at the bag in his hand, he realized they had just what they needed to kick the celebration off, right now.

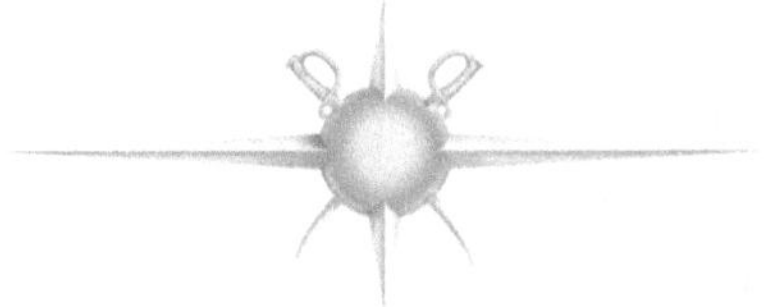

Chapter Forty-Two

Marta looked good. Real, real good.

As this was a special wardroom event, the CO directed semi-formal attire. So Matt had fished his one suit from the back of his closet and had it cleaned and pressed, and buffed his dress shoes until they shined.

His suit was charcoal grey with barely-perceptible blue pinstripes, his shirt white, and his tie the same shade as the pinstripes. When he got to her place to pick her up, the sun was still visible above the hills on the west side of Ventura Bay, so he had his shades on, and was feeling slick.

But when she opened the door and stepped out, he could only gape for a moment.

Her evening gown was a deep red, offsetting the highlights in her hair, with a single strap over her right shoulder and a slit in the left side so that her toned leg was just visible. A glimpse and a suggestion, riding the line between seductive and modest.

"You gonna catch flies," she said with a wry smile as she closed the door behind herself, and Matt forced his jaw shut.

He hadn't realized it had dropped open, he had been gawking so hard.

"You look great," he said, and her smile warmed.

"You as well," Marta said, and leaned in for a quick kiss, her lips brushing his cheek and then his lips in the flash of a moment that sent a little jolt through his body.

He took her hand, and they walked down to the car he had hired for the evening. It wasn't anything fancy, but the driver was dressed to the nines and he held the rear passenger door open for her with all the dignity of a seasoned chauffeur, despite him being just about Matt's age.

That seemed to please her, so he chalked it up as a win.

After she settled herself in, and as he closed the door, the driver looked at Matt with a, "Man you struck it rich," sort of expression, for a second.

Matt grinned at him, then got into the car on the other side.

Make that two wins.

Fifteen minutes later, they walked into La Trattoria and found a different, but just as attractive and friendly, woman working the hostess stand. She immediately recognized Matt and gestured toward the rear patio, which was roped off with burgundy-colored felt lines strung between brass stands. A single opening in the barrier, at its center, offered ingress to the patio, and Matt saw Vincenzo waiting there. He was also in a suit, though his was black, his tie a deep red, almost the same shade as the felt lines.

"All is ready, Mr. Gilbert," the hostess said, with a polite, professional nod.

"Thank you," Matt said, and he led Marta back to where Vincenzo waited.

After a pace or so, she leaned in and nudged him. "*Mister* Gilbert," she said, teasingly. "You coming up in th' world."

"About time you noticed."

She laughed, and they proceeded on to meet Vincenzo.

"Good evening, Matt," Vincenzo said as they reached him. It looked like he had taken a little extra time with his hair brush, and had he oiled his mustache? It was...more put together...somehow than the other times Matt had seen him.

"Nice to see you again," Matt said, and they shook hands. "Do you need anything from me?"

Vincenzo shook his head. "Everything is ready," he said. He seemed to puff up a bit as he added, "And I personally spent the afternoon with the chef making sure the sauce is perfect."

Matt found his mouth watering in anticipation at that. Everything Vincenzo's kitchen put out was great, but if he'd gone to extra lengths for this night's special...he could hardly wait.

He checked his watch. "Everyone should start arriving in the next ten or fifteen minutes," he said, and Vincenzo nodded, gesturing back to the patio bar.

"I've picked out a few special wines as well. Kieran will take care of you."

Matt recognized Kieran as the young bartender who had been on duty the other day. He was dressed up as well, though the way he was adjusting his tie shouted that he wasn't at all used to that sort of attire.

"Thanks, Vincenzo," Matt said, and he led Marta to the bar.

The wine was excellent, smooth and flavorful, and Kieran served it without spilling a drop this time, replicating, with aplomb, the technique Vincenzo had demonstrated.

Matt reminded himself to leave him a nice tip when the evening was over.

True to the schedule, the wardroom began filtering in. Though Matt would have expected the single JOs to be the early arrivals—no wives to wait on getting ready—CSO was actually the first.

He was in a dark green suit with a pale yellow tie, matching nicely with his wife's evening gown, which was a similar shade of creamy yellow, with a green sash at her waist. She was in her mid-30s, blond and slender, like she had been a dancer in her youth, and wore her hair in the local style, grown long on the left side. She had striking eyes, nearly as darkly green as her sash, and CSO's suit.

They came over to where Matt and Marta were nursing their drinks, and CSO crushed Matt's hand in a shake.

"You've met Stacy, of course," he said, gesturing to his wife.

Matt nodded and shook Stacy's hand, then introduced Marta.

"Cameron Kaminsky," CSO said, taking her hand in an obviously more gentle way than he had for Matt. He smiled mischievously. "How did this joker con you into being seen in public with him?" He gave Matt a wink as he said that, and Matt rolled his eyes.

Marta laughed softly, and gave Matt a sidelong look. "He promised good beer."

Stacy gestured toward Marta's wine glass and raised an eyebrow.

Marta nodded, turning accusing eyes on Matt. "I know. Quite upsetting," in a cold, accusing tone. It set him back for a second, then she broke and winked, the corners of her lips turning upward into a teasing grin.

CSO laughed.

The others arrived over the course of the next twenty minutes or so, congregating around the bar like it was the center of their own little gravity well.

Matt was just laughing at a joke that Charlie had told, when he noticed the CO and Cindy approaching the rope barrier. He slipped away from the JO group and headed over to where Vincenzo and he were shaking hands.

"Evening, Captain," he said, then smiled at Cindy. "Nice to see you, Cindy." Returning his attention to the CO, he added, "We're all here, sir."

The CO nodded, eyes sweeping the gathered officers, and their better halves. Matt could almost see him doing a mental roll call.

Finally, he said, "I'd say that calls for a drink," with a cheerful smile.

He led Cindy over to the bar, and once Kieran had set them up, Matt nodded at Vincenzo. Time to get things rolling.

The restaurateur cleared his throat loudly, and the murmur of conversation faded, all eyes turning toward him.

Vincenzo puffed out his chest a bit. "Ladies. Gentlemen. Welcome to La Trattoria, and thank you for choosing my humble establishment for your special evening." He swept his hand around the patio as he said that, indicating the tables that were laid out, awaiting occupants. "When you are ready, please take whatever seat you wish, and my people will see to your every need."

Someone off to the left said, laughter in his voice, "That's a dangerous promise to make, Vincenzo!"

Vincenzo laughed, and spread his hands in commiseration. "Everything within reason, I should say?" A ripple of chuckles swept through the officers, and a few of the women as well. "Enjoy your evening," Vincenzo said, by way of closure.

As if his words had unlocked a barrier between the bar and the waiting tables, people began selecting seats, and in just a few moments all were settled in.

Matt and Marta were at a table for eight. Charlie and his date sat to their right. She was a raven-haired girl named April, with slightly angular eyes that hinted at a bit of Han—or maybe Japanese?—heritage back in her family's history. Dan Flemming and his wife Rose, darker than someone from Carraway's World and striking in a crimson gown that showed off her curves extremely well, was across from them. And Gideon Schulz was to their left, with his fiancée, Yasmine. She had the look of a local, tall and bronzed, with well-toned muscles, and like Rose she wore her hair in the local style. But she was actually from the tropical region of Icarus, much to Marta's surprise when they were chatting to get acquainted.

Dinner exceeded Matt's expectations. It was a run of six courses. First a salad of greens topped with thinly-sliced cucumbers and peppers, and grumbled nuts and cranberries, with a vinaigrette that echoed and drew out the berries's flavor. Then came a creamy soup that had a just a hint of fire to it, followed by kebobs with chicken, beef, peppers, and onions drenched in a semi-sweet glaze. Then thick fettuccine noodles under the sauce that Vincenzo had been working on. Matt thought it was beef-based, but it was also tomato-ey, and it had peppers and meat and...whatever it was and however Vincenzo had done it, it was amazing.

Finally came cheesecake topped with strawberries with a strawberry cream sauce, and Matt thought he had died and gone to heaven.

They were...reluctantly...finishing up the cheesecake when the sound of a knife tapping on glass turned Matt's attention to the left, toward the CO's table. He had been sitting with XO, CHENG, CSO, and their wives, but now he was standing, his wine goblet in hand.

"Ladies. Gentlemen. I figured I should say something before things get too out of hand."

"Perish the thought, skipper!" said Gamal, two tables over from Matt.

The CO grinned. "I know. You are a well-behaved bunch." Chuckles from several people in the group made the CO pause for a moment. He continued, "I just wanted to say how pleased I am at the great work you've done these last few months. We had a lot of challenges to overcome, and you met them and, frankly, exceeded my expectations."

He paused, then added, "And the Commodore's too. He asked me to pass that along."

He took a moment to take a sip on his wine. "We're about to change gears completely though. It's going to be a lot of fun, but like the XO says all the time," he pointed his index finger at XO and grinned, and Matt could plainly see the teasing in that grin, "it's a change from what we have been doing. A big change. And not just for us, but for the ladies who are gracious enough to accompany us.

"We get underway on Monday and won't be back for several months. That's going to be tough on all of us, both on the ship and at home. Which is why we're here tonight." He grinned again. "Mandatory fun to take the edge off before we pick up the load on Monday. And also, it's a thank you, to you ladies who manage the home front while we're away."

The CO raised his glass. "We couldn't do it without you. Gentlemen, to the ladies."

The officers all stood, and raised their glasses. "To the ladies."

Matt sipped from his glass—it was a bit low for a lot of toasts—and sat. He took Marta's hand and squeezed it, and she returned the squeeze. But her smile was a bit restrained; he could see a darkness in her eyes.

He leaned closer. "What's—"

But the CO was speaking again. "And speaking of picking up the load. We have another reason to celebrate tonight. Far less pressing, but I can't ignore the fact that on Monday, Ivan is going to conn us away from the station for his first time as a qualified Officer of the Deck."

A couple of "Woot"s and "Oorah!"s rang out from the gathered men.

"But more amazing than that," the CO continued, "Matt is going to start up the reactor Monday morning for the first time as a qualified EOOW."

Charlie, sitting right next to him, gave Matt a light punch in the arm. "Hell yeah," he said, grinning.

From another table, Matt heard Ari Renquist's voice. "No more NUBs onboard!"

The CO half-smiled, half-winced, and shook his head. "That's right. No more NUBs." He sighed, then grinned more genuinely. He raised his glass again. "To the qualified Ensigns!"

Everyone else stood, and Matt was about to, but Charlie waved him back to his seat. "The toastee doesn't toast himself, dummy," he said quickly, before the "To the qualified Ensigns!" from the rest of the wardroom could drown out his words.

"Finally," the CO said, "I think we would be remiss if we didn't take a minute to thank Vincenzo and his staff." He turned to look at Vincenzo, who was now posted with Kieran at the bar. "I'd heard of La Trattoria. But I don't come to Ventura very often, so I never got to see if you lived up to the hype, until now. I have to say, your reputation understates the reality. To La Trattoria, with our thanks."

All the guys stood. It took a bit of beckoning for some of the ladies to as well, but after a minute, all turned and raised their glasses Vincenzo's way. He beamed a smile back at them, clasping his hands over his heart and making a small bow.

After everyone had settled back into their seats, the CO said, "Any toasts from the floor? Remember, this isn't a dining in, so keep them relatively printable."

Several of the the guys, and a few of the ladies, stood to offer toasts: to the Prime Minister, to the Navy, to their dog... It went on for a bit. But finally, after silence lingered, following a toast to the best football team in the Confederation—the Icaran Warriors, and that got some boos in protest—the CO stood again, and called an end to it. He reminded them not to get into too much trouble the rest of the night, and bid them a good rest of the weekend.

Charlie leaned back in his chair and eyed the others at the table. "I heard about a great little dance club at the other end of the beach. We were planning to go check it out. You guys up for it?"

Marta pursed her lips. "You mean TJs?"

Charlie nodded, and she winced, then shook her head emphatically.

"You not want t' go there," she said. "They overcharge off-worlders and water down th' drinks." Matt felt her fingers run over his. "We know a much better place: Melody Mavens, up the hill on the west side of the bay. Better view, better music, better company."

Charlie frowned as he considered that for a second, then he shrugged. "You say so." His grin returned. "I'm up for it. Let's go!"

Dan and Rose opted out, but Gideon and Yasmine decided to come.

Charlie stood up to spread the word to the other tables, and three other couples agreed to meet up there.

A few minutes later, Matt and Marta were in the back of his hired car. He looked over at her, and she had a little smile on her face as she looked out the car window, toward the passing buildings of Ventura. But he thought he saw that sadness he'd seen earlier again.

He reached out to touch her shoulder. "What's wrong? You've been a little sad the last little while."

She gave a little jerk, like she hadn't expected the touch, but just as quickly looked back at him. Her hand closed over his, and though the smile remained, the sadness in her eyes deepened.

"You told me you be leaving for a while, but it hadn't hit me until tonight. Gonna miss you."

"It's not going to be easy for me either."

She let out a little laugh that sounded half joking, but also half bitter. "You probably meet some girl in a port somewhere, and forget all about me."

Matt snorted. "Even if I wanted to, there won't be time. We'll maybe be stopping on Olifant for a couple days, but we'll be underway pretty much the whole time I'm gone."

She raised her eyebrows. "Then maybe a shipboard romance."

He snorted even louder, shaking his head emphatically. "Gross. You know better than that."

She laughed for real this time, and he slid a bit closer.

"The time will pass before you know it. But for now, let's enjoy the night, and Isaiah and Maleen's cookout on Sunday. Make some memories to carry us through."

"That sounds good."

The car pulled to a halt in front of Melody Mavens a few minutes later, and Matt led her inside to dance the night away.

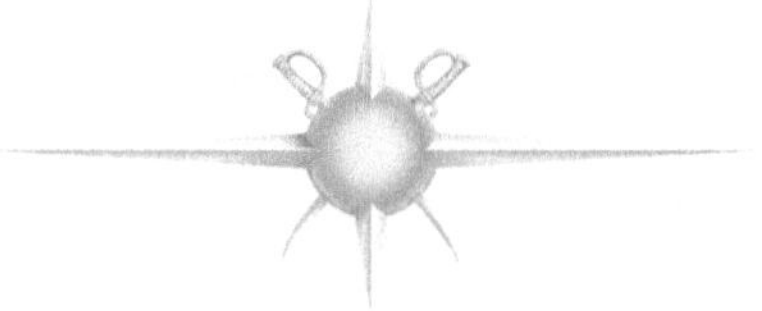

Chapter Forty-Three

Though the HALSWELL's VBSS team had done training for a full week while they were in port, Matt hadn't seen Eric Caldwell at all. The training had been in the classroom for the first day and then in the simulator spaces the remaining days, but conducted by senior enlisted, not the Lieutenant.

But when Matt entered HALSWELL's wardroom for lunch after completing his first watch as a qualified EOOW, he saw Eric waiting at the table, along with Zach Cornwell. Ivan was there as well, coming off OOD from the morning watch, and Terry. But that was it for lunch's second sitting.

Eric saw Matt enter and waved him over, and after getting his usual bacon-topped salad, Matt went to join him and Zach, away from the others.

"I was wondering if you were going to be getting underway with us," he said, as he picked a spot across the table from Eric.

Eric grinned. "Don't worry, I hadn't forgotten about you. There's lots to do before Commander Tolburt's assessment next week, so we'll be keeping busy."

Matt looked from Eric to Zach. "I guess I didn't realize there was an assessment?"

Zach chuckled. "This whole underway is for re-certifications, bro.

After the Control Tower and CIC controllers get checked out this week, it's us next week. Tolburt's coming aboard on the BSP next Thursday, to evaluate us on Friday."

Matt blinked. He had seen the Brief Stop for Personnel on the schedule for next week, but he hadn't put that together with anything the VBSS team was doing.

"Ok... So how does this work?"

Eric waved off the concern that Matt felt certain was showing on his face. "Just like you saw at the school. We'll—" He cut off as CS1 Davidson approached. He had the steward duty for lunch again this underway, apparently.

Davidson said, "That's everyone, sir. I checked with Commander Cafferly and he said to get started without him."

Cafferly was aboard as well? Considering his job at the FRIGRON, Matt supposed he shouldn't have been surprised to hear that. But he was, all the same.

"Thanks, CS1," Eric said, then looked down the table toward Terry and Ivan. "Dig in, gents."

They all did just that.

In between bites of salad, Eric said, "Like I was saying, it'll be just like at the school. This week we'll work on some planning exercises, and after the Boatswain's Mates knock the rust off, we'll practice gearing up and going out on the ship's boats. Next week we'll do boardings using REPTARVs. Simple scenarios Monday and Tuesday, more advanced Wednesday and Thursday. And then Friday, Commander Tolburt will observe and assess, and we'll forward our certification recommendation to the Commodore after he and I disembark Saturday morning."

"That's why you and I both have the morning watch this underway," Zach said. "We'll do the VBSS work on the afternoon watch." He pointed at Matt with his fork. "And you should work on your OOD quals in the evening."

That was going to be a lot to juggle.

Matt swallowed. He'd known this underway was going to be busy, but he hadn't fully processed what that would mean, practically speaking.

It was doable. He only needed three hours under instruction to count as a U/I watch for quals. So he could spend half of the evening watch on the bridge, like Zach suggested. Hell, he'd basically been planning on doing something like that anyway.

He just hadn't figured how many other things he'd have to do at the same time.

Well, that was space duty for you.

Zach must have seen the sudden realization on Matt's face, because he chuckled. "Don't worry, it's not as bad as it sounds. Or at least, it wasn't when we did it a year ago."

Matt nodded. "Ok. So what's first?"

Eric said, "Well, this afternoon Chief and I are going to do some one-on-one training with your boarding LPOs, while you guys go out on the boats. Then tomorrow we'll get started on the scenario planning evolutions."

Zach said, "I'm First Lieutenant, so I have to be there with my BMs, at least for their first time out today. But since you're going to be on the boats a fair amount as well, you should probably get to know them. And it can't hurt for you to get to learn a bit about how the boats work, too." He winked. "Plus, it's a lot of fun."

Matt had planned to get some divisional work done this afternoon, and then get started studying some of the forward systems that weren't covered by BEQ quals. The torpedo tubes, for example.

Looked like that was going to have to wait.

He didn't feel that bad about it. Zach was right; it sounded like fun.

He grinned. "Sounds like a plan."

Zach nodded. "We're briefing in Classroom #2 at 1345. Flight Quarters at 1430."

Matt looked at the chronometer. It was 1225. He'd be able to get some of that divisional paperwork done, at least. "Ok, see you there."

ICS FREDERICK HALSWELL had two boat decks, on the port and starboard sides of the ship on the 2nd deck, the lowest level of the ship. Though sized the same, the starboard deck, where Matt went, with BM1 Chavez and BM2 McCall, after Deck Division's pre-evolution briefing, was more cluttered than the port.

That was because in addition to the standard ship's boat that each deck housed, the starboard deck also moored the smaller, sleeker Captain's Gig. It was almost like a racer compared with the standard ship's boat's squat, almost blocky construction, and Matt wished for a second that was what they would be taking out today.

But that was not the plan. The VBSS team used the ship's boats for their boarding operations, not the gig, so no reason for him to take that out for a spin.

Maybe later.

"Was about to ask if you've ever been out on one of these, Mr. G," said Chavez as he opened the boat's outer hatch, about a quarter of the way down its port side from the bow, "but you did at VBSS school, right?"

Matt traced the length of the boat's hull with his eyes, and shook his head. "It looks similar, but this is a lot bigger."

Chavez frowned for a second, then shrugged. "Well, it don't matter I suppose. These are pretty easy to operate. We'll have you going in no time."

The hatch opened, and the three of them stepped into the boat's airlock. A moment later, they were inside the craft.

And yeah, it was quite a bit bigger than the Pegasus he had used at VBSS school. That barely had enough room for his team to stand up and turn around without clanging into each other. This was sized to accommodate about twenty people, and had actual seats in rows rather than just benches on either side of the boat's inner hull. And it only had the one airlock, as opposed to the Pegasus, which had one on each side. That left room on the starboard side of the boat for supply and emergency lockers opposite the airlock hatch.

"Are those removable," he asked, pointing at the rows of seats, "if you need to ship parts or stores on one of these?"

Chavez nodded. "Takes a bit of work, but yes." He looked at McCall and gestured toward the piloting bubble.

McCall slipped forward and got into the pilot's seat, then tabbed on the control panel mounted there, and began tapping out a number of commands. Meanwhile, Chavez pulled out a holopad from his thigh pocket and tapped a couple times.

"If you want to hang out, sir, we'll have the preflight checklist done in a minute," he said, without looking at Matt. "And then we'll be off."

Matt frowned, and shook his head. "I'm here to learn the boat. I'll do the checklist with you."

Chavez looked up from the holopad, a quizzical expression on his face. But after a second he seemed to drop whatever thought, or objection, he was about to voice. Instead, he shrugged and, turning the holopad around, he held it out to Matt.

"Your call, sir. Here's the checklist. I'll show you where everything is."

Matt nodded and accepted the holopad. "Thanks, BM1."

It took about ten minutes to do the checklist. Matt was sure BM1 would have finished it much quicker on his own. But it was good to learn what was where, and by the end of the procedure, he felt at a bit more comfortable with the layout of the boat.

Then they went up to the piloting bubble. McCall was tapping at the controls, referencing his own holopad.

"How's it going?" Chavez said.

"Just finishing up. Good to go in here."

Chavez nodded, and a moment later McCall made one last tap, nodded, and stood. Then he moved past Matt and Chavez, and Chavez made a sweeping gesture toward the piloting couch.

"Have a seat, sir."

"I don't think I'm ready to pilot this thing, BM1."

Chavez chuckled, and shook his head. "I don't think so either. No, we're going to do the checklist in here again, and he's going to double check the rest of the list back there." He jabbed a thumb over his shoulder, toward the rear of the boat that they had just checked.

"Oh." Matt should have seen that coming. "Makes sense. Watch team backup, right?"

Chavez nodded.

Another ten minutes later, McCall was in the piloting seat again and Chavez was in the rear of the boat. Matt was up next to McCall, to observe.

"HALSWELL, this is Fred-1. Ready to launch, over," McCall said, and Matt heard the transmission over his implants, which had tuned to the ship's controller frequency as part of the preflight checklist.

Matt raised an eyebrow. "Fred-1?"

McCall chuckled. "Gotta call the boats something. Fred's short for Frederick, so..." He shrugged.

"Fred-1, this is HALSWELL. Roger. Commencing boat deck depress."

Through the plasteel of the piloting bubble, Matt saw a crewman, another Boatswain's Mate he presumed, adjust three valves against the inner bulkhead of the boat deck. Then he gave a thumbs up to them, and he stepped out of the deck. The airtight door shut behind him, and an indicator light above it went from green to red.

Passing through that door earlier, Matt knew it was essentially a one-man airlock. The red indication meant the outer door, into the boat deck, was secured and dogged.

And then nothing happened for a while. Matt imagined he should be able to hear the atmosphere being suctioned out of the boat deck, but of course that was not the case. But...couldn't he almost hear the hissing anyway?

Just his mind playing tricks.

But finally, after what seemed forever, the controller's voice came back over his implants.

"Fred-1, this is HALSWELL. Boat deck depress complete. Opening the outer doors."

Below the boat, the hull of the ship seemed to crack, and then the doors separating the boat deck from the void beyond opened outward. The ship's orbital trajectory was such that the planet wasn't visible at all, just the blackness of space, with a myriad of pinpricks of white from distant stars.

The pilot's couch sat on a small steel platform jutting out into the piloting bubble. Not much to block the view, and for a moment Matt felt like he wasn't standing on that deck. More like he was actually floating, hanging onto nothing in that void below them.

His belly seemed to sink in on itself for a moment, and Matt swallowed, looking away toward the pilot's control console instead.

McCall tapped out a series of quick commands, and then said, "HALSWELL, Fred-1. Ready to detach, over."

"Roger, Fred-1. Disengaging docking clamps."

There was no sense of motion or acceleration, but the vector imposed on the plasteel of the piloting bubble went from a null indication to a small velocity along the z-axis, and the boat deck withdrew above them.

Or rather, they dropped down out of the bottom of the ship. And then all at once they were out in the void.

McCall took hold of the control yoke on his right and the throttle control on his left. Advancing both, the boat pitched downward and accelerated away from the HALSWELL. Then he turned left and right, and pitched back up, and the boat responded smoothly to his commands.

McCall nodded, a satisfied expression on his face. "HALSWELL, Fred-1. We are clear, and free to navigate. All control systems functional."

"Roger, Fred-1. Proceed as briefed."

For the next hour and a half, Matt watched as first McCall, then Chavez, took the boat on an excursion. They went out far enough that HALSWELL was just a barely-discernible smudge inside the blue circle that the piloting bubble projected over her, the strobes from her anti-collision lights the easiest thing to make out with the naked eye. Then they came back and shifted over to the control tower frequency, and made an approached to the hangar deck at the rear of the ship.

Fred-2 was out as well, and they took turns, putting the control tower personnel through their paces, even as the BMs driving the boats worked out the kinks in their Coxswain muscles.

Finally, after their third hangar deck approach, Chavez drove the boat about fifty kilometers away from the ship.

Then he stood up and stepped back from the pilot's couch.

"Your turn, sir," he said, gesturing toward the couch.

"Me?"

Chavez grinned. "Give her a whirl. There's nothing to it."

"Well, I guess we're far enough out that I won't crash into anything," Matt said, and he settled down into the couch.

It was cushioned with a foam that seemed to adjust to his body as he settled down into it, so that it felt completely natural, and the yoke and throttle control easily adjusted to his reach.

Taking a deep breath, he advanced the throttle.

The boat seemed to leap forward, and Matt found he was grinning ear to ear.

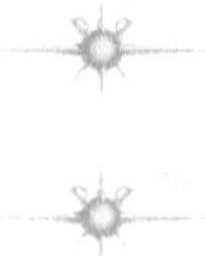

"Tell me that wasn't fun," Zach said, as Matt walked back to the wardroom with him.

Matt was still grinning. He shook his head. "I can't."

Zach looked sidelong at him. "Alas, there won't be much driving of the boats most of the time. Not unless you take First Lieutenant at some point. But it's good to have an appreciation for how they work."

"Makes sense to me." And it did. He still felt a pang of disappointment at the thought, though.

Zach laughed then, and clapped him on the shoulder. "Don't get too upset. The next couple weeks, we'll have plenty of other fun times."

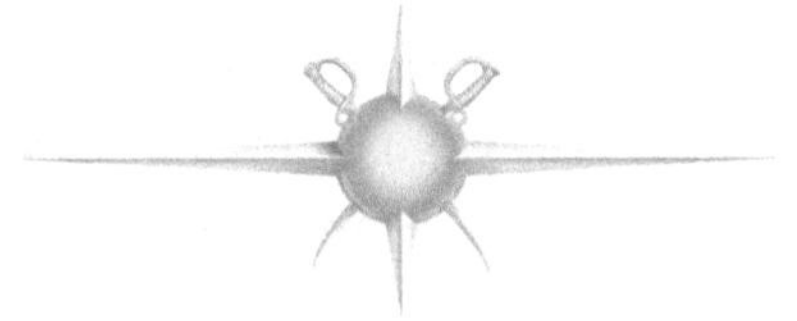

Chapter Forty-Four

Matt reminded himself to ask Zach exactly what he considered fun, because from his perspective the next week and a half didn't exactly fit the bill.

Oh, there *were* good times, and he certainly kept busy.

His under instruction watches on the Bridge topped the list, as far as he was concerned. He'd learned the basics of ship handling at OCS, and the rules of the road, but it had been over a year since he'd put that knowledge to use. So it was almost like starting over.

It was a good starting over, though.

As he announced to the bridge watch standers that he had the Conn for the first time, later in the evening the same day that he'd gone out on Fred-1, he got a thrill of excitement, and of accomplishment. This was what he'd signed up for the Navy to do: actually commanding the ship, not nurse-maiding a reactor.

Not that EOOW wasn't important. And not that he was actually in command; wouldn't be for another seventeen or eighteen years if he stayed in the Navy. But near enough to it. Taking the Conn meant the ship went where he ordered it. It didn't have the immediate tactile-level fun that driving Fred-1 had, but in Matt's mind it was actually better, in a meeting-his-goals kind of way.

Or at least, being on the path to it, anyway.

It immediately became apparent, even if he hadn't assumed it already, that he had a long way to go before he could expect to complete OOD quals, though, and stand the watch on his own. He remembered some of the rules of the road, but only a fraction of them. To say nothing about the navigation techniques he'd forgotten. Or the non-Engineering ship's systems he needed to learn. And their operating procedures, and the CO's standing orders, and...the list went on and on, in the form of a nearly-blank qualification card that was several pages longer than the EOOW card had been.

A long way to go, indeed.

He was eager to get to it.

If only the rest of the time had been so good.

Standing EOOW on his own wasn't bad, per se. But even though he had been de facto standing the watch for the last couple weeks, the O/I just standing back and counter-signing, suddenly, without the presence of that more experienced backup easy to hand, everything seemed more difficult, more momentous, than it had before.

It seemed like he goofed up more often than he got things right, and that was without the drill sets.

They hadn't discussed drills in OPS's breakdown of the plan for the underway, so Matt hadn't thought about them. But of course the ship was going to run drills. And he shouldn't have been surprised that he would see more of them than the other three regular EOOW watch standers. He was newest qualified, of course, and needed the most training.

It still turned his stomach into a knot when the drill team came back. Waiting on the drill set to commence, wondering how CHENG and the EDMC were going to screw with him today...

In reality, his section didn't really get more drills than the other watch sections, except for the midwatch. And it wasn't like they ran drills every day. In that week and a half, he was on watch for three drill sets.

It was still draining. Add on to that the additional Security Reaction Force drills the ship ran in the afternoons of the first week to complete Force Protection certification, his divisional duties, and having to cram in time to study all the new things he had to learn for his OOD quals, and Matt was dragging.

Felt like he hadn't had a moment's down time, or a good night's sleep, since they got underway.

And now, this week was VBSS missions every afternoon, taking all of that watch between pre-evolution briefings and post-evolution debriefings, so that he, Zach, and Eric always missed first sitting for dinner, and then spent a good chunk of the evening watches preparing for the next day's events. So he didn't get up on the bridge hardly at all.

Not that he minded the VBSS work. It was actually pretty fun, getting geared up and loading into either Fred-1 or Fred-2, intercepting the REPTARV, and conducting their assigned inspections. But by the time they finished the final event before Friday's evaluation, Matt was beginning to get even more worn down from it all.

Then LCDR Tolburt came into the wardroom Thursday evening. The ship had launched Fred-2 to pick him up from Copernicus Station while the VBSS team was using Fred-1 that afternoon, so Matt hadn't seen him come aboard.

He was just there for the evaluation the next day, so that meant the ordeal was almost over. It almost made Matt glad to see him again.

Matt was at the kiddie table, nursing a cup of coffee and reading over the technical manual for the ship's inertial navigation system, getting ready for a checkout, when Eric led him in.

Eric was talking with him about something, but he stopped when he saw Matt, and, grinning, gestured his way. Tolburt looked Matt over for a second, then the two of them walked over.

Matt stood. "Nice to see you again, sir," he said, and shook hands with him.

Tolburt cracked a hint of a smile, like he knew Matt didn't really mean it. "How've you been, Ensign?"

Matt shrugged. "You know, keeping busy, sir. Raring to go for tomorrow."

"I hope so." He looked around the wardroom for a second, as though assessing it. Then he nodded to himself and looked back at Matt. His eyes narrowed slightly. "Make sure you get some good rest tonight, Mr. Gilbert. Tomorrow's scenario is going to be challenging."

Matt nodded, and swallowed.

Tolburt held his gaze for another moment, then looked at Eric. "I have to go meet with the XO. I'll talk with you and Chief at 1930 in Classroom #4."

"Yes, sir," Eric said.

Matt waited until Tolburt had exited the wardroom, and the door closed behind him, before he blew out a breath and sat back down.

"Geez. Does that guy ever loosen up?"

Eric chuckled and took a seat next to him. "You have to get to know him. He's actually a pretty funny guy."

Matt looked at him, highly doubtful.

Eric didn't press it. Instead, he picked up the tech manual. "Studying for checkouts, huh?" He didn't wait for Matt to respond, but closed the manual. "He's right, you know. You're looking a little rough. Why don't you join us for movie night for a change, and then hit the rack."

"Eric, I've got a lot to—"

"There's always a lot to do. But you won't do the ship any good if you flub up the evaluation tomorrow because you're exhausted." He tapped the manual with his index finger. "There's always another checkout to get, but it's not a sprint. It's—"

"A marathon," Matt finished for him. "Yeah, I know. The other guys have told me that, too."

Eric raised his eyebrows at him.

After a moment, Matt nodded. "Ok, you're right."

And not just about the checkouts. Matt hadn't even considered joining in the evening movies in the wardroom, at 2000 each night. The rule about NUBs not attending wasn't really set in stone; it was more an implied truism.

But he wasn't a NUB anymore, was he? Not completely.

He nodded more emphatically, and Eric returned the nod.

"Ok. See you here at 2000, then." He stood. "I'm going to put my head together with the Chief." His grinned, a bit wickedly. "He's got a fun idea for you tomorrow."

Then he left the wardroom as well.

Matt was tempted to just open the manual up again and study until movie time. But screw it. Eric was right. He hadn't even called Marta since they'd been underway, and in the orbitals, as they currently were, there was no reason he couldn't have. He'd just...been sprinting.

So instead, he put the manual away and went to his stateroom, and his terminal, to make the call. She usually took dinner later than the ship; he could probably catch her before she went out.

That was a lot more appealing than inertial navigation, anyway.

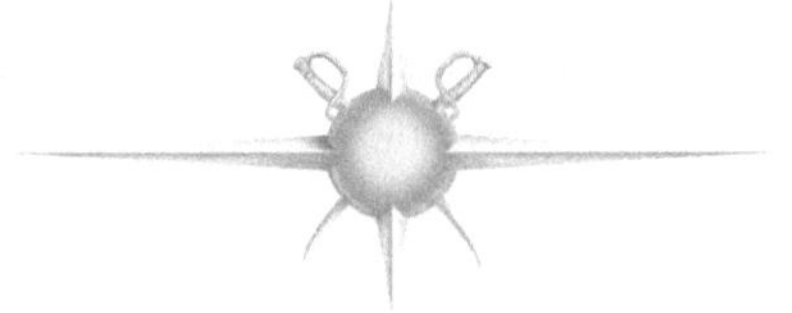

Chapter Forty-Five

Matt checked his rifle again. And just like before, it was fully loaded with practice rounds. And just like before, so were his pistol and spare magazines.

He checked his EVA suit status again, and the ballistic panels that the VBSS team added per procedures. And, of course, it was all good.

But as he stood next to Zach at the front of the passenger bay of Fred-2, as they made their final approach on the REPTARV that was pretending to be the S/V Torrance for their final evaluation, he had the nagging feeling that he had forgotten something, something major, that would screw up the entire exercise for the team, and the ship.

Over the private comm channel that linked him and Zach, he heard a bit of amusement in the older JO's voice as he said, "Calm down, Matt. We got this."

He turned to look at Zach, and of course he didn't look at all concerned. He was the image of confidence and surety. But then, he'd done this many times before.

Matt swallowed. "Hope so."

Through his visor, Zach grinned, and he reached out to put a light punch into Matt's shoulder.

"Just stick to the plan, remember the procedures. It'll be fine."

Matt inhaled deeply, and nodded, trying to force himself to calm.

Easier said than done.

Forward of him and Zach, he could see into the piloting bubble, where BM2 McCall was driving the boat. Past him, the blunted bulk of the REPTARV's hull was growing large in the port side of the bubble's view.

S/V Torrance was a suspected arms smuggler, and it was HALSWELL's job—Matt's team's job—to verify that she didn't have any contraband from the Tsago Dominance aboard. A routine inspection, in theory. But per the pre-mission briefing, there had been incidents with similar vessels in the past, so Matt and his team could leave nothing to chance.

Per the plan, Matt would take his team of five aft to inspect the engineering spaces, and Zach's equally-numbered team would take the living and cargo areas. So at least in theory, if there was going to be trouble, Zach's group should find it.

But there were lots of nooks and crannies on a starship. The suspected contraband—mostly crew-served equipment, so not especially bulky—could be hidden almost anywhere.

He had to be vigilant.

Matt looked aft, to where the enlisted crew was finishing their preparations. BM3 Peters, who he had gone to VBSS school with, was on his team, which made him feel more immediately comfortable since they already had known and worked together. He also had two other third-class petty officers, Chance and Bogarten, both Operations Specialists who normally stood watch in CIC when they weren't doing VBSS work. And then there was Storekeeper Second Class Feisel, who seemed to relish getting away from work in Supply Department, and Quartermaster First Class Vinz, the Navigation LPO, and Matt's right hand man in this arena.

They were grouped together on Fred-2's starboard side, since their team would board after Zach's forward team, and like Zach they had all appearances of being ready and confident—eager, even—to be about it.

Vinz stood closest to Matt, and seemed to notice his anxiety. He piped through on the team's channel, "Good to go, Mr. Gilbert," when Matt's eyes met his, and gave a thumbs up.

Matt returned it, and inhaled deeply again.

Somehow, seeing his team ready and steady made it easier for him to put aside his nerves than Zach's assurance had. Maybe because he knew he was expected to lead them, and the leader has to be cool and collected.

Or maybe it was just ego, not wanting to look the fool in front of them.

Either way, it worked.

McCall's voice came over Fred-2's internal comms circuit. "Velocity matched with the target. Initiating docking."

There was no way to sense the change in the boat's motion, not with the internal grav plates maintaining a constant gravitational vector. But Matt imagined he felt the leftward slip of the craft as McCall edged them over toward the Torrance.

Then there was a little shudder as the mating surfaces of two vessels contacted each other.

A moment later, McCall reported, "Good seal, sir."

Beside Matt, Zach straightened almost perceptibly, and turned to Chief Tennenbaum, the VBSS team's LCPO, when he wasn't doing duties down in the AMR with Auxiliary Division.

"Open her up, Chief," Zach said.

"Aye aye, sir," the Chief replied, and set about activating Fred-2's airlock sequence.

A moment later, Zach led his team aboard the TORRANCE. Two by two, they passed through the connector to the suspect ship, until the last of them passed within.

Then Matt, forcing his uncertainties aside yet again, followed, his team on his heels.

Matt crouched beneath a run of piping, his rifle at the low ready, and scanned the narrow space beyond.

He was deep into the engineering plant of the Torrance, and he had split his team into three pairs—himself and Peters, Vinz and Chance, and Feisel and Bogarten, to more efficiently sweep the compartment.

The space he had just entered ran forward and aft, just wide enough for two men to walk side by side if they squeezed, and was festooned with junctions boxes, wiring bundles, and more piping. There were myriad pipe bends that could make for hiding spots, but none even close to being large enough for a man.

Could hide a case of ammo, or a clutch of grenades or mines, though.

So carefully, peering into each spot with a flashlight and a sniffer that could supposedly detect combustible material at a short distance, he and Peters checked it all.

Nothing.

As expected, but not suspected.

It had been that way for the last half hour. Everywhere he and his team looked, every place that seemed as though it might contain the hidden cache, came up empty. It was enough to make him think maybe LCDR Tolburt and Eric had been putting him on, and this final evaluation was, in fact, going to be easy.

He tabbed the comm channel to his team. "Team Bravo, report."

A slight hiss of static, then Vinz came back, "Port and Starboard engine spaces clear."

Feisel reported a second later, "Maneuvering and switchboard areas clear."

Matt frowned, and glanced at Peters. The Boatswain's Mate shrugged, and said via the close-range suit-to-suit comm, "Maybe they're legit."

That was too good to be true, though. There had to be something amiss. Matt tabbed over to his channel with Zach.

"Team Alpha, Team Bravo. Engineering Spaces look good."

Zach's came back, "Roger. We're having a bit of—" Then the comm channel exploded in a scream of feedback.

Matt froze, a rush of adrenaline coursing into him.

"Team Alpha, say again."

Nothing but static over the channel, now.

Dammit.

He switched to the channel for the entire VBSS team. "Team Alpha, this is Team Bravo. Check in, over."

Only static came in response. But he thought he heard, faintly, a voice buried beneath the interference. He couldn't make out who, but he thought he heard panic in his voice.

Matt switched to the Team Bravo team channel. "Team Bravo, rendezvous at Maneuvering now!"

He turned and patted Peters on the shoulder and, since he was between Matt and the stand of piping they had passed through, indicated for him to take the lead.

He needn't have done so. Peters was moving almost as soon as Matt turned to him. He had his rifle shouldered and he moved in a half-crouch, his feet moving rapidly, but smoothly, to exit the narrow space he and Matt had been inspecting.

The passageway beyond was empty of personnel, but Matt now saw movement, where before he hadn't. Just his imagination playing tricks on him, as his nerves continued to amp up.

He tried Zach again. Again, nothing but static, interlaced with more feedback.

They hurried up a ladder and then down a wider passage between circuit breaker panels to the area outside of Maneuvering, and saw the other members of Matt's team arriving as they did.

The door to maneuvering was open, and the lone watch stander within was lounging on his chair, looking languidly at them as though completely uninterested in what they were doing.

Matt kept his eyes on the man as he addressed his team. "We've lost comms with Team Alpha. Have to assume they've run into trouble."

"Off to the rescue, sir?" said Chance.

Vinz replied immediately. "We don't know where they are, or what's going on. And we aren't Marines." He eyed Matt meaningfully as he said that last, his expression saying plainly that Matt needed to not be stupid.

Matt agreed completely. And anyway, procedure said clearly what they were supposed to do in a case like this. "No, we're not," he said, nodding to Vinz. He drew a breath. "Back to the airlock. We'll establish a strong point there while we try to regain contact with Team Alpha."

"Roger that, sir," Vinz said. He made to move forward, but Matt held up a hand to stop him.

"Peters and I will take the lead. Vinz, take rear guard."

ET1 Vinz almost looked like he was going to protest, but he just nodded. "Aye, sir."

"Move out," Matt said, and shouldered his rifle.

He moved in a quick but deliberate pace, so as to not force his heart rate higher than it already was. He covered each opening and hatch they passed, peering down his rifle sights to ensure no threats as he went. Peters, to his left, did the same on the other side.

They passed two crewmen, who froze, eyes wide, raising empty hands in an "I surrender" gesture, when they saw the ready weapons.

Matt's team passed them warily, but they made no moves against them, so the team left them behind.

Moments later, they were at the airlock, which McCall had sealed after they boarded the Torrance.

The space was semi-circular, with lockers for EVA suits lining the curved walls across from the hatch. Three passageways intersected with the space: the one leading aft that his team had just come through, one running athwartships, and one leading forward.

Matt gestured toward the two new passages.

Feisel took up position at the athwarships passage, rifle at the ready and trained down it. Peters took the forward passage, and Bogarten covered the passage leading aft.

Matt gestured toward Chance. "Tell McCall to prepare for launch, and see if he can raise Team Alpha on his gear. Tell them we've secured the airlock and will cover their return." There was a chance that Fred-2's communications gear, being more powerful than an EVA suit's, could punch through whatever was jamming his comms with Zach and Team Alpha.

Worth a shot, anyway.

Chance nodded and headed into the airlock.

Vinz and Matt shared a look. Matt could see Vinz was on edge, but he looked better than Matt felt.

He switched to the team-wide channel. "Team Alpha, this is Team Bravo. We have secured the airlock. Report status, over."

Again came static and feedback. But beneath, he thought he heard the report of weapons being fired.

No. No, he heard that separately, muffled by the helmet of his EVA suit. But clear, nonetheless. The sound of weapons firing, nearby.

The others in his team visibly stiffened, and then leaned into the stocks of their rifles. They heard the firing as well.

Matt brought his weapon up to the ready, aiming past Peters down the forward passage. In his periphery, he noted Vinz doing the same down the athwartships that Feisel was covering.

His heart rate accelerated, and no matter that he was trying to force himself to calm, or that he knew for a fact this was just an exercise. The world shrank down around him, coalescing solely on the site picture of his rifle, trained down the passageway ahead.

He spotted movement, an instant before Peters announced, "Contact!"

Matt felt the impulse to fire. His finger slipped into the trigger guard, alighted on the metal sliver that would send rounds flying toward the threat. He knew from many trips to the range it would take only the lightest pressure to unleash them, to save himself and his team from the coming attack.

Maybe save their lives.

He felt his finger pressing against that sliver...

Then he saw the figure coming down the passageway more clearly. It was wearing an EVA suit like his, and he saw the HALSWELL's ship seal atop its helmet.

A member of Team Alpha.

Relief flooded through him, and he slipped his finger off the trigger, as finally a transmission reached him on the team-wide channel, layered with static but now, finally, understandable.

"Team Bravo, Team Alpha. Hold your fire. We are inbound with two casualties."

Matt breathed out a sigh of relief and shifted the sights of his rifle away from the incoming figure, toward the corridor beyond.

Three more figures were following the lead man, two of them hunched over limp comrades that they were supporting as they hurried down the passageway toward Matt's team.

Finally, Matt gathered his wits about him. He transmitted on his team's frequency, "Alpha is coming in from forward." He didn't wait to hear replies before he shifted to his private channel with Zach.

"Dude, you ok? What happened?"

The last of the bodies that was being hauled along, limply, raised its head. "I'll tell you later," Zach said, resignation in his voice.

Matt's didn't reply; there wasn't really anything to say. Instead, he directed his men to help bring Team Alpha, and their wounded, aboard Fred-2. Then they evacuated.

As the airlock sealed shut behind him, and McCall slipped the boat away from the REPTARV, he felt his stomach, and his spirits, drop.

They were in the wardroom. Matt sat next to Zach, facing the briefing screen. To their left were WEPS, then XO, then the CO. CMC was on the other side of the CO, and then the Weapons Department LCPO, Chief Tennenbaum, and Petty Officer Linz.

Eric stood next to the briefing screen, looking grimly serious. LCDR Tolburt was seated at the end of the wardroom table closest to the door, his usual severe expression on his face.

For the last ten minutes, Eric had been presenting a re-creation of the VBSS team's activities aboard the TORRANCE, giving play-by-play commentary on their actions, and showcasing, with devastating detail, the results.

By the end of Eric's presentation, Matt was slumped in his seat.

They had blown it. Completely.

Two of Zach's team, including Zach himself, had been "killed" during the exercise, and they never had found where the stash of hidden weapons was located on the Torrance. Matt couldn't see how this could be anything but a complete failure.

"At time 54, the last of the VBSS team entered Fred-2, and the boat detached from the target vessel," Eric said. Then he drew himself a bit more erect. "That concluded the exercise."

The CO nodded slowly. He looked to his right, toward Matt and Zach, and Matt felt himself drawing back a bit more, as his Captain's gaze fell upon him.

"I see," the CO said. He paused for a moment, then looked away from Matt and Zach, toward LCDR Tolburt. "What is your assessment?"

Tolburt stirred. While Zach had been speaking, he had been completely impassive. But now, his expression slipped a little. "Your team acted appropriately."

Matt blinked. What had he said?

Tolburt continued, "Team Alpha, when confronted by the ambush, returned fire and fell back in an orderly manner. Team Bravo followed procedure and secured the airlock, instead of trying to play hero. Your team, overall, took two fewer casualties than we anticipated, and conducted an orderly retreat to the boat." The corners of his lips turned upward slightly. "I intend to recommend certification, Captain."

The CO nodded.

The sinking feeling in Matt's belly lifted, replaced by one of amazed disbelief.

He felt a nudge in his side, and looked to see Zach pulling his elbow back. He gave Matt a knowing grin. "We're not Marines, remember? Told you it'd be alright," he murmured, softly enough that it only carried to Matt's ears.

Matt was so focused-in on those few words that he didn't hear what the CO was saying until he was mid-way through a sentence that ended with, "Mr. Gilbert."

Matt whipped his head back around to see the CO looking at him, the expression on his face clearly expecting a response.

He cleared his throat. "Beg pardon, sir?"

The CO's lips turned upward ever so slightly. He clearly knew he had caught Matt out for not paying attention.

"I said, well done."

Matt blinked, then nodded, managing a little smile for the first time in what felt like ages. "Thank you, sir."

The CO's smile widened noticeably.

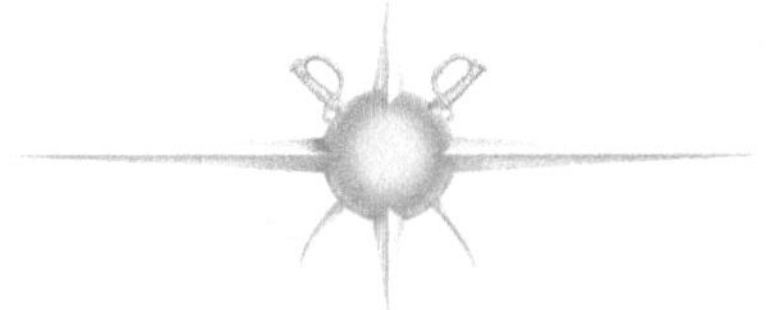

Chapter Forty-Six

The bridge of ICS FREDERICK HALSWELL had two bridge wings protruding out from its port and starboard sides. Closed off when the ship set condition Zebra for combat, they were accessible now, and Matt had to shove down a feeling of vertigo when he first came out to the starboard side blister.

On the bridge proper, there was a deck under his feet and the overhead above him, and while the plasteel observation windows made for a full-azimuth view of the surrounding space, he nevertheless never lost sight of the fact that he was, indeed, still on a solidly-built, and airtight, ship.

Out here, though...

The deck stretched out into the center of the bridge wing, and there was a terminal with controls for internal and external communications, and a display that showed the navigational picture and ship's status. But aside from that, the bridge wing was basically a sphere of plasteel, allowing an almost completely unimpeded view in all directions.

It also stretched out almost to the edge of the ship's hull, so when Matt looked down, he saw the curve of the ship drop away into the emptiness of the void, with the blue-white northern hemisphere of New California very, very far below.

Looking up, there was only blackness, and the starscape.

On their current vector, the sun was off the ship's port quarter, and that portion of the blister was polarized so that the star shown through only as a dim yellow-brown hued circle on the plasteel, not the eye-blindingly brilliant light source that the naked eye would see.

Matt had done EVAs in OCS. Several of them. He hadn't had any particular problem with vertigo then. But here, now... He almost felt like he did when he was standing at the top of a very tall building, looking down. That feeling, the fear of falling that somehow also contained a subtle urge to jump off, always made him want to pull back from the balcony in situations like that.

But here, there was no balcony, and no way to pull back except to go back to the bridge proper. But he couldn't do that. The supply ship, ICNS SPIRIT, was visible, even without the blue circle the tracking systems projected around it onto the plasteel sphere, ahead and to starboard.

HALSWELL had plasma medium and fresh food to bring aboard, and sanitary tanks to empty. And he was the Conning Officer. So backing away wasn't an option.

Still, he had to swallow hard, twice, to settle his stomach.

Beside him, Jerry Despirito, the OOD and his Over Instruct for this evolution, looked at him with a knowing expression on his face.

"Always a bit of an adjustment, coming out here," Jerry said.

Matt nodded, and swallowed again.

"Just keep your mind on what we're doing; you'll get used to it."

Jerry tapped the control terminal, and the supply ship's tracking information updated. The course vector that had been projecting from the center of the blue circle around the ship expanded, showing the vessel's velocity, acceleration, and direction of travel in bold digits that Matt couldn't have ignored if he wanted to. At the same time, a separate vector display appeared astern the supply ship, showing the relative speed between it and HALSWELL, and the variance in their course vectors.

They had executed an intercept procedure back on the bridge proper to bring HALSWELL around and onto the same plane as the supply ship's track, and closed to 10 kilometers, before transferring out here.

Now, Matt just had to bring HALSWELL along side and match velocity, while keeping her within 200 meters of the supply ship.

Their course vectors were mostly aligned, so it really came down to finessing the engine settings to approach her. Simple enough.

On paper, anyway.

"Small moves, Mr. Gilbert," said the CO. He was standing at the inner edge of the sphere, where it joined with the plasteel tunnel that connected the bridge wing with the bridge proper.

The CO came up to the bridge wing for every UNREP evolution. After all, maneuvering in such close proximity to another vessel inherently contained a risk to the safety of the ship. So he wasn't there just because it was Matt's first time doing this. Still, Matt felt the CO's eyes on him. It was both intimidating and comforting, knowing he was there.

"Don't rush it," the CO added. "Slow is fast, and we've got all afternoon if needed."

"Aye aye, Captain," Matt said. He inhaled again, then stepped forward and tapped the communications control panel, activating the direct comm link between his implants and those of the Helmsman.

"Helm, .5gs ahead," he said.

".5gs ahead, Helm aye," came the response. Almost immediately, the relative velocity vector began to creep backward, showing that HALSWELL was closing with the supply ship.

When the closing velocity reached 50 meters per second, Matt said, "Helm, all stop."

"All stop, helm aye."

Normally, the OOD or conning officer would issue standardized engine orders—1/3, 2/3, Standard, Full, Flank—and the RO in Maneuvering would answer the bell. This was to enable the RO to monitor reactor output and control the throttles to ensure the ship didn't exceed any power limits.

However, for situations like this, that required precision maneuvering and quick engine response, the Helm station had the ability to take direct control of the engine throttles. Doing that raised the risk profile for reactor operation, because the Helm couldn't monitor the plant's output, and wasn't trained to do so. But the designers determined that the small increase in risk from doing that was outweighed by the increased overall ship's safety margin gained by taking direct throttle control for close-quarters maneuvers.

Matt knew this, but it still felt a little weird giving the engine orders that way. Over the last three weeks since they got underway, he had gotten used to issuing the standard orders during his U/I times on the bridge.

"Always something new to learn," he mumbled under his breath as he watched the relative velocity vector.

It settled in at 65 meters per second, and he focused on the supply ship.

The computed Closest Point Of Approach (CPA) displayed beneath its circle blanked out momentarily as Matt watched, then flickered back to life.

CPA was 450 meters.

"Got to come a bit to starboard," Jerry said softly, and Matt nodded.

HALSWELL was steering 145 mark 25: 145 degrees clockwise from system north and 25 degrees depressed from the system zenith.

When the system had initially been charted and established, the survey team had selected a relatively nearby pulsar that lay along the system's ecliptic and designated that as system north, and then assigned the zenith as a point directly perpendicular to the ecliptic.

Thus all ships in the system operated within a standardized reference frame, which was automatically updated on newly-arrived ships by interfacing with equipment orbiting adjacent to the system's jump points.

Which was all well and good, but Matt needed to adjust his course, not replay the information he had regurgitated for a navigation checkout last week.

"Helm, come right to 145.5," he ordered.

The Helm responded, and Matt watched as the ship crept ever so slightly to the right. The change was not really perceptible to the naked eye, but the effect was immediate on the CPA. It ticked down quickly, then settled on 187 meters.

The CPA display turned yellow, indicating the need for caution. It would shift to red, and trigger alert notification windows at all stations, below 150 meters, indicating danger of imminent collision. Normally, the tracking and display system was set to provide the caution and danger alerts *much* further out than that.. But in UNREP mode, the alerts were tightened up, for obvious reasons.

"Ok, how long do you wait to come back left?" Jerry asked.

Matt frowned, then after a moment shook his head. There was a tool of some sort to help with that, but he couldn't remember which.

"Check this out." Jerry reached past him to enter a different command into the control tablet.

Immediately, the blister's display shifted, a dialog box opening in the clear area above the supply ship and to its left. The box was labeled "Trial," and Matt remembered.

"See? With this you can enter your intended new course and speed, and..." Jerry ran his finger along the control tablet, and the trial course swung far around to the left, away from the supply ship. The trial CPA increased and then, as he swung the course even further away, flashed to white text reading, "Past." He grinned. "Saves doing it in your head, or guessing."

"Yeah. I forgot about that," Matt said.

Still grinning, Jerry took a half step back, so Matt could more easily reach the control tablet. A moment later, he had it the new course calculated. He'd need to turn back to 145 in...

He looked at the chronometer display, and nodded to himself. Right about now.

"Helm, steer course 145."

They returned to the base course, and Matt was gratified to see the CPA computation show 192 yards.

The range was down to 5 kilometers now. He shifted over to the bridge to bridge channel.

"SPIRIT, this is HALSWELL, approaching from your port quarter. I intend to make up on your port side for stores transfer, over."

SPIRIT was much larger now. She wasn't sleakly-built like HALSWELL, all blocky like someone had just stacked a bunch of cargo containers together, slapped engines on it, and called it good. But she didn't have to look good, and that blocky configuration made a certain amount of sense, considering her job.

It took a few seconds for SPIRIT to reply.

"HALSWELL, this is SPIRIT, roger. Standing by to receive your lines, over."

The distance continued to close, and SPIRIT was becoming quite large now.

"Don't come in too fast," Jerry said. "You want to ease into it."

Matt pursed his lips, nodding. Their closing speed was still 65 meters per second, and two kilometers to go. Yeah, no need to rush.

"Helm, .5g astern."

The Helm acknowledged, and the close speed began lowering. 50 meters per second. 30.

"Helm, all stop."

"All stop, Helm eye."

One kilometer away now, and SPIRIT was dominating the forward-starboard view through the blister. Anti-collision strobes on her dorsal and ventral sections flashed red, and her stern light shown steady white, a contrast from the dull grey of her structure.

Now, Matt could see an open bay, one third of the way down her length from her bow, and small figures standing within, waiting to get started.

Speaking of which...

"Open the UNREP bay?" he asked Jerry.

"Yeah." Jerry replied, his tone saying, "Why didn't you do that five minutes ago?" as he gestured toward the control tablet.

Matt ordered the helm to reduce speed some more, then ordered the Chief Of The Watch to open the starboard-side UNREP Bay.

Now they were creeping up on SPIRIT at 10 meters per second, and she was half a kilometer away.

"Officer of the Deck, Chief DeFranco reports starboard UNREP Bay is open and personnel are standing by," said the Chief of the Watch.

Matt looked down and astern. He couldn't see it very well because of the curvature of the hull, but the UNREP Bay hatch was about fifty meters forward of the engine nacelle, and the primary cannon. Matt almost imagined he could see the glow from the Bay's interior lighting, but that was just his imagination, he was sure.

They were coming up on the SPIRIT's open bay now. The massive bulk of the supply ship, quite a bit larger than HALSWELL both in length and height, completely filled the void to HALSWELL's starboard.

Matt ordered the ship slowed again, and they crept forward at just over a meter per second.

"Now comes the fun part," Jerry said. He pointed at the open bay, now abeam HALSWELL's bow. There were markings on the supply ship's hull, forward of the bay. Like target reticles, labeled with big, blocky white letters so that Matt couldn't miss them if he wanted too.

"Stop us when the target marked SFG is directly abeam," Jerry said, reiterating the point they had discussed earlier, before Matt had taken the conn.

And Matt had read about the procedure, too, of course.

Different classes of ship were configured differently, naturally. So the designers of the supply ships had put those target reticles in place, to assist with the final approach. All one had to do to make sure the two UNREP Bays lined up was to position his ship so that the center of the target corresponding to his ship's class was directly lined up with a pylon that had been driven into the outer edge of the platform he was standing on.

Piece of cake.

But Matt's piece was a tad too big for him to bite it, apparently. Because when he got HALSWELL stopped, the target that bore the "SFG" label was about 15 degrees abaft the beam.

"Dangit," he said, and ordered a quick burst of reversing engines.

Slowly, the target moved back forward until it was where it was supposed to be, and Matt stopped the ship. She was now coasting through space, matching velocity vectors with the SPIRIT, 190 meters away.

"Not too bad," he said, and Jerry shrugged.

"Everyone misses the mark sometimes," Jerry said. "I'd say pretty good for your first time."

"Would be easier if we just used the auto systems."

"Not on this ship, Mr. Gilbert," said the CO. Matt turned to look back at him, and he raised an eyebrow. "You can't become a good ship driver if you never actually drive the ship," he said.

He stepped closer, looking down and astern toward where the SPIR-IT's personnel were busily swinging gear out from the hull. Then he looked back at Matt, a question on his face.

Oh yeah. Matt drew himself to the position of attention. "Captain, we are positioned for UNREP. I intend to send over lines."

The CO nodded. "Very well."

He passed the order to the Chief of the Watch, and informed SPIRIT over the bridge to bridge. Then it was a matter of sitting back and watching as HALSWELL shot pilot lines across to the SPIRIT's crew, and then used those lines to guide the plasma medium and sanitary hoses over from the supply ship.

While that was going on, drones began ferrying cargo crates across. Crates filled with fresh veggies, milk, and fruit, Matt presumed. He hoped.

A few minutes later, the Chief of the Watch reported, "Officer of the Deck, from the UNREP Station. Commenced pumping, time 47."

"Very well, Chief of the Watch."

Matt looked at the chronometer again. It was now 1448. They had computed earlier that to pump the amount of plasma medium they needed to bring aboard, and the amount of sans they needed to get rid of, would take about 30 minutes.

He grinned. They might have had all afternoon, but they were going to have the evolution done with plenty of time to spare. There would be no bagging the next watch with their unfinished work. Not this time.

And that, he had come to learn quite quickly, was rule #1 for managing your watch.

"Nice job, Mr. Gilbert," the CO said then, nodding approval.

"Thank you, sir," Matt said.

He was feeling pretty good about himself, right that moment. Between the VBSS eval last week and nailing the UNREP today, Matt was beginning to think he had this Naval Officer thing figured out.

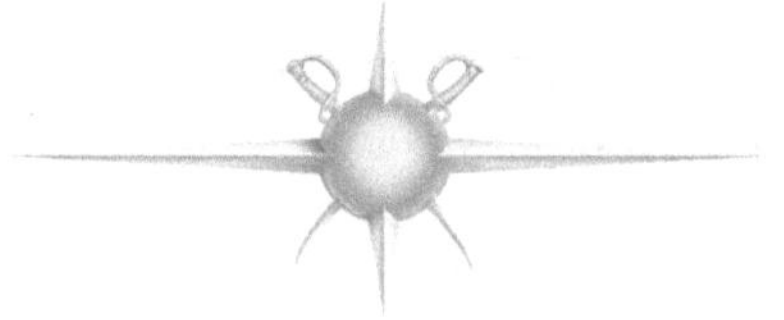

Chapter Forty-Seven

Officers Call was on the Plan of the Day at 1900 that evening, and Matt was still in pretty good spirits when he swept into the wardroom.

After completing the UNREP maneuver, there wasn't much to do for the rest of the watch except reposition the ship to the next regeneration point for the Track-Ex they were doing with RODNEY JACOBS. So Jerry spent the last hour and a half of the watch grilling Matt through checkouts on the visual navigation systems, and how to plot the ship's position from star sightings, and on the life pods. The checkouts were grueling, and he walked away with a page and a half of lookups—like usual—but also with a feeling of accomplishment.

It had been a good watch.

The wardroom was about half full when he walked in, and made a beeline to the coffee mess. Commander Cafferly had come through with a particularly good blend for this underway, but it was starting to get low, and Matt didn't want to miss out if he could help it.

CHENG was at the coffee machine when Matt walked up, looking a bit more frazzled than normal. And no wonder. With the start of the Track-Ex, the CO had stationed the TAO watch, so the Department Heads were four section in the CIC, on top of their other heavy duties.

CHENG had the afternoon watch, and from what Matt could see he was up really late each night to compensate for it.

"Matt," CHENG said, and handed the coffee pot over to him. "What the hell is going on with E-Div training?"

Matt paused midway through filling his cup. "Sir?"

CHENG narrowed his eyes at him. "Your monthly report was due yesterday. Since I didn't receive it, I checked the files myself. Half of the division hasn't completed the quarterly level of knowledge exam, and two haven't completed their upgrade from last quarter. The records for last week's training aren't updated either." His lips turned downward into a scowl.

Matt blinked. He'd turned in the report himself. He remembered it specifically...

Oh crap. That was the report for last month. Things had been so busy lately, he'd plum forgotten about it. It was probably still in his review queue, where Chief had sent it at the beginning of the week.

He opened his mouth to reply, but CHENG beat him to it.

"I know you've been busy working on quals, and the VBSS evaluation. And you should be. But you cannot let your other duties slide." He held his gaze on Matt for a few seconds, and Matt felt the ire burning into him. It was all he could do not to wilt on the spot.

CHENG said, "Get the reports done tonight, and don't let this happen again." Then his expression softened a tad. But just a tad. "I need you on the ball, Matt."

With that, CHENG went over and took a seat at the main wardroom table, next to the Chop.

Feeling chastened, Matt filled his mug, silently berating himself for his oversight.

Looked like he didn't have this Naval Officer thing fully down, after all.

He picked a seat at the other end of the table from where CHENG sat—he didn't want to sit under that disappointed, accusing gaze for whatever this meeting was about. The only open spot was between Gamal and Harry, across from OPS.

OPS raised an eyebrow at him as he sat. "How was the UNREP, Matt?"

Matt sipped at his coffee and shrugged. "Went well enough, I guess."

Harry chuckled and elbowed Matt in the side, softly. "We're not breathing vacuum anyway, so there's that."

Gamal laughed at the joke.

Matt just shrugged again.

A few minutes later, the CO, XO, and Commander Cafferly entered. XO was carrying a red folder that matched the tone of the wardroom tablecloth. He and the CO didn't sit, though. As Commander Cafferly took the seat to the right of the CO's chair, they moved over to the open end of the table, below where the briefing screen would lower in front of the sitting area and coffee mess.

All eyes turned to follow them as they came to a halt. The CO surveyed the group for a second before speaking.

"This is an important day, gentlemen. One that will go down in infamy, I'm sure."

Next to Matt, Gamal chuckled.

"XO?" the CO said.

XO nodded and opened the red folder. "ENS Linsky, front and center."

Ivan was sitting along the inner curve of the table, opposite where Matt was. At the XO's order, he rose and came to stand in front of the two of them, taking the position of attention.

XO read from the document in the folder, "By order of the Chief of Naval Personnel, ENS Ivan T. Linsky is promoted to the rank of Lieutenant Junior Grade, with all the rights and duties contained therein. Effective this day, the 1st of February, 2675." He looked up at Ivan. "Raise your right hand."

Ivan did so, and the CO raised his.

"Repeat after me," the CO said. "I, Ivan Linsky, do solemnly swear to support and defend the constitution of the Icaran Confederation. That I will bear truth faith and allegiance to the same. That I take this obligation freely, without any mental reservation. And that I will well and faithfully discharge the duties of the office I am about to enter, so help me God."

Ivan repeated as the CO led him through the oath.

At the end, the CO smiled broadly and held out his right hand. "Congratulations, Lieutenant."

"Thank you sir," Ivan said, and shook hands with him.

The CO and XO then took a moment to pin his new rank on his collars, on top of the sewn-on insignia that he was now no longer authorized to wear, and ordered him to about face.

The wardroom applauded, and Ivan's smile was ear to ear.

When the applause died down, the CO stepped forward to Ivan's side.

"Now, this leaves us with a problem, which if we don't solve will be the downfall of our wardroom. Jorge, get up here."

Jorge had been sitting next to Ivan, and he jumped to his feet, coming over to stand with the CO and Ivan.

"I am ready to relieve you as Bull," Jorge said, without waiting for the CO to ask.

Ivan replied, "I am ready to be relieved."

"I relieve you."

"I stand relieved."

They saluted each other, then shook, and the CO looked at them, bemused. "I won't ask if you guys did a turnover yet, then. Did you transfer the wardroom wallet permissions already?"

Jorge nodded. "This morning, sir."

"Of course you did," the CO said, rolling his eyes toward the overhead for a moment. "Don't let us down, Bull."

"Wouldn't dream of it, sir," Jorge said, as he and Ivan went back to their seats.

"He won't have much time to mess things up," OPS said. "Don't he and Vasili both promote next month?"

XO nodded and sighed. "And then Jeremy a couple months later. We're running low on Ensigns." His eyes swept to Matt, and his eyebrows rose. "Good thing we've got two more coming, or we'd have Matt as both Bull and George."

Matt had seen the messages about Ivan's, and then Vasili's and Jorge's upcoming promotions, so this wasn't exactly a surprise. He just shrugged.

"It'd be a step increase in performance, sir," he said, echoing the joke that he'd heard one of them make back at his Hail and Farewell.

Several of the men around the table laughed at that.

"Let's hope so," the CO said, then grinned at Jorge to show it was a joke. "That said, when are you planning to do your wetting down, Ivan?"

The wetting down was another of those traditions that Matt had heard about, but hadn't participated in yet. When an officer got promoted, it was expected that he would bring the wardroom out for a night on the town, and that he would spend as much on the drinks as the pay difference between his old rank and his new one.

Which for ENS to LT(jg) wasn't a huge amount. But it was the thought—and the tradition—that counted.

Ivan said, "We've got the one night at Copernicus before we roll to Olifant. There're a couple of good clubs down on the tourist levels I'm looking at."

The CO winced. "You want me to miss the one night with my wife that I'll have for months to come drinking with you?"

Ivan shrugged. "You don't have to come, sir."

"Woooo! He called you out, skipper!" said the CSO. He looked positively gleeful.

CO sent a dagger-like stare CSO's way, and he just smiled beatifically.

Finally, the CO sighed, shaking his head. "Have it your way, Mr. Linsky." He grinned then, his eyes twinkling in the lighting from overhead. "But there will be payback."

"Hope so, sir." Ivan replied, still grinning ear to ear.

The CO laughed, good-naturedly, and spread his hands in an "I give up," gesture. "Well since we're all here, let's talk business. OPS, how are we looking on the schedule?"

OPS had his holopad out on the table in front of him. He picked it up and tapped out a couple of commands, pursing his lips. "Tonight's phase of the TrackEx is on track to start as scheduled. We've got a series of ten regen points to run, then we need to depart for next week's events at 0900. Our starting position is at the jump point to Davidea. The JACOBS will be...somewhere." He put a bit of a mysterious, almost spooky, inflection into his voice there, and Matt bit back a laugh.

OPS continued, "We'll be stationing the Duty Captain for the final evolution with the JACOBS."

The CO nodded and looked around. "XO and I will be port and starboard for that, so we won't be as available as usual. Or at least, XO won't." The CO gestured toward XO. "XO gets the night watch."

XO winced a tad, and CO grinned at him. "That's why you get the big bucks, XO."

OPS also grinned as he continued, "Three days of playing hide and seek with the JACOBS, and then we have a 1000 mooring time at Copernicus Station on Thursday. We're underway for Olifant at 0900 Friday."

"That means we can't be out too late that evening," the XO said. "Fortunately for Ivan's wallet." More chuckles issued from around the wardroom table. "Have you heard from our new guy?"

OPS nodded. "The JACOBS is mooring ahead of us, at 0800. LT Phan will be waiting, seabag in hand, when we dock." He looked at the holopad again for a second, then shrugged. "And that's all that's new, skipper."

The CO nodded. "WEPS?"

WEPS shook his head.

"CSO?"

"SDMS is down for the next 24 hours. We've been running into a recurring error code. Chief thinks he's locked down the cause, but we've got to do a groom followed by a full system restart to clear it."

"Didn't we just get that thing?" Gideon said.

CSO shrugged. "Navy procurement. It is what it is."

The CO shook his head. "Well we shouldn't get shot at any time soon, so no real harm. CHENG?"

CHENG said, "Just the usual maintenance and training schedule, sir."

"Nothing broke?" The CO sounded incredulous.

"Knock on wood, sir," CHENG replied, rapping his fingers onto his temple as he did.

"Chop?"

"I've got rubbish removal and stores load scheduled for Thursday afternoon, at 1400, sir."

Which meant a sizable portion of the crew would have their liberty delayed, for their one night off the ship for weeks, to get that done.

"You are an evil man, Chop," XO said, and Matt thought he heard a bit of admiration in there.

"Price you pay for fresh apples, XO."

"Fair enough."

The CO gestured toward CDR Cafferly.

Cafferly pursed his lips, considering, then said, "Nothing for the entire group, no, skipper."

The CO's eyebrow twitched, but he didn't say anything. Instead he looked at the XO.

"Just my usual, sir." He ran his eyes slowly around to every man in the room. "We're out here doing it now, and it seems we've made that transition without too many hiccups. But don't let your guard down. Keep your standards high, and make sure your men are as well. The next month and a half will be challenging."

"But also fun," the CO said. "Tactical employment of the ship is the core of our job; it's the reason we have officers aboard at all. So as we complete the TrackEx and move into the Tactical Weapons Cert, make sure you take the opportunity to learn." He eyed the men with ENS bars, and then a few of the LT(jg)s as well. Then Gamal. "Especially those of you who are still working on your quals."

"Yes sir," Gamal said in a gravely serious tone.

The CO nodded. "Then let's be about it, gents. Dismissed."

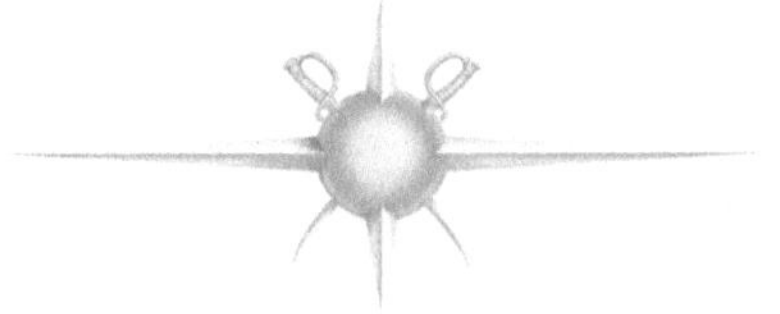

Chapter Forty-Eight

CIC was lit blue, like usual when underway, but there was an energy in the space that Matt hadn't experienced before. The stations were fully manned, ringing the TAO's station at the central fusion plot, and there was activity everywhere.

But it wasn't chaotic activity. The dialog was subdued, orderly, each station going about its business at a deliberate pace that nevertheless felt energetic. Communications were efficient, the primaries at each station talking with their support elements in other spaces, and making reports to the plot coordinator and TAO, in clipped phrases or with acronyms that Matt didn't fully recognize. Numbers and other data flowed in multiple streams, coalescing onto the fusion plot in as close to a sensible form as they could make it.

The fusion plot was laid out in a system-wide format. New California's sun lay at the center. New California herself, a small blue sphere riding a whitish-blue ellipse that depicted her orbital path, was about a third of the way out from the center. The Davidea Jump Point, where the ownship icon that depicted HALSWELL lay, was twenty degrees depressed from the ecliptic and about eighty percent out to the end of the plot, at 056 from system north. The jump point to Sollace, and the rest of the Confederation, lay at the edge of the plot, a few degrees above the ecliptic, at 285 from system north.

Unlike the system's two planets, the two jump points did not rest on ellipses depicting their orbital paths. The jump points were formed by variances in the gravitic profile of the system, and its relation to other nearby systems in the local star cluster...and some other astrophysical and quantum effects that Matt didn't completely understand, but obviously were correct because the jump points worked. Thus their positions were fixed relative to the central star, at least on time scales that mattered for human activity.

There were numerous contacts depicted on the plot. Mostly by the white squares of civilian vessels, but there was one other blue circle—ICS THOMAS LEFCOURT, CDR Cafferly's old ship. She was underway in the orbitals around the planet, and anyway wasn't involved in HALSWELL's operation.

But there was no JACOBS to be seen.

Taking the CO's suggestion as an order, Matt had come to CIC this time instead of the bridge. He needed another CIC Watch Officer U/I for his OOD qual card anyway, so it made sense. Brad Nelson, Assistant OPS, was CICWO, and Matt got permission to station himself U/I. It was the midwatch—all the other CICWOs had U/Is assigned on the watchbill—and WEPS was TAO.

Matt's previous CICWO U/I, on the maneuvering watch back to Copernicus Station, had been uneventful, to say the least. There had been almost nothing to do. He expected this time to be very different.

And he was not disappointed. With the TAO stationed, the CICWO became the plot coordinator, taking all the inputs from the various sensor stations, and the work of the fire control technicians who analyzed their data, and sorting it into a best fit track for each contact that the HALSWELL detected. And also integrating data from the system's Common Operating Picture; merging tracks that matched with HALSWELL's organic data to make sure the Fusion Plot was both accurate and not excessively cluttered.

It was a balancing act.

Brad and Matt were focused on the Gravitic Assessment Plot. It took the input from the gravitic sensors and presented that data on a 3-D plot that the technician manipulated to generate a target solution for the contact.

FC3 Jimenez was shorter than Matt by several centimeters, and broad-shouldered, though his belly strained at the fabric of his underway coveralls. He had a stylus in hand and was tracing the curves sent to him by the gravitic sensor array.

Brad gestured toward the pattern FC3 was making in the display. "Tell me about how gravitic assessment works," he said.

Matt immediately understood; GAP procedures were a checkout he needed for his stellar warfare qualification, the final hurdle he had to jump, after OOD, to earn his SWO pin. It wasn't exactly jumping ahead to go over it now, but it wasn't something he had been focusing on, since OOD focused on ship's systems outside of Engineering, the rules of navigation, and safety of ship.

Still, he'd learned all this in Tactical School, months ago, so he remembered it...mostly.

"It's not like radar ranging. It's passive receive only, so we can't immediately know the range to the contact, or its course. We have to analyze the changes in the gravitic pattern over time, compared with ownship's movement, to derive an area of uncertainty of where the contact is. Then as time goes on and we get more data, we can collapse that AOU and, using a time analysis of the AOU's movement, we can interpolate the contact's course vector."

Brad nodded slowly. "But every ship under thrust leaves a gravitic signature. How can we be sure we're analyzing the correct contact?"

Matt frowned. He knew they had talked about this back in school, but he couldn't quite recall. There was something about the relation of the ship's mass and...

Ah-ha! He remembered.

"Each class of ship leaves a specific signature. It's a function of the ship's mass combined with the output of its engines. That creates a resonance in the gravitic distortion that we can map, and then match to the ship class's signature."

"So how come Jimenez hasn't told us he's tracking the JACOBS already?"

Jimenez glanced up at Brad and made a knowing half-grin, but didn't speak. He kept about his job, leaving the question for Matt to answer.

But Matt's memory was coming back to him now. "The signatures overlap. A cargo carrier at 5Gs will make a similar distortion to a cruiser at 10Gs. But their maneuvering profiles will be different over time."

"So you're saying that there's a range, that the various classes of shipping will have overlapping signatures, and we have to look at it over time to be sure?"

Matt nodded.

Brad frowned. "But what if we're in combat conditions and we don't have the time to do that?"

"Then we interpolate with our other sensors. IR scans, transponder codes, radar returns. Visual from our drones or embarked ISR skiffs."

"JACOBS is running in stealth mode. What does that entail?"

Matt paused, considering. "They've set Condition Omicron. EMCON on all transmitters, so they don't send anything out. Darkened ship. All heat-generating equipment that isn't absolutely necessary secured, to minimize their IR signature."

Brad said, "True. Except they can't stop all transmissions. On an instrumented range like in Olifant they can, but not here. For safety reasons, unless they're in actual combat conditions they have to keep their transponder operating." He raised his eyebrows. "Rules of the Road, remember?"

Of course. Matt knew that. Why hadn't he thought of it? "So we can just pick that up!"

Brad grinned at him, and shook his head. "That would be cheating. For these sorts of exercises, we tell our transponder receiver to filter them out. Unless there is an imminent risk of collision, we won't see their transponder signal." He took a moment to look over the plot FC3 was making. "Anything else we could use to ID them?"

Matt considered. He wanted to say their IR signature.

But in Omicron that would be vastly reduced, because they would have secured so many ship's systems.

As well, the ship's hull was partially constructed of insulating material, to reduce the amount of heat transmitted out into space. Except in the ventral section, which contained the cooling coils for the air conditioning and reactor cooling systems. Those carried refrigerants that had absorbed the internal heat from the ship outside the hull to radiate away.

There was a thin superstructure surrounding those coils to shield some of that IR bloom, but there was only so much that superstructure could do.

So JACOBS would be transiting with their ventral section turned away from the HALSWELL as much as possible, to present the lowest IR profile they could.

That wouldn't be nothing, though. In fact, it would still be substantial. Just lower than what a civilian vessel would present.

"I guess we'll have to fit a bunch of pieces of data together," was all Matt could think to say.

Brad nodded. "And that's our job here as Plot Coordinator." He looked over at FC3 Jimenez. "What do you think, FC3?"

"I think, sir," said Jimenez as he made another notation with his stylus, "that the AOU for this transient does not correlate to any known track in the COP."

Matt looked more closely at the plot he had been working, and after a moment saw that Jimenez was correct. The AOU was a hazy red volume, elongated toward system northeast and southwest, and directing downward from above the ecliptic to just below it, about 60 percent of the way out from the star in HALSWELL's direction.

Numerous civilian ships were transiting in the AOU's general vicinity, but all but two were well outside it. One of those two were just beyond its border and traveling away from it, but had been at the very edge of it at the AOU's effective time. The other had just entered into the AOU fifteen minutes ago, five minutes after the AOU's effective time.

Whatever had caused the gravitic distortion that Jimenez had been working with, it wasn't any of the contacts they had in the system. So what did that leave, but the JACOBS?

Matt felt a thrill as Brad nodded agreement. "I concur. Have you assigned a track number?"

"Yes, sir. Track 25304."

"Press it to the fusion plot and rate it as POSSPA Low."

"Aye, aye, sir," Jimenez said, and began entering commands into his terminal.

"TAO, Plot," Brad said over the internal tactical net. "New contact, track 25304. Assess as possible space vessel, low confidence. Effective AOU time 0224."

Over at the fusion plot, WEPS perked up as the AOU popped up. He acknowledged Brad's report, then rotated the plot and zoomed in so the AOU and HALSWELL's position were more distinct.

Matt left Brad at the GAP and stepped over beside WEPS. He was thumbing his lips with his index finger, thinking the situation over.

"I think that's them," Matt said.

WEPS shrugged. "Could be. But we need more data to be sure."

"Ok, so what do we do?" Matt asked.

WEPS said, "That AOU is a bit too far away to send an ASV. If we had an air detachment embarked we could vector over a skiff to sniff around. But without those options? We change course. If that is JACOBS, she stopped her engines or we'd still be receiving the gravitic distortion. If she did that because she reached her desired vector to intercept us, and we make a large enough course change, she'll be faced with a choice: maintain course and lose the interception she'd planned, or maneuver to follow us. If she maneuvers, we'll get another bit of gravitic data, and we'll be able to reduce that AOU down a bit, and get a better feel for her overall direction of motion." He grinned wickedly. "If she does it enough, we'll reduce the AOU enough that one of our Hammerheads will be able to search it no problem, and she's done."

"That's a lot of ifs."

"And that's the fun of the game." WEPS shifted to the 27MC circuit, which went to all of the tactical support spaces, radio, and the bridge. "Bridge, Combat. Recommend course 223 mark 60 for target track analysis."

"Bridge, aye," said John Connelly's voice, over the same circuit.

"We're not going to shoot a torpedo at her, though," Matt said.

WEPS chuckled. "No, of course not. Once we get the solution tightened up enough, we'll send a tight beam to her, with her position and course vector. If we did our job right, she'll receive and acknowledge, and then we'll reset the scenario. If we didn't..." He spread his hands. "No response, and we look dumb."

As Matt watched, the ship's course vector shifted on the fusion plot, to the new course WEPS had requested.

"I don't like looking dumb," Matt said.

"Me neither. So let's make sure we do the job right."

Matt nodded, and went over to where Brad was reviewing the IR scanning data. There was nothing anomalous there. Or on any of the other sensors, either.

The ball was in JACOBS's court now. All HALSWELL could do was sit back and wait to see what she would do.

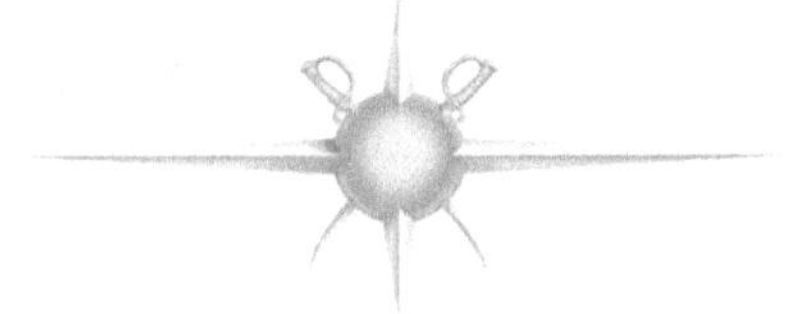

Chapter Forty-Nine

The rest of the watch passed more quickly than Matt expected.

Just as WEPS surmised, after only a short wait, they detected another gravitic distortion, which, after analysis, plotted partially within the first AOU and partly beyond its boundaries, but skewed toward the direction of HALSWELL's new vector.

Plotting the new AOU and interpolating it with the previous one, they narrowed down the possible volume that JACOBS inhabited to one that was much more localized. And closer to HALSWELL.

"Now," WEPS said, rubbing his hands together, "we send out the ASVs."

There was no need to set flight quarters. The ASVs were remotely-piloted from within CIC, and could dock autonomously when they came back to the ship. So within minutes, two of the drones departed their homes at the stern of the ship and sped toward the AOU, vectored to bracket it on opposite sides.

WEPS opted not to change course this time, but directed radar, visual, and IR scans toward the area of the AOU.

Then it became a waiting game again.

An hour passed, as the ASVs positioned themselves.

Matt paced the ring of stations surrounding the fusion plot, each moment expecting to hear one or another of the watch standers announcing a new detection. Brad kept pace with him, a slightly amused look on his face for the first few minutes.

Then he broke the tension by asking Matt to describe the firing sequence for the torpedo tubes.

That was one system Matt hadn't fully studied yet. He stumbled over his answers, and earned himself half a dozen lookups in just a few minutes before Brad gave up and shifted his line of inquiry to the High Pressure Air system.

Matt *did* know that one, and over the next twenty minutes he apparently satisfied Brad enough that he agreed to sign his qual card...after he came back with two lookups.

They stopped their rounds next to the weapons control station. Matt looked at the FC2 who was manning it, and the station's ready condition, and had a flash of memory from his final simulation back at Tactical School.

The station here wasn't that much different than the one he had used, although that was designed for a cruiser. HALSWELL had only two tubes compared with a cruiser's six, and space for far fewer reloads. But as he looked over the holographic interface, he saw that the control layout was mostly the same. Even the tube status indicators...

"Why do we have both tubes loaded for launch?" he said, and inwardly hit himself for not noticing that before. "We aren't going to be shooting at the JACOBS."

Brad chuckled. "Look closer."

Matt raised an eyebrow at him and bent forward, over FC2's shoulder.

The tube was colored red, meaning it was loaded...

Ah! The edge of the red circle in the tube was yellow. Matt had never see that indication at Tactical School. It was either read or green, never yellow. And the rest of the system looked the same.

Then he saw it. Adjacent to the tubes were status blocks for the weapon. At the top they both read "A/N TPS-45 Mk 7 (Training)."

He remembered the weapons load plan for the ship's last inport, though he hadn't been able to observe it because he was doing other things: two warshots for self defense and two training shapes. It was those shapes that were loaded into the tubes.

He looked back at Brad, and he saw that Matt understood, now.

"No use not getting all the training we can, right?" Brad said. "When we get a good firing solution, FC2 will get the training shapes spun up and ready. And if we get the tight beam response to show we were right, we'll fire a slug from the tubes and then practice steering the weapon toward the target, using the computer in the training shapes."

"Fire the tube? But won't that launch the shape out?"

Brad cuffed him on the shoulder. "When you get those torpedo tube lookups done, come back to me, and we'll talk about it."

Matt shrugged. He couldn't argue with that.

He turned to continue his round of the CIC stations, but only took two steps when a report came in from the watch stander on the other side of the room.

"TAO, SCCON. ASVs on station."

Matt turned around. Through the holographic fusion plot, he saw WEPS stand and head over to the control station that had made the report. The watch stander was obscured by the sun's icon, but Matt remembered he was an Operations Specialist First Class.

It took him a second to put the watch stander's station acronym together. But it clicked quickly.

The Space Combat Controller managed the flight paths and tasking for embarked Air Department skiffs and the ASVs. There were two control stations for that task, but with only the ASVs aboard, and not even a full compliment, the tasking was more than sufficient for one man to handle.

Now that the ASVs were on station, there was a much better chance they'd actually find the JACOBS. At least Matt hoped so.

He began getting that same thrill that he'd experienced earlier.

WEPS looked past the OS1, at his control display, and thumbed at his lip again for a moment. Then he nodded to himself.

"Commence active radar scan from ASV-1. Maintain ASV-2 in passive mode," WEPS ordered.

"Aye, sir," OS1 replied.

There was no immediate change in the plot display. In fact nothing happened for several minutes, and Matt began to think their search might end up being in vain.

Then multiple things happened at once.

"Plot, GAP. Strong gravitic distortion detected," announced FC3 Jimenez.

Almost at once, the radar station announce, "Plot, Radar, new radar contact, relayed from ASV-1."

And then, "Plot, IR. Strong IR bloom, relayed from ASV-2."

The activity in the CIC, so subdued just moments before, seemed to erupt into a frenzy. But it was a controlled frenzy. No voices rose, no reports came except in the same clipped, professional ways as before. But it seemed to Matt there was an extra life to it, an urgency of immediate actions taken, and decisions made.

In moments, he and Brad had the new radar and IR detections plotted and correlated...and sure enough, they triangulated almost exactly, into the closest edge of the previous AOU. And with the radar came a definitive course vector as well.

It would take several minutes more to analyze the gravitic detection, but was that really necessary with the other confirming data they had?

Brad apparently didn't think so.

"Press the solution to track 25304," he ordered, "designate as hostile and rate as PROBSPA."

A moment later the fusion plot updated. Instead of another AOU, a discrete red diamond appeared on the plot, with a course vector matching the one ASV-1 had relayed.

It was JACOBS for sure, and she was not on an intercept trajectory with HALSWELL. In fact, she was heading almost directly away from HALSWELL's track. She must have changed course away as soon as the ASV went active on radar, and she knew she was cooked. That explained the gravitic distortion and IR bloom; her turn must have placed her ventral section directly into ASV-2's view.

Brad said, "TAO, Plot. Evaluate track 25304 as hostile probable space vessel. Recommend killing with Hammerheads."

WEPS looked at the plot and grinned. "I concur. Weapons, make Tube 1 ready in all respects."

"Make Tube 1 ready in all respects, aye, sir," FC2 responded, and he began taking the preparatory steps that Matt remembered so well.

"Radio, TAO, prepare tight beam transmission. Data to follow," WEPS said over the 27MC. Then he shifted back to Brad. "Plot, transmit target solution to radio."

"Already sent, sir," Brad replied, and WEPS grinned tightly.

At the side of the fusion plot nearest the airtight hatch was cradled a wired handset. WEPS stepped over and picked it up, then hit a buzzer button next to it. A moment later, he straightened slightly.

"XO, TAO, confirmed track 25304 as hostile PROBSPA. I intend to transmit tight beam and kill with Hammerheads."

A moment of silence, then WEPS nodded. "Aye, sir."

As he put the handset back into its cradle, he said, "Radio, TAO, transmit tight beam."

"Transmit tight beam, Radio aye."

Seconds ticked by into minutes, during which time the airtight hatch opened and XO stepped into CIC. He moved to confer with WEPS, and a moment later FC2 reported Tube 1 ready in all respects.

And then, "TAO, Radio, tight beam response. Transmitted solution confirmed."

XO looked the plot over for a moment, then nodded at WEPS. "Weapons Release."

WEPS's lips twisted into something almost wicked. He keyed the 27MC. "All stations, TAO. Firing Point Procedures, Tube 1."

From there it went almost exactly the way Matt remembered it from Tactical School. Except the shudder that ran through the ship when the tube cycled was quite a bit stronger than the one the simulator had created.

He watched FC2 monitor the simulated weapon as it traveled to the vicinity of the JACOBS, then commenced homing.

If he didn't know better, he would have thought it was an actual torpedo homing on a real target, from the way the weapons control display reacted. Except that this target didn't take evasive maneuvers.

They could have zigged the generated solution, made it a harder engagement. Matt knew that. But for this first engagement, no. Keep it simple, stupid.

A few moments later, the system showed loss of telemetry from Tube 1, and the various sensors registered a simulated hit.

WEPS turned to XO with a satisfied look on his face. "XO, direct hit on track 25304. I assess as mission kill, based on weapon yield."

XO nodded. "I concur." He drew a breath, then looked around the room. "Nicely done, gentlemen."

There was not the kind of hooping and hollering that Matt's class had made in the simulator. The various watch standers merely nodded and kept on about their duties. They didn't even seem to acknowledge the compliment at all.

But Matt couldn't wipe the ear-to-ear grin from his face.

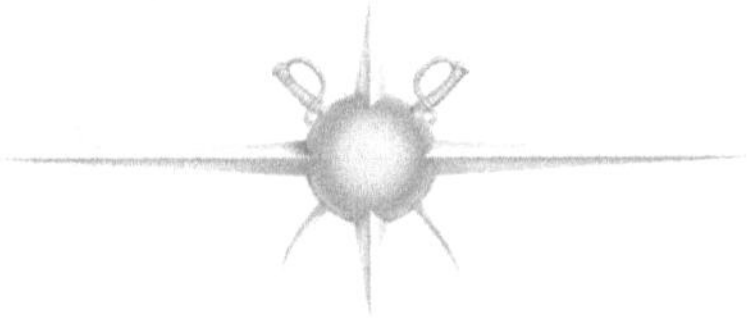

Chapter Fifty

att had EOOW for the Maneuvering Watch this time, and for the shutdown. But it didn't matter, because he had the duty that night. The one night in port between weeks underway.

He found out Tuesday afternoon. Normally OPS posted the duty watchbill at the beginning of each month, but since the ship had been underway for weeks before this inport, and was going to be underway for weeks after, he hadn't bothered. Instead, he posted the watchbill for the single night, after pulling the four unlucky guys aside after lunch's second seating.

Honestly, Matt wasn't all that surprised. He was still the new guy, and unmarried. None of the guys who had the duty that night were married.

It still sucked. But later that evening, he figured a way to make the situation more tolerable.

By the time he completed the reactor shutdown and set the inport watch, it was almost lunchtime. So he hurried forward, and just made it to the wardroom as the Captain was telling everyone to take their seats.

He slid in with the other three JOs who had the duty that evening: Jeremy, Charlie, and Brad.

Charlie noted his expression as he sat, and cocked his head, looking a bit surprised. "You look awful cheerful for a guy with duty on his only night in port."

"That's because I have my lookups," he said, nudging Brad with his elbow.

Brad gave him a sidelong look. "Is that right."

Matt nodded. "I spent the last couple days getting heavy on all things torpedo tubes."

"Sounds like a challenge to me," Jeremy said, between spoonfuls of creamy chicken and rice soup.

Charlie narrowed his eyes. "I don't buy it. No one's that excited for a checkout."

"Well, I am." Three sets of eyes locked onto him, and Matt felt their lack of belief for a long several seconds. Finally Matt shrugged, grinning. "And Marta's coming up to visit the ship for dinner."

The other three were silent. He looked from one of them to the other, surprised by their reactions. "What? You didn't ask your girls to come visit?"

Suspicious faces were lowering, turning more to chagrin.

"Seriously?" Matt felt his jaw dropping. He couldn't have been the only one to think of that.

Brad stood quickly. He looked over the CO's way. "Excuse me, Captain," he said.

The CO, looking a bit surprised, nodded. His surprise only grew as Jeremy and Charlie followed suit quickly thereafter.

"What, did you insult their mothers, Matt?" CSO quipped, from the other end of the table.

Matt just shrugged and dug into his soup. He watched the others leave the wardroom, and couldn't help but snort softly in amusement. He was the new guy, just barely not a NUB anymore, and he was able to think of how to make the bad deal duty night a bit better, but they couldn't?

It was a good lunch.

Marta arrived at the dockside hatch to HALSWELL's mooring just before 1600, as the last of the crew was heading ashore at the end of the stores load. The sentry stationed there passed the word, and a couple minutes later, Matt stepped through the hatch to meet her.

She was dressed casually in a light blue blouse and cream skirt that stretched to her calves, and she had a matching cream bag looped over her left shoulder. She beamed a smile when Matt arrived, and gave him a quick hug.

"Good t' see you again," she said.

"Feeling's mutual," Matt said, then turned to the sentry, a second-class Master At Arms. "I've got her, MA2."

The sentry glanced from him to her and back again, then he nodded with a sly smile. "Have a good evening, Mr. Gilbert."

It only took a moment at the quarterdeck to sign her into the guest log, and then they were past and on to the ship.

Marta's nose twisted slightly as they entered the main starboard-side passageway. "Now I know why your clothes smell the way they do."

Matt laughed. Boat smell was always a surprise to someone who wasn't used to it. "Come on, I'll show you around."

She had never been on a starship before, let alone a Naval vessel, so Matt decided to give her the grand tour. Or as much as he could within security requirements anyway. Since they were only in port for the night, the CSO had opted to keep the systems in CIC online, to avoid the hassle of having to restart everything in the morning. So much as he would have liked to, he couldn't bring her there. And Engineering was right out. So he toured her through the crews mess, one of the classrooms, the AMR and one of the boat decks, and then the torpedo room.

She gasped when she saw the torpedoes resting in their stows. As he led her forward to the tubes and the launcher control panels at the forward end of the room, she ran her fingertips along the length of one of them.

"They bigger than I thought they would be," she said, her tone and expression pensive as she looked on the bulk of the weapon. "How powerful is it?"

Matt shrugged slightly. "It packs a punch. One of these could probably split this ship in half, if it hit us square-on."

Marta pulled her hand away from the torpedo and shuddered slightly. She eyed the weapon with something approaching dread.

Matt stepped closer to her. "Don't worry. It's not dangerous. It can't arm, or explode, until after it's been fired." He put on what he hoped was a re-assuring smile. "There are lots of interlocks to make it impossible."

She licked her lips, and gave a little shake of her head. "No, that's not what I..." Marta drew herself up and swept her eyes around the room. "Can we get out of here?"

"Sure." He took her hand and led her out of the torpedo room, but even after they exited and proceeded aft toward the port-side ladder-well, the pensive, troubled look remained on her face.

Matt had thought to show her the rest of the unclassified spaces first, but he put that idea out of his mind. If there was one place on the ship that would restore her good spirits, it would be the bridge.

And he was right. When they mounted the final stair to the bridge, and she saw the sweeping panorama laid out on all sides, Marta's eyes widened and her mouth dropped partly open.

Even with the bulk of Copernicus station dominating the view on the starboard side, it was a magnificent sight. Despite his many hours up here learning the OOD job, Matt still hadn't fully gotten used to it.

The sun was nearly set when they arrived, its glow approaching the rim of the planet at the ship's stern. The plasteel bubble's polarization system reduced most of the glare, but even still it was breath-taking as it drew steadily closer to its final resting place for the night. On the other quadrants, thanks to the polarization, several of the brighter stars were visible; more would come into view as the flaming orb vanished over the next several minutes.

"Pretty nice, huh?" he said. Her hand was still in his, and he gave her a little tug toward the port-side bridge wing. "Check this out."

She was hesitant at first, walking the narrow steel path out to the wing. But as they reached the spherical conning space, the curve of the ship's hull fell away, and the blue and green, washed with white clouds, of New California stretched out beneath them.

She gasped.

"Oh my..." Her voice trailed off as she just looked down for a long moment. Then she inhaled slowly and looked at him. "I see why you like this."

"It doesn't suck," he said. Then he chuckled. "Well, this part, at least."

She nodded, and looked back down at her birth planet again. "I never come up here before," she said.

Matt chuckled again. "I guess you haven't hung out with too many Navy guys, huh."

She shook her head. "No, I mean... Never come up t' the station."

"Never?" He couldn't keep the surprise from his voice.

"Not my place." She made something between a shrug and a shudder. "Not my home." She gestured back toward the station. "Something made by off-worlders."

Matt blinked, confused. "Local people designed and built it, though."

Marta sniffed. "Would not have, if not for th' Confederation." She met his eyes, and he saw a hint of bitterness there that he hadn't detected before. "Many see it as sign of colonization, that we give up what was ours for money."

"And defense. The Dominance wouldn't be kind to you and yours, if—"

"I know. Some still resent it."

"Do you?"

She was silent for a long moment, staring at the bulk of the station again. Finally, she shook her head. "No. Makes me sad sometimes, though."

Matt wasn't sure what to say to that, so he kept silent. They stood there, hand-in-hand, and watched the sun creep ever closer to the horizon.

It was halfway down when two bells chimed over the 1MC. Matt stirred, and glanced up at the chronometer. It was 1700.

He squeezed her hand. "Come on, let's get dinner."

She returned the squeeze, and he led her down to the wardroom.

Marta brightened noticeably when she saw April again, and the two exchanged quick hugs of greeting.

The other two ladies, who Matt had met in passing but didn't know too well, introduced themselves to her. Siobhan, blond and short for a local woman, was Brad's girlfriend of two years. She worked at the

Marriott up here on the station, though she lived in Manoa. Kelly and Jeremy had only met a couple months ago. She was the shortest of the three women, and more plump, despite having moved to New California from Icarus a year and a half ago, to work at a bank in Ventura. She had taken up the local hair style, though, and greeted Marta in the local manner.

It was just the four couples for dinner, so they kept it less formal than a normal meal at the wardroom table. CS1 Davidson had the duty that night as well, and performed his steward tasks with his usual aplomb, but he also ramped up the joviality a bit.

Marta's melancholy, or whatever it was, had faded completely by the time they got through the soup course, and the room became full of laughter and good cheer.

So it was an enjoyable meal. Not quite as fun as it would have been at a restaurant off the ship, but Matt couldn't complain.

They sat for a few minutes after finishing up, sipping coffee, but soon Davidson cleared his throat meaningfully; he had to get about clearing the table and putting the place back into its usual working order. So they adjourned to the Engineering classroom to continue their conversation.

Matt had to leave briefly to do his 1800 tour of the Engineering spaces, but he hurried back to find more laughter and good cheer upon his return, and once they were sure Davidson was done, they went back to the wardroom.

With nothing going on aboard the ship, they did movie night early. Charlie picked out an old classic noir film that Matt had never even heard of before. It was dark, but witty, and the mystery compelling, and Matt found himself lost in the story.

Until the soft touch of Marta's hand finding his again interrupted his flow, and he looked over at her. Her eyes were soft as she looked at him, and she gave his hand a gentle squeeze. He smiled, and she returned it.

Later, as the evening was growing late, they escorted the ladies back to the quarterdeck. There they said their goodbyes.

"Going t' miss you," Marta said.

"Feeling's mutual. I won't be able to call anymore after a couple days." She nodded, understanding. Light speed latency was no fun, that way. "But I'll send you emails."

Marta sniffed and raised a teasing eyebrow. "You probably meet a girl on another world, forget about me."

Matt snorted. "All I'm going to see for the next two or three months are these ugly lunks," he said, gesturing toward the other guys, who were saying their own farewells. "Believe me, you have no competition."

She laughed, then leaned in for a kiss.

"See you when you back," she said, and he nodded.

Then she went to the hatch and waited for the other girls, who joined her a moment later. They all four waved, and then stepped off the ship.

Matt stood next to the other three guys, and they watched their feminine forms retreat down the docking umbilicus, and disappear out the dockside hatch. They were talking amongst each other, and April giggled about something right before they vanished from sight.

After a moment, Brad inhaled, and straightened. "Well," he said, then he turned and clapped Matt on the shoulder. "Let's go talk about those torpedo tubes."

Back to work.

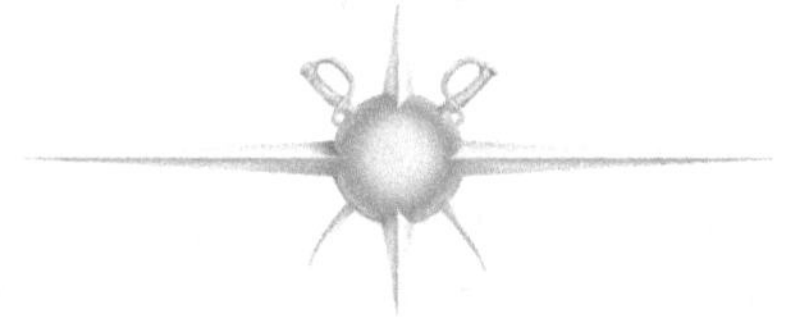

Chapter Fifty-One

Matt had made the transit between New California and Olifant not so very long ago. But he remembered that passage taking quite a bit longer the first time. Of course, he hadn't been standing watch, working on quals, doing divisional work, and missing out on sleep during that first trip, so he shouldn't have been surprised how different this passage felt.

But still, as he watched HALSWELL approach the jump to the Olifant system from the bridge, he couldn't get over the feeling that they had only just gotten underway.

He'd made jumps before, of course. Many times. But he'd never conned a ship through a jump point before.

Maybe that was the real reason for his strange feeling; not wanting to screw the maneuver up.

Not that there was much to screw up. The jump point, by itself, was merely a distortion in the local gravitic field, completely invisible to the naked eye. Or to all but the most specialized of instruments, and those were only carried on survey ships. None of HALSWELL's sensors would have been able to pick it up, if not for the equipment stationed at the point that made the jump possible.

The approach was fairly simple: align the ship perpendicular with the plane of the jump equipment, slow to less than 500 meters per second, and contact jump control once the ship closed to within 100 kilometers.

Jump Control did the rest, really.

Still, as he watched the white contact squares surrounding the eight jump generator satellites grow in size and spread out as the ship drew nearer, he felt a lump growing in his throat.

"Talk to me about how those things work," OPS said, at his side.

OPS had the watch as OOD this afternoon; a proficiency watch so he could remain current on his quals. But Matt had to wonder if it wasn't on purpose, to guide the new guy through on his first time.

And jump gate theory and operations was a checkout that only OPS could sign off, so it made sense to have him here, to knock out the checkout and pracfac all at once.

So it was probably a mix of all three reasons.

Fortunately, Matt had spent the last couple days studying up for the checkout. Still...

"I don't think I could explain the quantum and astrophysical effects completely," Matt said, and OPS sniffed, giving him a wry look.

"Use layman's terms." OPS's tone matched his look: amusement mixed with, "Don't be a dumbass."

Matt flashed a half-grin his way. He gestured toward the satellite labeled Olifant-1 on its contact data box. From the angle they were approaching, it was the lower-right contact of the jump generator's octagonal formation.

"Station number one coordinates with the other seven, to synchronize their activity. When we reach 20 kilometers, it will initiate the sequence. Emitters in the ventral sections of the satellites send a tuned gravitic pulse toward the center of the jump point that stimulates the quantum and gravitic instability there. If it's tuned right, the jump point will open, allowing passage to the connecting system."

OPS nodded slowly. "How do we know the correct tuning?"

Matt shrugged. "Jump points tend to respond to a narrow range of stimulation, but each one is slightly different. The survey teams that chart new systems basically use trial and error to figure out the proper tuning."

"How far apart are they?"

"The systems the jump points connect?"

OPS nodded again.

"If I remember right, the farthest ever charted was…five thousand light years? Something like that?"

"So, conceivably, if we didn't already know where this point was going, we might reasonably expect to find ourselves on the other side of the galaxy?"

Matt nodded.

"Why not in the Magellanic Cloud, or Andromeda?"

That was easy. "They are too far away. The gravitic interaction is so faint that even if a jump point were to form bridging that gap, it could not remain stable for very long. A few hours, at most."

"So how long will these jump points remain stable?"

Matt blinked. He hadn't thought of that before. The galaxy was in constant flux, as stars revolved about the galactic center, new stars were born, and old stars burned out or went supernova…

A chill ran up his spine as he considered that. At some point, all of the jump points they were currently using must someday shift as well…cutting off the star systems they currently inhabited from each other.

After all, the new jump point that formed in Davidea, connecting it with the Dominance, only came into being in the last few decades. If a new one could form, the old ones certainly could fade away.

Matt swallowed, shaking his head.

OPS must have seen the sudden uncertainty, nigh-on dread, that Matt felt, on his face, because he chuckled. "Don't worry, Matt. We've got thousands of years, maybe millions, before we have to worry about it." He gestured toward the control station. "How do the satellites stay in position?"

The new question brought Matt out of the existential thoughts that were starting to creep up on him.

"Well, the jump points are stable relative to the system's center of gravity. If the satellites are positioned close enough, they can take advantage of that stability so they only need small maneuvers to maintain their position."

From behind them and to the left, the QMOW spoke up. "Officer of the Deck, 30 kilometers to the jump."

"Very well, quartermaster," Matt said, and looked at the ship's status display. Their closure speed was 450 meters per second. Just over a minute to go.

"1MC," OPS prompted, and Matt nodded.

He could have used his implants, but he felt like being old-school about it. So instead, he pulled the mic for the 1MC down from the overhead. "All hands, prepare for jump," he announced.

The seconds ticked down. The jump point should be opening just...about...

"Jump Point activating," the QMOW announced.

But he needn't have.

Ahead of the ship, there was a pulse of white, and then a spiraling kaleidoscope of color, every color Matt had ever seen and more, like a rainbow that was running down a drain, losing coherence as it went so that the spectrum became of tumult of mismatched hues that normally would have never fit together.

Then it pulsed again, and the rainbow-swirl condensed into a shimmering circle that filled about half the distance between the jump point's center and the ring of control satellites.

Through that circle was the starfield. But even to the naked eye, it was different than the stars that he had seen in that same spot just a moment before. The new configuration of the sky, in Olifant system.

The satellites were now far enough apart that they were no longer visible in the plasteel bubble ahead of them. Their contact data boxes showed at the extreme top and bottom of the bubble, with arrow pointers showing their relative position off-"screen".

The jump point grew to engulf the ship.

The QMOW said, "Jump in 5...4...3...2...1..."

And then there was a lurch. Like jumping off a high-dive for a second, before the ship settled again.

They were through.

Matt turned to look astern and saw the jump point shrinking behind them, and the cargo ship that had been following them through, still on the other side, 100 kilometers astern. A couple hundred light years astern, now.

"LPSPS data updating," the QMOW said. He pronounced it, "Lip-Sips." As he did, Matt saw the ship's status display fluctuate, its numbers going to dashes for a second before returning to a new value, different from before, as their navigation system updated to reflect their position in the new system.

"Update complete," the QMOW said. "Local standard time 1947."

OPS blinked. "Fun, fun," he said under his breath. Then he grinned at Matt. "Looks like we *do* get the extra-long watch."

And he was right. It had been 1524 in Oliphant system, just about two and a half hours until the evening watch would relieve them. Now they had about four hours until the evening watch took over.

Wonderful. But not unexpected. The time difference between systems was transmitted between the jump control stations on each side when the jump point opened, along with email and other communications traffic that the control stations had in their buffers. So the guys who had the evening watch hit the rack early, and the afternoon watch had been given a heads up to expect a late relief.

Still kind of sucked to see it really come to pass, though.

"Anyway, while we get clear, tell me about LPSPS," OPS said.

Another easy one. "Lagrange Point Satellite Positioning System. It is what it sounds like: satellites positioned at stable Lagrange Points around the star system. They send out time-stamped radio signals, and our system receives them. Based on the satellites's known positions and the time difference between transmission and receipt, we can triangulate our position, on all three axes, within the system."

"How do they keep their reference times in synch?"

"Each of the satellites has an atomic clock, and the system traffic control station sends periodic time updates to account for cumulative errors and relativistic effects. The satellites know their positions and have the ephemeris data for the control station, so when they receive the time updates they apply a local correction to maintain their clocks in synch."

"And what determines system standard time?"

"The Prime Meridian of the most populated planet in the system."

In Olifant's case, that was easy since only one of the six planets in the system had an appreciable population center; the others had mining outposts and the like, but not enough of a presence to cause any competition.

OPS nodded again, slowly. His lips pursed, as though he was trying to find something to stump Matt with.

"Officer of the Deck, passing 30 kilometers outbound," reported the QMOW.

"Very well, Quartermaster." Matt walked over to the QMOW's plot.

As expected, the QMOW had the course to Olifant-d laid out already. It would be about a day and a half's travel. Better get to it.

"Helm, Ahead Standard. Come right to course..." He looked at the planned course vector on the plot again. "146 mark 105."

"Ahead Standard, come right to 146 mark 105, Helm aye," said the helmsman.

The view outside the bridge veered to the right and downward, and though there was no feeling of acceleration, Matt saw the projected course vector extend forward, growing steadily longer as the ship put on its economical 5Gs of acceleration. The indicated velocity value began to increase rapidly.

OPS had followed him to the plot. "Well, Mr. Gilbert, I'd say that went about as smoothly as we could have expected." He raised an eyebrow. "Let's talk about emergency abort procedures."

It was already going to be a long watch. Matt had the feeling it was going to feel a whole lot longer.

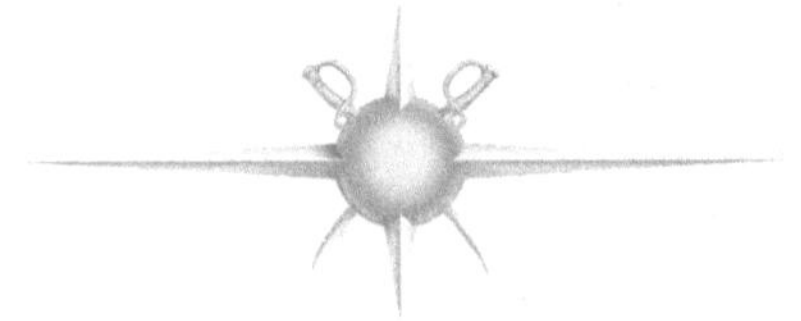

Chapter Fifty-Two

While Fred-1 and -2 could fit about twenty personnel, the Captain's Gig had seating for only six, aside from the pilot. But though it was more cramped, it was fitted out quite a bit more nicely. Faux-wood paneling in the passenger area and thicker, stuffed cushions on the seats made it nearly as comfortable as a high-end civilian transport, and the lighting was more muted, the LEDs tuned to a warmer frequency. So as Matt sat across the narrow aisle from where Charlie had taken his seat, he almost forgot for a moment that he was, in fact, still at work.

Both he and Charlie were in khakis, and it felt strange after months wearing only underway coveralls. But they were going ashore, and coveralls wouldn't do for that.

There was a slight lurch as the Gig detached from the ship, and then they were underway. Matt could see, through the pilot's station at the bow of the boat, the bulk of HALSWELL apparently ascend out of view, and then the Gig pointed down toward Olifant-d, below.

Since there were no elevators on Olifant, just an orbiting station for system traffic control and the docking of cargo and passenger vessels, the best way to the surface was the ship's boats. And since there were Ensigns to pick up from Tactical School, and a Hail and Farewell to plan for tomorrow night, Matt and Charlie got the good deal of heading down to the surface before anyone else.

Just as Jeremy had said, all those months ago.

"Do these guys know where to meet us?" Matt said.

Charlie nodded. "They checked out from Tactical School last week and have been on leave, but the school rogered up on our arrival time. They should be at the landing field when we get there."

Ahead, the planet was growing large through the piloting bubble. Quite large.

As though reading his thoughts, BM1 at the controls said, "30 seconds to re-entry," over his shoulder, and then pitched the Gig up.

The motionless movement of space flight began to give way. The Gig buffeted slightly, and then began to vibrate, and the glow of re-entry plasma began to show through the piloting bubble, growing brighter by the second until the polarization systems blacked out the brightest portions.

A click and a whir beneath Matt's feet, followed by a high-frequency hum that quickly spooled down to a bass tone, and then below, drew his attention, and he felt a momentary confusion. What had just happened?

Charlie must have seen the look on his face, because he gave a thumbs-up. "He just shut down the gravitic drive," he said. "Once we're through re-entry we'll be on the atmospheric flight engines."

"Oh." Of course. That made sense, and now that he thought of it, he knew that had to happen. This wasn't his first time going to and from orbit, after all. It was the first time on a vessel like this, though.

A bit abashed, he made a little shrug and spread his hands. "Never felt it like that before."

Charlie laughed. "Civilian rides are a bit more subtle about it." He waggled his eyebrows. "Don't want to freak out the women and children."

Matt snorted out a half-laugh.

It took another twenty minutes to reach the landing field, and Matt began to wish the Gig had windows in the passenger section. He'd seen the bay, and the peaks of the Hopkins Range, near Tactical School countless times before. But he hadn't bothered to look out at them on the civilian transport he'd taken up to the passenger liner that took him to New California.

Coming back, it would have been cool to have a look at them from above. No dice, though. All he got was the obstructed view through the piloting bubble.

Oh well.

The landing was uneventful. BM1 made a nice, gentle touchdown. There was a minute's delay while he secured the engines, then he turned around in his seat and grinned at them.

"Get ready to be light," he said.

He flipped a switch on his control terminal, and it felt like Matt's stomach leaped for a second as the Gig's internal grav plates secured. The immediate 10 percent reduction in gravity made it feel like he would fly up to the ceiling if he stood too quickly.

He hadn't thought about that. On the civilian transport out to New California, they had gradually increased the internal gravity to acclimate their passengers to what they would feel at the destination.

HALSWELL hadn't done that, and Matt hadn't thought to inquire about it. He supposed it made sense; they weren't going to be ashore on Olifant much at all on this outing.

"Man, it's gonna suck for the new guys," he said as he, slowly and carefully, got to his feet.

Charlie raised an eyebrow at him, then nodded as he got what Matt was saying. "We all went through it. They'll be fine."

The Gig's airlock was at the stern. Matt got it open quickly, then deployed the retracted set of five steps that led to the tarmac. But he felt like he could have just jumped out and floated down.

He didn't, though, and a moment later, he was blinking in the early afternoon light of Olifant's sun on a nearly-cloudless day.

Charlie and BM1 followed him down, and they conferred for a moment.

"How much time do you need to make the arrangements?" Charlie asked.

It had been easy to decide on a location for the Hail and Farewell. Might as well go back to his old stomping grounds, and The Score Zone had been eager to comply when he contacted them via email, earlier in the transit from New California. But he still needed to make the final arrangements face-to-face.

Plus, he wanted to break the new George in.

He looked at his chronometer. 1327.

"I told The Score Zone's manager I'd be there at about 1500. A half hour with him and then another half hour to get back here... Let's say 1600."

Charlie grinned. "The Score Zone, huh? I remember that place." He looked a question at BM1.

"An hour to refuel, then we can leave whenever you're ready, sir," he said.

Charlie nodded. "Ok. I've got a list of things to pick up for OPS and XO. I'll take ENS Price with me, and you and ENS Zenis can do your thing. Let's plan on a 1700 takeoff, BM1."

BM1 grinned broadly. "Outstanding, sir. Give me a chance to snag a couple things as well."

They parted company. Matt and Charlie headed across the tarmac to the passenger terminal, while BM1 went to hook up with the ground support people.

The terminal was large, with a couple dozen civilian gates supporting both orbital and atmospheric transports, and two smaller sections for private and military craft. The latter held just two gates, and with no other military craft on the tarmac, Matt and Charlie faced no delay getting inside.

It was laid out about the same as a civilian gate area: three rows of Naugahyde-upholstered chairs facing a broad, floor-to-ceiling window that looked out at the tarmac. But it was staffed by Navy personnel, and had the usual Navy pictures and notices up on the walls.

There was even a variety of damage control equipment scattered around in clearly-labeled storage bins, just like Matt had grown used to seeing on the ship.

Can take the Navy out of space, but can't take the space out of the Navy, Matt thought with amusement.

There was just one guy on duty in the terminal, an Air Crewman Second Class, complete with the silver "space wings" that enlisted aviation types wore as warfare devices, at the passenger control point just inside the first of the gates.

He looked up as Charlie led the way in, Matt on his heels, and straightened noticeably.

"Afternoon, gentlemen. You guys in from the HALSWELL?" he said.

Charlie nodded. "Afternoon, AC2. You got a couple Ensigns gaggling around here somewhere?"

AC2 chuckled, and gestured toward the far end of the gate area, where sliding doors led deeper into the terminal. "I think I saw them down at the bar, sir."

Charlie rolled his eyes. "No surprise there, I guess." He paused, then said, "We're on the ground for just a couple hours, then we'll take them off your hands."

AC2 nodded, glancing at his console. "Yes, sir. Looks like ground control has already updated you to an 1800 departure."

"We told BM1 1700," Matt said.

Charlie shrugged with a slight half-smirk. "It's not his first rodeo," he said. Then he waved Matt to follow. "Come on, let's go find our new guys."

There was a small bar a short way down the outer corridor from the military gates. And sure enough, AC2 was right. The crowd within was light, but it was easy to spot their quarry: a couple of guys in khakis by the window with a view of the parking lot beyond, with full seabags thrown down on the floor between their table and the wall. They each had plates full of hamburgers and fries, and tall steins of golden-colored beer on the table in front of them. The beers were more drained than the burgers were eaten.

The guy on the left was taller, and more muscular. He had sharply-angular cheekbones and a pronounced chin, and his hair was a deep, slightly reddish brown. The other Ensign was more dark-complected, midway between Jorge and a native of Carraway's world, with black hair and slightly-squinty eyes that were surprisingly light; blue almost to grey. He was of average height and build, and was just lifting his beer to his lips when Charlie and Matt walked up.

He stopped mid-drink, and hastily put his stein down. As he did, a trickle of beer spilled out onto the tabletop.

"Hello, gentlemen," Charlie said, as the Ensign hastily pulled at his napkin to wipe the spilled beer from his mouth and chin. "I assume you're Ensigns Price and Zenis."

The taller guy got up from his chair in a rush. His name tag said he was Zenis. "Ensign Paul Zenis, sir."

Finally collecting himself, Price stood as well. "Ybrahim Price," he said.

Charlie looked at them for a second, then shook his head and chuckled. "You can drop that sir stuff. We're all JO's here. I'm Charlie Vincente, this is Matt Gilbert."

Handshakes all around, but the two Ensigns still looked a bit awkward.

"How are the burgers here?" Matt asked, to break the ice a bit.

"Not bad," Ybrahim said.

"Overpriced," Paul added.

Matt chuckled. "It's spaceport food." He looked at Charlie, unsure where to go from there.

Charlie returned the look, then shrugged. "I guess we'll need to change plans a little bit." Looking back at the Ensigns, he said, "We have some errands to run before we take you up to the ship, but that can wait til you're done eating. Mind if we join you?"

There were two extra seats at their table, and Price waved Matt and Charlie into them. Matt took a seat as Charlie waved over a passing waitress.

"Two of what they're drinking," he said, gesturing toward the Ensigns's beers. He paused, then looked at Matt. "You hungry?"

Matt shook his head. He'd had lunch after watch, right before they left in the Gig.

"And a basket of fries," Charlie said.

The waitress nodded and hurried off, and the two Ensigns sat down as well.

Across the table from him, Charlie raised his eyebrows at Matt. "Told you it wasn't BM1's first rodeo."

Paul and Ybrahim exchanged confused looks.

Charlie's and Matt's beers arrived a minute later, and Charlie lifted his stein up in a little toast. "Welcome to the HALSWELL, gents."

Visibly more relaxed, Paul and Ybrahim raised their steins. Matt did as well, and they did a mutual toast in the air above the table.

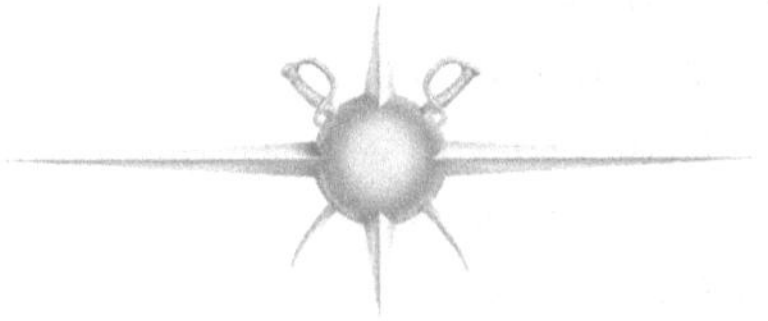

Chapter Fifty-Three

Matt was almost disappointed that the other guys in the wardroom didn't pull the same prank on Paul and Ybrahim as they had pulled on him when he first showed up to the ship. But circumstances were different; the underway watch routine was less flexible and conducive to that kind of joke.

And though Bo Phan, Gamal's relief from the JACOBS, had turned out to be a bit of a jokester, he was no Tim. So the new guys jokes did happen, but they were less...extravagant.

Paul was quick to pick up the gist of what his new duties would be as George. In fact, he gave a couple suggestions during their meeting with The Score Zone's manager that ended up making the Hail and Farewell party quite a bit better.

Still, it felt a little bit odd for Matt to pass over his port and starboard collar devices that evening. He'd kind of gotten used to them, in a weird way.

But very quickly after the ship left orbit the next morning, things got busy enough that Matt put it out of his mind completely.

The main reason Naval Tactical Training Command was based in the Olifant system was that the layout of the system made it ideal to set up an instrumented range for live fire training. Between the orbits of the second and third planet was a loose belt of asteroids and dwarf planets.

For most of the volume the belt took up, that meant almost nothing. But there *was* a cluster of gravitationally bound bodies that maintained a more or less stable orbit together in a portion of that belt.

When the survey teams mapped the system, the Admiralty of the then-growing Icaran Confederation almost immediately recognized its potential.

So over the course of almost a decade, the Corps of Engineers placed active and passive sensor arrays on the surface of every one of those bodies, in the end creating a volume of space where nothing larger than an ASV could traverse without being detected and accurately tracked. They then constructed a control and logistics station adjacent to that volume, and voila! The Olifant Training Range was created.

Every ship and squadron in the ICN had to come to the range periodically to renew their tactical certifications using real weapons against real (un-manned) targets. It allowed for high quality training, as well as quality control testing of the various weapons systems the ICN employed.

Well worth the time and expense, from the Navy's perspective anyway.

Matt had heard about the range, of course, but had never visited or operated in it. That was a thing prospective Department Heads, and XOs and COs, did during their training pipeline, not raw JOs. So he was pretty eager to participate.

Big explosions are always fun.

There was a lot of work involved, though.

It was almost a two day journey from Olifant-d to the range. That time was filled with briefings, range safety training, and more briefings, on top of the usual routine. By the time HALSWELL moored, port side to the logistics and control station, it was almost a relief to get through it all.

The ship moored at 0830. At 1000, they had an Officer/LCPO call in the crews mess.

It seemed to Matt, as he sat down between Chief Evans and EM1 Brossard, that there were more people at this briefing than there had been for the pre-sea trials briefing at the end of their maintenance availability.

There certainly were a lot of unfamiliar faces. Staff members from

TACTRACOM, he was sure. But surely there couldn't be more of them than there had been yardbirds for the sea trial?

He must be imagining it; maybe because, honestly, he was more interested in this exercise than he had been in that testing period.

Two minutes before 1000, the CO walked into the mess, followed by a man with three silver bars on his collar. A full Captain, not just Captain by position. He had the space command pin beneath his warfare insignia, so he had been a CO in the past, and a different pin, the one denoting command ashore, above his name tag. The CO of the range?

After everyone got settled, that question answered itself. OPS started the briefing, as usual. But he deferred to the Captain, who rose from his seat next to the CO, and moved center stage.

"Good morning, gentlemen. I'm Captain Hugo Bishop, Commander of the Olifant Range. I wanted to take a minute to welcome you to our home. We're happy to have you here, and have prepared a full schedule for you over the next three weeks. I'm sure you're excited to get to it. But keep in mind *the* primary rule on the range. Safety. You are here to train, and my team is here to evaluate. No one is here to get hurt or killed. You've all been briefed on the safety rules."

OPS nodded emphatically, and CAPT Bishop continued in a stern, forceful tone, "We will not hesitate to immediately abort any event if there is a violation of those rules."

He didn't need to say what that would mean for the ship's certification. He didn't have to; it was plain even to a new guy like Matt.

CAPT Bishop nodded. Then his stern facade broke a bit, and he gestured toward the starboard side of the room, where a group of officers from TACTRACOM was sitting. "This is Commander Josef Lazlov, head of the combatant tactical evaluation team." A balding man, whose remaining hair was completely grey and who boasted entire canyons of smile and frown lines on his round face, raised his hand in response to the Captain's introduction. "He and his team will be riding you for the duration of your certification. Unless they intervene during a scenario or ask you a question, while you're on watch, please act as if they are not there." He flashed a little half-smile. "They are evaluators, not instructors. That said, if there is a problem with the simulations or scenario presentation, or something is not clear, feel free to bring it to the team's attention, and ask for clarification."

He took his seat again, and OPS took center stage again.

"Thank you, Captain Bishop," he said. Then he nodded to the CO. "Captain, this brief will cover our schedule of events and plan for the Tactical Weapons Certification." He tapped his holopad, and the lights dimmed as the briefing display came to life.

The first slide showed a lot of weapons movements. A lot.

"First order of business is we will be loading and offloading ordnance. WEPS?"

WEPS had been standing off to the side. Now he moved to stand next to OPS. "We currently have two SDMS training canisters, two warshot torpedoes, and two torpedo training shapes loaded aboard. For the first phase of the certification, we will be replacing the SDMS training canisters with warshots, and replacing the warshot torpedoes and training shapes with a full load of eight exercise torpedoes. The SDMS canisters will be swapped this afternoon. Torpedo load is tomorrow. Start time for tomorrow's load is 0600, and we will continue until the load is complete, probably about 1800."

He gestured toward the bottom half of the slide. "For phase two, we will return to the station to load six exercise and two warshot torpedoes. During that time, we will also load anti-ship weapons packages for Air Department assets that we will be embarking. At the completion of the certification, we will moor again to load point defense turret ammunition, offload any unused exercise torpedoes, and load our self-defense torpedo and SDMS loadouts, along with the two SDMS training canisters and torpedo training shapes that we came here with."

WEPS's face was dead serious. "That's a lot of weapons to move in a very short period of time. The weapons reload teams have been drilling in the torpedo room for the last several weeks, but this will require focus from everyone. TACTRACOM will have safety monitors and evaluators with the reload teams in the torpedo room and for every evolution. But this is our ship; I expect everyone to be focused. Safety first."

The CO nodded. "Slow is fast, gentlemen. If we have to delay getting underway to get the loads done safely, we will. So don't feel you have to rush it."

Matt was behind him and CAPT Bishop, so he couldn't see the

CAPT's expression, but something in the way he shifted in his seat when the CO said that made Matt think he didn't entirely like something about what he said. Or maybe it was the way he said it?

WEPS nodded. "Yes, sir." Then he stepped back as OPS tabbed to the next slide, which showed a 3-D chart of the range, divided up into four sectors.

"The first thing to know is we are not alone on the range. Two squadrons, SSR-61, the Silver Eagles, and SSA-25, the Warthogs, are completing their own certifications. There will be no tracking or engagement outside of our assigned area, and we cannot direct any live fire in the direction of an occupied area."

He tapped his holopad, and three of the four sectors became shaded in Red, Silver, and Brown.

"For Phase One, we will be in Sector 2," the Red sector, "SSR-61 will be in Sector 3," the Silver sector, "and SSA-25 will be in Sector 1," the Brown sector.

"Phase One will begin with gunnery scenarios. For two days, we will track and engage target drones with the primary cannons. The scenario events will begin with basic target geometries and work up to complex geometries involving multiple targets. The next two days will involve SDMS tracking and engagement, with similarly increasing levels of difficulty. Following that are two days of point defense turret engagements. Day seven is level of knowledge exams and evaluation team working time.

"Week two is torpedo engagement scenarios. Days one and two will be simple tracking and engagement scenarios, two per day. Days three and four are intermediate-difficulty scenarios involving a single hostile target with one or more interfering contacts."

OPS advanced the slide again, and the sector assignments shifted. Now the sectors that had been shaded Red and Silver merged so they were shaded with alternating Red and Silver hash marks.

"On Day five, the sector assignments shift because SSR-61 will be joining us for the event in Sectors 2 and 3. That day will be an advanced scenario with multiple hostile targets and interfering contacts, with SSR-61 in direct support of our operation. Day six is level of knowledge interviews between our watch standers and the evaluation team, and evaluation team working time. Day seven we moor for the second phase weapons load.

"For Phase Two we will embark a personnel detachment and two surveillance and reconnaissance skiffs from SSR-61, and they will operate as our Air Department for the duration of the scenario. We will again operate in Sectors 2 and 3 for four days of complex integrated tracking and engagement scenarios in coordination with the SSR-61 detachment."

The slide shifted again, and this time all four sectors were shaded in Red.

"The end of Phase Two uses the entire range. It is a Sink-Ex against a decommissioned cruiser hulk. Elements from SSA-25 will participate with us and SSR-61. TACTRACOM will position the hulk, and then it will be engaged in the following order. SSR-61 will make strafing runs using their anti-ship weapons package. Then SSA-25 will engage with their standoff anti-ship missiles. Assuming the hulk has not been destroyed, we will finish it off with our warshot torpedoes."

WEPS smiled thinly at that.

OPS continued, "SSR-61 will disembark their skiffs during our transit back to the station, and we will offload any of their remaining ordnance during our self defense package load."

OPS looked at his holopad again, to see if he'd missed anything, then nodded to himself and looked back up at the CO. "Pending your questions, sir, that's the plan for the event."

The CO nodded slowly. Then he stood up and turned to look at the assembly.

"As you can see, we've got a lot on our plate for this. Complex operations, and real weapons. But it's not a real fight, and as Captain Bishop said, the most important thing here is safety. Remember the watchstanding fundamentals. Watchteam backup is going to be paramount. I want you to review the range safety procedures before every watch, and every evolution. And if anyone—and I do mean anyone—sees, or thinks they see, a potential safety issue, I expect that person to sing out. Loudly." He paused, then said, forcefully and in his no-nonsense Captain voice, "Any member of this crew is authorized, and expected, to stop one of these evolutions in the name of safety. Understood?"

A general murmur of, "Yes sir," rumbled throughout the room.

"Make sure your people get that word, and understand it, as well." He looked around the room slowly, then nodded. "XO?"

"I think you summed it up nicely, skipper."

The CO flashed a quick grin at him, then looked back at Captain Bishop. "Captain?"

Captain Bishop paused, then stood again. He joined the CO, facing the crew. "Again, welcome to the range. Good luck." He paused, then genuinely smiled. "And don't forget to have fun."

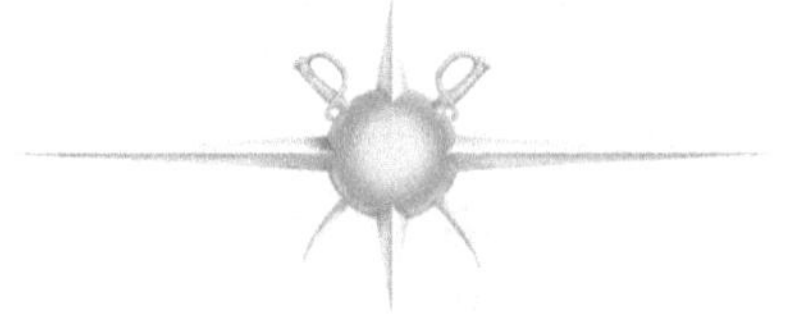

Chapter Fifty-Four

Matt noticed Paul was walking a bit stiffly as he climbed the ladderwell ahead of Matt, on his way back to officers country. When they reached the O-1 level, Matt came up next to him in the corridor.

"You ok, dude?"

Paul looked at him and winced. "I am sore everywhere," he said, in a pained tone.

And Matt understood. It was the increased gravity. Doing anything was harder than he was used to, so he was feeling the same thing as when you've not been lifting weights for a while and start up again... except all over.

That sucked.

Matt clapped him on the shoulder. "Look at it this way: you're getting a workout in, every minute of every day."

"Great," he said, but he chuckled, at least.

Matt grinned at him. "You'll adjust soon enough." Then a thought occurred to him. "Hey, OPS!"

OPS was just opening the airtight door into the wardroom area ahead of them, but paused when Matt called out to him. He cocked an eyebrow Matt's way.

"I was just thinking about the eval team. Did they adjust to our higher grav somehow, or...?"

OPS looked from Matt to Paul and back again. "Or are they going to be feeling it like the George here?" He shook his head, then shrugged. "If they didn't, they're just going to have to suck it up, like everyone else."

Then he ducked through the door.

Matt followed, holding the door open so Paul could grab it before hurrying to catch up the OPS.

"We aren't worried that they'll be grumpy, mark us down?"

OPS snorted. "They're professionals, Matt. But if it makes you feel any better, the gravity difference isn't a surprise to them. They have to deal with ships from different systems all the time, and I've been told the grav plates in some of their spaces are separately adjustable from the rest on the station. So if they're smart—and they are—they probably made some preps."

OPS rounded the bend in the corridor beyond the wardroom and stopped at the cork board where the watchbills and other information sheets were posted. Then he stopped and pulled a printed page from the binder he was carrying, and tacked it to the board with an available thumbtack.

"What's that, the new watchbill?"

OPS nodded, and proceeded to his stateroom door.

Matt scanned the page, and frowned. "What happened to the U/I watches?"

OPS stopped, turned around, and looked at Matt like he was daft. "It's an evaluation, Matt. An inspection. No under instructions in tactical watch stations until it's done." He gestured toward Paul. "Just like Paul won't be EOOW U/I when we have the reactor safety inspection after we get back to New Cali." He grinned, almost wickedly. "That'll be your time to shine."

Disappointment flooded through Matt, though his rational mind screamed that he shouldn't be. That it made perfect sense, and he knew it. But dangit, he had gotten fired up hearing about all the cool things the ship was about to do. And now he'd...have to hear about it all from Maneuvering?

That sucked worse than being sore, like Paul.

OPS must have seen it on Matt's face, because his expression softened a bit. "Look, you can probably watch the gunnery evolutions from the bridge, if you're off watch for it. And maybe the Control Tower will let you squeeze in for flight quarters with the SSR-61 guys." He paused. "Maybe. But we're out of instruction mode right now. Besides, you're almost pracfac complete for OOD, right? Better use of your time to study up for the rest of your checkouts, and get ready for the exam."

Matt nodded. He was right, of course. And certainly there would be more opportunity to do the fun tactical stuff down the line, once he was fully qualified.

Suck it up, the rational, professional voice in his head told him. Suck it up, and do your job.

It was right, also.

OPS took his nod for the end of the conversation and clapped Matt on the shoulder, then he went into his stateroom and pulled the door closed behind himself.

Matt looked at the watchbill again, more carefully. OPS really hadn't been kidding; everything had been shifted around, and as he looked at it in light of what OPS said, he saw why.

EOOW was the four junior-most guys: him, Jeremy, Jorge, and Vasili. And no matter that Vasili and Jorge had both finished their OOD quals in the last month. Matt had the evening watch. Paul was U/I under Vasili on the morning watch, and Ybrahim U/I under Jorge on the afternoon watch. Jeremy had the midwatch.

Up forward, of course the Department Heads were TAO. Gamal was CICWO instead of TAO U/I. The other three most senior JOs were CICWO as well. The rest were OOD or Conning Officer.

Stacking the deck for the inspection. Made sense.

"Well, just have to make the most of it," Matt said to himself.

Beside him, Paul was also perusing the watchbill. "Oh hell yeah, I got a U/I already?"

Matt looked sidelong at him. Had he sounded as eager for reactor duty as Paul did, when he first came aboard?

Paul noticed the look. "What?"

Matt shook his head. "Nothing. It good that you'll be with Vasili. He's pretty heavy on the plant. You'll learn a lot from him."

Paul grinned. "I can't wait."

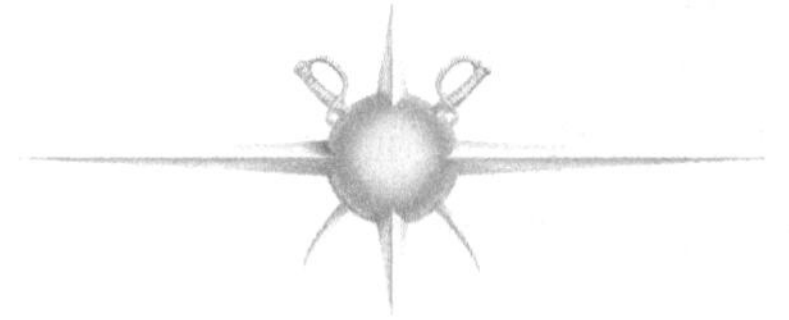

Chapter Fifty-Five

OPS was right. There really weren't many more pracfacs that Matt had to accomplish on his OOD card. He hadn't conned the ship into a mooring yet, and he had to do three more drill sets. He did have quite a few more knowledge checkouts to get through, though. And the qualification exam was looming.

So over the next two weeks, he hunkered down and studied. Hard. And despite the time crunch of the evaluation schedule, he managed to get several of those checkouts completed. He also got OPS to consider putting him on the maneuvering watchbill for their final docking at the logistic and control station, to knock out that mooring pracfac.

If that panned out, Matt figured he might have his OOD quals done before they got back to New Cali. That would just leave some high-level tactical checkouts with WEPS, CSO, and CO, and a few odds and ends pracfacs, and he'd be done with his SWO quals as well.

Maybe he'd manage to pull that off before he got promoted in a few months. Maybe.

So Phase One was productive. But it still was less than satisfying being back in Maneuvering instead of on the Bridge, or in CIC, the whole time.

He managed to get up on the bridge for one of the gunnery exercises, though.

Jerry was the OOD for that evolution, and Rasheid the conning officer. But the evaluation team was mostly down in CIC, with just one observer up on the bridge. So he got permission to observe, from one of the bridge wings. Ybrahim and Jorge came along as well, since it was the morning watch.

The three of them stood, surrounded by the panorama around them, and tied their implants into the Tactical comms network—muted, of course, so they couldn't speak over anything. Jorge showed Matt a neat trick that he hadn't learned yet, and called up a dialogue window on the outboard side of the bubble showing a representation of the fusion plot down in CIC, so they had a good idea of what was going on.

It was the second day of gunnery, so there were three targets in their area of the range. One was flying a solo track through the area. The other two were transiting in tandem.

CSO was the TAO, and he opted to engage the solo target first, then come back for the pair. At first it seemed like a simple interception, but at the last minute the solo target made a hard turn to port and downward, and accelerated away faster than HALSWELL's maximum of 18Gs.

It turned into a tail chase, with the target's red diamond directly ahead as the ship pressed forward at Flank acceleration. Matt watched as the range to the target steadily crept up, and felt a growing concern.

Very soon, it would have pulled out beyond the maximum range of the primary cannons. And then what? He imagined not successfully engaging the target wouldn't bode well for their evaluation.

Next to him, he saw similar concern on Jorge and Ybrahim's faces.

It looked like this was going to be a wash-up.

Then CSO ordered a 30 degree turn to port. The target moved rapidly off to the starboard side, and its range began ticking up even faster.

"What's he doing?" Ybrahim said, and Matt didn't know how to answer.

Jorge's eyes widened then, and he grinned. "Watch this," he said, and Matt cocked an eyebrow at him.

"When you qualify OOD, you'll understand," Jorge said in response. He raised his nose slightly as he said it, like a man putting on airs.

Matt snorted, and was about to respond, when CSO ordered all stop, and hard to starboard.

The ship's acceleration dropped to zero, and she yawed about, so now the bow was pointing just ahead of the target.

And the primary cannons opened up.

Matt knew how the cannons worked. They projected plasma pulses from the cation and anion flows in the engine room, separated in time and on opposite sides of the ship so they wouldn't attract each other instead of heading on to the intended target. But he'd never seen them fired before.

The flare of the cannons were brilliant, even with the polarization function of the plasteel bubble, and Mat blinked away purplish after-images for a second.

The projectiles lanced forward, the first two shots even with the ship's plane of motion. Three more sets of projectiles followed, angling upward and downward as the cannons tracked through their—very limited—training range.

The CSO ordered flank again, and steadied on a course astern of the target.

Quickly, Matt realized what CSO had done. By changing the ship's course, he had opened up the angle between the target's vector and the ship's, so he could get a leading angle for the shot while also bracketing the target's motion in the vertical axis.

But surely the target could maneuver, and evade...

The ship fired another salvo just as the target zigged, turning away from the incoming fire, and from HALSWELL. Which put it on a course toward CSO's new chosen vector, and the new salvo he had just sent down range.

Matt thought for a second the target would be able to evade again, and it did try. But this second salvo was more dense; CSO had fired over a dozen times.

The target zigged and yawed, shifting its course wildly as it veered past the income fire. But the salvo was too large, and last of the plasma balls struck it.

There was no sound, of course, but the flash of the impact was distinct. Then the red contact diamond winked out.

"Yes!" Ybrahim said, clenching his fist.

Jorge gave Matt a little punch to the shoulder. "Ye of little faith."

"I stand corrected."

The pair of contacts was a tougher nut to crack. They were tracking through the other side of HALSWELL's area, so CSO kept the ship at flank, to close the distance to them as quickly as possible. But as HALSWELL approached, they broke formation, each zigging away in opposite directions.

They led a merry chase, and CSO ordered several salvos that missed each of the targets. But finally, after what seemed an age, he settled HALSWELL down onto a course vector that brought both of the targets on a converging track ahead of the ship.

The cannons each fired a salvo of four shots, and as the projectiles flew forward, Matt immediately saw that each cannon had been targeted on a separate drone. And the fire hit both of them, almost as their courses would have crossed ahead of the ship.

The three of them stood there for a minute after the event ended. Finally, Matt blew out a breath.

"That was pretty awesome," he said.

The other two nodded agreement, then they left the conning bubble and went below.

After that, Matt decided not to bother observing the SDMS and point defense turret events. No way they would be as dynamic as the gunnery was, from the bridge, so he just set to his studying instead.

During the brief in-port period between Phase One and Phase Two, Matt focused on divisional work. Two of his junior EMs were up for maintenance quals, and he and Chief convened two mini qual boards for them, in preparation for their time with the CHENG after the evaluation.

They were in the Engineering classroom in the middle of the second board when the CO came on the 1MC.

"Good afternoon, HALSWELL, this is the Captain," he said, and EM3 Venai stopped what he was writing on the briefing board.

"First, I want to say well done. Phase One of our Tactical Weapons Certification is complete, and I'm pleased with all of your efforts and hard work. With that said, we just received a message from our Commodore, and I have good news and bad news."

Chief raised his eyebrows, and Matt could see the question on his face. Probably the same as Matt was thinking: what kind of bad news?

He didn't have to wait long, because the CO said, "The bad news is we're going to be away from our families for longer than we expected. We have been ordered to the Melrose system for a two-week goodwill visit at the conclusion of the Tactical Weapons Certification. What that means is we'll be receiving official visitors from the Melrose government, and many of us will be attending various receptions and functions on the surface of Melrose during that time. So I hope you have your dress uniforms ready. Between the transit to Melrose and our time there, we'll be getting back to New California about a month and a half later than planned. But we'll get the chance to show the flag to a friend of the Confederation, and take some well-earned liberty." He paused. "That's the good news, in case you were wondering."

The CO said, "That said, Phase Two of our certification starts tomorrow, and it will be very challenging. So keep focused, and let's show the evaluation team what HALSWELL is made of, so we can enjoy that liberty on a high note. Carry on."

The 1MC winked out, and EM3's face looked like it was about to split, from the size of his eager grin. "Melrose? I've heard that place is awesome. Man, this is gonna be great!"

Chief shrugged. "Probably. But what does that have to do with scheduling monthly maintenance?"

EM3's smile vanished, wiped back to a look that almost approached professional stoicism. Almost. "Aye, Chief. As I was saying..." He turned back to the briefing board, and what he was writing a moment ago.

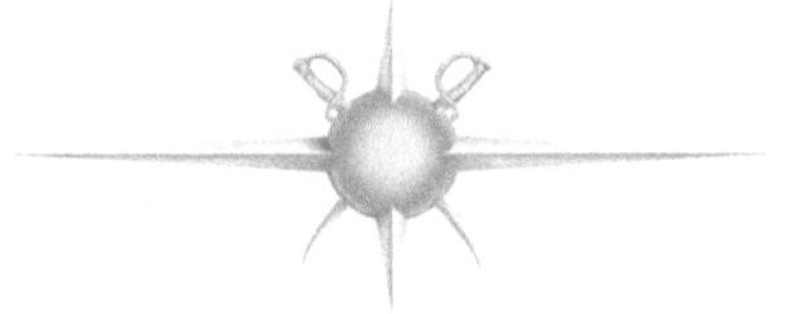

Chapter Fifty-Six

When Matt first came aboard the HALSWELL, there were a number of open bunks in the various officers staterooms. Since then, some had been taken briefly by members of the shipyard testing team, and the FRIGRON personnel, who had come underway with the ship before. During Phase One, between Paul and Ybrahim coming permanently aboard and the TACTRACOM evaluation team staff, the wardroom was noticeably more crowded.

Now, in Phase Two, it was packed to the gills. The SSR-61 detachment consisted of six officers—three crews to rotate between their two skiffs—and they all needed places to rack out. The senior-most of the group, a Lieutenant Commander and Officer in Charge of the detachment, ended up bunking down in Harry and Matt's stateroom. It was the first time since Tim left that all three racks were filled.

Shouldn't have been a big deal, and really it wasn't, but it was an adjustment, one more body to squeeze past when coming in and out, or maneuvering around.

The LCDR and his assistant OIC, a full LT, came aboard directly from the station as the ordnance load completed, along with a couple dozen enlisted crewmen who maintained and supported the skiffs. After the ship got underway, the skiffs landed with the remaining pilots.

Remembering OPS's words from earlier, Matt decided to observe flight ops from the Control Tower while the skiffs were landing on the ship.

Turned out, that was the right time to do it. Since the evaluation didn't technically start until the next morning, the eval team wasn't observing and assessing the Control Tower team that evening, so there was actually room for Matt to stand in the corner and watch.

The Control Tower protruded slightly from the stern-most point of HALSWELL's upper deck. It was enclosed in transparent plasteel, allowing observation down to the flight deck below and up almost to the zenith above the ship, and almost 180 degrees in azimuth. So the controller could see every move the incoming craft made, and assist as necessary...and possible. A flashing red strobe was mounted at the peak of the tower's protrusion, to indicate to the bridge that flight operations were in progress, and help provide a reference to the pilots as they made their approach.

Lighting along the perimeter of the flight deck helped with that as well.

The process was certainly not very simple. Matt had never flown anything but the ship's boat that one time, and he imagined it wasn't exactly easy to do what those guys did. But it wasn't dramatic, at all.

The Tower crew, when Matt was there, consisted of Operations Specialist Chief Bruckman, who led the Sensors Division under Jorge, and OS2 Nielsen. Nielsen operated the flight deck equipment while Chief handled comms with the pilots, and supervised, coffee mug in hand. Of course.

When the skiffs were 100 kilometers out, they contacted the tower, and OS2 activated the landing lights and radio homing systems. Chief talked the skiff in until they were ten kilometers out, then OS2 opened the hangar bay doors.

The pilots took it from there. There were systems in the tower that could remotely interface with the skiff's controls to land it automatically, or via manual control from the tower, but those were backups, for emergencies.

No pilot wanted to have the computer land for him. Or at least Matt assumed not.

The landing was slow, until it was not.

One moment the skiff was way out there, seemingly creeping toward the ship. Then it was close, real close, just off the stern. It paused there for a moment. Through the piloting bubble at its bow, Matt could just make out the pilot making some adjustments.

And then it was down. It just swooped on in, and for a second Matt thought it was going to crash into the hangar. But at the last second, it slowed to a bare crawl and lowered until it was just above the flight deck. Then it eased on into the starboard side hangar bay.

It was smaller than Matt expected, actually. Halfway between the Captain's Gig and Fred-1 and -2, with a body that was basically a rounded-off box, two snubby wings with what looked like mounts for weapons or equipment, and a short, cruciform-style tail and elevator arrangement at its stern. From that, Matt assumed it was capable of atmospheric, as well as space, flight.

The second skiff followed about five minutes after the first, landing in the port-side hangar bay.

And that was it.

Matt thanked the Chief, who promised to sign his qual card later, and headed down to his stateroom. There, he opened up the POTTER-class tactical procedures manual on his terminal, and got to reading.

Or tried to. Fifteen minutes along, the 1MC piped to life. "Officers Call in the wardroom. All off-watch officers, your presence is requested."

There wasn't an O-call on the plan of the day. What was the deal?

Matt closed out his terminal.

The wardroom was mostly full already when Matt arrived, and the new faces stood out plainly.

Five guys from the aviation squadron were clustered around the kiddie table. They wore olive green jumpsuits, to contrast the navy blue everyone else wore, and their "space wings" were different from the SWO pins Matt was used to seeing. The starburst effect was the same, but the horizontal tines were instead curved, feathered wings.

The pilots were chatting amongst themselves, while HALSWELL's officers did the same, and while there was no hostility between the two, there was a gulf that Matt immediately sensed. It was different from other riders who had come aboard. The FRIGRON and shipyard people were not part of the crew, but...almost?

Probably it was familiarity, and the fact that all of them were SWOs, so immediately spoke the same language and were part of the same tribe. In a sense.

Or maybe someone just needed to break the ice.

Matt walked over to the kiddie table. A couple of the pilots spotted him and nodded.

"Hey guys. I just watched your landing from the control tower. Is that as fun as it looks?"

The pilot nearest him shrugged. "You kind of get used to it after a while, so it just becomes routine."

The guy sitting next to him rolled his eyes and nudged the speaker with his elbow. "He means yes. But then, he's in the back all the time, so the fun's kind of lost on him."

This close, Matt saw a subtle difference between their warfare devices. The first guy's had crossed spears, instead of the crossed sabers that the SWO pin and the second guy's had. Then he got it. The first guy was a Naval Flight Officer, not a pilot. His job was running the sensors and electronic systems, not actually flying the skiff.

The NFO smirked. "Good thing for you I am, Skittles. You'd get lost crossing the street."

The pilot looked at him for a second, then shrugged. "Fair."

"Skittles?" Matt asked.

"It's my call sign," Skittles said.

The youngest-looking of the group, a LT(jg) who also wore pilot's wings, said, "In flight school, he brought some candy up with him during a zero-G training flight, and the bag burst."

Skittles nodded, wincing slightly. "You wouldn't believe how long it took to clean all of them out of the cockpit. Damn things found their way into places I couldn't imagine. One of them even managed to pop a circuit breaker, somehow."

Matt chuckled, shaking his head. "That sounds—"

He stopped talking as the wardroom door opened and the squadron detachment's OIC walked in, along with the CO and XO. The OIC made a beeline for his guys, nodding greeting to them, and Matt.

"Jeepers, you have the package?" he asked.

The guy who had told the skittles story nodded. He reached down to the deck at his feet and came back up with a thin rectangular object, wrapped in brown paper.

The OIC took it—Matt noticed he was an NFO also—and headed over to the CO's side.

The CO hadn't taken his seat. He stood in the space between the main table and the kiddie table, and surveyed those present for a moment before nodding.

"Looks like we have a quorum, so let's get started." he said. He gestured toward the OIC. "I wanted to welcome aboard Lieutenant Commander Julio Vargas, call sign Vegas, and his team. They are going to play a key roll in Phase Two's events, and he is now our Air Boss. I want you all to consider them fully a part of the crew while they're here. Commander?"

LCDR Vargas said, "Happy to be here, Captain. I brought a token from our CO, if you don't mind." He held out the package to the CO.

He accepted it and tore the paper off, then held it up for the wardroom to see.

It was a plaque, showing the Silver Eagles's squadron seal set on darkly-stained wood.

The CO handed the plaque off to the XO, who traded it for an object he was carrying. No surprise what that was: the HALSWELL's command plaque, which the CO gave to Vegas.

That bit of formality aside, Vegas introduced his team.

Matt had already met Skittles and Jeepers. The NFO who had spoken first went by Turbo. The other two were Freebie and Hound Dog. They all had real names too, of course, but Matt focused more on remembering their call signs, since it seemed that's mostly how they referred to each other.

But over the rest of the week, Matt didn't see much of them. The ship had an office space and pilot's ready room set aside for the Air Department down on the O-1 level, adjacent to the airlocks into the hangar bays, and they spent most of their time there, except for meals and the evening movies.

And since Matt had the evening watch...he mostly interacted with them in passing. Which was a shame, because they seemed like good guys, who were having fun doing what they did.

Well, if the ship really did get sent on deployment later on in the year, like OPS alluded to before they left New Cali, they would embark an air detachment then, as well. And he'd be complete on his quals by then, so he'd have a lot more time to get a peek at their world.

So Matt continued to focus on his job, and not hobnobbing.

And so the days passed, with the ship occasionally shuddering from torpedo launches, until it came time for the Sink-Ex.

They had a separate pre-evolution briefing for that the evening before, again down in the Crew's Mess. The main thing that came out of the briefing was the CO announcing that he was authorizing off-watch personnel to observe from the bridge or the Navigation Observation Spaces on the O-5 level, the uppermost space on the ship above the bridge, and at the ship's keel on the 2nd Deck. In those spaces, Navigation Division kept optical astronomical observation equipment, so the ship could take star sightings to navigate by, should the other navigations systems fail.

Apparently the Sink-Ex was actually separate from the evaluated portions of the certification; it was a good deal that the ship got to participate in it. So observers would not get in the evaluation team's way.

Did that include CIC as well?

Matt asked OPS after the briefing, and OPS thought it over for a moment, then nodded. "Just keep to the sidelines."

The Sink-Ex was scheduled for the morning watch. So once again, Matt, Jorge, and Ybrahim observed together, from the back of CIC.

HALSWELL remained at station-keeping half the morning, outside of the planned engagement zone for SSA-25's missiles. It was an exercise in anxious semi-boredom as Matt watched the chronometer tick through minutes, and then hours. And then, finally, the range gave clearance to commence.

Vegas and Freebie, the assistant OIC, were in CIC monitoring at the SCCON station. Letting their JOs have the fun; Matt approved of that.

Matt had his implants tied into the Tactical and SCCON nets, so he heard the order to launch both skiffs. A few minutes later, Eagle 504 and Eagle 505 appeared on the fusion plot, moving away from HALSWELL, toward the cruiser hulk in the center of the range.

SCCON ordered Jeepers, in 504, to make the first pass, and the skiff accelerated quickly ahead.

One thing Matt had learned during his brief encounters with the pilots was that, though the skiffs were usually configured for surveillance and reconnaissance, they did have a self defense cannon. It wasn't good for much more than scaring a small civilian ship, but it was better than nothing. But they could be re-configured to a limited anti-ship role as well. That entailed removing most of the skiff's sensor and electronic countermeasure pods and installing a pair of missile cannisters. The missiles were the same as the SDMS system fired, just with a different software build. SDMS could configure the missiles either for threat intercept or anti-ship mode; the skiffs could only access anti-ship mode.

The missiles weren't all that big, and didn't pack a very big punch individually, but a salvo of multiple missiles could do some nice damage to a small combatant.

A cruiser could shrug it off, though. For a while, anyway. Which is why SSR-61 went first on the Sink-Ex.

Jeepers completed his pass, and scored five hits out of six. One of his missiles had an error of some kind and lost tracking, flying completely past the hulk and on into open space.

"And that, right there," Jorge said, leaning in closer to Ybrahim and speaking softly so his voice wouldn't carry and disturb any nearby watch standers, "is why we have the range safety rules, and why they set up the geometry for the shot the way they did."

Ybrahim frowned for a moment, then nodded. "The missile will run out of fuel and shut down before it exits the range."

Jorge nodded. "So there's no danger of it homing in on some poor schlub somewhere. The range will keep track of it, and pick it up after the event's over, and no harm, no foul."

"Makes sense," Ybrahim said.

A few minutes later, Eagle 505, piloted by Skittles, hit with all its missiles, and the skiffs turned back toward the HALSWELL.

Thirty minutes passed while the skiffs cleared SSA-25's engagement zone and the range checked again to ensure the area was clear of unexpected traffic, and that the hulk was in a fit condition to receive the next round of attacks.

No worries on the latter, not from just the skiffs's small missiles. But civilian traffic sometimes didn't see the cautionary Notice To Spacemen that system traffic control sent out to announce the exercise, or ignored it. There were plenty of stories about some clueless civvie wandering into an exercise and messing it up, by mistake. And unlike the skiffs, the missiles SSA-25's interceptor/attack fighters carried were no joke. They didn't pack as much of a punch as HALSWELL's torpedoes, but just one of those missiles would ruin even a large civilian vessel's entire day.

Still, it felt like forever before the control station declared the range hot, and ordered SSA-25 in.

The engagement zone for the missiles was a red-shaded conic section on the fusion plot, extending halfway between the hulk and HALSWELL, widening as it approached the hulk.

The plan for the shot entailed a section of two fighters approaching from astern HALSWELL, and launching as they drew abeam her port side. That way, even if the missiles malfunctioned and commenced their target search earlier than planned, HALSWELL would be outside of the visible window of their sensors, so there was no way a missile could home on her by mistake.

Unless something went really, really wrong.

The CO was next to the CSO at the fusion plot, watching as the fighters appeared from astern, and Matt noticed that SDMS was powered up and in standby, as were the point defense turrets.

Just in case that really, really wrong thing happened, he supposed.

It was very unlikely. So unlikely it probably wouldn't happen in the remaining lifetime of everyone aboard, combined. But if it did...

Good to be ready, just in case.

The two fighters launched at the designated point, and adjusted their vectors to exit the range as their missiles flew toward the hulk.

The specs said that those fighters could carry two missiles each, but each only fired one, depicted on the fusion plot as the upper half of a blue semicircle above a blue M, from which the missile's course vector extended.

The missiles approached the planned activation point, and Sensors reported that the ESM suite had picked up side lobe from their targeting radars.

Matt felt a tension depart that he hadn't noticed he'd been feeling. If they only detected the side lobe of the radar, the main beam wasn't directed at HALSWELL. No malfunction, at least not one that was dangerous to them.

That was good.

The missiles streaked forward, and Matt was impressed at the acceleration they were putting on. Much quicker than a torpedo could manage; harder to evade.

A moment later, it was over. Both missiles converged on the hulk, and their contact icons winked out.

"Sensors, Captain. Project visual onto the fusion plot," said the CO over the tactical net.

Besides the telescopes in the Navigation Observation Spaces, which were not especially powerful, the ship had a bank of high-powered, trainable telescopes for just this purpose, and a moment later, an image appeared in the fusion plot.

Chagrin flooded Matt as he took in what the telescope was showing. The cruiser hulk was shattered, broken into three large pieces and uncountable smaller ones, scattering in all directions from the force of the missiles's explosions.

CSO shook his head. "She's done, skipper," he said, and the CO nodded agreement.

Then he sighed. "No torpedo shoot for us."

The range confirmed it a few minutes later. They declared the hulk destroyed and the range cold, and better luck next time.

"Sorry about that, HALSWELL," the range safety coordinator said over the event control circuit. And he sounded like he meant it.

A moment later, the CO got on the 1MC to break the bad news to the ship, and Matt could feel the letdown practically seeping through the bulkheads as everyone got the word.

"Well, shoot," Jorge said, as the three of them left CIC and headed back to the wardroom. "That sucks."

It did.

Oh well, like the man said. Maybe next time.

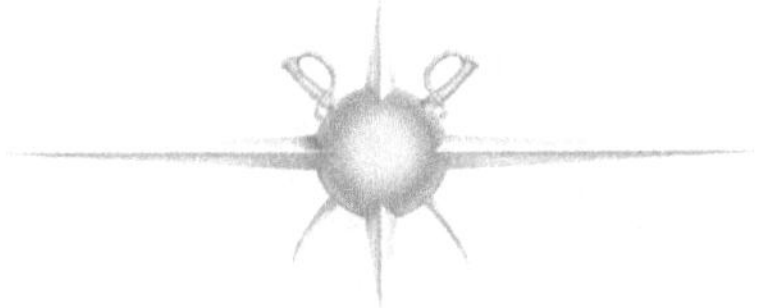

Chapter Fifty-Seven

The range logistics and control station was close, very close, off THALSWELL's port side. Matt watched it creep closer from the port-side bridge wing, with Harry beside him, and tried not to let the CO's presence behind them make him nervous.

No reason to be nervous. Of course not. Just his first time ever conning the ship onto a mooring, was all.

OPS came through, and posted Matt as Conning Officer for the maneuvering watch, and the approach had gone pretty much flawlessly up to this point. Harry had given a few gentle nudges here and there, but Matt had been conning the ship enough that he was comfortable, now, with how she responded to helm and engine commands.

And he'd observed mooring maneuvers several times before, read all the procedures. So he knew what to do, and when.

Still, with less than two hundred meters between the ship and the station's massive bulk, completely taking up the entirety of the view to port, he was becoming keenly aware of the small margin for error in this evolution.

The main engines were in standby and he was maneuvering with quick puffs of reaction thrusters that were placed along the length of the hull. It really didn't take much; there was no resistance to slow the ship down, after all.

Still...

Matt licked his lips and checked the closure rate. 1.5 meters/second, with 175 meters to go. About a minute and a half. He figured he'd need to apply thrust to stop the ship in about—

"You're a little fast," Harry said, softly.

Matt looked at him, and Harry made a, "Get on with it," spin of his hand.

Ok, apply thrust now.

"Helm, fire port thrusters."

"Fire port thrusters, helm aye."

Down the length of the ship's hull, grey-white plumes shot out as the thrusters fired.

"Thrusters firing," reported the helm.

The closure rate began to reduce, slowly at first. 1.25 meters/second. 1.

"Helm, secure thrusters."

The plumes stopped before the helm reported back, and the closure rate stablized at 0.8 meters/second.

Range was down to 100 meters now. The ship needed to be stopped between 25 and 50 meters for the mooring gear at the bow and stern to clamp onto the station's anchor points.

He looked back at the alignment markings painted on the station's hull. The SFG point was slightly forward of his alignment pylon. But not by much; based on the markings on the deck adjacent to the pylon, it was within the tolerance of what the mooring gear could adjust for.

75 meters. He ordered another burst from the port thrusters, and the closure rate settled at 0.2 meters/second, 60 meters from the station.

The earlier bout of nerves was gone now. He had this.

As the ship passed 50 meters inbound, he ordered the thrusters again, and the closure rate essentially zeroed out. He had the impression that the ship was still moving slightly, but the indicator only read to one decimal place, so it was just a gut feeling. But even if they were, it was slow enough that it wouldn't be an issue for the mooring gear.

Speaking of which...

"Chief of the Watch, deploy forward and aft mooring gear."

"Deploy forward and aft mooring gear, Chief of the Watch, aye."

Matt couldn't see the hatches containing the gear open; they were beneath the curve of the hull forward, and the stern gear deployed directly from the ship's transom. But the gear themselves came into view quickly enough.

It was like a pair of great robotic arms—because that's pretty much what the mooring gear was—reaching out toward the anchor points on the station. Multi-fingered claws opened at the end of each arm...

And then there was a subtle shudder in the deck as the claws closed and the ship was made fast to the station.

Matt checked the alignment again, and sure enough they were right on the SFG marker. He grinned at Harry, who nodded.

"Range Control, this is Halswell. We are moored at Station 5. Ready to receive support umbilicals," he said, over the bridge to bridge.

The station acknowledged, and Matt turned, coming to the position of attention as he faced the CO. "Captain, sir, the ship is moored."

The CO stepped forward and looked at the alignment, then at the mooring gear themselves, and how they were gripping the anchor points. Then he nodded. "Yes, it is." He grinned then, and clapped Matt on the shoulder. "Nicely done."

They had Officers Call in the wardroom after the ship secured the maneuvering watch and stationed the normal in-port watch.

The JOs from SSR-61 had flown off, but Vegas and Freebie were still aboard, and joined the rest of HALSWELL's officers. Matt noted that the evaluation team did not.

The CO didn't take his seat immediately. Instead, he called the meeting to order from the space between the main table and kiddie table.

"We've got a lot on our plate, gentlemen, so let's get to it. First, we received a message from the Commodore that requires immediate action." He looked aside at XO, who was standing with a pair of blue folders in his hand.

XO came to attention. "LT Linsky. LT Kusnetsov. Front and center."

Ivan and Vasili got up and came to stand in front of the CO, at attention.

"Attention to order," XO said.

Everyone stood and came to attention.

XO flipped one of the folders open, and began to read.

"Commander, Frigate Squadron Four, takes pleasure in recognizing Lieutenant Junior Grade Ivan Linsky and Lieutenant Junior Grade Vasili Kusnetsov, Icaran Confederation Navy, for having satisfied the demanding technical and professional requisites, and demonstrated a thorough and proficient knowledge in starships and starship operations aboard the ICS FREDERICK HALSWELL (SFG 1271). I hearby certify that the above named officers are entitled to wear the golden starburst of an Icaran Confederation Navy stellar warfare officer."

From his pocket, the CO pulled out two SWO pins, which he pinned onto Ivan's and Vasili's left breasts. Then he stepped back and smiled.

"Congratulations, gentlemen."

The CO began to clap, and the rest of the wardroom did as well. Vasili and Ivan tried to keep a stoic military bearing. But only for a minute, then they looked at each other, grinned broadly, and shook hands.

The applause subsided after a short while, the CO said, "Seats," and the two of them went back to their chairs.

"Now," the CO said, "Gamal wasn't going to be leaving us until after we get back to New Cali. But with our orders to Melrose, he won't be able to do that and still fulfill his transfer orders. So he's going to leave us here at Olifant. Fortunately, we already had his hail and farewell, but there is one more matter of business to attend to." He looked at Gamal and crooked his finger. "Front and center."

Gamal knew what was coming, clearly. With a slight smile on his face, he came to attention in front of the CO. So did everyone else, a moment later.

XO opened another of the folders.

"The Commanding Officer, ICS FREDERICK HALSWELL (SFG 1271), takes pleasure in presenting the Navy Achievement Medal, gold star in lieu of third award, to Lieutenant Gamal Simpson, Icaran Confederation Navy, for service as set for in the following citation.

"For exceptional performance as Assistant Operations Officer and Fire Control Officer aboard ICS FREDERICK HALSWELL. LT

Simpson performed his demanding duties in an exemplary and highly professional manner. As Assistant OPS, he was instrumental in the planning and execution of two combined exercises with the Royal Davidean Navy, and the preparation for a major maintenance availability. As Fire Control Officer, he successfully managed the installation, testing, and certification of two major combat control system upgrades, and the successful completion of the ship's Tactical Weapons Certification. LT Simpson's unmatched professionalism, unswerving devotion to duty, and impressive tactical acumen reflected great credit upon himself, and upheld the highest traditions of the Naval service. Signed, J C Berkley, Commander, ICN."

As XO was reading, the CO pulled a blue, white, and yellow ribbon that supported a gilded replica of the ICN's starburst from his pocket, and pinned it to Gamal's breast, below his warfare device.

More applause, and the CO waved him back to his seat.

"XO gave away the goods there. As you know, I spoke with Commander Lazlov before we set the maneuvering watch. We won't have the full report for about a week, but we did pass the certification."

CSO let out a little whoop, and several of the others followed suit.

The CO waited patiently for that to subside, then turned toward Vegas and Freebie, at the kiddie table. Vegas seemed to anticipate what the CO was about to say, because he stood and came over to him, before he could call.

XO came over and handed the CO a small pile of thinner folders. He took them and turned back to Vegas.

"Vegas. We didn't work together for very long, but I appreciate all the help you and your team gave. Without your assistance, and your backup, I don't think Phase Two could have come off as well as it did." He held out the folders to Vegas. "These are letters of appreciation for each of your team."

"Thank you, sir," Vegas said, and they shook hands.

"With that," the CO said. "We have some business to discuss. You're welcome to stay, but—"

"We've got a lot to take care of as well, sir," Vegas said.

"Well then, I won't keep you. Thanks again."

Vegas nodded, then he looked across the rest of the men in the wardroom. "If any of you guys swing through Montecino, come by SSR-61 any time. We'll have a chilled beer waiting for you."

Then he nodded at Freebie, and the two of them left.

The CO went around the table to his chair, and sat. He was silent for a moment, and Matt thought he was mulling something over. Then he nodded quickly, to himself.

"Another message came through that you should know about. Orders for my relief. His name is Colby Mackenzie, and he's been serving on the Second Fleet staff for the last couple of years. I haven't met him, but I've heard of him through the grapevine. He's very competent and professional, and apparently one hell of a poker player." He grinned a bit ruefully. "So you won't be able to take the Captain's money for much longer."

WEPS laughed at that.

"When does he get here?" asked Terry.

"October. We'll have a month of turnover, and then he'll take command sometime in November."

"If we do get that deployment, that'll be almost right before we leave," OPS pointed out.

The CO shrugged. "That happens sometimes. The vagaries of Navy personnel scheduling." He inhaled then, straightening a bit. "But in the meantime, you'll still have to deal with me for the next six months or so. Now," he looked at OPS. "This visit to Melrose is a bit of a change in plans, but not completely unexpected. Walk us through the voyage plan real quick, OPS."

This clearly wasn't a surprise to OPS, as he nodded and tapped his holopad, which had been lying on the table in front of him.

The wardroom lights dimmed and the briefing screen lowered, and everyone turned to see it better.

"Melrose is three jumps from here. It'll be about a two and a half week transit. We'll take the jump point to Carraway, and then to Haspastus." He raised his eyebrows. "At that point, we will be leaving Confederation space."

"Question, OPS," Paul said, and OPS nodded. "I thought Melrose just controls a single system?"

"It does, but there's basically nothing in Haspastus. It's a white dwarf orbiting a neutron star, with no real usable resources. We tried claiming it for a while, and they did as well, but both of us realized there wasn't much point. So the system is basically unclaimed space. We maintain the jump point to our space and Melrose maintains the jump point to theirs." He tapped his holopad again as he was saying this, and a chart of the Haspastus system came up on the screen.

Matt squinted to make out some of the fine details, but OPS was right. There was basically nothing there. But there was a third jump point.

"Who maintains the jump point to Vialobos?" he asked.

OPS shrugged. "It's a joint venture between us, but there's not much in Vialobos either, so your guess is good as mine how long both governments will even bother. Regardless, Haspastus will get us to Melrose. Now, coming back..." He tapped his holopad, and the screen shifted, showing a map of jump points. "Coming back, we'll go through Occent Prime, and then back to Sollace, then home."

Matt blinked. Occent Prime was another non-Confederation system, and he had heard some sketchy things about it.

"That going to be a problem?" Harry asked, echoing Matt's thoughts. "There was that big trade dispute with them a few years ago."

OPS shook his head. "They are favored trading partners, and allies."

"Officially," the CO said. "But the Admiralty thinks it's a good idea to show the flag, and a few guns, every now and then, just to keep them aware that we're paying attention to them. We won't be stopping, just transiting through as a freedom of navigation operation."

CSO said, "But if we happen to gather some ELINT or the like on the way through..."

"CSO," the CO said, levelly.

CSO shrugged. "Can't fault me for thinking it, sir."

The CO looked at him for a moment, then sighed, nodding. "If something of interest occurs during our transit, we will of course take appropriate action." He gestured for OPS to continue.

"Now," OPS said, "as the Captain said on the 1MC, we will be hosting official parties from the Melrose government, and they have invited us to attend several functions as well. We will be stopping at Olifant-d to drop off Gamal, and a few others who are transferring. That will be the last chance to pick up uniform items, if anyone needs something."

"Not that any of you would get underway without a full set of uniforms," XO said, dryly. "That would be against regulations."

"But if you *do* need anything, make a list and give it to me," OPS said. "When Zach and Matt bring Gamal down, they'll make a run to the exchange."

Matt blinked, surprised that he was included with Zach in that plan. Zach was the First Lieutenant, so he owned the boats. Matt wasn't.

"We will?" he said.

"Yes," OPS said.

"Aye, sir."

The CO looked amused at that exchange, but he didn't say anything.

OPS referred to his holopad for a moment, then looked back at the CO. "I've scheduled an UNREP for the day after tomorrow, as we're leaving Olifant, and another in Carraway, just before we jump to Haspastus. And that's all I have, sir."

The CO nodded and looked around the room. "Any other questions?"

Shaking heads all around.

"Good job on the certification, gentlemen. Dismissed."

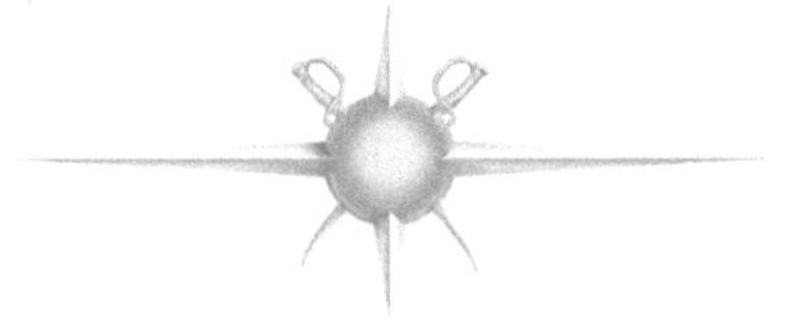

Chapter Fifty-Eight

Matt took the written exam for Officer Of The Deck two days after HALSWELL jumped to the Carraway system.

It didn't feel as crushing as the EOOW exam had. Maybe all the information he'd been cramming into his head over the last eight months had finally had time to percolate, so it fit together more coherently. Because there wasn't a single question that he felt completely lost on.

Or maybe it was because he just liked the OOD stuff more than the EOOW stuff.

Either way, Matt was feeling good as he finished up the exam and left Classroom #2. He didn't ask himself if he passed or not; no, he'd nailed it. And with that, there were just a couple drill sets and three knowledge checkouts left, and he'd be card complete.

And he got the drills.

The ship was in standard transit routine, except they had shifted to a three-section watch rotation to support putting more guys into U/I spots for the more advanced qualifications. They ran drill sets three days a week, with dedicated training days in between, and a tactical scenario on Saturday. With drills thrown into the tactical scenario, of course. Thus, he saw lots of drills, both in the plant and on the bridge.

So as the ship made the jump to Haspastus, Matt began to think he might just get completely done with OOD before they hit Melrose. That wouldn't suck.

The transit through Haspastus, though certain to be almost completely uneventful, was the longest of the voyage—a full week through that mostly empty and lifeless space. If not for the drill and training routine, it promised to be pretty boring.

Until, on the third day of the transit, while Matt was reviewing his divisional training report in Maneuvering, the 1MC came to life.

"Muster the VBSS team on the port boat deck. Muster the VBSS team on the port boat deck."

Matt blinked, straightening up in the EOOW's chair.

EM1 Brossard was his Electrical Operator again. He looked back at Matt with a raised eyebrow, as if to say, "Did I hear that right?"

A moment later, the internal comms receiver beside Matt whooped. He picked up the handset.

"Maneuvering, Engineering Officer Of the Watch."

"Engineering Officer Of the Watch, Captain. Lieutenant Covington is coming back to relieve you. Report to me on the bridge as soon as he does."

"Report to the bridge, aye sir," Matt said. He replaced the handset back into its cradle, and just looked at it for a second.

Whatever was going on, it was beginning to feel...interesting wasn't exactly the word.

Brossard said, "Shit's getting real, huh sir?"

"Guess so," Matt said.

Sam Covington showed up two minutes later. He spent exactly fifteen seconds looking over the EPCP and RPCP, then he nodded and turned to Matt. "I relieve you. Get moving."

"I...stand relieved." The deviation from the normal formality of the watch turnover routine was throwing him off even more than the unexpected muster.

Well, he'd find out what was going on soon enough.

Matt made a beeline for the bridge. When he got there, he immediately spotted the CO, standing beside his chair in the forward starboard corner, in company with Bo and Zach. They stopped their conversation as he hurried to them.

"Reporting as ordered, sir."

The CO nodded. "Let's get started."

He gestured toward a contact symbol on the bridge display ahead of the ship and to port. It was a white square, so a civilian vessel. A dialog window was open adjacent to the symbol, showing an image from one of HALSWELL's telescopes. The image was grainy, but Matt could easily identify the ship as a mid-range cargo carrier, Icaran flagged from the markings he could see on the hull.

"On the midwatch we received a distress call from the Space Vessel Daisy, and diverted to render assistance."

Which was required under the law: all spacemen were obligated to provide aid to vessels in distress. Still, Matt liked to think they'd do so even if it wasn't a requirement.

"We haven't heard anything from her since," the CO went on. "Not on bridge-to-bridge, not on tight beam. She appears to still have power, though her engines are apparently in standby." His face tightened visibly. "We will intercept with her in just under two hours, and I'm sending you over to ascertain what's going on, and assist if possible." He turned serious eyes on Zach, then Matt. "I don't mind telling you I'm a little bit nervous about this. We have no idea what's happened there, if anything. So be careful. Don't take any unnecessary risks, and if you come upon anything dangerous, don't try to be a hero." He raised his eyebrows. "I need information about what's going on, and an intact crew, not casualties. Understood?"

"Yes, sir," Matt said immediately.

"Yessir," Zach said.

The CO nodded. "Get your team ready, and make sure everyone understands what they're getting into."

Zach nodded, then he clapped Matt on the shoulder. Together, they hustled down to the boat deck, where the VBSS team was assembling.

The waiting was the worst part.

Zach briefed the team on the situation. It didn't take very long, and as Matt watched, he could see the seriousness of the situation settle on each man, as their faces became stolid, focused. Not like when a guy is standing at attention doing the military bearing bit, but like when it's getting real and he knows it. The swallowing of doubt and focusing on what has to be done; that expression.

Matt saw all of his team go through that as they got ready, and he was sure everyone was prepared.

And then they waited for an hour, and the grousing started.

"Jesus," said OS3 Bogarten, as he pulled at the collar of his EVA suit —no one had donned his helmet yet; no reason to while still on the ship —and winced. "This thing's biting into me." His nostrils flared as he breathed out in annoyance. "Are we going to do this, or what?"

ET1 Vinz, standing next to Matt, glared over at him. "Can it, jackass."

Bogartern, for a second, looked like he was going to retort, or maybe even turn things physical. But he caught himself with his mouth half-open—to say something that would have forced Matt to have him thrown in the brig, he was sure—and, with a visible effort, shut it, then, shaking his head, he turned away.

He gestured for BM3 Peters to come closer. "Help me adjust this damn thing, will ya?"

Peters didn't say anything, he just got to work helping Bogarten with the fit of his suit.

Matt and Vinz exchanged looks, and Vinz raised an eyebrow that said, "He's got a point, though."

And he wasn't wrong.

They were still on the port boat deck. Fred-2's airlock was open, but they hadn't boarded yet. Better to be able to stretch out a bit while they could. And who knew, the operation might get called off.

Matt didn't think that was very likely, though.

His Team Bravo was hanging out separately from Zach's Team Alpha. Not out of animosity, but just a natural sorting as the two groups prepared, and talked through what they were going to do, together. But looking over toward Zach's group, he could see signs of discontent like were beginning to appear in his group.

He walked over, and Zach rose from where he had been sitting, leaning up against the ship's hull.

"What's up?"

Matt spread his hands. "Any word? Some of the guys are getting antsy."

Zach frowned slightly, and shook his head. "CO said two hours, so we should be coming up on her any minute now. Tell them—" He cocked his head slightly, and his eyes lost their focus on Matt, as a call came in over their implants.

"Fred-2, this is HALSWELL. Load the VBSS team and prepare for launch."

All around, the team roused themselves; all of them had their implants tuned to that circuit as well.

Zach straightened, and grinned at Matt. "Let's mount up."

BM1 McCall was flying the boat again, and Matt was glad of it. All the same, as he eased Fred-2 toward the hull of S/V Daisy, Matt's nerves were firing intensely.

He flexed his fingers on the grip of his rifle almost reflexively, and swallowed to keep his stomach from lurching as he felt, ever so subtly, the slight shudder in the deck as the boat made contact. A moment later, another, louder, clicking sound announced the sealing clamps latching in place.

Through the visor of his EVA suit, Matt looked at Zach. He was outwardly calm, but Matt could see a drop of sweat easing it way down Zach's forehead.

It was comforting, to know he wasn't the only one who was feeling it.

"Hard seal, sir," BM1 said over the internal comms net. "But I'm not getting an internal airlock permission code. You're going to have to use the manual override."

Zach nodded, frowning slightly. "Thanks, BM1."

It wasn't unexpected. With no contact from the Daisy at all, how would they know to expect the VBSS team's arrival?

A space vessel wouldn't just open its airlock on a whim. The crew had to activate the system from inside for a visiting vessel to cycle their lock, for obvious safety reasons. There *was* a mechanical override, for use in case of a loss of power, or other emergency situations. It took longer. Quite a bit longer. And it was a safety and security gap.

But the designers had decided that its benefit in the event of an emergency outweighed the security risk, so all space vessels had it built in.

That would be how the VBSS team got aboard, looked like.

Over the team-wide comm circuit, Zach ordered the Chief to get the airlock open, and Chief and BM3 Peters set to work.

Five minutes later, they were inside.

Like most vessels, the Daisy's airlock opened to a semi-circular area stuffed with EVA and Emergency Supply lockers everywhere a guy could see. And there were passages running forward and aft, and another running athwartships, connecting the quarterdeck area to the rest of the ship.

The first members of the team to board—Chief, Vinz, and Peters—immediately took up station at each of the passages, weapons raised, and covered them until the remainder of the team entered, and then they all stopped to take stock.

The quarterdeck area was spotless, almost like it had never been used, and the atmosphere sensors built into Matt's EVA suit reported pristine conditions. The gravity felt light, but that was to be expected; Daisy was registered out of Carraway's World, which boasted a gravity well slightly below Terran-standard, almost the same as on Olifant.

Compared with New Cali, that was light indeed; Matt had experienced the difference already, twice.

"No one's home," Chief said, cautious uncertainty in his tone.

Matt and Zach exchanged looks. "Reminds me of the final scenario we did for our cert," Matt said over their private channel.

Zach frowned, and nodded slightly. "Me too." He inhaled quickly. "Stick to the plan, and let's get this done." Over the team-wide circuit, he said, "By the numbers, guys. Team Alpha checks cargo and operations, Team Bravo takes Engineering. Check in at five minute intervals."

"Five minutes, aye," Matt said. Then he switched to his team's circuit. "Team Bravo, let's move out."

One thing that the TACTRACOM scenarios missed out on, that Matt now had, and grew to appreciate immediately, was the ship schematic view that he had popped up in the upper left quadrant of his helmet's visor. Since the REPTARVs were re-configurable at will, and often were changed from one scenario to the next, there wasn't a standardized layout that they could reference. But every ship of a class coming from the same shipyard was built more or less the same, with only minor differences. And those plan view schematics were on file in public databases that the Navy, of course, had access to.

Once HALSWELL ascertained Daisy's design, it was simplicity itself to pull those schematics, so the VBSS team wasn't going in blind to how the ship was laid out.

It made getting back to Engineering quick and easy. Down the passageway leading aft until it turned athwartships. Then left at Daisy's central corridor and down a ladderwell to the airtight hatch leading back into the plant.

Daisy was a mid-range cargo vessel. Most of her internal volume that wasn't Engineering was dedicated to the cargo hold, and she had a small crew compliment: just fifteen people. But still, Matt would have thought his team would come across signs of someone being aboard during their trek back to the plant.

But there was nothing.

Until they descended the ladder.

The level below was just a round anteroom in front of the hatch to Engineering. There were damage control lockers on either side of the room and a communications panel adjacent to the hatch. And that was it; nothing special, equipment-wise.

But the hatch was damaged. The locking mechanism for the hatch dogs was burned through; black scorch-marks marked the lock. The leavings of a cutting torch, Matt was sure. The hatch itself was ajar, not closed like it should have been, and...

Peters whistled softly. "Geez, there's shell casings everywhere."

He wasn't kidding. Matt counted at least a couple dozen casings, all over the anteroom. Someone, or several someones, had fired off a lot of rounds.

He moved slowly to the hatch and pulled it more fully open.

The passage beyond ran between racks of breaker panels, and Matt could clearly see some of them were damaged. There was at least one bullet hole, and several dents and scorch marks. Further back, toward the end of the panels, the space opened up a bit, and he saw yellow-ish glints on the deck. More casings, standing out plainly against the grey linoleum floor.

And there was something darker on the deck as well, just obscured by the edge of the right-hand side panel.

"More casings back there," he said. "Looks like they were defending Engineering against a breech."

Vinz moved up next to Matt and peered through the hatch with him. "But defending against who?"

They traded looks. Vinz looked nervous; no wonder, Matt was feeling spooked himself.

Part of him wanted to say screw it, fall back to the airlock and get the hell out of here. But they had a job to do.

He was about to order his men in, when he received a call over the team-wide comm circuit.

"Team Bravo, this is Team Alpha, over." Zach's voice was tight, his tone clipped.

"This is Team Bravo. We're at the hatch to Engineering. There's evidence of a firefight here."

There was a short pause, long enough for Zach to say, "Shit," before he transmitted. "Up here too, and we've got three bodies in the Mess," Zach reported. "All shot."

Matt wished he could say he was surprised, but of course there would be bodies if there was a firefight aboard. He looked back down the passage between the breaker panels, and swallowed. Probably there were going to be more dead people down that passage as well.

"Do we fall back to the airlock? I think it's safe to say we know what happened here."

"No," Zach said immediately. "Finish your sweep. There might be survivors, someone who needs help." His voice hardened. "But be careful. Don't hesitate to defend yourselves."

"Team Bravo, aye."

Matt turned to look at the rest of his team. They had heard the discussion. Whatever humor they may have had before was gone. They looked like Matt felt: anxious, scared even, but committed.

"You guys ready?" Matt asked.

"Let's get it done, Mr. G," said Vinz.

"Ok, let's go."

He turned, and led the way into Engineering.

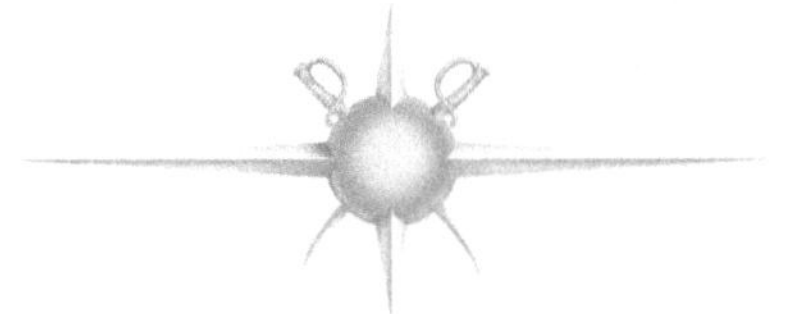

Chapter Fifty-Nine

There were no survivors.

The dark spot on the deck that Matt spotted turned out to be blood, from a body that was leaned back against a stand of piping, a few meters past the breaker panels. He was a man in his 30s, light complected with a bushy brown beard, and he had been shot in the chest and abdomen. From the look of things, he had managed to crawl his way out of the line of fire, and sit back against that pipe. He'd left a blood trail all the way, but he still had a pistol in his hand.

Maybe he'd thought to make his last stand there. Take out some of his attackers before he went. But it looked like he had passed out before he could do that; there were no spent casings anywhere around where he sat, and the pistol was still loaded.

They found three more bodies in Engineering. Two in the Maneuvering area and another on the lower level between the plasma condensers.

Team Alpha found a similar situation up forward. Besides the shot people in the Mess, there were two more bodies on the bridge, three in one of the passages near the port-side airlock, and signs of a fight everywhere.

There was a problem, though. That made twelve dead, but the crew compliment was fifteen.

Where were the other three?

The CO met the VBSS team on the boat deck upon their return, his face tight. They had reported their findings over the radio circuit, but he quizzed Zach and Matt extensively all the same.

XO, WEPS, and CSO were with him, and after Zach and Matt finished their story, the CO turned hard eyes on the three of them.

"I want answers, gentlemen. What happened to the other three crew, and who was responsible for this?" His eyes flicked from WEPS to CSO and back. "Get over there, pull every log, every security file, I don't care what. But get those answers."

"On it, skipper," CSO said. His normal joviality was gone, replaced by cold focus. "Chief Bruckman's getting a team together. They should be able to access Daisy's network real quick."

WEPS added, "Chief Tanton is sending over an evidence team to document everything." Tanton was HALSWELL's Chief Master At Arms. "He needs to do that first, though, before we start anything too intrusive."

The CO nodded. "Fair enough. XO, there's a lot of bodies to deal with. Does Senior Chief Roos need to draw any additional help?"

Roos was the ship's Independent Duty Corpsman, the head of the medical division. He had three junior Corpsmen working for him, and that was fine for bruises, scrapes, the common cold, and other minor medical issues. They were not coroners, though, by any stretch of the imagination.

XO said, "After Chief Tanton's done, I think Senior Chief's just going to move them into the Daisy's frozen stores, until a salvage team can arrive to get her to port."

"Well, give him whatever he needs." The CO's lips compressed, and his right cheek quivered slightly; it was like he was struggling to not show the anger that was clearly beginning to boil over. Matt had never seen such an expression on the man before.

"And get me answers. Quickly."

For more than a day, HALSWELL remained adjacent to the Daisy. Forensic teams under the CMAA visited first, to document and collect all the evidence of the atrocity that they could, and then CSO's team followed, to dig into the ship's computers and logs.

For Matt, that time crept by. On watch back in Maneuvering, he felt continually peppered with questions and speculation by his watch standers and people who had to come to Maneuvering on business. After the first hour or so, his watch team gave over asking, as much from his demeanor, he supposed, as from the terse and short answers he gave them.

Did they really want him to describe how that one guy's guts were spilling from his body because he'd been shot in the belly four times? Hell, he didn't want to remember it at all, let alone tell anyone else about it.

But the visitors to Maneuvering didn't let up. They kept coming and coming, and always asking the same things, until finally he ordered the doors to Maneuvering closed and dogged, no one in or out except on urgent business.

Fortunately, Ivan showed up to relieve him not long after that, and he didn't ask about anything but turnover business. And then Matt was able to escape back to officers country, and his stateroom.

Harry was there when he arrived, lying in his rack with his back propped up against the bulkhead and reading a book, an old-school fantasy novel. The kind with dragons and knights, and damsels in distress. Or at least, those things were prominent in the cover art.

Harry's eyes left the page as Matt closed the door behind himself, and his eyebrows rose. "Good thing Vegas isn't here anymore. You'd have woke him, slamming the door like that, and you know how prissy those flyboys are."

Matt scowled at him, and pulled out his desk chair. He intended to lose himself in tactical manuals, studying for his SWO quals. And he didn't need to hear jackassery from Harry, on top of everything else.

"What's got you so riled up?"

Matt just scowled deeper. Chapter Seventeen contained torpedo preset guidance, how to select the best settings for a given scenario. He dove in there.

But several minutes later, he was still on the first paragraph. He'd read it, realized he had no idea what it said, then re-read it with the same result, at least six times. Much as he wanted to, his mind simply wasn't on it. He was instead replaying the scenes aboard the Daisy, and getting more and more angry.

"Those motherfuckers," he muttered.

Harry stirred on his rack. From the edge of his vision, Matt saw him swinging his feet over the edge, and then hopping down onto the deck.

"Dude, what's up?" Harry wasn't joking around now; he sounded more concerned than humorous.

"You don't know?"

Realization came over Harry's face, and he nodded. "You're pissed about that civvie ship, huh."

Matt looked him askance. "And you're not?"

Harry shrugged. "Sure I am. But you're taking it personally," he said, in a tone that screamed, "Why, dude?"

"Yeah, well, if you saw what those bastards did up close, I guess you'd take it personally, too."

Harry nodded slowly. "You want payback." He sighed. "Well I hate to break it to you, but there's a good chance there won't be any. Whoever did that was long gone when we got here."

Matt shook his head. "Only by a few hours."

"Which in another system might not matter, but here?" He gestured toward the outboard bulkhead. "Unclaimed space, remember? There's no system traffic control, no COP. Only what a ship can pick up with her organic sensors and transponder. And pirates," he raised his eyebrows, "don't run with their transponders on. Soon as they were done they lit out at their ship's maximum Gs for an hour or two to clear datum, then put engines to standby to coast to wherever they're going, so no one can track their gravitics."

"They'll have to slow down again," Matt objected.

"They'll be hell and gone from here before they do that. Best face facts," Harry clapped him on the shoulder. "Odds of us, or anyone, finding them are pretty low this time."

"So they're just going to keep on getting away with it?"

The clap became a squeeze. "I said this time. Now that we know they're in the area, ICN and the Melrose Navy will start taking steps. In the long run, these guys are done. They just don't know it yet."

In the long run. That was small comfort. But, Matt had to admit, it was some. It might take months, or even years, but there was no way a pirate gang—if that's really what they were—could escape justice, in today's world.

That wouldn't do those poor bastards on Daisy any good, though.

But nothing will, dude, said that annoying, rational voice in Matt's head. Justice is for those who remain; the dead won't care either way.

"Well, hopefully it'll be sooner rather than later," Matt said.

"Amen to that, brother."

Harry hopped back up onto his rack, and opened his novel again. Matt got back to studying, and found that he was actually able to do it this time.

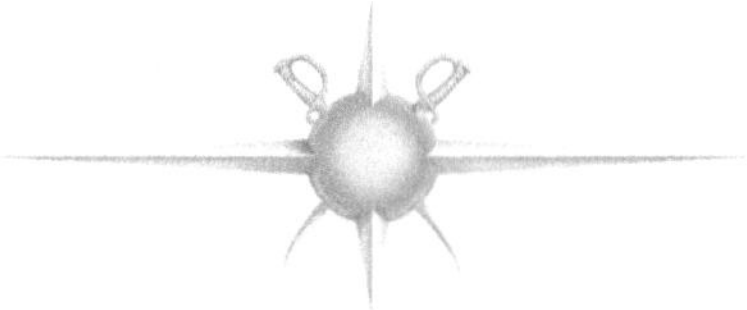

Chapter Sixty

XO came on the 1MC a short while later to announce Officers Call in the wardroom at 2000. That made Harry whistle in surprise, and Matt couldn't disagree.

The nightly movie was an almost sacrosanct part of the ship's schedule. Stomping all over it for a meeting was unusual, to say the least. But then, it wasn't every day the ship came across a pirate attack, was it?

There was little small talk as the men assembled, and the CO wasted no time calling the meeting to order.

"WEPS and CSO have been investigating the events on the Daisy. I want all of us to know what they found, so we're all on the same page moving forward." He gestured toward the pair of Department Heads, who were center stage, where OPS normally stood for one of these kinds of briefings.

CSO did the holopad tapping that lowered the lights and brought up the briefing screen, but WEPS spoke first.

"As you all know, the crew of the Daisy was murdered by a force or forces unknown. Twelve of them were gunned down in what appears to have been a rolling firefight that spread throughout the ship. At first we thought it might have been an internal squabble, or mutiny of some kind, because there were no signs of damage to the exterior of the ship's hull. But the internal security footage shows clearly that another vessel docked with the Daisy on her port side, and a force of armed men stormed aboard. The crew attempted to resist but were overcome, and corralled into the ship's Mess.

"The security footage records video, not audio, but from the footage it appears that the leader of the boarding team threatened the Daisy's master with the lives of his crew, and the master provided them with an access code to a specific item of the ship's cargo that was locked away into a specially secured space."

XO's eyebrows rose. "What was the item?"

WEPS shook his head. "The cargo manifest doesn't list it, and when we reviewed the schematics of that ship class, the secured space the master led the boarding team to doesn't correspond to any space on the plan view."

"So the Daisy wasn't just an honest cargo vessel bringing trade from Melrose to Carraway and back," said the Chop.

"Doesn't look that way," WEPS agreed. "If I had to guess I'd say they've been smuggling illicit material for some time, a rival organization found out about it, and..." He snapped his fingers.

"So what happened to the three who weren't shot?" the CO asked.

"From the personnel files, they were the master, the mate, and the cargo master," WEPS said. "It looks like they were in on it. As soon as the boarding team leader got what he wanted, he issued an order and his men began firing on the gathered crew. But once that started, the crew fought back. They overwhelmed the attackers in the mess, took their weapons, and scattered throughout the ship." He scowled. "And the attackers methodically hunted them down and killed them."

"Would have had more of a chance if they'd stayed together," CSO said, grimly.

"Maybe," WEPS said. "But they didn't have very many guns, just what they got from the bad guys in the mess."

"The bodies in the Mess were pirates?" OPS asked.

WEPS shook his head. "No, the security footage shows the boarding team taking their dead back onto their ship with them."

The CO's face was getting darker by the second. "So the master set his own crew up for the slaughter."

XO said, "He would have to know he couldn't cover that up, and he would become a wanted man." He traded a look with the CO. "Whatever was in that smuggler's hole, it must be worth a fortune. Enough for him to cash out, go someplace far from the Confederation, and live without putting his face out where we could see, ever again."

"Well, he didn't get very far," WEPS said. He nodded to CSO, who pulled up a video on the briefing screen.

It showed the three Daisy turncoats, the leader of the boarding team, and two of his men. They were smiling, and several were laughing over a joke of some kind. The men entered the anteroom for the Daisy's port side airlock, to go back to their ship from the look of it. The three turncoats went first, but as soon as they were through, the boarding team members shut the inner airlock hatch and dogged it. One of them hit the control panel adjacent to the hatch and activated its override.

The screen split then, showing the interior video of the airlock, synched with the anteroom. The three turncoats stopped, confusion on their faces, because the outer hatch was shut. Then panic as the inner hatch closed behind them. They rushed at the inner hatch, the master grasping desperately onto the hand wheel that would open it manually, but it was too late.

The outer hatch opened, and two of the turncoats were sucked out into the void immediately.

The master managed to hold on to the inner hatch's hand wheel for a few seconds, but he lost his grip as his body went into spasmodic convulsions. A short while later, he drifted out into the void. But he was clearly dead well before that happened.

"Got his just deserts," said Bo.

Heads bobbed in agreement all around the room.

"The docking ship must have detached once the boarding team was aboard," WEPS said. "Maybe a security precaution, in case some of the Daisy's crew got loose, so they couldn't take over the boarding team's ship." He smiled viciously. "But it worked nicely to turn things around on the master and his guys as well."

"Can't say I feel sorry for him," the CO said. He gestured toward the split video showing the boarding team leader and his men. "What did we learn about them?"

CSO said, "As we suspected, the ship was running darkened, with her transponder off, or in receive-only. She was right on Daisy before her crew knew it. But they should have; the radar got returns off her for an hour before intercept. If the mate hadn't been part of the plan, Daisy might have been able to try to escape. She wouldn't have got far, but the crew could have at least prepared to defend themselves."

He tapped his holopad, and a new image came up. This was an exterior shot that must have come from one of Daisy's scopes. It showed a long, sleek vessel that was shaped almost like a missile, except that its bow was flattened, and it boasted short delta-shaped winglets at its stern.

Matt saw two turrets that looked trainable, mounted on its dorsal and ventral sections, and another pair of guns protruding from the flattened section of the ship's nose. And he wasn't sure, but it looked like there were pods mounted to the bottom of the winglets. Missile canisters, maybe?

"This is the attacking ship," CSO said. "It's an old COTARI-class corvette, built in the same yards as we were, but twenty-five years earlier."

OPS let out a long, low whistle. "I thought the last of those were scrapped fifteen years ago."

WEPS shrugged. "The Confederation authorized a foreign military sale version of the ship, for sale to friendly systems. Who knows how those systems disposed of them. And...well, let's face it. Not everything that gets reported scrapped or destroyed always really is. A few credits change hands, signatures get blazed, someone looks the other way..." He spread his hands as though to say, "What can you do?"

"If these people were able to get their hands on a vessel like that," XO said. He paused, then shook his head. "This is not just some fly by night outfit." He glanced at the CO. "Not run of the mill pirates, improvising as they go."

The CO shook his head, his expression dark.

"I asked Chief Tanton to run a check," WEPS said. "There are few pirate reports within the Confederation. But along the border systems, and in unclaimed areas like Haspastus, it happens sometimes. There have been two dozen reports of pirate attacks within the last five years, total. Two of them stand out. They were both in the outskirts of Occent Prime. The first left no survivors. One man survived the second one, by wedging himself into a crawl space under the main plasma medium condenser in the engine room. He got in so tightly that he got stuck, and waited there until the rescue and salvage team eventually found him, two days later."

Oof. That would really, really suck. Matt winced, considering it.

"He gave a description of the vessel that attacked his ship." WEPS pointed at the corvette on the screen. "Sounds a whole lot like that. But his ship's systems were damaged enough that they couldn't get good imagery from them, so we cannot confirm it. The other ship, though..."

He nodded at the CSO, who tapped his holopad. A new image of a vessel came up. This one was darker, much darker; the attack location must have been quite a bit farther from the system's star than the attack on Daisy. Because it was so dark, it was difficult to make out, but Matt thought he saw a flattened bow with cannons protruding from it, and small winglets at the stern.

"I think it's safe to assume this is the same ship. Now, this attack occurred three years ago. After talking it through, CSO, Chief, and I think the best explanation is that the vessel is owned by a criminal syndicate, most likely out of Occent Prime. Because of the cost to acquire, maintain, and operate a ship like that, it is probably used infrequently, for high profile, highly profitable operations." WEPS gestured toward the port side of the ship, the side facing the Daisy. "Apparently, like this one."

The CO nodded slowly. "It's speculation." WEPS opened his mouth to reply, but the CO held up a hand to forestall him. "But good speculation. It matches the facts, at least." He leaned back in his chair, frowning. "Do we have any idea where they got to?"

WEPS stepped aside and took the holopad from CSO, who took center stage now. A tap brought up a capture of the GAP display in CIC.

"The night of the distress call," CSO said, "we detected a strong but distant gravitic distortion that falls within the expected engine parameters for the COTARI-class." He sniffed. "Of course, that also overlaps some civilian classes as well. That said, the distortion began about two hours after the distress call, and lasted ninety minutes. At the time we only did a rough analysis, but I had FC division do a reconstruction on it, and we came up with this."

The GAP showed an AOU that encompassed Daisy's position at the time as well as an arc that extended from about a third of the way inward toward the neutron star and about the twice that distance out from the Daisy toward...

Matt felt his eyes widen. The AOU was angled toward the jump point to Vialobos.

"There have been no detections since then, which makes sense if the attackers wanted to clear datum quickly, and then minimize the possibility of detection."

Exactly the thing Harry had said. Matt reminded himself to not discount Harry's ideas so easily in the future.

Everyone else could see what Matt had seen. Even Paul and Ybrahim seemed to be focusing in on the icon depicting the jump gate.

The CO jumped straight to it. "What's in Vialobos, OPS?"

OPS frowned and tapped at his holopad. He scrolled through some data for a moment before replying.

"It's a binary system with two K-type stars. Two planets: a hot Jupiter type gas giant with an orbital radius of 0.77 AU and a second, smaller gas giant at 3.75 AU. There's a sizeable asteroid belt just outside the orbit of Vialobos-b, and numerous dwarf planets in the outer orbitals. Apparently the system is known for high comet activity. There are a couple dozen mining outposts in the asteroid belt, and on one of the dwarf planets, but the latest reports say only six are in active use. Both are Melrose-flagged. Cargo and supply vessels come through a couple times a month, according to shipping records."

The CO pursed his lips. "So. Lots of places to hide, but no real place to stay for an extended period of time." He focused back on CSO. "What's the endurance of a COTARI-class corvette?"

"She can outrun us in a short race, but we'll take her in the end," CSO says. "Flank speed will give her 20 Gs to our 18. But she's only good for two days doing that, while we can do five." He chuckled. "Course, we'd both be screwed if we went full-out like that. Heading straight out toward interstellar space with no way to slow down, and set to run out of power real quick."

The CO looked at him levelly, and CSO cleared his throat. "She can run for eighteen days at her economic engine setting: 5Gs, like ours is. We can last twenty-five, so again, we got her."

"And we just had an UNREP before we jumped to Haspastus," OPS put in. "She doesn't have the logistics setup to schedule

UNREPs like we do, so she certainly doesn't have full plasma medium tanks."

"That's a dangerous assumption," XO said. "If you'd asked me an hour ago, I'd have told you that only governments own ships like that. Assuming you guys are right," he looked back at WEPS and CSO, "the syndicate that owns her could very well also own a tanker ship of some kind."

CSO nodded, conceding the point. "It's possible they set out on a vector toward the Vialobos jump point as a diversion, and that they intend alter course to Melrose once they think they're clear. There's no COP in the system, but their transponder must have received our transmissions, so they know we are here, and they'll be cautious because of that. That said, there's no way to know how proficient they are at some of our tracking methods, and their equipment is older. The sensitivity of our sensors, and our GAP techniques, have come a long way since the COTARI was decommissioned. So they may not know how well we can track them at distance."

WEPS shifted to another shot of the GAP. This time there was an overlay of red dots on a vector arc running from Daisy to the Vialobos jump point.

"Assuming they burned at max-Gs, which the strength of the distortion we detected supports, on a direct course to the Vialobos jump point, they should be right about here." CSO indicated one of the dots about two-thirds of the way to the jump point. "They will have to slow to access the jump gate. So if they intend to jump there, we should detect another distortion sometime late tomorrow. If they instead intend to divert to Melrose, and then Occent Prime, they'll probably wait to adjust course until after they've passed the jump point, to maximize their distance from the attack datum."

He paused. "Or at least, that's what I would do."

The CO nodded, considering. After a moment, he said, "I concur. Her armament, WEPS?"

WEPS shrugged. "Assuming they haven't made changes from the class's baseline configuration, she has dorsal and ventral magnetically-driven projectile cannons, not too dissimilar to our point defense turrets. Two forward firing plasma cannons about one half the strength of ours. And two missile canisters with a total of twenty IR and radar-homing missiles. The missiles are the easiest things to upgrade, so it's probably safe to assume they approximate the capability of our SDMS."

"Torpedoes?"

WEPS shook his head. "The COTARI was built for speed, not combat power."

"So we can take her," XO mused.

"With a full combat load?" the CO replied. "For certain." He nodded emphatically at that. "But we have only two warshot torpedoes and twenty SDMS missiles aboard." He raised an eyebrow at the XO. "That puts us a bit closer to parity."

"Well, we don't actually *have* to engage them, do we?" asked Terry Dixon, sitting over next to the Chop.

WEPS rolled his eyes. "Oh, come on, Terry!"

"I'm serious, WEPS. They relied on a stealth operation, and surprise. But we know they're here now, and where. We've already told system command in Carraway and the Melrose government what happened, and there's nowhere this ship," he gestured at the corvette's inferred course vector, "can actually go. So we wait them out. They'll have to leave to go home sooner or later, and both governments can set up a cordon at their side of the jump gate to snatch them up when they do."

Several people were staring at him like he was a loony.

Terry hadn't made a big thing about his pacifist stance since that first day's O-call, and Matt had kind of dismissed it as a novel way to view the world, especially as a military officer, but hadn't thought of it since.

But now...

Memories of the dead men on the Daisy returned in a rush, and Matt felt a wave of revulsion even considering what Terry had just said.

"Dude, Terry. Grow a pair," said Vasili. A couple others shared the sentiment, vocally.

Terry scowled at them, and shook his head. "I'm not a coward, guys. I just think there's a way to do this without getting a whole bunch more people killed."

"Gentlemen," the CO said, raising his hands for quiet.

Everyone stopped staring at Terry and looked back at the CO.

"That's not a bad idea, Terry," the CO said. He met Terry's gaze and nodded. "And it's good to consider alternatives, especially if it can avoid an unneeded fight. But I think you're forgetting something. What about the people in those mining outposts? We have no idea what these pirates...or whoever they are...will do once they're in Vialobos." He sniffed. "For all we know, they could have converted one of the abandoned outposts into a base, where they can remain for months. I can promise you, neither government will maintain a cordon for more than a couple weeks. It's too costly."

The CO looked around at the rest of the officers. "So we're going in."

Matt felt a shiver of adrenaline go up his spine at the CO's words.

"For the moment, we'll split the difference. We'll go halfway between the Melrose and Vialobos jump points. If they slow to make Vialobos, we'll follow. If not, we can position ourselves ahead of them, to intercept before they jump to Melrose.

"If we get to Vialobos and find conditions are not suitable for an engagement, we will retreat here, and implement Terry's plan. But if not..." His lips tightened into a mask of determined aggression, "I intend to seek them out and destroy them."

"Damn right," Matt said, and the guys near him nodded emphatically in agreement.

"CSO, draft messages to Carraway system headquarters and the Melrose government. Inform them of our findings, and our intention to pursue and engage. Express our regrets to Melrose, but we will be tardy for our goodwill visit. And request reinforcements from Carraway. I want those messages out within the hour."

"Aye, sir," CSO said.

"OPS, plot a—"

"Already on it, sir." OPS was tapping away at his holopad. "Looks like...321 mark 025 is good for now."

The CO nodded. Reaching down beneath the wardroom table, he picked up a handset that he pressed to his ear. The CO's line to the bridge. A moment later, he spoke.

"Officer of the Deck, Captain. Set course 321 mark 025, Ahead Full. Set Condition Omicron throughout the ship."

A moment's silence while the OOD acknowledged the order, then the CO replaced the handset into its cradle.

Then Matt heard the Chief of the Watch over the 1MC. "Set

Condition Omicron throughout the ship. Set Condition Omicron throughout the ship."

"He knows we're here from our transponder. Let's take that away from him." The CO sniffed and looked at WEPS. "WEPS. Muster the reload team in the torpedo room. Backhaul the training shapes from Tubes 1 and 2, and load warshots into tubes 1 and 2 for launch."

"Backhaul Tubes 1 and 2, and load warshots into Tubes 1 and 2 for launch, aye sir," WEPS replied.

The CO smiled, a thin, focused smile. "I guess it's a good thing we just had our weapons certification, because we're going into battle, gentlemen."

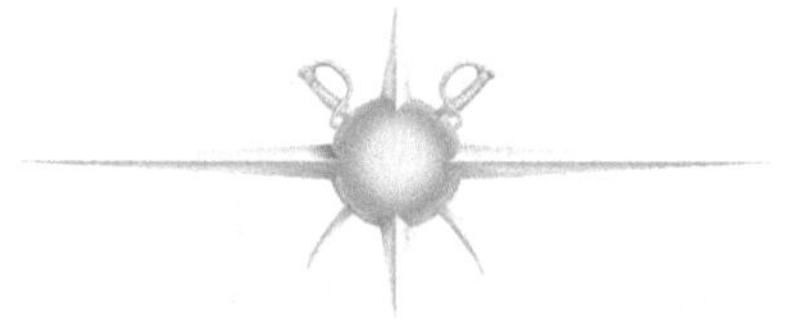

Chapter Sixty-One

The meeting broke up, but Matt remained in his seat for a bit.

They were going in. They would hunt down the monsters who massacred the crew of the Daisy and bring them to justice. It would be a righteous hunt, the kind of thing he envisioned when he joined the Navy.

"And I get to watch a reactor the entire time," he said, softly.

He sipped from his coffee cup. It had grown lukewarm during the briefing, but it was a good blend, so it still should have been a pleasure on the tongue.

But it wasn't.

He kept replaying what he'd seen on the unfortunate freighter. The dead men, lying where they'd fallen in their vain attempt to escape the verdict the pirates handed down to them.

It demanded justice. It demanded he help meet that justice out. But instead…just a reactor.

As usual, the rational part of his mind shouted at him that he was being an idiot. Every job on the ship was important, and making sure the reactor was up and available to power the engines at need, and it was operated safely, was one of the most important jobs on the ship. Nothing the tactical guys in CIC did mattered, if that didn't happen.

It wasn't a very satisfying thought.

On the other side of the room, the CO was leaving, OPS and XO in tow. They were not talking loudly, but Matt heard, "...in my stateroom..." from the CO before he stepped out.

About a third of Matt's coffee remained, but he decided he didn't really want it. He stood, went over to the coffee mess, and dumped it out, then set the mug on the rack for dishes and utensils that needed cleaning.

He couldn't just sit in Maneuvering for this.

So he left the wardroom and went the few paces to the CO's stateroom door. Finding it closed, he knocked three times.

A few seconds later, the door opened, and Matt found himself looking eye to eye with the XO. Past his shoulder, he saw the CO seated at his desk, and OPS standing off to the side. OPS was in the middle of saying something, but stopped when he saw Matt at the door.

"What's up, Matt?" XO said, "We're in a meeting."

"I need to talk to the Captain. It's important."

XO gave him a weird look, then turned to look over his shoulder.

The CO frowned slightly, but nodded. XO stepped aside, pulling the door fully open so Matt could come through.

"What can I do for you, Matt?" the CO said.

Matt drew himself to attention. "Sir, I request to be moved from EOOW to CIC for the duration of this operation."

The CO blinked, and there was silence for a moment.

OPS spoke up. "You're not qualified for the CIC watch, Matt."

"I know that. But I can help the plot coordinator, like I did during the Track-Ex. It sounds like we'll need as many people working the problem as possible if we're going to find these guys, and..." He trailed off, unsure how else to say what he was feeling.

The CO smiled slightly. "Everyone wants to be at the pointy end of the spear, all the time. But we have to take the needs of the ship into account, not personal preferences. Otherwise, everyone would be either on the bridge or in CIC, and nowhere else."

"Yes sir. But in this case, I think—"

"You're emotional about this," XO said. Matt wasn't sure if that was a statement of fact or an accusation. "Understandably so. It's a hell of a thing to deal with on your first real boarding assignment."

Matt shook his head. "That's not what I'm saying."

"The fact is, EOOW is important," OPS said. "If we take damage, the man in Maneuvering will become critical to the survival of the ship."

Matt snorted. "And I'm the right guy for that? OPS, I've been standing the watch on my own for all of three months, and you still have to put the most senior watch standers with me, in case I screw up."

OPS's brow furrowed.

XO said, softly, "If you don't feel you're competent to do the job, maybe you shouldn't be qualified."

Something snapped within him, and Matt spun, jabbing his index finger at XO. "Oh fuck off, XO! You know what I'm saying. And don't give me any of that crap about how every job is important and vital to the ship. I've been telling myself that all day, and it's bunk! You weren't over there. You didn't see what those sons of bitches did, but I was. And I can't just sit, twiddling my thumbs in Maneuvering when I could be doing something *useful* to—"

The XO's eyes had gone wide, and his jaw dropped open...in shock?

Matt realized he had been shouting. The pit fell out of his stomach, and he let his arm fall limply to his side. He looked back at the other two men.

The CO's face was an expressionless mask.

OPS was pissed. Beyond pissed. He had turned beet-red, like he was becoming a towering pinnacle of fury.

"Mister Gilbert," OPS said, his voice quivering with rage, "you are out of line. Turn around and march your ass out of here, right now. And you better pray we don't write you up for—"

"OPS."

OPS's tirade cut off before the CO's icy tone.

Swallowing, Matt realized he was shaking as he turned to look at him.

The CO just stared at him for what felt like an eternity.

Finally, he said. "XO is right. You're emotional. There's no place for emotion in combat. It can get us killed. We have to be calm, so we can do the correct thing, at the right time." He let that sit for another short eternity. "And OPS is right. You're not qualified for watch in CIC, and you have a duty to the ship, not yourself."

Matt's heart was pounding in his ears, and that pit in his stomach was opening up wider and wider and...

The CO looked away from him, toward the XO and OPS. "But he's right, too, gentlemen. If we do take fire, it will be in the interest of the ship to have the most experienced person available in Maneuvering to coordinate the casualty response."

He looked fully at Matt again. His face remained stern, but Matt thought he saw something shift within his eyes; a flash of empathy.

More quietly, he said, "And sometimes a man sees an affront so bad, he cannot live with himself unless he does everything he possibly can to make it right."

The CO held his gaze for a moment, then he turned away from all of them, swiveling in his chair until he was facing the ship's status display mounted adjacent to his computer monitor. He was silent for almost a full minute, and Matt saw the little vein on the side of his temple pulsing, but his face remained a stern mask. Finally, he let out a little sigh.

"OPS, what is the navigation picture in Vialobos? Any particularly difficult areas?"

OPS shook his head, without ever taking his eyes off of Matt. "No, sir. It's pretty straightforward."

The CO nodded to himself, then he swiveled back to face them fully. "In that case, I don't think we need to have the Conning Officer stationed. The OOD can handle it on his own. I want you to write up a watchbill change. Move the men who are currently penned in as Conning Officer to EOOW, and move Matt, Jeremy, Jorge, and Vasili to Assistant Plot Coordinator in CIC. They missed out on valuable tactical training during the weapons certification, and this will help make up for it."

OPS's jaw worked for a couple seconds, then he nodded. "Yes, sir."

The CO looked Matt square in the eye. That flash of empathy was gone, leaving just stern command. "You want a chance to take a more active role? To bring these criminals to justice? Well, you've got it." His brow furrowed, and he leaned forward ever so slightly. "Don't fuck it up."

Matt brought himself back to as much a position of attention as he could, as badly as his arms and legs were shaking. "Yes, sir. Thank you, sir."

"Dismissed."

Matt glanced aside at the other two men. OPS was still trying to slice him in half with sword blades from his eyes. XO's face was unreadable.

He fumbled at the door handle, then got out of there in a hurry, while he still could.

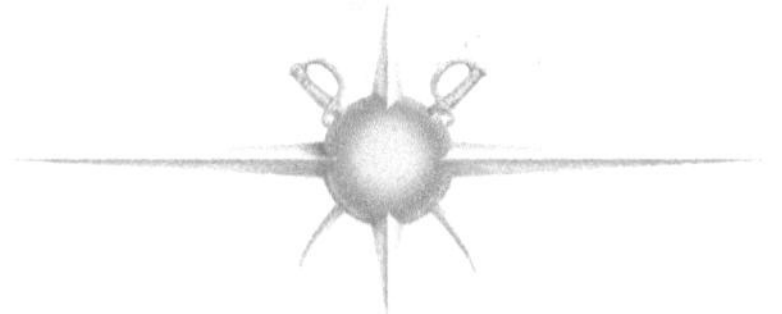

Chapter Sixty-Two

It didn't take long for rumors about the events in the CO's stateroom to start spreading, and Matt intentionally stayed out of the wardroom for several hours. He felt the eyes on him, the speculation, and he didn't want to talk about it. Hopefully it would blow over.

Then OPS posted the watchbill change, and that caused quite a stir.

Matt didn't see it get posted; he was in his stateroom reading the tactical manuals. But he knew immediately when it was. His stateroom door flung open, and Vasili and Jeremy rushed in.

"Jesus, Matt," Vasili said, holding up the printed-out copy of the watchbill. He had apparently taken it off the board; a thumb tack was still stuck in the top of the page. "What the hell did you do?"

Matt sighed, and shrugged. "I asked the skipper to move me to CIC for the operation in Vialobos."

"That's it?"

"Yeah, pretty much."

Vasili and Jeremy traded skeptical looks, and were silent for a few seconds. Then Jeremy shrugged.

"Well, Brad, Rasheid, Sam, and Ivan are not exactly happy with you right now." He smirked. "They didn't expect to have to come down to the galley and row."

"Great." XO and OPS were pissed at him, and now a bunch of his fellow JOs were as well. Matt looked up at the overhead and sighed. "Well they can blame the skipper, not me. It was his decision."

"Uh-huh."

From the expressions on their faces, they remained unconvinced, and, if possible, even more speculative. But after a moment, Vasili shrugged. "Whatever, I guess." He grinned. "I'm just looking forward to kicking some pirate ass."

Matt could agree with that. "You and me both. But speaking of which..." He gestured at his terminal, and the open tactical manual.

Vasili took the hint. "We'll let you study." He clapped Jeremy on the upper arm, and then they turned to go. Vasili stopped before pulling the door closed behind them. "Whatever it was you did, thanks. We owe you one."

The soft click of the door latch snapping into place put the exclamation point at the end of Vasili's words, and Matt found that was...somehow...comforting.

Matt had the evening watch next. Then, depending on whether they detected the pirates again or not, the new four-section combat rotation would start the next day, and he would move to the afternoon watch, in CIC with CSO and Harry.

That promised to be entertaining.

But for now, and despite his stomach grumbling, he didn't want to have to face OPS and XO, and the no-doubt JO speculation. So he skipped dinner, and went back to the plant for his final EOOW watch for a while.

He hadn't considered how strongly the enlisted gossip flowed, though. Especially since all drills and training evolutions, and all but the most essential maintenance evolutions, were canceled until further notice, due to setting Condition Omicron and being about to enter a real combat scenario. That left very little to do in Maneuvering except shoot the breeze, for six hours straight.

On the bright side, Matt very quickly became pretty well numb to the barrage of speculative questions and attention. On the other hand... well, he knew there wasn't really any such thing as a secret among such a relatively small crew, who were cooped up together for weeks and months at a time. But it was quite a bit different to know it, and to actually experience it, in real time.

The CO helped. Halfway into the watch, he came on the 1MC with an update. The ship had detected a gravitic distortion that matched the signature they'd seen at the "crime scene," and had evaluated it as indicating that the pirate corvette had, indeed, slowed to make the jump to Vialobos.

HALSWELL would therefore begin pursuit, and shift to the new combat routine. They would maintain Condition Omicron until further notice, and station the Duty Captain. As before, XO had the night shift and CO the day shift.

"We are burning hard for the Vialobos jump gate," the CO said, and that was a fact. The OOD had ordered Ahead Full just before the CO came on the 1MC: 12Gs to push the ship toward the jump point. "We expect to make the jump in the middle of the morning watch tomorrow. Once we transition to Vialobos, we will be in a combat environment. So be about your duties smartly, and be ready for the unexpected."

The CO paused. "I'm cannot tell you how long we'll be in Vialobos, except that it will be for as long as it takes to find these pirates, and either convince them to surrender or engage them in battle. At our current fuel state, barring relief by the fleet units from Carraway, that could be several weeks, if we're careful in our maneuvers. So keep yourselves sharp, and don't lose focus. Carry on."

And that put the end to chit-chat about what may or may not have happened in the CO's stateroom yesterday evening.

But not to Matt's own speculation.

The Duty Captain started tonight. Which meant he would have to give his post-watch turnover report to the XO, not the CO. It would have been awkward enough facing the CO after what happened earlier. But Matt hadn't told the CO to fuck off; he'd told the XO.

This was not going to be a fun post-watch process.

Except...it wasn't awkward at all. The XO was his normal, calm self, and took his and Jerry Despirito's relief reports with a couple routine questions and a professional, "Thank you, gentlemen," from his desk in his stateroom.

Matt could have just left with Jerry, and counted his blessings. But he needed to clear the air, so he remained.

XO must have expected both of them to leave, because he immediately went back to reading the document he had been working on when they walked in. It took him a few seconds to realize that Matt was still there.

He looked at Matt quizzically. "Was there something else?"

Matt cleared his throat. "Sir, I... I wanted to apologize for...yesterday. OPS was right, I was out of line. I was just..." He ran out of words, and spent a bit trying to think of how to say how he had been burning up over what went on aboard the Daisy. But finally he just shrugged slightly and said, "Sorry, sir," a bit lamely.

XO looked at him in silence for a few seconds, then he nodded. "Yes, you went up to that line and leaped straight over it. Far over it." He raised both eyebrows to emphasize the point. "I get it; we all do. But you need to work on your professional thick skin. There will be many times in the future when you will strongly disagree with a superior officer, or a course of action. And that's fine, take it up with him in private. Maybe he is wrong and you can help him change course for the better. Or maybe you just don't have the right perspective to be able to see the reasons behind what he's doing. But what you *can't* do is disrespect his rank and position."

Matt felt that; it was like a verbal slap, because it was, and an earned one, at that.

"Again, sorry, sir."

"Take it as a learning point, of what *not* to do next time." His expression became a bit more mild. "But don't beat yourself up over it. Done is done, and I'm not going to hold it over you. Neither will the skipper." He paused, then chuckled. "OPS might. You really pissed him off. But not for long. Once we nail these guys, no one will remember that conversation even happened." He grinned mischievously. "Until the Hail and Farewell, anyway."

Oh great. Matt hadn't thought about that. But then again, the funniest stories are usually the most awkward or weird at the time... Matt realized he was smiling, and felt a lot better.

XO saw it, because he nodded again. "Get some rest. Tomorrow, we're going to catch us some pirates."

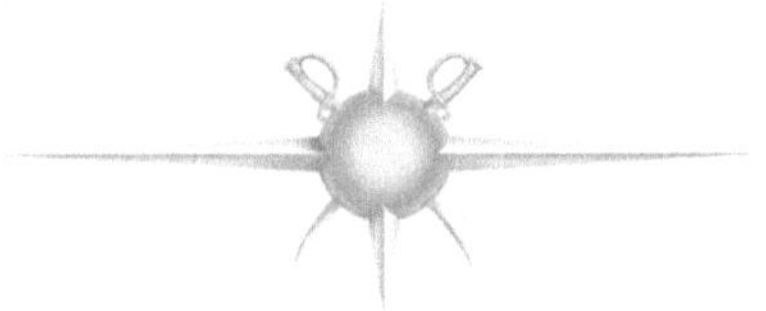

Chapter Sixty-Three

But the XO was wrong. They didn't catch the pirates the next day. At least, not immediately.

HALSWELL jumped to the Vialobos system a few minutes before 1000, and local time became 0845. Normally, this would cause consternation with some watch standers. But today, feeling like they were hot on the trail of some major bad guys, it felt like everyone was down for whatever time they got to spend working the problem.

Matt spent the last couple hours of the morning watch on the bridge, watching the goings-on through the ship's status display and tactical overlays built into the bridge display system.

He really should have been taking care of some divisional work, but screw it.

And he wasn't the only one. Several Chiefs who almost never spent any time up on the bridge filtered through, sometimes lingering for just a couple minutes and sometimes staying for a good half hour before going back to their normal duties.

But the only thing the ship got out of the morning watch was confirmation that the pirate corvette had, in fact, made the jump yesterday, as they had assumed.

The way they got that confirmation was pretty neat, though, and

Matt learned something new; something he never even imagined to ask about, before the events of the last couple days.

He knew the jump gate equipment logged communications events for transmission through the gate when it opened. He didn't know it also logged a complete record of each ship that passed through: name, port of registry, place of construction, owner's contact information…and multi-angle visual scan results, and passive IR, Radar, and gravitic signatures.

It was the gravitic part that really surprised Matt, until he thought it over. Of course a ship passing through a jump point would leave a gravitic signature, and since the jump gate satellites were essentially just great big gravitic pulse generators, they would be able to detect it; they would almost have to, to do their job correctly.

He just hadn't considered the implications of that fact.

So, after interfacing with the jump gate satellites, HALSWELL knew for certain the corvette was in Vialobos, and had about a day's head start on them. That made for a large volume of space that they would have to search. But it was a known volume, and the tactical displays had the pirate's AOU plotted, growing at their maximum engine output, before HALSWELL even made the jump.

In reality, the AOU was much smaller than that estimate. The corvette wouldn't be running at flank the entire time. In fact, she couldn't, not without running out of fuel, fast. So while the volume to cover was large, it was not unmanageable.

By the time he left the bridge to get lunch before going on watch, Matt felt like he had a pretty decent grasp on the situation, and was confident about their chances of success.

CSO and Harry apparently did as well. They ate together, along with Bo Phan, who was their OOD, at the end of the wardroom table closest to the door, and Matt noticed the others were chewing quite a bit more quickly than normal. But between bites, they discussed their plan of attack for the watch.

"Too bad Vegas and his gang aren't here," Harry said.

CSO nodded. "They would make this one hell of a lot easier. Those skiffs can cover a lot of space, quickly, and their ESM suite is top notch. We could have docked one of our ASVs in their rear compartment, and then they could probe off-axis of our direction of travel with the ASV slaved to their control…" He made a little finger-gesture of a fun firing. "Like ducks in a barrel."

"Well at least we've got the ASVs," Matt said.

"And they will help. But we'll only be able to have one out at a time. WEPS left one in standby mode at the jump point, to alert us if the pirates double back, just in case." CSO raised his eyebrows. "Hard to do, but they've had a day to position themselves, and if they suspect we're following them—and I would if I were them—they could be hunkered down in their equivalent of Condition Omicron not far from the gate. And then when we zoom past," he waved his hand toward the wardroom door, "they duck behind us back to Haspastus, and burn for home…and then we're in a tail chase again."

Matt frowned as he thought that over. Normally the ASVs were only good for twelve to eighteen hours of use before they needed to dock and recharge. Which was more than a crewed skiff could comfortably do, but it was still a limitation. But in standby mode an ASV could lurk for almost a week, waking every couple hours to send a wellness message to the ship, but just passively "listening" aside from that.

But that left HALSWELL with only three units immediately usable…so CSO was right. It would be best practice to only have one of them out at a time, to retain a surge volume. And because things break, and having a backup is always a good idea.

Harry frowned as he considered CSO's words, then he shook his head. "I don't think they'll do that. There's not as many places to hide there, and they must have at least some idea of our capabilities. They have to know we'll catch them if they just run. I think they're going to zip toward one of those asteroids, maybe one of the mining outposts, and hope to get tucked in before we get there."

"Well, we'll find out soon enough." CSO took a long swallow of water from his cup and pushed his plate away. "All set?"

Matt and Harry both nodded, and CSO looked over toward the CO. "Excuse us, Captain."

They left the wardroom together, almost before the CO finished nodding permission for them to leave.

Because Matt was already familiar with most of the tactical picture from his time on the bridge, turnover with Jeremy was pretty quick. The situation was much as it had been before lunch, except they had finished launching ASV-2, and it was now off on a forty-five degree offset from the ship's course vector.

HALSWELL was on course toward the nearest of the active mining outposts, but was moving relatively slowly. When WEPS came through the jump gate he had put on a quick half hour of acceleration at Ahead Full, and then left the engines at standby since then. It made for a slower transit, but also didn't put out a consistent gravitic distortion that the corvette could detect, and maybe track.

"I have to wonder how good they are at GAP techniques though," Matt said, as he and Jeremy were looking over their own GAP—which was depressingly devoid of any data from the corvette so far.

"We have to assume they know how to use their ship's equipment," Jeremy said.

"True enough. Well," he straightened fully and turned to face him. "I'm ready to relieve you."

"I'm ready to be relieved."

"I relieve you."

"I stand relieved." Jeremy grinned. "How's lunch?"

"Chicken pucks and fries."

Jeremy's smile grew two sizes larger. "Sweet! I love those things."

Matt could only chuckle in amusement. Not that there was anything wrong with chicken pucks, per se. It was basically a hamburger, but with breaded chicken instead of a ground beef patty. But there was something about the chicken...it always felt a little too squishy, to him. Kind of fake.

Tasted pretty good, though. Matt couldn't deny that.

"Enjoy."

Jeremy lifted his index finger to his eyebrow in a little salute. "Knock 'em dead, man."

"We'll do our best."

A minute later, CSO came over the tactical net. "All stations, TAO. The Combat System Officer has relieved as TAO."

All the various stations rogered up, and they were off.

Time to catch some pirates.

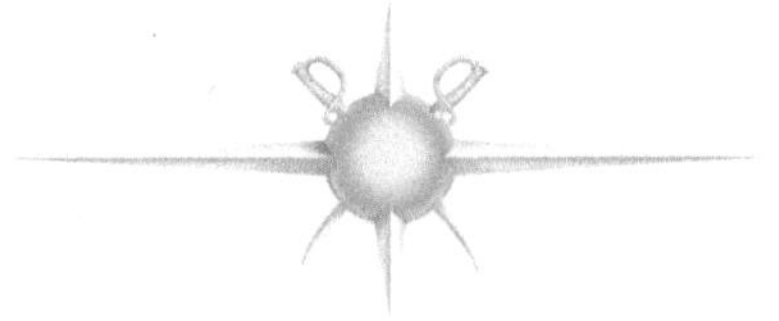

Chapter Sixty-Four

Matt joined Harry and CSO beside the fusion plot. It was zoomed out to show the entire system, with its one jump point back to Haspastus, two gaseous worlds, and twin suns. The Hot Jupiter world was on the opposite side of the system's center of gravity from the jump point at the moment. The other world was about sixty degrees to spinward from the jump point. And of the six manned mining outposts, all but two were similarly distant, well outside the corvette's expanding AOU, and unreachable for several days, regardless.

The abandoned outposts were another matter. Two were close enough that it would be a toss-up whether it would be quicker to go to the manned station HALSWELL was vectoring toward, or not.

At the GAP, he had noted gravitic intercepts from the vicinity of the manned outposts, and those were displayed on the fusion plot, as yellow squares for unknown vessels. But the nearest of them were at the extreme edge of the corvette's AOU, so it was all but certain they did not correlate to HALSWELL's quarry.

"We'll be in tight beam range of that outpost in two and a half hours," Harry said. "I assume that's the plan?"

CSO nodded. "They may have monitored the pirates's entry to the system, or at least they should have picked up their burn as they left the gate. Their sensors probably aren't top of the line, but they can't have missed that."

Matt scanned the fusion plot again, frowning. "Here's hoping."

He focused in on the blue half-circle that denoted ASV-2, vectoring away from HALSWELL's track. It had showed up clearly on the GAP as it accelerated away, but its signature faded quickly as it gained distance from the ship. And now that it was coasting, it left none at all, and sent out no transmissions except for its tight beam link back to HALSWELL.

"Well," CSO said, rubbing his hands together. "Nothing much to do but wait, and keep a close eye out." He raised an eyebrow at Harry. "And don't forget about the IR and visual scan." Radar, of course, was right out, because Condition Omicron meant EMCON—no transmissions off the ship, except tight beam, without CO's permission—for obvious reasons. "I've been in a few engagements where that was the first indication of the enemy, until it was too late."

"You got whacked?"

CSO nodded. "The first time." He sniffed, then added, "But only the first time. Don't want a repeat here. We're not on the range anymore."

Harry winced as he considered what CSO just said. "Agreed, sir."

They got about their business. Matt and Harry had agreed to divide up the work. He would cover the GAP and ESM, while Matt would cover visual, IR, and SCCON. The controller had things pretty well in hand with ASV-2; there wasn't all that much to do. So Matt bounced between the IR and visual systems. Personnel back in the Sensors shack were doing in-depth scans, supported by automatic analysis systems, so he knew he really wasn't contributing all that much. But he still tracked through it all on one of the control stations in CIC.

Over time, he developed a routine, dividing the space around the ship into eight segments, and carefully looking through all the data from each segment in sequence, so in the space of fifteen or twenty minutes he had done a survey of the entire volume around the ship.

Had the support personnel, or the automated systems, picked up anything, it would have made that routine less dry. But it was all he could do at the moment.

At some point, after his second full survey, he looked over and saw that the CO had joined CSO by the fusion plot. That was expected; where else would the CO be in a combat scenario? But it still gave Matt a rather tense feeling, like he was being watched an evaluated.

Don't fuck it up, the CO had said.

Well, he didn't intend to. Even if he hadn't said that, back in his stateroom. The memories of the dead men on the Daisy were reminder enough.

The CO's presence gave some more, though.

But despite that, the watch began to drag. There was no indication that the corvette was anywhere in the system. But the jump gate equipment had been clear: she had made the jump. So where was she?

Perhaps the pirates had figured a way to spoof the jump gate. Make it think they had jumped, when in fact they had just gone dark back in Haspastus, and watched, laughing up their sleeves, when HALSWELL went through to pursue them.

They could be well on their way to the Melrose jump point by now if that were the case. Maybe—

"TAO, Radio. Tight Beam connection confirmed," came the Radioman of the Watch's voice, over the 27MC.

Matt turned to look back at the fusion plot, and did a double-take. More time had passed than he thought; he hadn't checked the chronometer in a while. And now the plot showed a dotted yellow line connecting HALSWELL with the mining outpost they had been vectoring toward, an indication of the communications link.

CSO acknowledged, then picked up the comms handset and called up the mining outpost.

They responded as close to immediately as light speed latency would allow. Matt was on the other side of the space, and couldn't hear what CSO was saying very clearly. And the outpost's replies came only over the handset. So he watched in curious ignorance for a minute or so, until a broad, satisfied smile appeared on the CSO's face.

Matt thought he heard a thank you, then the CSO hung up the handset. He turned to face the CO.

"We've got 'em, skipper," Matt could hear more plainly. Then CSO's voice came over the 27MC. "Plot, Radio, TAO. Prepare to receive uploaded gravitic data from mining outpost Conway's Crush."

Radio rogered up, and Matt hurried over to Harry at the GAP.

It took a few minutes, but the gravitic data began to populate.

Harry whistled as he looked at it. "Man, they weren't screwing around."

And he was right. The gravitic distortion Conway's Crush had recorded, and was now forwarding on to them, was blatant, it was so strong. The corvette wasn't even trying to hide.

And there could be no doubt the corvette was the source. FC2 at the plot pulled up the signature HALSWELL had recorded from the Daisy incident, and this new data matched it exactly. And the beginning of the distortion plotted exactly at the jump point, beginning just after the time of the corvette's passage.

We've got 'em, indeed.

There was a lot of data to sift through, and it took the majority of Matt, Harry, and FC2's attention. At Harry's prompting, Matt split off periodically to check the other sensor data, but it only took a cursory look to see there was nothing there; the new GAP data was all.

Half an hour later, they had a clearer picture, and pressed it to the fusion plot.

CSO looked even more satisfied as he studied it.

The AOU was tight at the jump point, and expanded into a conic section that projected from the jump point toward the inner system. But it was much tighter, overall, than the AOUs Matt had plotted during the Track-Ex, and in other scenarios. It helped to have a definitive starting point. And since they knew the corvette's operating characteristics, and were able to match the data with that from the Daisy's location, it was all but certain the corvette had executed a flank speed burn as soon as they exited the jump gate.

That made the AOU quite a bit tighter, indeed. And it pointed straight at one of the abandoned mining outposts, just like they had suspected.

"She'll be there late tomorrow afternoon or early evening, looks like, skipper," CSO said, pointing at the outpost on the fusion plot. "She burned for three straight hours after leaving the gate, so I would expect her deceleration burn to start sometime late tomorrow morning."

The CO nodded agreement. "Train all the passive systems on that bearing. I want to know the instant she maneuvers."

"Aye, sir," CSO said. "I'm going to recover ASVs 1 and 2. We'll redeploy them when we're closer, to give us a heads up on what they have waiting for us."

"I concur." The CO picked up the handset to the bridge and pushed the call button. A moment later, "Officer of the Deck, Captain. Have the quartermaster plot a course to the position Combat is sending up, then execute at Ahead Full. Time the engine bell orders so that we will arrive tomorrow at 1500, with a maximum deceleration burn."

It took Matt a second to get the reason for the CO's order, but not a long second. The fuel consumption at Flank compared with Full was greater than the acceleration benefit, over the long run. So a bit of a longer burn at Full would still burn less, and get the inbound velocity up quickly. But the CO wanted to hold off braking toward the mining outpost for as long as possible, so the QMOW would be planning for a flank-speed deceleration at the end of their run.

Doing it that way would get HALSWELL there as fast as possible, while also maintaining as much speed and surprise as possible.

And getting there just as the corvette was arriving, and maybe in the middle of her docking, would mean she would not have time to refill her plasma medium tanks, if the pirates had indeed refit that outpost as a base. Which Matt was beginning to think was the most likely scenario.

Made a lot of sense, now that he fully thought it through.

Bo acknowledged the CO's order, and the CO hung up the handset. Then he turned to CSO. "I'll be down in Classroom 2 if you need me." He looked from CSO to Matt and Harry, and gave a quick nod. "Good work."

Then he turned and left the space through the aft airtight hatch.

On the fusion plot, HALSWELL's course vector began to shift, rapidly, as Bo carried out the CO's order.

"SCCON, TAO, recall ASVs 1 and 2," CSO said. Then he grinned at Matt and Harry. "Just a matter of time, now. They can run, but they can't hide."

The rest of the watch went by more slowly. With their quarry's likely destination firmly established, there was not much to do but monitor the various sensors, and wait. And as expected, by the time Vasili, OPS, and Charlie showed up to relieve the watch in CIC, they still had not detected anything from the corvette. But that would change soon enough, as HALSWELL closed the distance between them.

Unless the pirates had another trick up their sleeves. Time would tell.

Turnover with Vasili was quick, and Matt went to leave. But as he passed the CSO and OPS, still in their turnover discussion by the fusion plot, he felt OPS's eyes on him.

"Mister Gilbert."

Recalling XO's words, he stopped with a feeling of trepidation, and turned around. "Yes, sir."

OPS's expression was neutral. "Charlie finished grading your OOD exam this afternoon."

Matt hadn't exactly forgotten about that, but he hadn't been thinking about it either, what with all that had been going on the last couple days. "Hope I didn't fail."

OPS made something between a sniff and a snort, and shook his head. "No, you crushed it, actually. What else do you have left on your card?"

Matt shrugged. "Just a couple checkouts with you about the Rules of the Road and navigation principles, and one with Doc Roos about medical emergency procedures."

OPS considered for a moment, then made a quick half-nod, almost to himself. "Those won't take long. Hook up with me tomorrow morning and we'll knock them out. I'll get your board scheduled as soon as all this," he waved his hand at the fusion plot, "is done with."

"Yes, sir. That'll be good."

Next to him, CSO grinned, and gave Matt a thumbs up.

OPS turned back to him to continue their turnover, but paused when he saw Matt wasn't moving along. He raised a questioning eyebrow.

Might as well get it over with. Matt cleared his throat softly. "Sir, about the other day."

OPS shook his head. "I'm not sure what you're talking about, Mr. Gilbert." His expression remained neutral, but there was a glint in his eyes that said he did indeed, but he wasn't going to press it, so just let sleeping dogs lie.

Matt got the hint. "I guess it's nothing, sir."

OPS nodded. "Carry on, then."

As Matt left for the post-watch routine, and dinner, he felt a rising senses of relief. Looked like OPS wasn't going to stay pissed at him, after all.

It was only as he was spooning out his salad in the wardroom that the rest of the conversation fully sank in, and that relief fled before a sense of excitement...and apprehension. He'd been anticipating his OOD board for months, and now it was almost here.

He was ready. He thought.

But still, there was the thinking about a thing and then there was the doing of it.

Well, at least the guys wouldn't be able to con him into rushing off the ship at the last minute, this time.

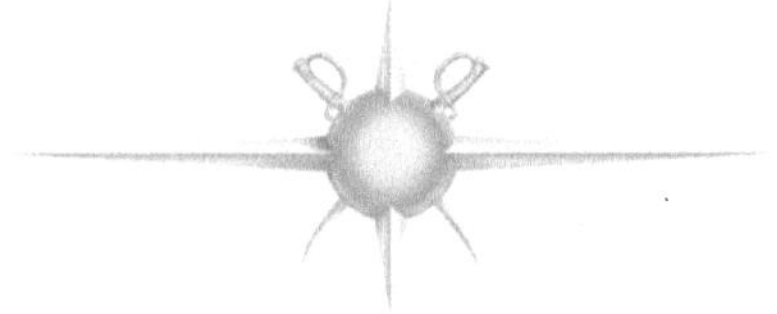

Chapter Sixty-Five

HALSWELL was racing through the Vialobos system at a greater velocity than Matt had ever seen her achieve before. They'd maintained Ahead Full for just over ten hours, driving the distance to the abandoned mining outpost downward at a herculean rate.

Intellectually, Matt knew the kinds of speeds starships like HALSWELL could attain. But up to this point they had only done acceleration burns for brief periods, to get their velocity up to a reasonable rate, to get where they needed to be on time.

No need to drain the plasma medium tanks dry for a standard transit, after all.

But this was no standard transit.

At breakfast, the conversation was muted, despite the palpable energy emanating from the other men in the wardroom. It seemed like everyone stopped to glance at the ship's status display every other minute, as though something dramatic would change in that brief span, and everyone seemed ready to spring into action the moment it did.

Hard to engage in small talk, when you're feeling that way.

Matt and OPS hooked up mid-morning, and the checkouts were similarly stilted. He asked his questions and Matt gave his answers, but it felt like neither of them were fully engaged in the exercise. At least

Matt wasn't. His mind kept flicking ahead toward this afternoon, and what would happen when they arrived at the mining outpost.

Would the pirates be there, or had they detected HALSWELL's approach and changed their plans? If they were there, had they fortified the outpost? Maybe there were other ships besides the corvette, or defense platforms, or...

The possibilities were legion, and he was sure he could drive himself mad chewing on them all. So it was hard to put the speculation aside and focus on the checkouts. Maybe that's why OPS gave him so many lookups.

Regardless, that left just the one more checkout with the Doc before his board, so as Matt was going through his list of lookups with OPS, to make sure he didn't miss anything, before leaving to get them done, he felt pretty good.

"Ok, I think that's—"

An electronic beep interrupted what Matt was about to say. Both he and OPS looked away from each other, toward the ship's status display that was mounted adjacent to OPS's desk in the Operations Department Office, where they had been meeting.

Engine output and ship's velocity were two major items on display, and Matt immediately saw what had triggered the alert. -18Gs, and the overall velocity was ticking down, rapidly.

"We've started our deceleration burn," he said.

OPS nodded. "Looks like."

He reached over to a control pad that was built into the corner of his desk. A couple quick taps brought up a 2-D rendering of the fusion plot.

It was zoomed in to more closely show the mining outpost, and HALSWELL. The corvette's old AOU filled most of the display, shaded a light red.

"They should be slowing any time now, also," OPS said. "And then it's game on."

"Assuming they don't change course."

OPS shrugged. "If they do, we'll see it, and we've got more fuel than they do." Everyone kept saying that. And it was true, Matt knew that. Still... OPS went on, "But they have to know that. If I were them I'd hope I could get into my fortifications before we arrive, and maybe wait us out."

"You think they've built up a base there."

"It's the only thing that makes sense." He smiled thinly. "We'll find out soon enough." With an obvious effort, he pulled his eyes away from the display. "But for now," he gestured toward Matt's holopad, where he had been taking his lookup notes.

Taking his point, Matt looked back down at his list again to double-check. But yeah, he'd verified everything. "That's all I've got."

OPS nodded. "Then get to it."

He only had time to find three of the lookups before he had to roll to the wardroom for lunch, and then head out to take the watch. But even that small amount of studying felt like pulling teeth, it was so hard to maintain his focus.

Lunch was bland. Or rather, he hardly noticed it, so in a rush he was to get through it. And his stomach was starting to do flips in his belly, as the reality of what they were about to encounter fully set in. When he pushed his plate away and rose, with the others in his watch team, he was surprised to see how little he had actually eaten, but yet he felt full.

Nerves starting to get to you, his inner, rational voice said. Calm the hell down.

Easy to say; hard to do. And when he stepped into CIC, he felt like he was bouncing a foot into the air with each step, from the tension and energy flowing through him.

That didn't stop him from zeroing in on the fusion plot, and recognizing the import of the changes there.

ASVs 1 and 2 were out again, zipping away from HALSWELL at opposite 30 degree offsets so they would be able to bracket the target with their sensors.

And the target was drawing near. Zoomed in as the fusion plot was now, it was easy to see the details.

The mining outpost was carved into a deep crater in what passed for the southern hemisphere of a dwarf planet labeled Vialobos-4253. The display indicated it was about 1/12 terran standard mass, and about 400 kilometers in radius.

But more important than that, there was a new AOU for the corvette. This was assigned a track number—84762—and it was tight, taking up about a third of the remaining volume between HALSWELL's position and the dwarf planet. That was almost small enough that the ship could fire now, and just let the Hammerheads do the search for the corvette themselves.

If they had more than two onboard, that was. With such a small load-out, they would have to pick their shots more carefully, which meant refining their targeting solution quite a bit more.

Jeremy was over by the weapons control station, and Matt hurried over to him.

"How's it going?"

Jeremy flashed a quick grin. "They kicked on their engines about twenty minutes ago. Initial GAP solution looks like they're slowing, so I guess we were right, and they're intending to dock at that old outpost."

Matt nodded. Made sense. "We're still passive only?"

"Captain wants to wait until the ASVs are on station. Then we'll light 'em up, and be able to triangulate them like that," he snapped his fingers.

That made sense, also. "Have the ASVs detected their gravitics?"

Jeremy shook his head. "They put on full thrust to get there more quickly."

Which was a drawback to the ASV's small size. They could accelerate much more quickly than a ship like HALSWELL. But the amount of gravitic distortion that acceleration created relative to their mass made for a sort of self-noise that reduced the capability of their gravitic sensors. They same thing happened to HALSWELL, but the ratio was different enough that the effect was much less pronounced.

That, and the limitations imposed by fuel consumption, was the main reason why the ship's maximum engine output was set the way it was. Theoretically, HALSWELL could accelerate quite a bit faster than she was limited to. But it would make her blind, and leave her completely out of fuel in a very short time, so it wasn't worth it.

"How long til they're on station?"

Jeremy checked the chronometer and purse his lips for a second. "About 45 minutes."

Matt nodded. "Anything else?"

Jeremy gave a quick shake of his head, and Matt relieved him.

It took a few more minutes for CSO to relieve WEPS, and then they all gathered at fusion plot with the CO and, Matt was surprised to see, the XO as well.

XO must have noticed his look because he said, "Today was not the right day to be in the rack on the afternoon watch."

CO nodded agreement. "You got the briefing, gentlemen. Once the ASVs are on station, EMCON is secured, and I want a full active scan on that entire region of space."

"Aye, sir. We'll find them," CSO said.

Matt looked at the fusion plot again. The distance between HALSWELL and the dwarf planet was far less than the distance from his home planet of Trinity to its nearest planetary neighbor, at its perigee. Even backyard telescopes could make out details of the planet... so how come HALSWELL's visual or IR scan hadn't picked up anything?

The corvette was painted dark, like HALSWELL was, and was almost certainly running darkened ship, and in their equivalent of Condition Omicron. But as close as she was, and as fast as she still had to be moving...

He stepped over to the sensors section at the forward semicircle of the room and studied the IR and visual displays. The OS1 on watch at the console gave a quick shake of his head.

"Know what you're thinking, sir, but we've been doing nothing but sweep the area of her AOU ever since she started her engines up again. Not a damn thing, yet."

"I would have thought she'd leave an IR trace for certain, at this range."

OS1 shrugged. "Those corvette's are small ships, sir. Much less internal heat than we put out, even when we're at Omicron. If she turned her belly away from us after she detected our engines, it'll be several million more kilometers before we'll likely see her."

"You think she detected us?"

A loud snort was the petty officer's first reply. "She'd have to have thrown her gravitic sensors away, or have no idea how to use them, to avoid it."

Matt frowned, but couldn't deny his point. "Ok," he said. "What's going on at the outpost?"

"It was below the horizon when we checked it last. Let's..." He took control of one of the telescopes and panned it over, and his eyebrows rose. "Hot damn, look at that."

Either as a result of the dwarf planet's rotation or the change in HALSWELL's angle of approach as she slowed, the crater housing the deserted mining colony was now partially in view.

But it was obviously not deserted anymore. As OS1 zoomed in on it, Matt saw multiple set of lights illuminating stout-looking structures, and beside a lighted landing pad, three—no, four—rounded humps that looked like fuel tanks.

OS1 shifted to IR, and the place was glowing almost as brightly as the lights that illuminated it.

"Definitely someone there," Matt said, and OS1 grunted. "Press that to the fusion plot." Then he switched to the tactical channel on his implants. "TAO, plot. Visual on the mining outpost, and it appears to be manned."

"TAO, aye," CSO said, and Matt heard a stirring behind him.

"Keep an eye on that," he said to OS1, then stepped back to the fusion plot.

As he approached, the XO was talking. "—are those?"

He was pointing at a smaller object out past the body of the dwarf planet itself. Matt hadn't noticed it before, because they had zoomed in so far to make out the base. But now he saw two other objects, oddly shaped and barely visible, in the area.

CSO frowned and tapped on the fusion plot controls, and a dialog window opened. "The system chart says Vialobos-4253 has four satellites, smaller asteroids that it captured at some point."

XO said, "Good place to put defensive batteries."

The CO frowned, deeply. "IR?"

CSO tapped the controls again, and the IR spectrum of that same image came up, overlaid on the visual. The base was glowing like before, but the satellites were dark.

The CO sniffed. "We have to assume there's something there. Maintain a constant IR monitor on those satellites."

CSO said, "We only have so many scopes."

The CO just looked at him, and after a moment, CSO nodded. "Aye, sir."

As CSO passed the order to the Sensors cell, the CO moved over to the handset for the 1MC.

"Attention, HALSWELL, this is the Captain."

All around the CIC, conversations stopped, and Matt could feel that growing silence spread through the ship.

"We are just over two hours from our destination, and we have the target in sight. The pirates appear to have fortifications in place, so I expect we will encounter resistance. We will be manning battlestations in thirty minutes. Off-watch personnel, hit the head or grab some chow now, because I cannot tell you how long the engagement will last." He paused, clearly pondering for a moment. "Carry on."

The CO placed the handset back in its holder and looked gravely at the XO. Matt hurried back to his duties.

Minutes passed like seconds, and still there was no sign of the corvette on visual or IR. Matt was beginning to wonder if they were really there.

And then...

"TAO, SCCON, ASVs 1 and 2 nearing station and reducing thrust. Both units report gravitic detection, passing to plot."

At the GAP, the new data came streaming in. It matched the signature that HALSWELL's organic systems had been tracking. But now, with three receiving stations instead of just one, FC2 was able to reduce the AOU almost immediately.

That solved the question that had been burning in Matt's mind, because instead of an AOU, a solid hostile red diamond appeared on the fusion plot. But it was off-axis to the dwarf planet. Instead of burning straight in, the corvette had altered course to pass above it, so the visual and IR scopes had been looking in the wrong place.

It wasn't a large course change, enough to put the corvette on the edge of the AOU the team had plotted. But it was enough.

Had they intended to slip around the other side of the planet from HALSWELL and then come up on them from the rear? It seemed like a good idea, to Matt.

But now they had her, dead to rights, and still far enough away from the mass of the dwarf planet that if that was her intention, it was not going to work.

At the fusion plot, the CO smiled thinly. "Light them up."

CSO returned the grin and ordered a full active scan, and the CO said, over the 27MC, "Officer of the Deck, Captain. Man battlestations."

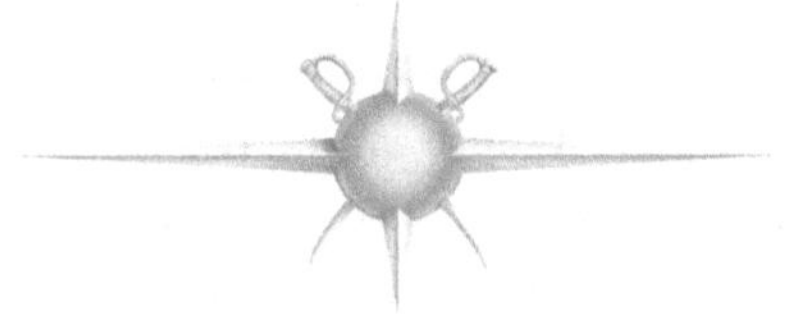

Chapter Sixty-Six

"Man battlestations. Set Condition Zebra throughout the ship."

The order went out on the 1MC, followed by the thirteen electronic gongs of the ship's general alarm. Then the Chief of the Watch repeated the order.

Throughout the ship, a controlled wave of frenetic activity was taking place, everyone scurrying to get to where they were supposed to be. Matt was already in his place, but he could feel the rush that must have been passing through the body of every other man on the ship as they moved smartly to their places.

On-watch personnel would not see much of a difference. But the off-watch, on the other hand, had a lot to do.

The off-going—meaning, the guy who had the watch before this one—EOOW would go to Damage Control Central, to manage any needed DC efforts. The torpedo reload team, consisting of Torpedo Division and a few selected personnel from other Weapons Department divisions, would muster in the Torpedo Room. Damage Control Division, augmented by a few non-divisional personnel, would muster at the various Repair Lockers on the ship, and suit up. Doc Roos and his personnel would bring their emergency medical equipment to the Chief Petty Officers's mess, which doubled as the ship's hospital. Other offgoing personnel went back to their previous duty stations to augment the on-watch personnel. Oncoming watch standers, and others who were not specifically assigned elsewhere, mustered in Crews Mess and Wardroom, awaiting orders to assist wherever they were needed.

The standard was for everyone to be on station in five minutes, after which the Chief of the Watch would activate all of the airtight doors and hatches on the ship, sealing them shut to maximize the ship's airtight integrity. Once that was done, no one could move around on the ship without coordinating with the COW on the Bridge, who would make sure no one would open a door or hatch unless the space on the other side was intact.

The time flew past, all the more because as soon as HALSWELL went active on her radar, ESM detected a whole lot of emissions from the corvette, and the base.

"They must have been talking via tight beam only," said the OS2 who was manning the ESM station in CIC. "But they're not hiding now."

Both the corvette and the base had multiple radars emitting now, several of them falling into the area of the spectrum that was reserved for military, fire control radars.

Matt swallowed a growing lump in his throat when he registered that, but the three senior officers around the fusion plot seemed nonplussed.

"I guess they mean business, skipper," CSO quipped.

The CO grunted. "Let's find out." He picked up the handset for the bridge-to-bridge radio circuit. Not a tight-beam transmission, it would be received by anyone and everyone in the system.

"COTARI-class corvette on approach to Vialobos-4253, this is the Icaran Confederation Ship FREDRICK HALSWELL. You are ordered to cut thrust and surrender your vessel, and answer to charges of piracy and murder aboard the Icaran-flagged Space Vessel Daisy. Over."

Almost half a minute passed, much longer than light speed latency should have required at their current range. The CO and XO traded looks, then the CO raised the handset again. But before it was halfway to his mouth, an answer came through.

"Hey there, HALSWELL, this is the Singing Josie," said a high-pitched male voice with a strangely folksy drawl that made Matt remember camping trips out in the wild when he was a kid, for some reason. "Don't know nothing about no Space Vessel Daisy. Y'all caught us about to make a run for supplies for our mining camp, here, over."

XO snorted, and CSO rolled his eyes.

"Do they think we were born yesterday?" CSO asked, incredulously.

"They're just stalling for time," the CO said. He keyed the bridge to bridge. "Singing Josie, this is HALSWELL. We have tracked you from Haspastus, and the outpost you are approaching is not officially sanctioned. I say again, cut thrust and surrender your vessel, or you will be fired upon. This is your only warning. Over."

He lowered the handset and said, "TAO, make tubes 1 and 2 ready in all respects."

"Make tubes 1 and 2 ready in all respects, aye, sir," CSO said, and he relayed the order to the Weapons station.

Much less time passed before Singing Josie responded this time. "Hold your horses, there, HALSWELL. No need to get ornery. I don't rightly know what it is you're looking for, but I ain't looking for no fight, neither. Cutting thrust now, and you're free to come on over."

"Roger, Singing Josie. Standby. HALSWELL out."

The CO looked over at the XO and raised his eyebrows.

XO looked skeptical. "I don't buy it."

The CO opened his mouth to reply, but a report on the tactical net interrupted him.

"TAO, Sensors, gravitic distortion faded. Assess target has reduced engine output to standby."

"Well I guess that answers that," the CO said, ironically.

CSO snorted. "No way they're just going to wait for us to waltz on over." He called up the visual of the dwarf planet again.

Its rotation had continued, and now the mining outpost was almost directly facing HALSWELL. And a third of the suspect satellites had come into view from behind the dwarf planet's bulk.

CSO pointed at the new satellite. "Probably just want us to get in range of those, so they can blast us."

Damn skippy that's what they wanted, even Matt could see that. But what other choice was there?

Before anyone could say anything, though, the CSO continued.

"Plot, TAO. Run a maneuvering problem. Assuming the satellites have plasma cannons equivalent to ours, give me a course to intercept the Singing Josie without passing within firing range of them."

Harry's voice came back on the tactical net. "Plot, aye." He sounded uncertain, downright doubtful.

Matt checked in with the visual/IR station again, then headed over to give Harry a hand.

He had a maneuvering trial solution application up and was fiddling with it, a frown on his lips. "It would help if we had good ephemeris data on those satellites," he said as Matt reached him.

"We've got their orbital velocity from the radar returns, right?"

Harry nodded. "Yeah but that thing," he pointed at the dwarf planet, "is not exactly symmetrical." Which was a true statement. The hemisphere containing the formerly-abandoned mining outpost was decidedly lopsided, hardly a hemisphere at all. "Makes for a distorted gravity well, so who knows how their next orbits will look."

Matt shrugged. "Well, I guess we'll just going to have to use a good, old-fashioned engineering approximation." By which, Matt meant a guess.

Harry snorted out a laugh, and they got to it.

About 10 minutes later, they had a solution. Not a very elegant one, and it didn't completely answer the mail, but the best they could do. Harry pressed it to the fusion plot, then they went to talk it over.

CSO was frowning as he looked the solution over. It would have HALSWELL shift course, in azimuth and elevation, half a dozen times before falling in behind the latest-appearing satellite as it transited the face of the dwarf planet. It was convoluted, and didn't seem to make intuitive sense at first, but when they plotted the assumed firing ranges of the satellite emplacements, it did the job.

Right up until the end.

"When we're on the final approach to intercept, we'll be skirting the engagement bubbles of both these satellites," XO pointed out, indicating the second and third of the satellites.

He was right. This was because the second satellite's orbit was highly inclined from the dwarf planet's equator, and slower than the others, so its arc and the third's ended up overlapping for an extended time.

Harry spread his hands helplessly. "Best we could do, sir. If we wait to clear them both completely, the first satellite will have cleared the back side of the planet, and it will be able to engage us, as well."

"And we still haven't seen satellite #4, so we don't know what it's about," Matt added.

Silence loomed for a few seconds as the senior officers pondered that. Then the CO sighed.

"They say a good plan today is better than a perfect plan tomorrow," he said. "CSO, pass that track to the bridge."

"Aye, skipper," CSO said.

The CO then called the OOD on the bridge and filled him in on the plan, and HALSWELL's vector began to shift on the fusion plot, to follow Matt and Harry's track.

As they approached the final turn to intercept Singing Josie, Matt stopped by the Weapons station. A look over the FC3's shoulder confirmed what he had assumed, but also wanted to verify. Both tubes were ready in all respects, their indications fully red, and the track data for the corvette was assigned to both weapons. SDMS and the point defense turrets were powered up, but in standby. And the primary cannons were charged, safety systems off, ready to fire.

They were as ready to go as could be.

He watched as the range ticked down, and noted with approval that FC3 shifted the torpedoes from long range tactics to short range almost immediately, when HALSWELL came within two-hundred fifty thousand kilometers of the corvette.

LT Tolson would be proud.

Matt chuckled to himself as that thought crossed through his mind. Why he should ponder what his former instructor would have to say about it, if he were here, escaped him. But there it was, all the same.

At the fusion plot, the CO nodded to himself as they completed their final turn, and picked up the bridge to bridge. "Singing Josie, this is HALSWELL. We will come up on your starboard side. Prepare to receive boarders, over."

"Sounds like a plan, HALSWELL. We'll be waiting, over."

XO quirked his eyebrow at him. "You're not sending the VBSS team over?"

The CO let out a sardonic laugh as he shook his head. "They won't give us the chance."

XO frowned, and traded glances with CSO, who matched his expression.

"You mean to let them take the first shot," CSO said. It was almost an accusation.

"No one will be able to say we didn't give them a chance to surrender."

CSO snorted. "No one will be able to if we just blow them out of space right now. We know who they are, and what they've done, for a fact."

The CO nodded slowly, giving CSO a grave look. "Maybe. But the forms must be followed."

Matt had to admit, he came down more on the CSO's side than the CO's, right that moment. How could anyone fault them for taking the shot now?

But then he thought it through for a moment, and changed his mind. The bridge to bridge conversations had been in the clear, so any other vessels in transmission range—which effectively meant everyone in the system, sparsely populated as it was—would have heard the Singing Josie essentially surrender. Firing on her after that would be untenable.

CSO must have come to that conclusion as well, because he nodded understanding. He still had a frown on his face, though.

"Well, guess we'll see what they do." He thought for a moment. "Should we launch one of the ship's boats? We could rig it for remote piloting from the SCCON station, so it would be unmanned."

The CO nodded. "Good idea. Make Fred-1 ready for launch."

"Aye, skipper," CSO said, and he relayed the order to the Boat Deck, where elements of Deck Division were at their battlestations muster.

Minutes passed, and the range ticked down, until HALSWELL came to a relative halt two thousand kilometers off the corvette's starboard quarter. That was much farther away than would be done for a standard boarding, but it kept the ship outside the minimum torpedo engagement range of one-thousand, five-hundred kilometers. So they would be prepared to respond if...when...the pirates started the fight.

But as he watched Fred-1 depart on one of the visual relays, and head toward the corvette, Matt couldn't help but wonder what if they didn't? They couldn't exactly dock Fred-1 to them with no one aboard; it would reveal that they were bluffing.

OS1 chuckled, and Matt realized he had said that last bit out loud.

"If they don't take the bait, Fred-1 will have a mechanical problem and have to return to base," the petty officer said.

Matt raised an eyebrow at him, and he shrugged. "Not my first rodeo, sir."

Matt shook his head, feeling a bit silly, and went over to the radar console.

Fred-1 was two-thirds of the way to the corvette when something new came up on the radar. The OS2 who was manning it perked up and compared the new contact with the system chart, and blanched.

"TAO, radar," he said, "new radar contact, correlates with satellite #4."

At the fusion plot, a new contact block appeared. It was coming out from behind the mass of the dwarf planet almost exactly at its south pole, and moving quickly enough that it must have had a much longer, and more eccentric, orbit than the other three.

That explained why HALSWELL hadn't seen it yet. But it also meant that now there were three satellites to potentially contend with, instead of two. And its higher velocity meant that if it had a weapons emplacement, it would be able to add its fire to the first two in mere moments.

"Crap," Matt said, as the new engagement bubble for the satellite appeared.

Fred-1 was closer to the corvette now, and SCCON hailed them, slaving the boat's radio to his own console. Visual data from Fred-1's cameras were being pushed to the fusion plot, and the corvette appeared to be dormant, waiting.

They responded to Fred-1's hail in the same cheerful, welcoming tone as before, though. And despite the knot of anxiety growing in Matt's stomach, he dared to hope that maybe they really were going to surrender, and spare themselves a fight they couldn't win.

Unless they thought they could?

The engagement bubble for satellite #4 swept northward, overlapping those for #2 and #3.

And then HALSWELL was at the locus of all three.

"TAO, Sensors. IR blooms from satellites 2 and 3."

On the visual from Fred-1, the dorsal turret on the corvette rotated, to face the boat.

"TAO, SCCON, taking evasive on Fred-1," said the SCCON, just as the visual display showed the turret begin to fire.

Then the HALSWELL's vector shifted drastically on the fusion plot, elongating as the engines came up and the ship pitched upward and to the left.

At the same time, Bo's voice came over the 27MC. "Combat, Bridge. Incoming plasma fire from," he listed coordinates that correlated to all three satellites, "executing evasion pattern epsilon."

Matt had learned that pattern as part of OOD quals. It was specifically designed to evade fire from multiple sources, and supposedly did a good job of it.

Guess they'd find—

"Vampire, Vampire, Vampire," said Radar. "Incoming missiles from Singing Josie."

At the fusion plot, the XO and CO traded looks.

"Here we go," XO said.

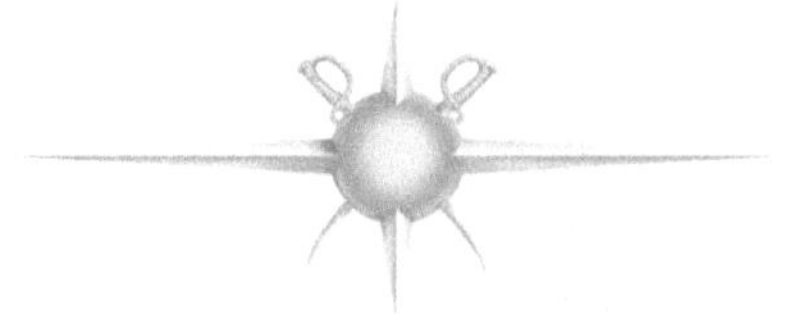

Chapter Sixty-Seven

CSO barked out a series of orders.

"Weapons, point defense to auto-engage. ESM, commence countermeasure jamming." And then, "Firing Point Procedures, Tube 1."

Weapons responded, "Target inside minimum engagement range, sir."

And it was true. The visual had showed the corvette turning toward them to fire its missiles, and now its vector had elongated to exceed HALSWELL's, and it was coming up on them from astern.

And ten missiles were tracing their way from the corvette toward them, closing distance rapidly.

Over at the weapons station, Matt could see the ammo counters on the point defense turrets counting down, and he thought he could not so much hear as feel the report of their fire, through the deck and into the soles of his feet.

Two of the incoming missiles vanished from the plot, then a third, as HALSWELL's defensive fire did its job. But the range was so short—

CSO said, "Launch countermeasure."

Matt hadn't thought about the countermeasures they had loaded at the end of sea trials in a while. But he knew how they worked, both from Tactical School and his studies since checking aboard. They were not terribly dissimilar to ASVs, though smaller and with much less endurance. But they had powerful radar jammers, and gravitic generators that were tuned to match the ship's signature, as well as heating elements that would hopefully draw the eye of an IR system.

Supposedly they worked pretty well, but Matt had never seen them in action for real, so...

The countermeasure popped out of HALSWELL's stern and ran orthogonal to their course at full acceleration, then commenced transmitting, and the ship jerked to starboard and downward as Bo continued with his evasive maneuver.

Three of the missiles diverted from their pursuit of HALSWELL, chasing after the countermeasure.

One of the visual cameras was locked onto the corvette. It was still astern, and maneuvering to remain there.

"They're faster and more maneuverable than we are," XO said. "They can hang there forever, until they run out of fuel, and—"

On the visual display, the corvette did exactly what XO presumably was about to say: it opened up with its plasma cannons.

Bo pitched the ship down and to the left, and point defense took out two more of the missiles. Then the ship lurched, and Matt stumbled against the radar console.

"Combat, bridge, plasma impact astern."

The CO's lips compressed.

"Their cannons aren't all that strong," CSO said. "One hit won't make it through our armor plating."

"There won't be just one hit," the CO said. "Get them off our stern. Engage with SDMS."

CSO nodded. "Weapons, lock SDMS on the corvette. Five missile spread."

"Weapons, aye." A pause, then, "Locked, sir."

"Fire."

In Matt's mind's eye, he saw five missiles streaking upward in a rapid salvo from the humpback behind the bridge tower. He remembered thinking, when he first saw the ship, how that humpback screwed up the ship's looks a bit.

He didn't think that anymore. The ship's cannons only fired forward, and while point defense could fire aft, it was engaged with the missiles, and anyway was not much of a threat to even a lightly-armored warship like that corvette. Without SDMS, they would have had no way to engage Singing Josie unless they managed to out-maneuver her.

And Singing Josie had tucked inside minimum engagement range of HALSWELL's torpedoes right away, which screamed that the guy captaining that ship knew what he was doing, and what HALSWELL was capable of.

But SDMS was new; maybe he didn't know about that.

HALSWELL's missiles arced up and then toward the corvette. On the visual, the corvette almost seemed to flinch, then it pivoted to port and thrust away, its dorsal point defense turret rotating to track toward the missiles.

The CO said, over the 27MC, "Bridge, Captain. Cut thrust and 180 about. Now."

On the fusion plot, HALSWELL's acceleration vector dropped to zero, and the little puck that showed the ship's bow began to rotate.

The CO looked at CSO. "Fire as she bears."

"Fire as she bears, aye sir. Weapons, engage with primary cannons."

"Engage with primary cannons, Weapons aye." Weapons sounded decidedly satisfied in that acknowledgment.

The cannons began firing moments later, and the CO ordered, "Bridge, Captain, maintain the corvette on our bow."

On the fusion plot, the corvette was zigging and zagging to evade HALSWELL's missiles. But Matt realized he had almost forgotten about the last two that the corvette had fired. One streaked past HALSWELL, apparently tracking on her projected position before she cut thrust, then winked out of existence as a point defense turret took her.

The second...

The ship lurched again, harder this time, and Matt bounced off the edge of the fusion plot console and hit the deck.

His head swam and his tongue hurt; his mouth was filled with an iron taste, and he realized he had bitten his tongue, and was bleeding. But something was dripping down the side of his face... He reached up, and saw that he was bleeding from his scalp as well.

Son of a—

"Emergency Report, Emergency Report," came an amplified voice.

Must have been over the 4MC, the emergency reporting system. It had stations all over the ship, and would override any, and all, announcing circuits so that word could be passed of casualties. "Fire in the Auxiliary Machinery Room. Fire in the Auxiliary Machinery Room."

As Matt was pushing himself to his feet, he heard the Chief of the Watch repeat the report over the 1MC.

The CO looked at XO. "XO."

"On it," XO said. Then he rushed to the hatch at the rear of CIC. He spun the hand wheel dogging it, then pulled it open and left the space without looking back.

He was heading to the Auxiliary Machinery Room, to take charge of damage control efforts at the scene; the XO's job in the event of a major casualty.

Matt shook his head to clear it. It took a second, but eventually he had his bearings again. Sort of.

"TAO, Weapons, Point Defense Turret number 4 is off-line."

Matt focused in on the Weapons station, and saw the icon for that turret flashing red, with an error bar over top it. That wasn't good.

"Dammit," CSO said. "Status of primary cannons?"

"Firing, sir."

Matt could see that. On the visual, plasma balls were streaming toward the corvette, even as she dodged to evade. What about the missiles?

The fusion plot told the story. Three of HALSWELL's missiles had vanished, taken by the corvette's point defense. Two remained. One...

Matt saw the final missile explode on the visual, and he couldn't tell if it was hit by fire from the corvette's turret, or if it had struck the hull. But as the corvette cleared the blast area, it looked like she was off-gassing a bit.

"Was that a hit?" he said.

CSO shook his head. "Hard to tell. If—" He really saw Matt then, and stopped. "You ok, Matt?"

Matt waved him off. Or tried to. He still felt a bit groggy, so the gesture wasn't nearly as brisk as he intended it. "Good to go."

CSO looked doubtful, but right then the 7MC interrupted.

"Bridge, Maneuvering. High temperature alarm in the forward Air Conditioning heat exchanger. Recommend rig for minimal electrical."

The CO scowled, and shifted to the 7MC. "Bridge, Maneuvering, Captain, maintain a normal full power lineup." Then he barked on the CIC circuit, "Range to target?"

There was a pause, during which Matt grasped the sudden tension in the CO's voice. The Air Conditioning system was possibly the most important system on the ship, though one wouldn't think it at first. All of the electronics on board created heat, that was radiated into the air or into chilled water piping running through the electronics cabinets, or both. Without the AC system, that heat would quickly build up to the point that it would be difficult to man the ship, let alone fight it. Computers would trip off-line, screens would go blank, and that would be it. HALSWELL would be down for the count, while the crew gradually succumbed to heat exhaustion.

But the corvette would blast them to kingdom come well before they died of that.

Matt ran a ship's schematic through his head. Point Defense Turret number Four was the lower aft turret. The air conditioning radiative heat exchange, in its housing to mask as much of its IR signature as possible, was amidships, a bit forward of the turret.

If the missile hit the turret itself, little chance the heat exchanger would be damaged. But if it struck between the turret and the heat exchanger...

On the bright side, there were multiple flow paths through the heat exchanger, and each could be isolated from the main supply and return headers. So if one or more of the flow paths were damaged, they could be isolated, and the system restored to at least a portion of normal capability.

But those headers, and the isolation valves, were located in the Auxiliary Machinery Room, which was now on fire.

"XO, don't let us down," Matt said under his breath.

The Weapons station answered the CO's query. "Two thousand, two hundred kilometers, sir."

CSO perked up. He hadn't noticed the range increase that much. No one had. He ordered, "Firing Point Procedures, Tubes 1 and 2."

The torpedo firing litany passed quickly, though it seemed to take forever. Finally ship, solution, and weapon all reported ready, and CSO looked at the CO.

"Fire," the CO said.

"Fire Tube 1."

Weapons actuated the tube launch sequence, and a moment later the ship shuddered as the weapon left the tube.

"Fire Tube 2."

Again the ship shuddered, and two Hammerheads appeared on the fusion plot, heading toward the corvette.

"TAO, Weapons, Ownship clearance maneuvers complete, Hammerheads are enabled."

CSO said, "TAO, aye," and kept his eyes locked on the plot.

Visually, the corvette was definitely off-gassing now. And its acceleration vector was shorter than it had been. Matt guessed their missile had been a hit after all. And now the corvette was fleeing, not bothering to zig-zag, running straight away from the torpedoes.

Then she did something surprising. She spun 180 degrees, launched another salvo of missiles, then spun back around to keep running.

"That's a neat trick," CSO said, as the six missile salvo split up, half going toward one torpedo and half toward the other.

Torpedoes are designed to maneuver to throw off point defense target acquisition, and to see through decoys and countermeasures. But they weren't designed to evade missiles. They had onboard radar, IR, and gravitic sensors, though, so were not blind to the incoming fire. Both torpedoes altered course radically, and two of the missiles missed.

But in the end, the two torpedoes were blasted from the sky, and the corvette veered about to vector toward HALSWELL.

The satellite batteries opened up again. Matt had hardly noticed they stopped firing while the corvette had been close in, but it made sense that they had. No need to risk hitting their own ship. But now that there was plenty of clearance between HALSWELL and Singing Josie, HALSWELL was fair game once more.

On the bright side, satellite #4 was almost out of range, and would be for some time due to its elongated orbit. On the down side, satellite #1 was just coming out from behind the dwarf planet, and would be in range again in just a few minutes.

"SDMS," the CO said, and CSO ordered another salvo of five missiles.

The corvette vectored straight toward the HALSWELL this time, and revolved on her forward-to-aft axis so that now her ventral turret was unmasked to the incoming missiles, even as her forward plasma cannons also fired.

"Does he think he's going to win with a glorious final charge?" CSO muttered, and ordered, "Fire primary cannons."

After the corvette's earlier caginess, the lack of subtlety in this new line of attack struck Matt as odd, also.

On the fusion plot, two of HALSWELL's missiles vanished, and then radar called out, "Vampire, Vampire, Vampire," again.

This time the corvette's missile volley was only four missiles. Bo drove the ship downwards, so both dorsal point defense turrets could bear on them, and they were quickly dispatched. Then it was back to facing the corvette, and applying plasma fire.

But even as the ship steadied back up to face her, the primary cannons ceased to be needed. First one, then a second, of HALSWELL's missiles struck home. The first smashed a hole in the corvette's nose, above her plasma cannons and where Matt assumed her bridge would be. The second struck amidships, just aft of the the turret.

There must have been a magazine there, or something, because a secondary explosion whited out the visual for a second.

After the glow faded, Matt could see that the corvette was split in two, and off-gassing mightily from both sections, which were tumbling away from each other erratically.

"Got her, sir," CSO said.

The CO just gestured toward the satellites on the fusion plot. "Silence those batteries."

CSO ordered two SDMS missiles toward each of the active plasma cannons. Shortly, explosions on the captured asteroids announced the missiles's impact, and the end of those threats.

Matt felt like cheering, but the look on the CO's face put that desire down.

He was studying the fusion plot, and the crater containing the base. Then he picked up the 27MC. "Bridge, Captain, maneuver us into strafing position over the base."

Bo acknowledged the order, and before long, the ship was in a parking orbit above the base. Satellite #1 was almost in range, but Matt didn't think that was any real concern anymore.

CSO pulled up the visual of the base and expanded it so he and the CO could look at it more closely. After a moment, the CO said, "Take out the fuel tanks."

CSO smiled thinly, and soon the fuel tanks were no more.

Then a voice came over the bridge to bridge. "Icaran Warship, this is Honey's Home. Stop shooting, for the love of God. We surrender."

Matt couldn't help but chuckle at the base's name. It seemed too quaint to be a den of pirates.

"Congratulations, skipper," CSO said, and held out his hand to the CO.

They shook, and the CO smiled with satisfaction.

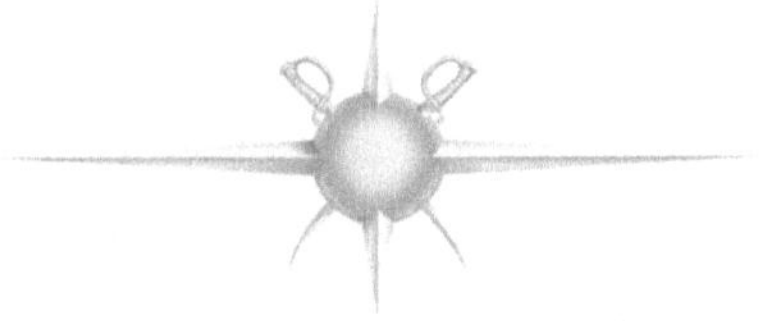

Chapter Sixty-Eight

In the immediate aftermath of the battle's end, Matt felt nothing but elation. Elation, and relief, because it could have gone much differently. And looking around CIC, he saw from the expressions on everyone's face—even the CO's—the same feeling.

But then another feeling eclipsed that. Warmth.

It was getting decidedly hot in CIC, and it only took a moment to realize why. The AC system. And the fire. The fire was almost exactly three levels below CIC, and heat would easily transmit through the bulkeads and decks.

How long had it been burning?

Matt's mind swept to the fire fighting training his class had endured back in Tactical School: both in the classroom and in simulation rooms, where the entire room could be set on fire to provide whatever scenario the training staff desired. A single statistic came to his mind, of a small fire lit in the torpedo room, not much larger than a trash can.

It had rendered CIC unlivable in less than ten minutes.

But Matt couldn't see even a whiff of smoke. So what...?

Then the rest of his training leaped back to mind.

The first step in fighting a fire on a ship was to isolate the ventilation ducts into and out of the affected space, so as to limit oxygen flow to the fire and retard the spread of smoke throughout the ship. That wouldn't stop the heat flow, though.

As if the CO were reading his thoughts, he picked up a sound-powered handset and pressed a call button. Matt heard him say, "DC Central, Captain. Report status of the casualty."

A heartbeat later, the 1MC came to life. "The status of the casualty is as follows. XO is the man in charge in the Machinery Room. No further assistance is required. Five personnel have been evacuated to the Chief's Mess for treatment. The fire is contained to the aft port section of the Machinery Room, in the vicinity of the #2 Oxygen Generator. Power has been secured, and firefighting teams are fighting the fire with fire hose #3 and #4."

Matt took all that in, and nodded to himself. They had it contained and were attacking it with two different hose teams. With power secured, the fire should be out momentarily.

At the fusion plot, the CO seemed to share Matt's notion, because he nodded emphatically and replaced the handset, then turned to CSO.

"Recall ASVs 1 and 2," the CO said. "Have ASV-1 find Fred-1 and evaluate its status, and have ASV-2 do a flyby on us." He winced slightly. "Let's get an idea of the damage."

CSO nodded. "Aye, skipper," he said, and issued the orders.

Long minutes passed as the air continued to get warmer, and the drones returned from their positions, out past the dwarf planet's outer orbitals. Then DC Central came over the 1MC again.

"The fire is out."

Sighs of relief issued from several personnel around CIC, Matt included.

A moment later, XO came over the tactical net; his implants must still have been tuned into it.

"Captain, XO. The after third of the AC heat exchanger's flow paths have been destroyed. We've been venting coolant out into space, and the main AC coolant tank is nearly at the low level alarm setpoint. The Damage Control team has isolated flow to the damaged section of the heat exchanger, but I can't tell if there's another leak. Recommend rigging for minimal electric as soon as feasible, and conducting an external inspection to confirm the existence of more leaks."

The CO scowled, and nodded. "Very well, XO. ASV-2 is enroute to conduct the inspection. Standby."

He and the CSO traded looks, and CSO shook his head. "We just got the old girl out of airdock, and now we have to go back in."

The CO nodded. "Looks like."

CSO sighed. "So much for liberty at Melrose."

The CO chuckled. "I think that's the least of our worries." Then he drew a breath, and picked up the 1MC.

"Attention, HALSWELL, this is the Captain. We have engaged the pirates and destroyed them, but we've taken damage to our Air Conditioning heat exchanger. We're evaluating the extent of the damage, but I expect we will need to dock to make repairs." He released the transmit button and frowned pensively for a moment, before continuing.

"On the down side, it looks like our visit to Melrose will have to wait. But on bright side, that means we'll be heading home sooner than expected. Once we've mopped things up here, we'll set course for New California. In the meantime, expect to be on a minimal electric regime until further notice, while we get the air conditioning situation under control." His jaw worked for a moment, then he just said, "Carry on," and set the handset down again.

"CSO, draft a message to Carraway headquarters. Give them a preliminary engagement report and request Marine support." He gestured toward the base on the visual display. "That's not a nut our VBSS team is equipped to crack."

CSO nodded. "Aye, sir. I'll get right on it."

The CO nodded, then shifted to the 27MC. "Bridge, Captain. Secure from battlestations with the exception of damage control and medical efforts. Rig the ship for minimal electric."

Bo acknowledged the orders, then passed them over the 1MC.

Around CIC, secondary and support stations flicked off, as personnel secured them in accordance with the minimal electric bill. They secured some of the lighting as well, leaving the space, already dimly lit normally, even darker.

"Mr. Gilbert," the CO said, looking Matt's way.

"Sir?"

"Secure yourself, and go have the Doc look at your head."

Matt tried to wave it off. "I'll be fine, sir."

"Let the Doc make that determination. Get below."

"Aye aye, sir."

Reluctantly, Matt circled around the fusion plot toward the aft hatch. Although the engagement was over, it still felt like he was abandoning his duty to leave.

On the other hand, his head was really beginning to throb, and his tongue as well. So his stubborn side didn't push back too hard, this time.

It turned out that he might as well have stayed in CIC. Doc Roos and his team were dealing with three smoke inhalation cases and five burn cases of varying severity. They didn't have time to do more than take a quick look at him, verify that the bleeding had stopped on its own, give him a bottle of ibuprofen, and order him to come back if he began to feel nauseous, or have other symptoms of a concussion. Then they kicked him out of the Chief's Mess.

So he made his way back to officer's country and the wardroom, through passageways that were dimmed like during the ship's night routine. In the wardroom, his head wound elicited several comments that quickly turned to jokes, and before he knew it he had a new nickname.

So that was a plus.

Over the next few hours, the ship completed work overhauling the fire, then conducted an emergency evacuation of the AMR and surrounding spaces, to vent the smoke and other gasses released by the fire into space, and ASV-2 did its damage survey.

The plasma hit to the stern didn't look too bad. Scorch marks and shredded armor plating, and buckled access hatches to four of the ship's ASV bays, were the obvious effects of the hit. Nothing that should impede the ship's immediate operation.

The missile hit was another matter entirely. The XO's report from inside the AMR was bad, but outside was worse. The superstructure between turret #4 and the heat exchanger was ripped away, and the heat exchanger tubes were shredded. The turret was scored in multiple places and knocked off true, and sections of the hull were twisted and burned all the way out to the edge of the hull, where it curved upward.

Looking at the imagery of the survey on the screen in the wardroom, Charlie shook his head and whistled. "Good thing it hit there, where there's a gap between the pressure hull and the outer skin. Otherwise..."

He didn't finish the thought, but he didn't need to. Matt had seen what that final SDMS missile strike had done to the corvette. HALSWELL might not have been ripped in two, but the hull very likely would have at least been breached, and at least one or two compartments opened to the void.

And who knows how many of the crew lost overboard in the process.

"Thank the Lord for good luck and good design," said Terry in reply, and no one could contradict him.

The survey also showed that the XO had been right, and several more of the heat exchanger tubes were still leaking. But with the imagery, Auxiliary Division was able to determine which were affected, and as soon as the AMR was re-pressurized, they got in there and closed the required isolation valves.

So the ship had Air Conditioning again, but the system was woefully low on coolant, so they remained on minimal electric for most of a week. During that time, Deck Division went out in Fred-2 to retrieve Fred-1. The boat had taken a burst from the corvette's turret and was holed in over a dozen places, its control systems completely shot. But it wouldn't do to leave the boat floating around as a navigation hazard, so they towed it back and spent a good hour and a half almost literally pushing it by hand up into the starboard boat deck.

At the end of that week, reinforcements from Carraway arrived: A Marine Landing Ship (MLS) and another frigate, ICS CARENA, of the more modern TYPHON-class.

Matt had gotten so used to HALSWELL, and the other POTTER-class ships at New California, that CARENA looked decidedly odd to him, now. She lacked the tall bridge tower; instead, her bridge was just a small hump atop her more angular hull. Also, her engine nacelles were mounted on the ventral section of her hull, instead of on the sides, like HALSWELL.

More importantly, her primary cannons were not mounted at the front of her engines, but on the sides of her hull, so they were trainable through a much larger arc. They probably could fire almost directly astern.

That would have made engaging the Singing Josie a lot easier at the beginning of the battle.

But the thing that most caught Matt's attention was the voice that came over the bridge to bridge when CARENA hailed them: a woman's voice.

Matt knew there were female ships in the ICN, of course. But with none of them stationed at New Cali, it had been so long since he'd heard a female voice associated with anything Navy, it threw him for a loop at first.

And it got him thinking about how long it had been since he'd seen a woman at all. The other guys in the wardroom apparently felt similarly, to judge by the discussion at the wardroom table after the two ships linked up.

Alas, there was to be no socializing, though, except for the personnel of Deck Division. CARENA had loaded extra bottles of AC coolant aboard before heading out to relieve them, and the BMs—and Zach, of course—got to go over in Fred-2 to pick them up.

Certainly, it was because after that trip, HALSWELL had at least a serviceable AC system again, that the guys who made the trip looked especially happy for the next day. It had to be that.

Turnover between HALSWELL and the arriving ships went quickly. In the days since the base had surrendered, there had been next to no activity from the base. No calls on any radio circuit, not to HALSWELL and, at least that the ESM systems could detect, not to any other station either. No one tried to escape; not that they could go anywhere with their fuel depot destroyed. And no one tried to fire on the HALSWELL. It was like, after surrendering, the pirates had just gone to sleep.

Or maybe decided to end it all before they were taken into custody?

There was no way to tell until the Marines entered the base, and Matt didn't really care to speculate. But if he were to make a bet, it would be that they were just waiting, dejected, for their fate.

HALSWELL wouldn't be sticking around to find out, though. A few hours after CARENA and the MLS arrived, HALSWELL set course for the jump gate and accelerated away at Ahead Standard.

And Matt had a new reason to be anxious: his OOD board was in five days.

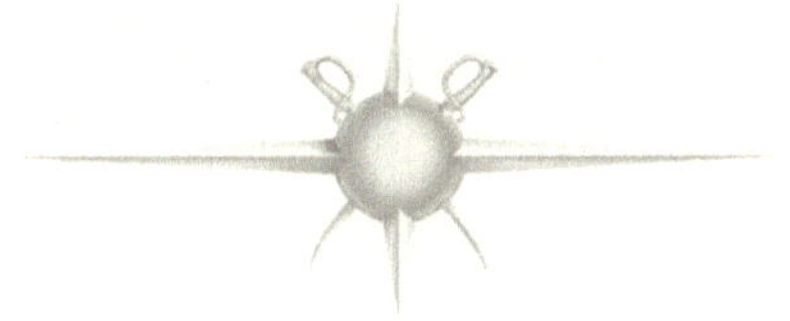

Chapter Sixty-Nine

Breakfast was rich this morning. Thick cuts of bacon and even thicker pancakes, with strawberries and whipped cream on top, and just a dab of syrup. A trio of eggs over-hard, well peppered. A bowl of freshly-sliced melon. And a tall glass of orange juice.

They had an UNREP yesterday afternoon, and that had replenished HALSWELL's food stores, which after almost three weeks had been severely lacking in things like fresh fruits and veggies.

But that wasn't why the breakfast seemed so much better than any of the meals Matt had eaten recently.

Tomorrow, they were jumping back to New California, and just a couple days later they'd be mooring at Copernicus Station for inspection and evaluation before going into one of the air docks to conduct repairs. OPS had posted the inport watchbill last night, and Matt wasn't going to have duty for two days after they pulled in. So he and Marta had made plans for a grand reunion that first evening back, and Isaiah had invited him to join a group of his friends on a sailing adventure the next day.

But that wasn't the reason either.

There were rumors of a special welcome from the Commodore, and maybe the Governor of New Cali, to honor the returning heroes, the pirate-slayers.

But those were just rumors, probably originating from the third class petty officers's gossip committee.

No, today's breakfast was grander than any Matt could remember because he was about to take the watch.

On the bridge.

By himself.

For the first time.

Across the table from him, CSO gestured with his fork toward Matt's bowl. "You taking up cannibalism, Melon?"

Matt rolled his eyes, and chuckled. Looked like the nickname was going to last.

Oh well, it could be worse.

The meal was a bit rushed, by necessity because he did have to take the watch. But it felt like a banquet, anyway. And when he pushed back his seat and asked permission to leave the mess, he felt charged and ready.

His pre-watch tour of the ship was a blur, but somehow as he ascended the ladder to the bridge, he recalled every detail. Which torpedomen were doing maintenance on tube #2, who was manning the ship's store for the morning watch. The pressure indications on the CO_2 scrubber outlet manifolds. All the little things that said the ship was going about its routine without difficulty.

As long as you didn't look too closely at the Air Conditioning system, at least.

The view out the bridge's observation windows was breathtaking, as always. Sollace's green-yellow star dominated the port side, about twenty degrees below what passed for the horizon. It shown so brightly, from HALSWELL's position, that its small K-dwarf partner was invisible, even though from the charts it lay about fifteen degrees forward of the primary from here.

It was unusual for a jump point to be as close to the system's center of gravity as the New Cali jump point was in Sollace. There were all manner of physics reasons for the anomaly, and Matt supposed he could think of them if he really wanted to—but he probably wouldn't understand them.

But it didn't really matter. It was what it was, and it made for a dynamic approach to the jump point.

Like the star was actively blazing their trail back home.

Matt found himself laughing at the thought as he went to the check the plot at the QMOW's station. QM1 Jaboly looked at him quizzically.

"What's so funny, sir?"

Matt shrugged and waved the question away. "Just a silly thought. We looking good on the PIM?"

The Plan of Intended Motion was the driver that wielded the whip against the OOD's, and QMOW's, back. Rule #1 was get the ship where it was supposed to be, when it was supposed to be.

Well, Rule #2, anyway. Be safe was Rule #1, always.

Jaboly nodded. "We're about thirty minutes ahead, actually."

"Outstanding."

Business was equally on track with the Chief of the Watch, and Matt went to join CHENG over by the CO's chair.

CHENG didn't get to stand watch up here all that often, with all of his duties back in the plant. But he had to maintain proficiency, like everyone else, and Matt had the idea that he cherished every moment he got to really drive, really be a SWO.

"I've toured the spaces and reviewed the logs, and am ready to relieve you, sir," Matt said.

CHENG grinned at him. "I'll bet you are. Feels good to be qualified up here, doesn't it?"

Matt nodded. "Been working toward this for a long time."

"I remember my first OOD watch." CHENG sounded almost wistful as he said that, and his eyes grew distant for a moment. Then he shook himself, and cleared his throat. "I'm ready to be relieved."

CHENG spent the next couple minutes giving Matt the rundown on the status of the ship's rig, what maintenance items were being performed and how long each should take, and how the ship stood with respect to the navigation and contact picture.

There wasn't much of a contact picture to speak of; just a couple passenger liners on their way to the New Cali jump point ahead of them, and another on a reciprocal course toward Olifant. Not exactly hard to manage.

But CHENG gave a thorough breakdown of each contact, more thorough than was strictly necessary, and Matt wondered if he wasn't drawing the turnover out on purpose.

If so, Matt couldn't blame him. He wouldn't want to have to go back to reviewing log packs, maintenance packages, and all that, when he could be up here instead.

But there was only so long CHENG could draw it out, and eventually he ran out of things to say.

"I relieve you, sir," Matt said.

CHENG nodded. "I stand relieved." He paused, then added, "You've had quite a first year aboard, haven't you."

It wasn't a question, but Matt nodded emphatically. "And it hasn't even been a full year yet."

"Well, don't get your expectations too high. Most of the time it's not nearly so eventful." Chuckling, he patted Matt on the shoulder, then moved toward the ladderwell.

Matt considered his words for a moment, then decided CHENG was probably right. After all, he could count the number of ships who actually had engaged in real combat in the last five years on two hands. At least, that were widely spoken of, anyway.

And that was a good thing.

But for now, it also didn't matter. He was here, where he'd dreamed of being for a long, long time. OOD qualified, with his final SWO board probably within the next month.

So whether the future was going to be full of thrills and chills, or just routine, it was going to be a good future, either way.

Matt drew a deep breath, nodded to himself, and said the words he'd been dreaming of saying for longer than he could remember.

"Attention on the bridge. Ensign Gilbert has the deck and the conn."

A thrill went up his spine as he heard himself. And then again as, around the bridge, his watch standers responded.

"Helm, aye."

"Chief of the Watch, aye."

"Quartermaster, aye."

Matt crossed his arms and looked ahead, at the contact boxes for the passenger liners and, beyond, the navigation icon that marked the jump point. And past that, to the future.

And he smiled.

Artwork

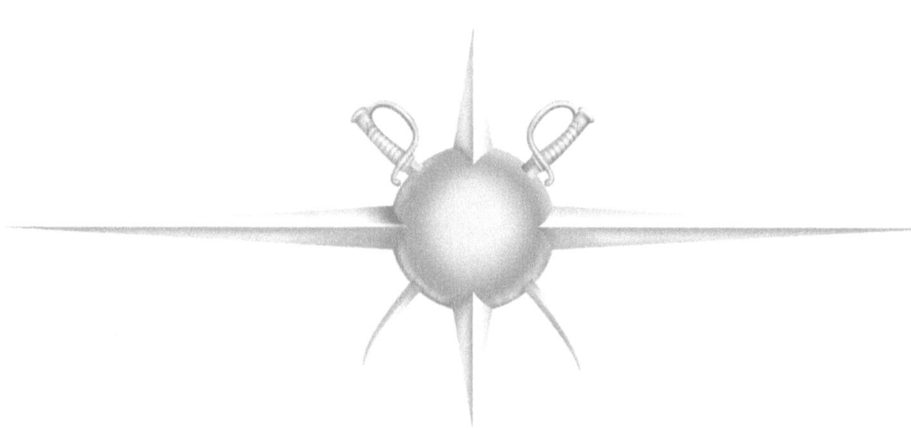

ICS FREDERICK HALSWELL
"FOLLOW ME"
SFG 1271

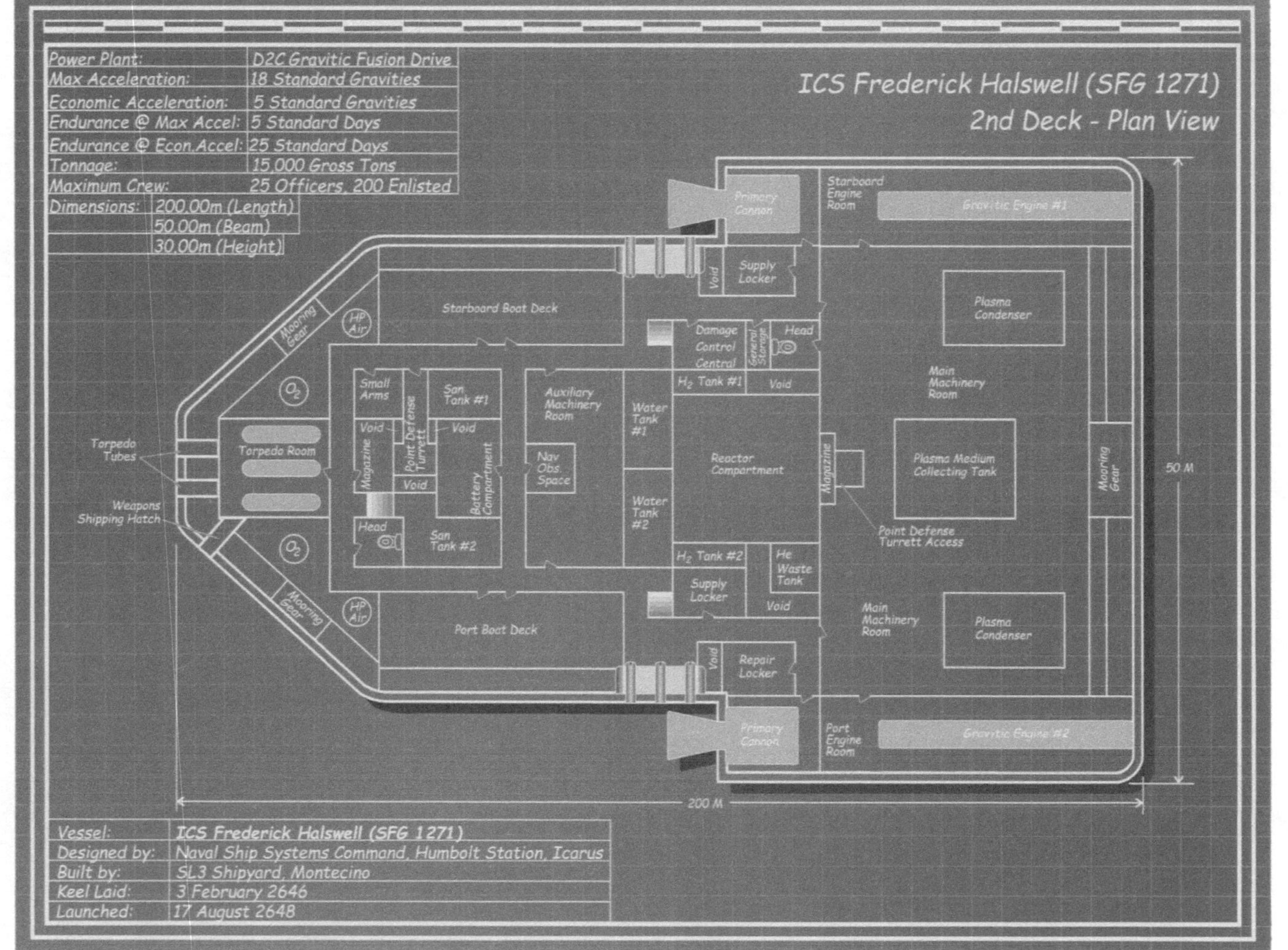
ICS Frederick Halswell (SFG 1271)
2nd Deck - Plan View
Power Plant: D2C Gravitic Fusion Drive
Max Acceleration: 18 Standard Gravities
Economic Acceleration: 5 Standard Gravities
Endurance @ Max Accel: 5 Standard Days
Endurance @ Econ. Accel: 25 Standard Days
Tonnage: 15,000 Gross Tons
Maximum Crew: 25 Officers, 200 Enlisted
Dimensions: 200.00m (Length)
50.00m (Beam)
30.00m (Height)
Starboard Engine Room
Gravitic Engine #1
Primary Cannon
Void
Supply Locker
Plasma Condenser
Main Machinery Room
Starboard Boat Deck
Mooring Gear
HP Air
O2
Torpedo Tubes
Torpedo Room
Weapons Shipping Hatch
Small Arms
Void
Magazine
Point Defense Turrett
San Tank #1
Void
Void
Battery Compartment
Auxiliary Machinery Room
Nav Obs. Space
Head
San Tank #2
Damage Control Central
General Storage
Head
H2 Tank #1
Void
Water Tank #1
Water Tank #2
Reactor Compartment
Magazine
Plasma Medium Collecting Tank
Point Defense Turrett Access
Mooring Gear
H2 Tank #2
Supply Locker
He Waste Tank
Void
Main Machinery Room
Plasma Condenser
Port Boat Deck
O2
Mooring Gear
HP Air
Void
Repair Locker
Primary Cannon
Port Engine Room
Gravitic Engine #2
50 M
200 M
Vessel: ICS Frederick Halswell (SFG 1271)
Designed by: Naval Ship Systems Command, Humbolt Station, Icarus
Built by: SL3 Shipyard, Montecino
Keel Laid: 3 February 2646
Launched: 17 August 2648

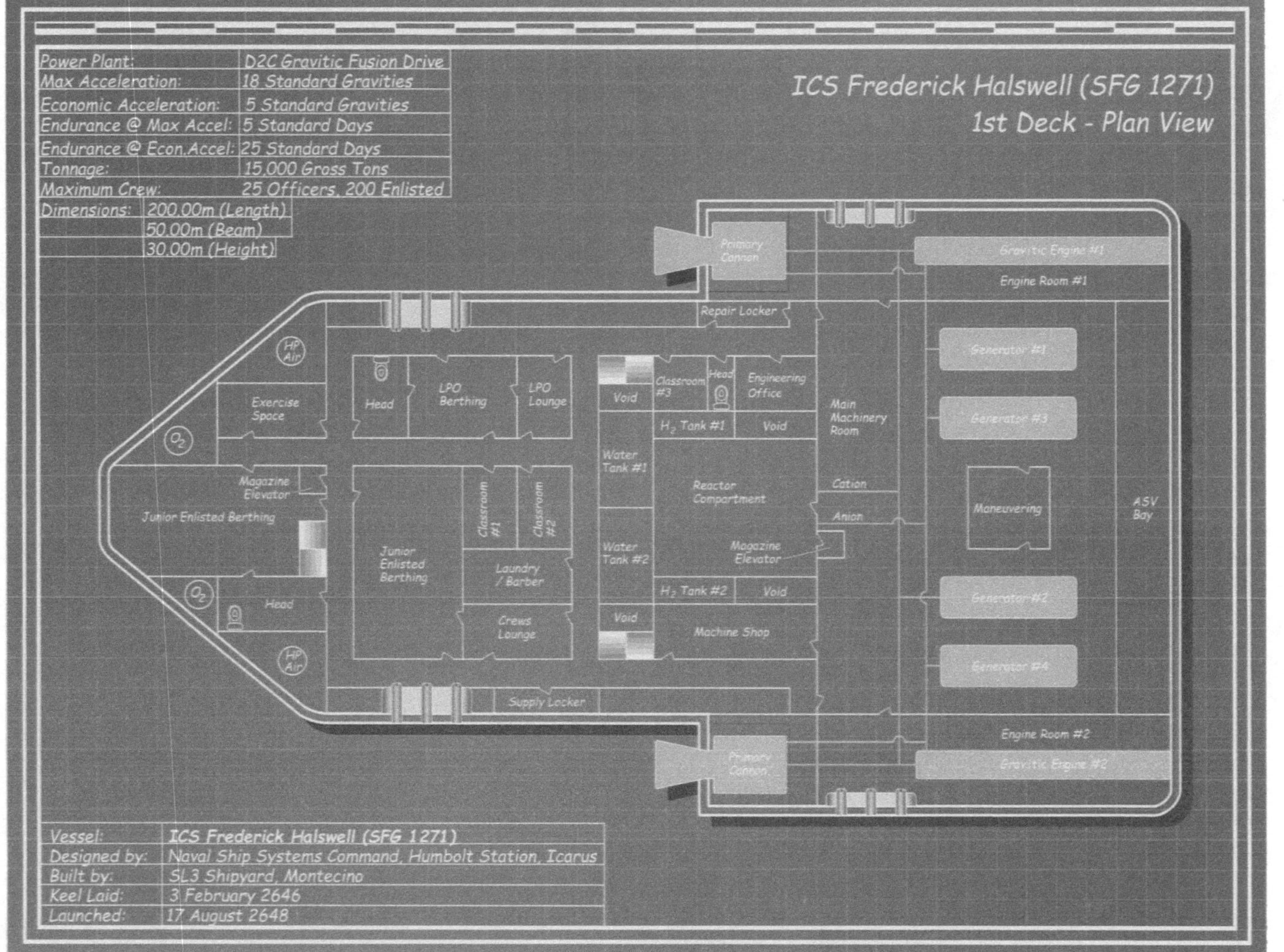

ICS Frederick Halswell (SFG 1271)
1st Deck - Plan View
Power Plant: D2C Gravitic Fusion Drive
Max Acceleration: 18 Standard Gravities
Economic Acceleration: 5 Standard Gravities
Endurance @ Max Accel: 5 Standard Days
Endurance @ Econ.Accel: 25 Standard Days
Tonnage: 15,000 Gross Tons
Maximum Crew: 25 Officers, 200 Enlisted
Dimensions: 200.00m (Length)
50.00m (Beam)
30.00m (Height)
Primary Cannon
Gravitic Engine #1
Engine Room #1
Repair Locker
Generator #1
Generator #3
HP Air
LPO Berthing
LPO Lounge
Void
Classroom #3
Head
Engineering Office
Main Machinery Room
Exercise Space
Head
H₂ Tank #1
Void
O₂
Water Tank #1
Cation
Maneuvering
ASV Bay
Magazine Elevator
Junior Enlisted Berthing
Classroom #1
Classroom #2
Reactor Compartment
Anion
Junior Enlisted Berthing
Water Tank #2
Magazine Elevator
Generator #2
O₂
Head
Laundry / Barber
H₂ Tank #2
Void
Generator #4
HP Air
Crews Lounge
Void
Machine Shop
Supply Locker
Engine Room #2
Primary Cannon
Gravitic Engine #2
Vessel: ICS Frederick Halswell (SFG 1271)
Designed by: Naval Ship Systems Command, Humbolt Station, Icarus
Built by: SL3 Shipyard, Montecino
Keel Laid: 3 February 2646
Launched: 17 August 2648

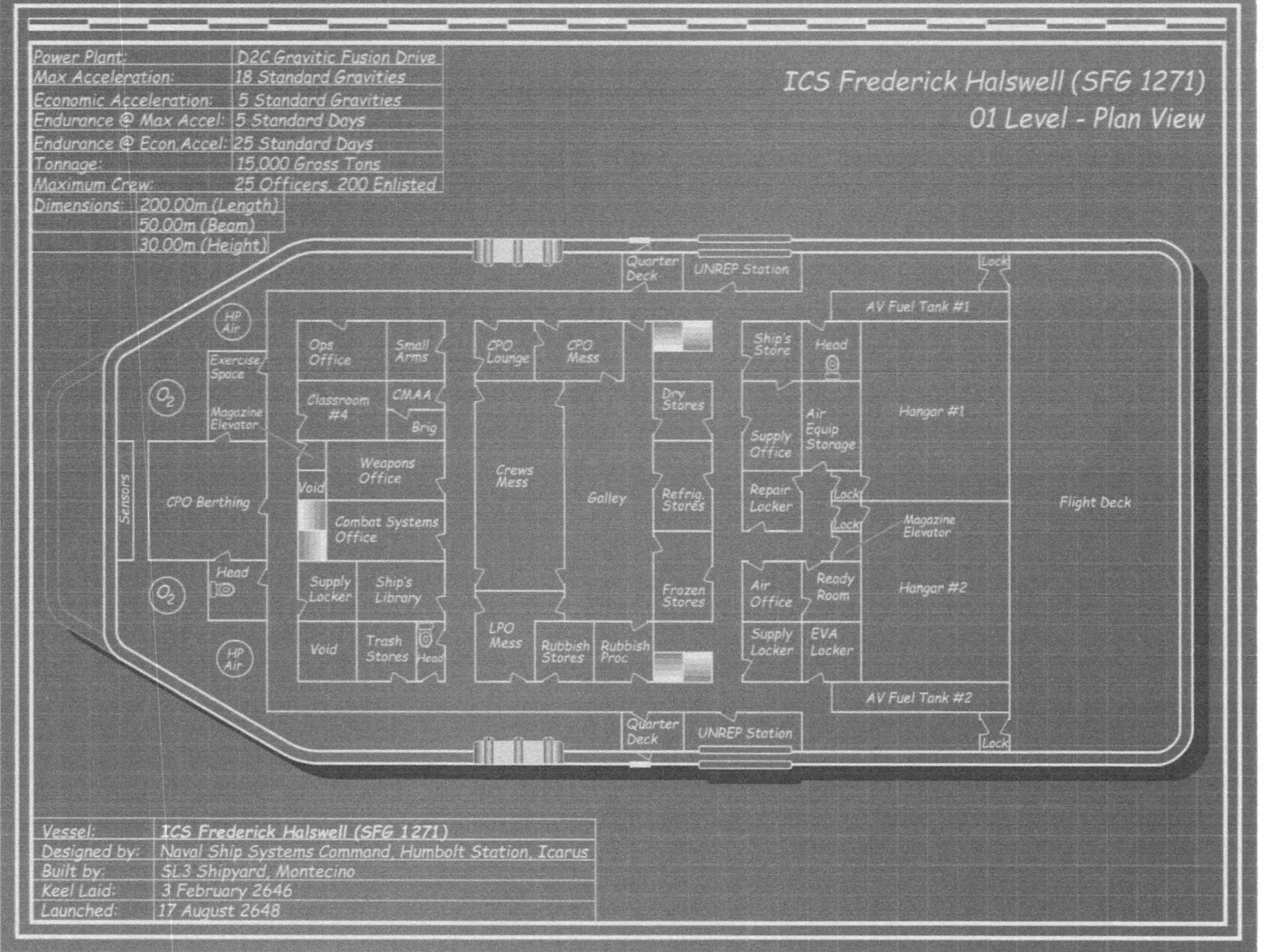

ICS Frederick Halswell (SFG 1271)
01 Level - Plan View

Power Plant: D2C Gravitic Fusion Drive
Max Acceleration: 18 Standard Gravities
Economic Acceleration: 5 Standard Gravities
Endurance @ Max Accel: 5 Standard Days
Endurance @ Econ. Accel: 25 Standard Days
Tonnage: 15,000 Gross Tons
Maximum Crew: 25 Officers, 200 Enlisted
Dimensions: 200.00m (Length)
50.00m (Beam)
30.00m (Height)

Vessel: ICS Frederick Halswell (SFG 1271)
Designed by: Naval Ship Systems Command, Humbolt Station, Icarus
Built by: SL3 Shipyard, Montecino
Keel Laid: 3 February 2646
Launched: 17 August 2648

HP Air
Exercise Space
O2
Magazine Elevator
Sensors
CPO Berthing
Head
O2
HP Air
Ops Office
Small Arms
Classroom #4
CMAA
Brig
Weapons Office
Void
Combat Systems Office
Supply Locker
Ship's Library
Void
Trash Stores
Head
Quarter Deck
UNREP Station
CPO Lounge
CPO Mess
Crews Mess
Galley
LPO Mess
Rubbish Stores
Rubbish Proc
Quarter Deck
UNREP Station
Dry Stores
Refrig. Stores
Frozen Stores
Ship's Store
Head
Supply Office
Air Equip Storage
Repair Locker
Lock
Lock
Air Office
Supply Locker
Ready Room
EVA Locker
AV Fuel Tank #1
Hangar #1
Magazine Elevator
Hangar #2
AV Fuel Tank #2
Flight Deck
Lock
Lock

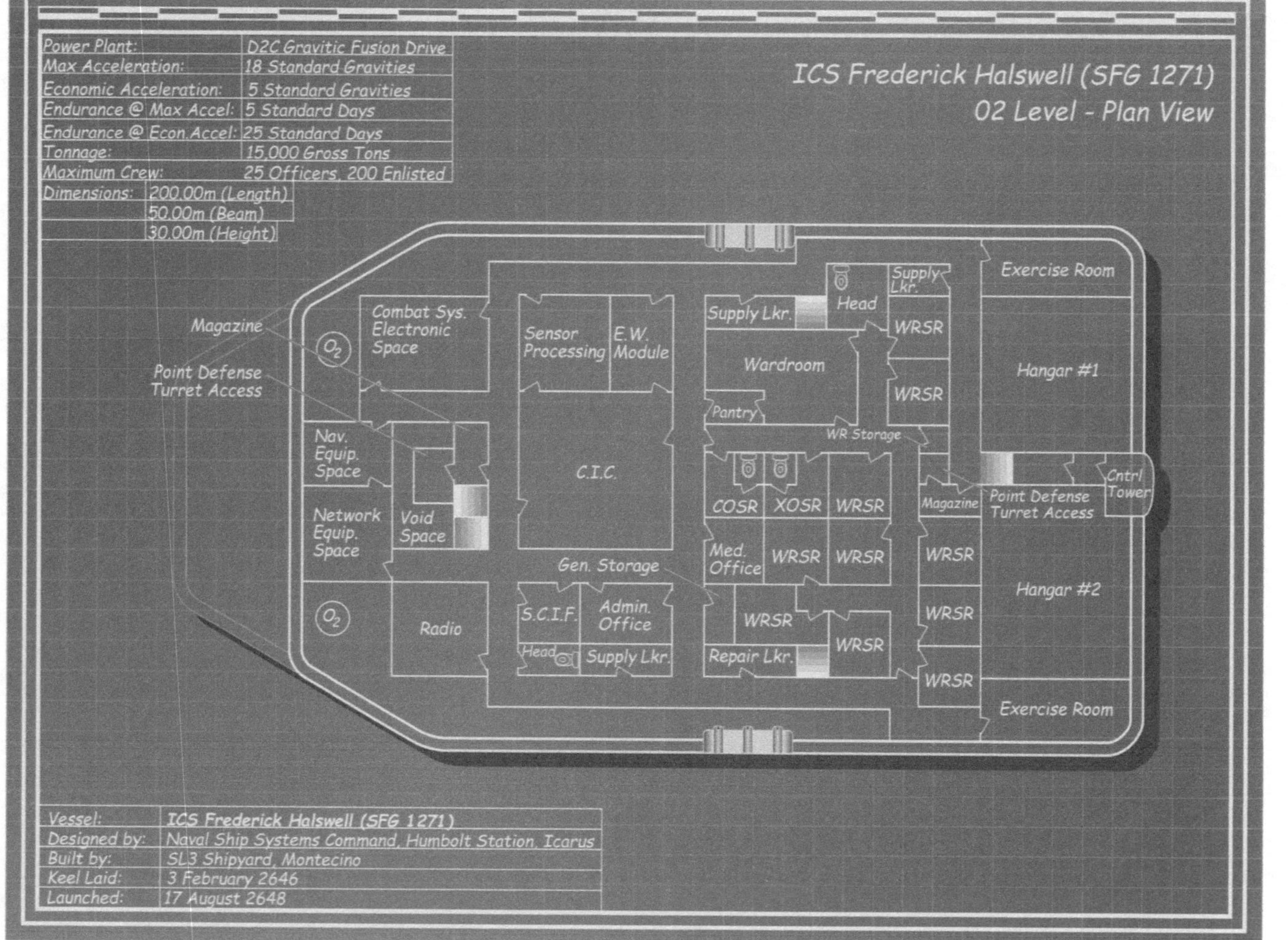
ICS Frederick Halswell (SFG 1271)
O2 Level - Plan View
Power Plant: D2C Gravitic Fusion Drive
Max Acceleration: 18 Standard Gravities
Economic Acceleration: 5 Standard Gravities
Endurance @ Max Accel: 5 Standard Days
Endurance @ Econ.Accel: 25 Standard Days
Tonnage: 15,000 Gross Tons
Maximum Crew: 25 Officers, 200 Enlisted
Dimensions: 200.00m (Length)
50.00m (Beam)
30.00m (Height)
Magazine
Point Defense Turret Access
Combat Sys. Electronic Space
Sensor Processing
E.W. Module
Supply Lkr.
Head
Supply Lkr.
WRSR
Exercise Room
Wardroom
WRSR
Hangar #1
Pantry
WR Storage
Nav. Equip. Space
C.I.C.
COSR
XOSR
WRSR
Magazine
Point Defense Turret Access
Cntrl Tower
Network Equip. Space
Void Space
Med. Office
WRSR
WRSR
WRSR
Gen. Storage
Radio
S.C.I.F.
Admin. Office
WRSR
Hangar #2
WRSR
Head
Supply Lkr.
Repair Lkr.
WRSR
WRSR
Exercise Room
Vessel: ICS Frederick Halswell (SFG 1271)
Designed by: Naval Ship Systems Command, Humbolt Station, Icarus
Built by: SL3 Shipyard, Montecino
Keel Laid: 3 February 2646
Launched: 17 August 2648

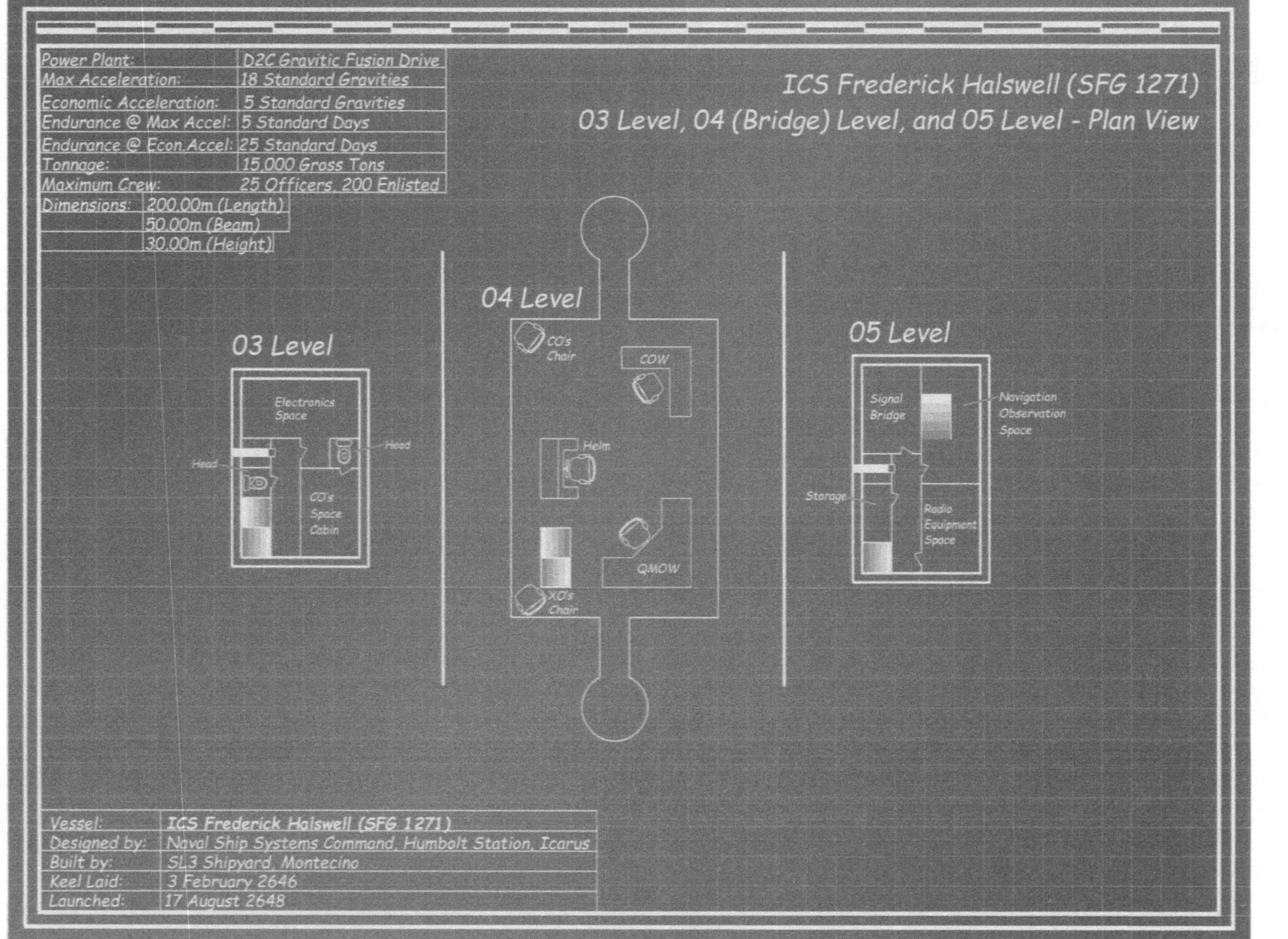

Power Plant: D2C Gravitic Fusion Drive
Max Acceleration: 18 Standard Gravities
Economic Acceleration: 5 Standard Gravities
Endurance @ Max Accel: 5 Standard Days
Endurance @ Econ.Accel: 25 Standard Days
Tonnage: 15,000 Gross Tons
Maximum Crew: 25 Officers, 200 Enlisted
Dimensions: 200.00m (Length)
50.00m (Beam)
30.00m (Height)
ICS Frederick Halswell (SFG 1271)
03 Level, 04 (Bridge) Level, and 05 Level - Plan View
03 Level
Electronics Space
Head
Head
CO's Space Cabin
04 Level
CO's Chair
COW
Helm
QMOW
XO's Chair
05 Level
Signal Bridge
Navigation Observation Space
Storage
Radio Equipment Space
Vessel: ICS Frederick Halswell (SFG 1271)
Designed by: Naval Ship Systems Command, Humbolt Station, Icarus
Built by: SL3 Shipyard, Montecino
Keel Laid: 3 February 2646
Launched: 17 August 2648

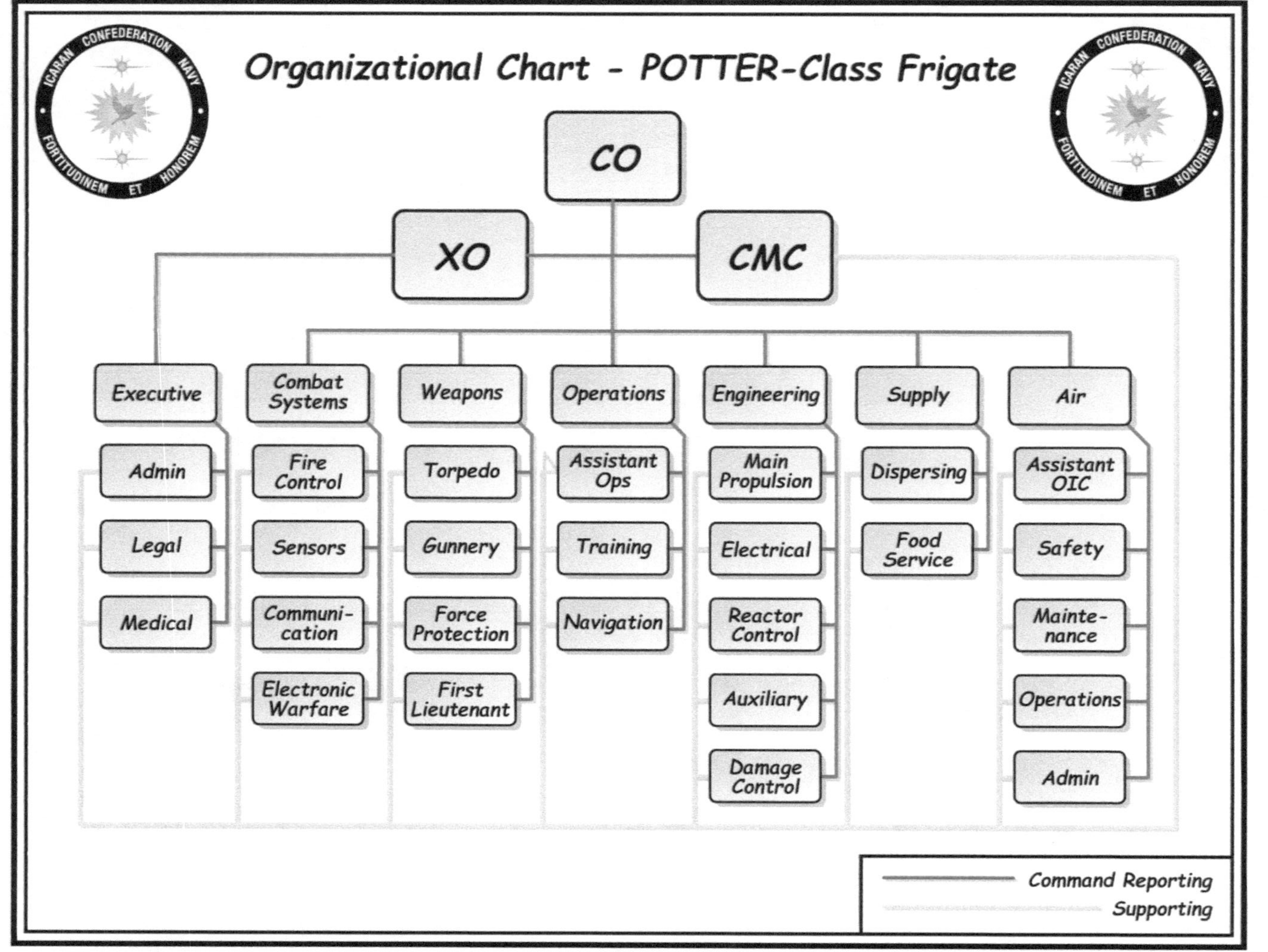

Organizational Chart - POTTER-Class Frigate
ICARAN CONFEDERATION NAVY HONOREM ET FORTITUDINEM
CO
XO
CMC
Executive
Admin
Legal
Medical
Combat Systems
Fire Control
Sensors
Communication
Electronic Warfare
Weapons
Torpedo
Gunnery
Force Protection
First Lieutenant
Operations
Assistant Ops
Training
Navigation
Engineering
Main Propulsion
Electrical
Reactor Control
Auxiliary
Damage Control
Supply
Dispersing
Food Service
Air
Assistant OIC
Safety
Maintenance
Operations
Admin
Command Reporting
Supporting

Message From The Author

Thank you for reading my book. I hope you enjoyed reading it as much as I enjoyed writing it.

Feel free to come say hi at my website, on Twitter, or on Gab. I always enjoy hearing from readers, especially since you all are, collectively, my boss.

Also, come check out my podcast, Story Time With Michael Kingswood, where I read stories and talk through some of the latest goings-on in my world.

Find it on YouTube, Rumble, Bitchute, Odysee, or through your favorite podcast feed.

Subscribers are always welcome, and encouraged!

Thanks again. My best to you and yours.

Warm Regards,
Michael Kingswood

Mailing List

If you enjoyed this book and would like word on new releases and special deals from Michael Kingswood, sign up for his newsletter on his website. Guaranteed to be spam-free, you can opt out at any time. And you can rest assured he will not share your information with anyone, for any reason, without a court order.

https://michaelkingswood.com/newsletter-signup/

About The Author

Michael Kingswood has published more than 100 short stories, novellas, and novels. He has appeared in anthologies from WMG Publishing, Stark Press, and Knotted Road Press. A twenty year veteran of the US Navy's submarine force, he has four children and currently resides in San Diego.

Fans can contact him through his <u>website</u>, on <u>Twitter</u>, or on <u>Gab</u>.

Michael has a weekly podcast, Story Time With Michael Kingswood, where he reads his work and discusses writing, philosophy, and generally has a good time. Subscribers are always welcome!

Listen on: <u>YouTube</u> <u>Rumble</u> <u>Bitchute</u> <u>Odysee</u> <u>Podcast</u>

More Books By Michael Kingswood

Glimmer Vale Chronicles

Glimmer Vale

Out-Dweller

Tollard's Peak

Robbed Blind

The Falconer's Stairs

Campaign Season

Bardsong

Stories From Glimmer Vale

Legacy

Hidden Magic

Captive Hearts

Wedding Gifts

Lost Credit

The Pericles Conspiracy

Passing In The Night

The Pericles Conspiracy

52 Stories In 2023

Volume One

Volume Two

Volume Three

Volume Four

Volume Five

Dawn Of Enlightenment

Masters Of The Sun

Novellas

What Lurks Between

The Necromancer's Lair

The Champion

Veritas Morte

Story Collections

Tales Of Adventure #1

Tales Of Adventure #2

Short Story 10-Pack

A Jar Of Mixed Treats

Short Mystery 10-Pack

Stories From Glimmer Vale, Volume 1

Short Fiction

Michael has also published a number of shorter works, which can be found at michaelkingswood.com/store.